Praise for Alexandra Potter

'Nobody does it quite like Alexandra Potter'

Daily Mail

'Sure to score points with all you hopeless romantics out there'

Heat

'The type of fun fiction we can't resist'

Stylist

'Great fun'

Closer

'A touching, funny love story'

Company

'Funny, romantic . . . tale about what might happen if all your wishes suddenly came true'

Daily Mirror

'A winning formula of chaotic heroine meeting eccentric hero, and, after misunderstandings, finding love. Sharply written, pacy and funny . . . pure self-indulgence'

The Times

'I loved it – it's fun, fast and feel-good – the perfect three! Positively dripping with humour and heart'

Helen Lederer

'The perfect reading romcom'

Daily Mail

About the author

Alexandra Potter is an award-winning author who previously worked as a features writer and sub-editor for women's glossies in both the UK and Australia. In 2007 she won the prize for Best New Fiction at the Jane Austen Regency World Awards for her bestselling novel, *Me and Mr Darcy*. Her novels have been translated into seventeen languages and her latest novel, *You're the One That I Don't Want*, is being adapted into a film. She now lives between London and Los Angeles and writes full-time.

Also by Alexandra Potter

You're the One That I Don't Want
Who's That Girl?
Me and Mr Darcy
Be Careful What You Wish For
Do You Come Here Often?
Calling Romeo
What's New, Pussycat?
Going La La

DON'T YOU FORGET ABOUT ME

Alexandra Potter

First published in 2012 by Hodder & Stoughton
An Hachette Livre UK company

4

A CIP catalogue record for this title is available from the British Library.

B format Paperback ISBN 978 1 444 71211 7
A format Paperback ISBN 978 1 444 75580 0

Typeset in Plantin Light by Hewer Text UK, Ltd

Printed and bound by Clays Ltd, St Ives plc

Hodder & Stoughton policy is to use papers that are natural, renewable and recyclable products and made from wood grown in sustainable forests. The logging and manufacturing processes are expected to conform to the environmental regulations of the country of origin.

Hodder & Stoughton Ltd
338 Euston Road
London NW1 3BH

www.hodder.co.uk

For my dad
Ray Potter

Who loved and laughed and lived and left
And nothing will ever be the same again

ACKNOWLEDGEMENTS

As always, huge thanks to my agent Stephanie Cabot, my editor Isobel Akenhead, and everyone at Hodder for all their hard work, enthusiasm and commitment. Behind every new book is a team of people working hard behind the scenes and I am forever grateful to have the best team there is.

Sadly, during the course of writing this book, I lost my dad and I want to thank all my wonderful friends whose outpouring of love and support got me through the darkest of times: Sara, Rachel, Beatrice, Rhian, Dana, Chris, Bev, Katie, Kate, Mishky, Pete, Matt, Saar, Charlie . . . to name but just a few. Thank you from the bottom of my heart, I am so lucky to have you guys.

And finally, to my amazing mum and my sister Kelly – I couldn't have done this without you. Thank you for being there every step (or should that be 'word') of the way. For your strength, your unconditional love and your unwavering belief in me as a writer.

We make a good team. Dad would be proud.

A NEW YEAR'S EVE RITUAL

Many ancient cultures believe in the magic of New Year's Eve to cleanse yourself of anything from the old year that you don't wish to take into the coming one. Be it fears or regrets, heartache or painful memories, ill-health or bad habits, this is the time you can leave the past behind and move, unburdened, into the future.

First light a fire. Then take a piece of paper and write a list, or use pictures, or some other symbol to represent the things you want to be rid of and, at the stroke of midnight, throw them into the flames.

As they burn away, sparks will well and truly fly. So make a wish. Because it will be carried on these sparks, sending your hopes and dreams out to the universe, to be blown by the wind, into the New Year . . .

Dear Diary,

Seb and I broke up.

Well, that's not strictly true. He broke up with me. He said he loved me but wasn't in love with me, that it would probably be better if we break up, how he hopes we'll always remain friends . . .

But you know the worst thing of all? When he told me he couldn't see a future with me. That pretty much broke my heart.

I'm not sure what to write now. Shall I write that I still feel numb? That it's only been a few hours and I still can't believe it's over? That I know that soon the shock is going to wear off, like an anaesthetic at the dentist, and I'm terrified of the pain?

Or shall I write that I know it's all my fault. That there are so many things I wish I'd done differently. So many regrets. So many 'what ifs'. But now it's too late. I've never loved anyone like I love Seb, and now I've lost him.

I miss him already.

I

What's on your mind?

Sitting at my desk, I rest my chin on my hand and stare glumly at my computer screen.

Facebook stares back.

Correction: Taunts me with everyone else's marvellous love life.

Scrolling down, I read through my friends' status updates:

Chrissie Hattersley is loving the Gucci handbag her boyfriend bought her for Christmas.

Jenny Hamilton-Proctor Looking forward to celebrating New Year's Eve with my perfect hubby and baby. I am so blessed.

Aneela Patel ♥ Imran Butt

Melody Dabrowski Andy popped the question, and I said yes!

Sara Jenkins Since I can no longer fit into my jeans, it's time to spill the beans, John and I are pregnant!!!!

Emily Klein Only two sleeps before my Bali honeymoon. I CAN'T WAIT!!

Emily's going on honeymoon? I didn't even know she'd got married!

I'm distracted by an email pinging into my inbox. It's from my boss, Sir Richard, reminding me about his visa for his upcoming trip to India in the New Year.

Shit. I'd forgotten all about it.

'All under control,' I type breezily, hitting reply.

It's 3 p.m. on New Year's Eve, and while most people are either at home on the sofa, watching repeats on TV and finishing off the rest of the mince pies, or thousands of miles away on a beach in Goa, enjoying some winter sunshine, I'm ensconced in an office block in southwest London.

The office is home to Blackstock & White, drinks merchants famous for their whisky and other brand-name spirits, where I'm PA to Sir Richard Blackstock. *PA.* That sounds rather swanky, as if I should look like something out of *Mad Men* and be terribly efficient, but in reality I'm not the best PA in the world. In fact, to tell the truth, I'm pretty rubbish. But that's not really my fault. I was working here as a temp about a year ago, when his PA left to go on maternity leave, and Sir Richard offered me her job.

From the start I told him I wasn't PA material. I'm not entirely sure what PA material is, but I'm pretty sure it's not someone who types with two fingers, has a 'filing system' which consists of shoving everything in a drawer and then forgetting about it, and for the life of her can never remember whether it's supposed to be 'faithfully' or 'sincerely' at the end of a letter.

But Sir Richard waved away my concerns with one of his jovial smiles. Fifty-something, with a penchant for shiny brown suits and a comb-over that's fooling no one, he's the nicest boss I've ever had. Which is why it's such a shame he's retiring in a few months, I reflect, scribbling myself a reminder about his visa on a Post-it note and sticking it onto my computer which is fast becoming covered with them.

Staring at the pink and yellow Post-it wallpaper, I feel a niggle of worry. I should really start addressing some of them, otherwise pretty soon I won't be able to see my screen.

Or Facebook.

Spotting a friend's album entitled *Paradise*, I start idly clicking through the pictures: there's one of a sunset . . . a view of the infinity pool . . . having his'n'hers henna tattoos . . . him with his arms wrapped around her, gazing lovingly into her eyes . . .

I heave a deep sigh. If I felt depressed before, now I feel even worse. Faced with the gift-bearing boyfriends, perfect husbands and romantic holidays, my love life, or lack of it, is thrown into sharp contrast. I mean, I know I'm lucky in lots of ways. OK, I might not have a high-flying career, but I've got a job. I've got a roof over my head (well, technically it's my flatmate Fiona's roof as she owns the flat and I rent her spare room) and, as my mum is always fond of telling me, 'You've got your health, Tess.'

Still, it would be nice to have my health *and* an adoring boyfriend.

Abandoning their album I look back at the nagging question next to my profile picture, '*What's on your mind?*', I feel a familiar knot in my stomach. I've been trying to ignore it, but it's impossible.

One word: *Seb*.

To tell the truth, he's never off my mind. He's on it from the moment I wake up in the morning to the moment I go to bed. Ever since we broke up two months ago. Well, actually it was two months, one week and three days.

Yes, I'm still counting.

Two months, one week and three days since we had 'that conversation'. Well, I call it a conversation, but that implies a communication between two people. In actual fact it was mostly Seb telling me he loved me but wasn't in love with me, whilst trying to avoid eye contact and staring uncomfortably down at his trainers, and me sitting across from him on the sofa, fighting back tears and trying not to let him see my heart was breaking.

We'd been together for nearly a year and I really, *really* loved him. I loved that he was American and so different to me, with his strange cultural references, addiction to soy lattes and habit of mispronouncing the tube stations (he once called Leicester Square *Lie-ces-ter* Square). Loved that he was successful and smart and had these big broad shoulders that I could snuggle up against, into what I used to call 'the nook'. I even loved his terrible guitar playing – his rendition of 'Wonderwall' was his favourite – and it was so cute and rather adorable how he could never remember half the chords.

And then of course there was the sex. At the memory I feel a familiar tugging inside. I *really* loved that bit.

Some people grow to love each other. Start out as friends. But with Seb it was instantaneous. He was The One. From the moment we'd gone on our first date, and I'd been so nervous I'd clumsily knocked my glass of red wine all over his lap, I knew I was a goner. There was no point trying to resist. I was going to fall in love with him and there was nothing I could do about it.

What I didn't know was just how hard I was going to fall.

Since 'that conversation that wasn't really a conversation', I haven't heard from him, apart from the odd text 'just to say hi' and an e-card wishing me a Merry Christmas. But I only have myself to blame. Although he never said it, deep down I know it's all my fault we broke up, I'm the reason it didn't work out between us, and I can't help thinking if I'd done things differently we'd still be together . . .

Feeling the tears prickling my eyelashes, I hastily blink them away. Anyway, there's no point going over it all. You don't get to rehearse a relationship so you can get it right second time around. Seb and I are over and I need to forget all about him and move on.

'Wow, it's like a ghost town in here.'

I look up sharply from my computer screen to see a tall figure wearing a neon green vest and bicycle helmet striding through the foyer. Reaching into the messenger bag strapped across his chest, he pulls out a package and, seeing there's no one on reception today, heads down the corridor towards me.

'Where is everyone?' he asks in a thick Irish accent, glancing around the office and the empty desks strewn with the remnants of Christmas decorations.

'Getting engaged . . . going on honeymoon to Bali . . . having his-and-hers henna tattoos . . .'

He frowns in confusion. 'Henna tattoos?'

'Sorry, just ignore me.' Batting the question away with my hand, I force a smile and take the package from him. 'Thanks—'

'Fergus,' he prompts, unprompted.

'Oh, right . . . Fergus,' I nod.

He's one of our regular bicycle couriers. I've seen him popping in and out of reception, but we've never really spoken before, apart from a couple of times when Kym, our receptionist, has popped to the loo and I've had to sign for urgent parcels. We used to employ a firm of motorcycle despatch riders and van drivers, but about six months ago Sir Richard, the CEO, went all green and sent out a memo insisting we use 'pedal not petrol power' and we started using bicycle couriers.

'Grand,' replies Fergus cheerfully. 'Nearly had a punch-up with some wanker in a Porsche who doesn't know his arse from his indicator, but other than that . . .' Tugging off his helmet, he runs a gloved hand through a tangled shock of black hair. It's the first time I've seen his face properly and I realise he's actually quite good-looking. 'How's about you . . . ?' Raising an eyebrow he glances at the little nameplate on my desk. 'Tess Connelly.' He looks up and flashes me a flirtatious grin.

'Oh fine,' I fib, and begin briskly shuffling random papers around on my desk. I've seen him flirting with all the office girls in reception and I'm not going to fall for his charms. 'Busy.'

'Right, yeh,' he nods, glancing dubiously around the empty office.

'In fact, I haven't stopped all afternoon,' I say haughtily.

Which is a blatant lie. Work's been dead. Nothing ever happens between Christmas and New Year and most people have taken it off as holiday, especially as they're doing a bit of an internal refurb upstairs. I only volunteered to come in because I thought it would help distract me, keep my mind off things and give me something to do other than sit on the sofa with Fiona watching daytime TV and working my way through the giant tin of Quality Street her grandparents sent her.

But I don't want this cheeky Irish bicycle courier knowing that, I decide, picking up a sheet of paper and pretending to study it. 'Ooh look, an important fax from one of our clients in Brazil.'

See, I can at least *look* like I'm a super-efficient PA.

'What's bums, tums and thighs?' he asks, peering over my shoulder.

'*What?*' I glance down at the 'important fax' and see it's a list of aerobics classes for the gym I keep thinking about joining. *Thinking* being the operative word. Only with the New Year just around the corner, I'm determined it's going to be one of my resolutions. 'Oh . . . um . . . it's a new kind of Brazilian rum,' I fluster.

'Get away,' grins Fergus, his bright green eyes flashing with astonishment. 'Seriously?'

'Well, you know what they're like in Brazil,' I fib, crossing my fingers underneath my desk. 'It's all about the body, I mean look at Gisele . . .'

'Wow, you learn something new every day, don't you?'

'Um . . . yeh,' I nod, avoiding his gaze.

'Fancy asking for that in the pub – I'll have a large bums, tums and thighs.' He lets out a throaty laugh and shakes his head. 'Jeez, wait till I tell my mates back in Dublin about this one.'

Oh fuck, me and my big mouth.

'So, did you go back to Dublin for Christmas?' I ask, quickly trying to steer the subject away from Brazilian supermodels and made-up drinks.

'No, I didn't make it back this year,' he replies, scratching the little patch of stubble sprouting on his chin. 'Thought I'd have a quiet one here instead.'

'Quiet? *In London?*' Coming from the country, I could never describe London as being quiet.

'I've got seven sisters, eleven nieces and two nephews,' he explains. 'Imagine them all in one room. All shouting over the top of each other. Trust me, compared to that, *anywhere* is quiet.'

He rolls his eyes and I can't help but smile at his woeful expression.

'What about you? Big family knees-up?'

'No,' I shake my head. 'My parents flew out to Australia to visit my brother who's backpacking around the world, so I spent it with my granddad.' My earlier resolve not to engage with Fergus is fast disappearing and I can't help being drawn into opening up.

'So you had a quiet one then too, hey?'

I think about Granddad Connelly. There're a lot of words I'd use in conjunction with him, but quiet isn't one of them. 'Not exactly,' I smile ruefully, my mind throwing up an image of me and half a dozen of his eighty-something friends clustered around a fold-up table in his nursing home room, feasting on mince pies and a couple of bottles of Blackstock & White whisky I brought with me, while he entertained us with his repertoire of terrible jokes.

'My grandpa's ninety-two and he's always trying to lead me astray,' he grins. 'And there was me thinking he should be sitting in a rocking chair feeding me Werther's Originals.'

'Yeh, I know, right?' I laugh, despite my mood. His cheerful humour is infectious.

'So where's the craic tonight?'

I stop laughing and look at him blankly. '*Craic?*'

'You know, the party . . . New Year's Eve,' he prompts.

'Oh, right, of course.' I've been trying to block it out all day. New Year's Eve isn't exactly the best date in the diary for someone nursing a broken heart. 'I'm going to a party with my flatmate.'

'Great,' he nods enthusiastically. 'Where's that then?'

I falter. Fiona's been going on about it for weeks, but I haven't been paying much attention. To tell the truth, I've been secretly hoping that if I ignored it, it would somehow go away. A bit like I do with credit card bills, and those extra five pounds I put on over Christmas. 'Um . . . actually I'm not exactly sure . . .'

Thankfully I'm interrupted by the loud crackle of Fergus's radio, and the voice of his controller instructing him on another job. 'OK, well, better hit the road.' He throws me an apologetic smile. 'Have fun tonight . . .'

'Right, yeh, you too,' I nod, watching as he straps on his helmet, battling with the spikes of black hair that are determined to escape its confines. 'See you later.'

'See you next year,' he winks jovially and, turning on his heel, he quickly strides across the office.

I watch his neon figure disappearing through reception, then turn back to my computer and Facebook.

Suddenly my insides freeze.

Seb's been tagged in a photo. *At a party.*

My stomach lurches. I stare at it, like a rabbit caught in headlights.

Oh my god. While I've been holed up on my sofa, surrounded by soggy tissues and empty Malteser packets, wearing my scruffy old sweatpants and no make-up and feeling so depressed that even the cast of *EastEnders* appears cheerful by comparison, Seb's been out having fun. Without me.

My mind immediately goes into free-fall. Where is he? Whose party is it? Did he go on his own? Did he meet anyone? What other pictures are there?

For a moment I gaze at the photograph, torturing myself with all kinds of thoughts, before pulling myself together.

God, this is ridiculous. I've got to forget about him.

Impulsively I hit delete. A message pops up: '*Are you sure you want to remove Sebastian Fielding from your friends?*' And before I can change my mind, I click confirm and his photograph disappears.

He's gone. Just like that.

For a few seconds I stare at the space where he used to be, then briskly turning my attention back to work, I peel off a Post-it note.

If only it was that easy to delete him from my heart.

2

At four o'clock Sir Richard declares the office 'officially closed' and shoos me off home. 'Haven't you got a party to go to?' he booms good-naturedly, smoothing down the errant piece of hair that flaps around on his head, like a restless bird threatening to take flight. Unfortunately yes, I feel like answering. But of course I don't. Feeling depressed is one thing, letting your boss know you're a heartbroken wreck who wants to go home and hide under the duvet until the year is over is quite another.

'Um . . . yes,' I nod, avoiding his gaze and shutting down my computer. Standing up, I grab my coat from the back of my chair.

'Ah, to be young, footloose and fancy-free,' sighs Sir Richard wistfully. Perching his large frame on the corner of my desk, he folds his arms and gazes at me with a faraway look in his eyes.

I force a smile. Bundled up in my duvet coat, with Seb firmly on my mind, and a New Year's Eve party looming, there are many ways I can think of to describe how I'm feeling right now, and fancy-free is not one of them.

'I remember when I was your age, the things I'd get up to on New Year's Eve . . .' He trails off with a chuckle. 'You know, I once got arrested for dancing in the fountains at Trafalgar Square?'

'You did?' I look at my boss's ill-fitting suit, the thick, oversized glasses teetering on the end of his ruddy nose, his sensible brown lace-up brogues that look a hundred years old. It's hard to imagine.

'Indeed I did,' he nods, with more than a hint of pride in his voice. 'Actually I streaked.'

'*You did?*' My voice comes out at a higher pitch. I suddenly have a vision of Sir Richard running through fountains. *Naked.*

Arggh. *No.* I bat the vision away furiously.

'Oh yes,' he nods gravely. 'I was quite the rascal in my youth.'

I'm not quite sure where this trip down memory lane is heading, but I don't want to stay and find out.

'Well bye,' I say briskly, pulling up my fur-trimmed hood as if in an attempt to protect my ears from any more naked streaking stories. 'Happy New Year!'

'Ah yes, indeed, indeed,' he nods vigorously, snapping back and pushing his glasses up his nose. For a moment he remains there, perched on my desk, and for the first time I notice his suit is slightly more crumpled than usual, and if I'm not mistaken, he hasn't shaved this morning. 'Well, Happy New Year, Tess,' he says, reverting back into boss mode. Straightening up, he stuffs his hands firmly in his pockets. 'Have a wonderful evening.'

'You too,' I reply. He cuts a rather sad figure, standing by my cheese plant, alone in the office, and it suddenly strikes me that if I've escaped to the office, is Sir Richard escaping too? And if so, what from?

No sooner has the thought popped into my head than I dismiss it. Don't be silly, he's been happily married to Lady Blackstock for the past twenty years, what could he possibly be running away from? And, grabbing my bag, I give a little wave and walk towards the lift.

After the central-heated warmth of the office, outside is like stepping into a chiller cabinet. I set off briskly walking. It's too cold to wait for a bus, even in my duvet coat, plus I only live twenty minutes away. Digging out my iPod, I untangle the earphones and, to the sounds of Paolo Nutini, head towards the river.

Two tracks later, I see the majestic arch of Hammersmith Bridge up ahead, the ornate gold detailing picked out of the darkness by the stream of car headlights. Icy blasts whip up from the river and around my frozen ears and, turning up my collar, I bury my face into my mohair scarf and keep walking. Below me the Thames is inky black, but dotted along the riverbank I can see pubs with their strings of coloured fairy lights and make out the shapes of people spilling out from the beery warmth, braving the cold to smoke cigarettes.

I turn off my iPod. I can hear the sounds of chatter and laughter carried on the gusts of wind and for a moment I pause to lean against the railings. I let my gaze drift outwards. There's something magical about being suspended high above the river, looking down on London and life. A sense of freedom and quiet, even with the hum of the traffic behind me, that allows my mind the space to wander. To daydream. To think.

As usual I think about me and Seb. It's getting to be a bit of a habit, replaying scenes and conversations in my head, imagining if I hadn't said or done that, imagining if I'd reacted this way instead . . . It takes two people to make a relationship, and two people to break it, but there's so many things I did wrong. Not great big things, just lots of little random things.

Like, for instance, that stupid argument about marriage. With a stab of regret my mind flicks back to the summer. We'd gone to a friend's wedding and what began as jokey banter after I caught the bouquet about how 'we'll be next', turned sour when he said he didn't believe in marriage. I got all upset and took it personally, even though we'd only been dating for six months and I wasn't in any rush to get a ring on my finger. But that's what happens when you're a hopeless romantic and drink too much champagne . . . God, I'm such an idiot.

I feel my heart tug. Staring out into the velvet darkness I wonder where he is. What he's doing. If he's thinking about me. Missing someone has to be one of the worst human emotions. All the other feelings like anger and fear and horror get so much more airplay, as if their intensity gives them more value, but whereas those emotions come in violent bursts and are gone again, the gnawing ache of loss has to be simply endured. It's like background noise, it's always there, it never goes away. You just have to try to block it out, distract yourself, hope that tomorrow the hole they left behind has grown a little smaller.

Suddenly aware of how cold my fingers are, I unwrap them from the frozen railings and, shoving my icicle fingers in my pockets, cut down from the bridge and head towards a large red block of Victorian mansion flats on the corner. Above the doorway a sign in stained glass reads *Arminta Mansions*.

From the outside it looks very grand, very moneyed and very posh, but in reality the communal stairwells are a bit shabby and some of the neighbours are a bit dodgy. Fiona bought her flat years ago, with some money she was left by an old aunt, and it's up four flights of lung-bursting stairs, is in desperate need of a lick of paint and more than a little bit cramped.

Which, to be honest, is *very Fiona*.

Seriously, she's just like her flat. Grand on the outside, and anything but on the inside. To the outside world she's a successful health and beauty journalist, with a column in a national newspaper's Saturday magazine, where she extols the benefits of exercise, three healthy organic meals a day and SPF45. To those on the inside – i.e. me – she freelances from our kitchen table in her pyjamas, smokes twenty a day and, when she's not slathering herself in Hawaiian Tropic at the first glimmer of sunshine, she's trying to lose weight on some crazy fad diet or other.

I've tried telling her she's gorgeous just the way she is, but she'll never listen. Last month it was nothing but Tom Yum soup. 'It's the cabbage soup diet for the millennium,' she'd explained enthusiastically, 'only without the flatulence', and three times a week she'd walked to the Thai takeaway to collect huge vats of it. Still, I guess that's regular exercise.

Fiona is my oldest and closest friend. We met at our local primary school when we were both eight years old, and by way of introduction she told me she could play the piano and that her parents had a holiday home in the south of France. Which they do.

Sort of.

If you can count towing a caravan across the Channel every year.

As for playing the piano, it was more 'Chopsticks' on a Yamaha keyboard.

But that's Fiona. She's always been like that. And yes, OK, it can be a bit embarrassing when she puts on her posh voice and tells people she went to Cambridge, but omits to mention it was actually the poly. Or like, for example, the other night when I heard her on the phone saying she must go as she 'had Pilates', when in actual fact, what she really meant was she *has a Pilates DVD* and it's stuffed underneath the telly gathering dust along with all her other exercise DVDs. Not only that, but I've only ever seen her do it once and she switched it off halfway through to watch *Dragon's Den.*

Yet, despite her affectations, underneath it all she's one of the sweetest people you'll ever meet. She's got a huge heart and when the chips are down, I know she'll always be there for me – I call her the fourth emergency service; but it's as if she feels she has to put on this big act to the public. As if, for some reason, she's ashamed of who she really is. To be honest, I think a lot of it has to do with her mum. She was one of those classic pushy mothers who nagged her about her puppy fat and had her doing all this extracurricular stuff.

Poor Fiona used to turn up at school every day nearly collapsing under the weight of about four musical instruments, a tennis racquet, hockey stick, ballet outfit and swimming gear. When she complained her mum told her, 'Marilyn Monroe never got anywhere by being Norma Jean.' Which was a bit confusing for an eleven year old. And a lot of pressure. I don't think Fiona's ever really got over it.

'Tess, is that you?'

Breathless from the climb, I push open the door of the flat to be greeted by a loud holler coming from her bedroom. Strangely, when it's just me, her voice is a lot less *Made in Chelsea* and a lot more *The Only Way Is Essex*.

'Why? Who else are you expecting?' I puff, dumping my bag on the table in the hallway. Flea, our ginger cat, appears and begins wrapping himself around my legs and purring loudly. Picking him up, I'm tickling him under his chin when a thought strikes: *Oh no! Maybe she's invited one of her recent dates to the party too.*

Mentally I whiz through a Rolodex of men who've trooped through the flat in the past few months: there was Karl the diplomat who was six foot ten and nearly knocked himself unconscious on the kitchen doorframe; Gavin, who wrote poetry, and insisted on reciting it; Carlos the Spanish guy, who turned up to take her out to dinner, smoked a joint on the sofa, then promptly passed out . . .

To tell the truth, I can't remember them all. After years of dating the old-fashioned way without much success, Fiona has recently discovered online dating and is going through men at an alarming rate of knots.

I listen out for her reply but there's no answer.

Oh god, don't tell me one of them's here *already*. Well, it wouldn't be the first time I've walked in and unexpectedly come face-to-boxer-shorts with a half-naked man in the kitchen.

'Fi . . .' I say cautiously. I cock my ear for the sounds of *you-know-what* coming from her bedroom. I can hear a lot of rustling; poking my head around the corner, I peer down the corridor. 'Are you . . . um . . . decent?'

There's a loud thud, then her door's abruptly flung open.

'Ta-daahh!'

Flea gives a high-pitched screech and jumps out of my arms in fright. But instead of a strange man in boxer shorts, there's Fiona in a nurse's uniform.

'What do you think?' She does a little twirl on her vertiginous heels. 'It's for the party tonight,' she continues, fiddling with the white nurse's cap. It's perched on top of her blonde hair which has been highlighted, tonged and hairsprayed to within an inch of its life.

And to think she just wrote an article about hair and how it's time to 'throw out the colouring and styling products' and go *au naturel.*

'What's your costume?' She looks at me expectantly.

I stare at her for a moment, vague memories of her talking about the party trickling back: 'huge roof terrace with amazing views . . . works for Moët so there'll be tons of champagne . . . invite says to wear a costume . . .'

I get a really horrible sinking feeling.

'You hadn't forgotten it's fancy dress, had you?'

'Well no, not exactly—' I begin, but she cuts me off excitedly.

'So, come on, don't keep me in suspense, what are you wearing?' Turning to study her reflection in the built-in microwave, she applies another coat of lip gloss.

'Well, that's the thing you see, I was going to wear my jeans, I mean no one will ever notice—' I reason, tugging off my coat and hanging it over the back of the chair.

'Tess!' She lets out a gasp and rounds on me. 'You cannot go in your jeans! It's New Year's Eve!'

'What's wrong with wearing jeans on New Year's Eve?' I try

arguing, but I'm met with a look. I know that look. It's the one she gave the gas man last winter when he told us he couldn't fix the boiler and, 'Sorry luv, you'll have to take cold showers until I order a new part.' She didn't say anything – she didn't have to. Not with *that* look.

Suffice to say he spent all afternoon taking apart and rebuilding our ancient combi-boiler and she spent all evening soaking in a long hot bubble bath.

'But you have to wear a costume,' she says. 'It's a fancy-dress party.'

Suddenly seeing my opportunity, I grab it with both hands. 'You're absolutely right,' I nod gravely, 'Only, I don't have one, so you know what, I probably shouldn't go. I'm not really in the mood anyway . . .'

I feel almost giddy with relief at the thought of staying home in my pyjamas with Flea and the TV.

For like a second.

'Nonsense. Of course you should go,' she says, batting away my objections with her lip-gloss wand. 'You're depressed. A party will make you feel tons better.' She flashes me an encouraging smile.

'I'm not depressed, I'm heartbroken,' I point out.

Her smile is replaced with a look of concern. 'Oh Tess, you've got to stop mooning over Seb. You need to forget about him. Pretend like he doesn't exist. It's been months now—'

'It hasn't been *months*, it's only been two months, one week and three days . . . or thereabouts,' I add, trying to sound vague and failing, 'and I'm not *mooning* over him. I just miss him, that's all.'

'Of course you do,' she says, giving my arm a squeeze. 'And I know how it feels, I've been there. Remember when Lawrence broke up with me?'

'It's hardly the same – you went on two dates.'

'I was still heartbroken,' she replies, looking hurt.

'Fiona, the only time I've ever seen you heartbroken is when they didn't have your size in the L. K. Bennett sale,' I point out.

It's not that Fiona doesn't have feelings, but when it comes to failed romances, she only allows herself twenty-four hours to be depressed/delete all his texts/eat everything in the cupboards. At the end of which she does her Tracy Anderson DVD, changes her Facebook status back to Single and goes back online.

'Love isn't measured by time, you know Tess,' she continues sagely, ignoring my last comment. 'You can fall in love at first sight.'

'You can fall in *lust* at first sight,' I correct, thinking about those two dates of hers with Lawrence, which, if I remember rightly, were mostly spent sub-duvet.

'I've got a spare costume you can borrow,' she says, ignoring me. 'It's a bit too snug for me, as that Tom Yum diet didn't work. I put *on* four pounds . . .' She glances down at her stomach in dismay and tries to suck it in, expanding her ribcage so that her cleavage looks even bigger than before. 'But it will fit you perfectly,' she adds, looking back at me pointedly.

'What costume?' I ask cautiously.

'You'll love it! It's a sexy kitten!' she beams.

My heart plummets. 'How can a kitten be sexy?' I wail but, even as I'm asking, I'm not sure I want to find out.

But before she can answer, we're interrupted by her BlackBerry ringing and she snatches it up from the table. 'Pippa, sweetie,' she squeals, switching into her posh voice. 'How are you?'

Pippa is one of Fiona's posh new friends that she met at the Cartier International polo last summer. Fiona was there to write an article – apparently 'polo is the new Pilates' – and Pippa and her mates were there because they're friends with the royals who were attending. Pippa used to date Prince Harry. Or *knew* someone who had dated Prince Harry.

Whatever, it's still a connection, however tenuous, and it's brought out the Marilyn Monroe in Fiona's Norma Jean.

'Absolutely, I can't wait for tonight. Are Tiggy and Rizzle coming too?'

That's one of the things I've noticed about Fiona's posh friends. No one's got a normal name; they all sound as though they should be characters from a kid's cartoon. Even Fiona isn't plain old Fiona when she's with them – instead she turns into 'Fifi'. I know this as I once answered Fiona's BlackBerry for her when she was in the bath and it was Pippa asking for someone called Fifi. At first I thought it was a wrong number.

'Christmas?' trills Fiona. 'Oh, I spent the day at Mummy and Daddy's.'

Mummy and Daddy? Since when did John and Liz, Fiona's parents, go from being plain Mum and Dad to 'Mummy and Daddy'?

Bemused, I listen as she starts flicking her blonde hair about and chattering on about 'how wonderful it was to spend some time in the country'.

The country being her parents' pebble-dashed semi in Kent, by the way.

I weave past her and start filling up the kettle. Forget champagne and canapés, I'm dying for a cup of tea and some Jaffa Cakes. I bought a fresh packet just the other day . . . Standing on tiptoe I begin rummaging in the cupboard, while she continues her conversation.

'I know, I'm exactly the same! I just adore the long walks and fresh air.'

I try not to laugh. Fiona doesn't do fresh air. She does scented candles and Marlboro Lights. And as for long walks . . .

I glance down at her teetering heels. Fiona is barely over five foot, but what she doesn't have in stature, she makes up for in skyscraper stilettos. She's the only person I know who sticks up for Victoria Beckham. She calls her a 'kindred soul'. In fact, only the other weekend I caught her flicking through a copy of *Hello!*, and out of the corner of my eye I saw her looking at another photo of Posh in another pair of ridiculously high heels. Not realising I was listening, she let out a deep sigh and murmured, 'I feel your pain, Victoria, I really do,' and rubbed her bunions in solidarity.

'OK, super! Can't wait to see you too. I just need to help my flatmate with her costume.' She shoots me *that* look, and I shield myself with the packet of Jaffa Cakes. 'OK, *ciao*, *ciao*.' There's lots of kissing into her BlackBerry, then she hangs up and turns to me.

'Oy, stop stuffing your face!' Seamlessly reverting from *Made in Chelsea* back to *The Only Way Is Essex*, she snatches the packet out of my hand. 'We need to turn you into a sexy kitten.'

'But I don't want to be a sexy kitten,' I yelp, clutching onto my tea before she swipes that as well.

'It's New Year's Eve,' she says firmly. 'You don't have a choice.'

For a moment there's a standoff in the kitchen, and I briefly think about holding my ground.

But Fiona can be very scary, especially in that nurse's costume.

'OK, OK.' Holding my hands up in surrender, I get up from the table. 'I give in.'

'I knew you would,' she nods with satisfaction. 'Now hurry up, I've got a cab coming.' Pushing me towards my bedroom, she disappears into hers and emerges with a black leotard and a pair of furry ears. 'A party is the perfect cure for heartbreak. You'll have so much fun tonight you'll be able to put this whole thing with Seb behind you.' And, passing me my costume, she gives me a quick hug. 'Trust me, you'll wake up tomorrow and it will be like it never happened.'

3

I have a theory about New Year's Eve.

All over the world it's hailed as the biggest and best night of the year. A night to celebrate, to have fun, to party like you're Prince and it's 1999. And with it comes all this expectation and anticipation. All this build-up. All this pressure to have an amazing time.

To be honest, it's a bit like losing your virginity.

But what happens if you don't have an amazing time? What if it's actually all a bit of a letdown, and while everyone else appears to be having a blast, you can't help thinking 'is this it?' and worrying there's something wrong with you.

(Now I think about it, it really *is* like losing your virginity.)

Except I have a sneaking suspicion that secretly *everyone* is thinking the same thing. It doesn't matter whether you're doing the hokey cokey in Trafalgar Square, getting drunk at a club in New York or raving on a beach in Goa. All over the world, millions of people are faking it. It's like one great big conspiracy.

Then again, maybe my theory is completely wrong and everyone else really *is* having a fab time, I decide, glancing over at a very drunk Marie Antoinette, who looks to be thoroughly enjoying snogging the face off Elvis. Maybe it's just me and I really *am* the odd one out.

It's an hour later and I'm in one of those huge white stucco houses in Chelsea. Inside it's like something out of a glossy magazine shoot: there's a picture-perfect Christmas tree in the marble hallway, a roaring fire, and a large terrace that stretches out from the grand drawing room, decorated with thousands of twinkling fairy lights.

The party is in full swing. On arrival Fiona was swooped upon by Dan, a former online date from KindredSpiritsRUs who'd stalked her in cyberspace and was now holding her hostage in the corner of the kitchen. And, after a few failed attempts at small talk, here I am, standing on my own in the living room, not knowing a soul, and trying to look all cool and relaxed.

I mean, there's only so long you can pretend to be texting, isn't there?

Spotting a passing tray of champagne, I lasso a glass and drain half of it in one go.

'Thirsty, hey?' grins the waiter with a thick Aussie accent.

'Sort of,' I smile, grateful for a friendly face. I think about trying to engage him in conversation, but before I can muster up anything to say, he's already weaving his way through the rest of the party.

Glugging back the rest of the champagne, I scan the room for someone to strike up a conversation with. Now I'm here I'm really trying to get into the party spirit and have a good time, but despite my best efforts I'm not doing very well so far. I don't think this outfit is helping. Fiona's argument that everyone would be wearing a costume and I'd 'blend in' is proving to be no comfort from the fact I'm wearing what is effectively a giant 60-denier body stocking and a pair of furry ears.

Plus I'm trying not even to *think* about the whiskers she drew on my face with eyeliner. Or the fact that she insisted I wear a tail she'd made out of tinsel.

I'm just wondering where I can get another glass of champagne before I die from embarrassment that everyone can see my bottom, when Fiona emerges from the kitchen. 'Oh god, sorry about that,' she gasps apologetically. 'I couldn't get away; he kept insisting we were soul mates.'

'But I thought you only went on one date and it was terrible.'

'Worse than terrible!' She pulls a face. 'He told me he doesn't drink, doesn't smoke, and is still a virgin!'

'So you were a perfect match,' I say with amusement.

'Well that's just it,' she says, looking pained. 'He kept going on about how our profiles were a ninety-nine-per-cent match and he didn't understand why I didn't want to go out with him as the computer says we're meant to be together—'

We're interrupted by a loud shriek of laughter and both turn to see a gaggle of girls outside on the terrace. All wearing suspenders, fishnets and push-up bras, they're quaffing champagne and clustered around a skinny, horsey-looking blonde in a red devil's costume.

'Oh look, it's Pippa and the rest of the girls,' says Fiona with surprise. 'She mustn't know I'm here.'

I glance across and feel a snag of doubt. I've never actually met Pippa, but she looks like one of those people for whom everything is irrelevant apart from themselves, and that includes Fiona's presence at this party.

'Still, it is very busy, she probably just didn't see me,' continues Fiona brightly, though somewhat unconvincingly. 'Come on, let me introduce you – you're gonna love her!' And before I can protest, Fiona has looped her arm through mine and is enthusiastically steering me outside.

'Hi guys,' she waves, tottering up to the group, which breaks apart at our appearance and eyes me suspiciously. But Fiona doesn't seem to notice. 'Tess, this is Lolly, Rara and Grizzle,' she beams, flinging out her arms like a presenter on one of those shopping channels when they're presenting some hideously fake-looking item and trying to convince you how wonderful it is.

Funny that.

There's a murmur of hellos and lots of flicking of hair.

'And this is Pippa!' she gushes, with the verbal equivalent of a drum roll.

Pippa leans in to kiss me on both cheeks, whilst her eyes run over me like radar scanners. 'Tess, I've heard *soooo* much about you,' she coos, giving me a smile that's as fake as her friendliness. 'How wonderful to finally meet you.'

'You too,' I smile. 'I've heard so much about you too.' (I swear if Fiona tells me the Prince Harry story one more time . . .)

'Do you know Pippa's a jewellery designer?' continues Fiona. 'Isn't that amazing?'

'Um . . . yes,' I nod. 'Amazing.'

'Look, she made this ring!' Fiona points to Pippa's finger and something that looks as if it fell out of a cracker.

'It's an emerald,' says Pippa nonchalantly. 'Five carats. Flawless.'

I look again in astonishment. That great big green piece of glass is *real*?

'I get all my stones from Raji,' she continues blithely. 'It was originally in an antique necklace but I reset it.'

'Raji? Oh, is that the jeweller's on the high street, near Putney Station?'

'Rajasthan, in India,' she says, looking at me as if I'm stupid.

I feel my cheeks colour.

'Though I'm thinking of taking a break from designing as it's so *exhausting*.' Heaving a sigh, she takes a sip of champagne.

'I can only imagine,' I nod, trying to imagine how tiring it must be making emerald rings all day – and failing. 'All that flying, and backwards and forwards to India. I get knackered just walking across Hammersmith Bridge to the office.'

Hearing the sarcasm in my voice, Fiona glances at me nervously, but Pippa is immune.

'I know, right! Absolutely!' she wide-eyes. 'And air travel is so dehydrating for the skin. My facialist is forever telling me' – she adopts a stern voice – '"Pippa, think about your pores!"'

There's a muttering of sympathy and someone gives her shoulder a reassuring squeeze.

'That's why I'm thinking of setting up an animal sanctuary and working with rescue animals.'

'Pips, you're so incredible with animals,' pipes up Grizzle. Or is it Lolly? I can't tell them apart: they're all blonde, skinny and wearing push-up bras.

'We've got a rescue cat!' enthuses Fiona, trying to join in. 'She's called Flea.'

'Really? How cute,' sniffs Pippa. 'But I was thinking of something a bit less *domestic*.' She gives a little derisory smile.

I watch Fiona's face fall. God, Pippa is such a horrible, condescending snob. I don't understand why Fiona wants to be her friend. For some reason she's impressed by her.

'Mummy breeds llamas, and horses are in my blood, so flea-ridden old moggies aren't *exactly* me.' She gives a little titter and the rest of the gang join in like a load of braying donkeys.

I feel a sudden flash of protectiveness. For both Flea *and* Fiona.

'Oh I don't know, I'm sure you can be very catty if you feel like it,' I reply with an innocent smile.

Abruptly the laughter stops and there are a few nervous giggles. I catch sight of Fiona's horrified expression as Pippa turns and stares at me, as if seeing me for the first time. Narrowing her eyes, she asks sharply, 'What exactly is it that you do again?'

'Nothing nearly as fascinating as you—' I begin breezily, but I'm interrupted by Fiona who almost tackles me to the ground.

'Oh, look, Tess, you've got an empty glass,' she exclaims in a shrill voice. 'Let's go get some more drinks.' And, grabbing me by the elbow, she hurries me inside.

* * *

'I'm sorry,' I say, as soon as we're inside. 'I know Pippa's your friend, but I had to stick up for Flea.' And you, I add silently.

'Oh, she doesn't mean anything by it, that's just her way. She's just a bit shy, that's all,' says Fiona defensively.

'*Shy?*' I repeat in disbelief. 'If Pippa's shy, then so is Lady Gaga.'

Diving on a waiter with a tray of champagne, Fiona pretends not to hear me. 'Two glasses, please.'

'Actually, not for me, I think I might go home,' I interrupt.

With a glass already in each hand, Fiona twirls around to face me, spilling the champagne over the sides. 'Go home?' she exclaims. 'You can't go home: it's not even midnight yet! You'll miss the countdown.'

'That's the idea,' I smile ruefully.

She looks so crestfallen that I feel a stab of guilt. It's not her fault I'm not enjoying the party. Try as I might, broken hearts and New Year's Eve just don't go together.

'I'm sorry,' I shrug apologetically, 'but I don't think I can face that moment when we get to 'one' and I've got to find someone to kiss.'

'You can kiss me,' she offers solemnly, 'as long as it's not on the lips.'

'Thanks, Fiona, that's really kind of you,' I say with mock gratitude. 'I love you, but not that much.'

'It's OK, I can take the rejection,' she shrugs, burying her nose in her glass of champagne. She takes a few gulps, then elbows me in the ribs. 'Oh c'mon, Tess, stay and have another drink,' she cajoles, waving a glass of champagne under my nose. 'Let's just get smashed and have a laugh.'

In the past, getting drunk with Fiona has always made me feel better – until the hangover the next day, of course – but tonight my heart's just not in it. Not even with the offer of free champagne.

'Another time,' I say, shaking my head.

'But it's New Year's Eve, you'll never get a taxi,' she argues. 'So you'll have to stay.'

At that precise moment, I see the headlights of a cab pull up outside, and a couple of late partygoers spill out onto the pavement. Perfect timing: it's my getaway car.

'Now listen, you're under strict orders to enjoy the rest of the party and get horribly drunk,' I instruct, giving her a big hug before she can protest any further. 'And, by the way, I think Henry the Eighth has got the hots for you.' I gesture across the room to a guy who's wearing breeches, a fake-fur cape and has a big ginger beard stuck on his face.

'That's what they said to Anne Boleyn, and look what happened to her,' she pouts sulkily, finishing off her glass and starting on mine.

She glances across at him.

He winks.

'Then again, maybe he's worth losing my head over,' she says and, as I watch her sucking in her stomach, I leave her to flirt and dash outside to the waiting cab.

4

'Hey fleabag, I'm home.'

One good thing about New Year's Eve, everyone's so busy partying that there's zero traffic on the roads, so it's not long before I'm letting myself into the flat, shutting the door behind me, and kicking off my high heels.

God, it feels good to be home. Padding into the kitchen in my stockinged feet, I flick on the kettle. Even if the kitchen is a mess, it's Fiona's turn to do the washing-up. We're out of milk, too, I realise, tugging open the fridge and surveying the empty bottle left on the shelf.

I say empty, but there's a tiny dribble, courtesy of Fiona, who always makes sure to leave a bit so she can't be blamed for finishing it off. 'But there's some left,' she'll bleat when accused, referring to the couple of drops in the bottom.

Chucking the bottle in the recycling, I nose around in the cupboards for something that doesn't require milk. There's a bunch of Fiona's herbal teas, but they're not actually for drinking, they're just for appearances. She gets them out whenever she's got 'guests', and makes a little virtuous display with them, along with her Diptyque candle and speciality jams, which she got from a Fortnum & Mason's gift hamper about four Christmases ago. And which I once mistakenly nearly opened when we ran out of our usual Tesco's strawberry.

I'll never forget it. She literally leapt across the kitchen in her silk kimono dressing gown, like something from *Crouching Tiger*, and with a howl snatched the cognac and elderflower marmalade from my hands before I could get the knife under the seal. I'm not kidding, it was actually pretty scary.

Oh hang on, what's that? Behind the nettle and burdock root infusion, I spot a bottle of something that looks like—

My emergency bottle of tequila.

I eye it triumphantly. I'd forgotten all about that. Sir Richard gave it to me last year for my birthday and I'd stashed it away in the cupboard. Not that I don't drink tequila, but usually when I'm at home and I fancy a drink, I'll share a bottle of wine with Fiona, not start doing slammers on the kitchen counter.

I eye the bottle.

I said *usually* when I'm at home. But tonight's different. There's nothing usual about it. It's New Year's Eve. I'm heart-broken. Home alone. And I'm wearing a sexy kitten costume.

Sod the herbal tea. It's going to take something a lot stronger than that tonight.

OK, to do this properly I need salt and a lime. That much I do know. I glance at our pathetic excuse for a fruit bowl. With Fiona being a health and beauty writer, you'd think it would be overflowing with exotic fruits. Instead we've got two blackened bananas and a Granny Smith that's so shrivelled it should be on display in the British Museum. And I can't find the salt. Or a clean glass.

Oh well, never mind, I muse, grabbing my Keep Calm and Carry On mug from the mug tree, and pouring myself a shot. Actually, it's probably more like about four shots, I realise, looking at the amount of tequila in the bottom of the mug before slugging it back. I slam my mug down on the kitchen counter and wince. The tequila is like liquid fire, burning a path to my stomach. Whoah. Talk about strong. This stuff really blows your head off. A few more shots like that and I'll be so completely blotto I won't know what day it is.

Perfect.

Pouring another large mugful, I head into my bedroom. This used to be the living room, but because Fiona's flat is really only a one-bedroom, she converted it into another bedroom when I moved in. Which works fine as the kitchen is one of those big eat-in kitchens, and I've got my own little portable TV that I like to watch lying on my bed, plus I've got the original Victorian fireplace in my room, *and* it works.

In fact, I think I'll light it now, I decide. A real fire always cheers me up. Throwing on some firewood, I busy myself with twisting up bits of newspaper, a trick my granddad taught me as a little girl, and in no time at all I've got a decent fire going. On a roll, I turn my attention to my candles, only my favourite scented one is finished.

Damn. Chucking it in the bin a thought strikes me, but immediately I dismiss it. No, I can't. Fiona will kill me.

She'll never find out, whispers a drunken, rebellious voice in my head. *You can put it back before she comes home. You're only borrowing it.*

Now normally in my sane, rational mind I would never entertain such an idea. Borrowing 'The Diptyque', as Fiona reverently calls it, is a bit like borrowing the Crown Jewels. In other words, you just don't. It's meant to be displayed on the little corner table in the hallway, along with the white orchid in a pot, and Fiona's Smythson address book which she got as a gift from a PR.

But I'm not sane. Or rational. I'm a glass of champagne and two very large tequila shots down already, and now it seems like a bloody marvellous idea. As does finishing off that entire box of Jaffa Cakes, I suddenly remember, tripping happily into the kitchen and returning with the contraband goods. Munching on a biscuit, I light her Diptyque candle with a flourish. There. Perfect.

Inhaling the expensive scent of fig, I stand back from the fireplace. With the fire flickering away and the candle lit, I feel a warm glow. It all looks so lovely. So cosy. *So romantic.*

I wish Seb was here.

Boom. It hits me again. For a few moments he hadn't been in my head, but now he comes flying back in again, almost knocking the breath out of me. Feeling my eyes prickle, I try quickly distracting myself by grabbing the remote and switching on the TV. I'm not going to cry, I tell myself firmly. I am *not* going to cry.

I force myself to focus on the TV. It's the usual New Year's Eve-type stuff: a reporter standing by the Millennium Wheel, freezing cold in her silver dress and trying to look all jolly . . . *flick* . . . an old black-and-white movie . . . *flick* . . . Jools Holland's New Year's Eve show . . . *flick* . . . another reporter, only this time she's on the other side of the Atlantic, '*even though we have a few hours to go until the ball drops, we're gearing up for it here in New York . . .*'

Perching on the end of my bed, I watch as the camera pans around the dazzling lights of Times Square and the crowds of revellers all cheering madly, until it focuses back on a grinning couple.

'*. . . and here we have Tiffany and Brandon who are getting married tonight, live in Times Square!*'

Argh no, we don't. Hastily I flick channels. Now I'm back to the reporter freezing her arse off at the London Eye.

'*So I'm with Andrew Cotter, a lecturer in Cultural Studies, to talk about all the different New Year's Eve traditions and rituals that are happening across the globe.*'

Cut to Andrew, a short balding guy with glittery space-hopper ears. I'm presuming they're part of a fancy-dress costume. At least I hope so.

'*So tell me, Andrew, how is the rest of the world celebrating?*'

'*Well, Kerrie,*' he begins jovially, '*in Denmark you throw broken plates at people's doors, and in Venezuela everyone wears yellow underwear for good luck—*'

'*Yellow underwear!*' giggles the reporter. '*Have you got yours on tonight, Andrew?*'

'*I have indeed, Kerrie*,' he winks. '*What about you?*'

'*Well that would be telling!*' she gasps with mock indignation, and they share a flirty giggle, before seeming to remember she's live on TV, and she clears her throat briskly.

'And of course here in the UK we have fancy dress! So let's take a look at some of the best ones here this evening . . .'

As a parade of people in whacky costumes troop by the cameras, I take a glug of tequila.

Fancy dress.

I mean, it's not much cop, is it? Wearing yellow underwear and throwing plates sounds like way more fun than wearing a black Lycra catsuit and pair of furry ears. Tugging mine off, I chuck them on my dressing table. Sexy kitten indeed. Quite frankly I look more like an old moggy. Speaking of which, where's Flea?

Suddenly I hear a loud screech from outside and, glancing out through the window, I see an explosion of coloured lights. Of course. *Fireworks.* Flea must be hiding somewhere. He hates fireworks – they absolutely terrify him.

I'm about to go on a hunt when I hear the teeniest of meows coming from under the bed and, unsteadily getting down on all fours (the tequila has gone *right* to my head), I peer underneath. Out of the dimness, a pair of huge green eyes stare back at me, unblinkingly.

'Hey buddy,' I cajole, reaching out to stroke him. He doesn't budge. Paws curled under his chest, sphinx-like, he gives me a stubborn look that says, 'Hey buddy nothing, I'm staying right here.'

Which is fair enough. I don't blame him. Given the choice, hiding under the bed is how I would have chosen to spend my New Year's Eve.

Giving him one last tickle, I'm about to get up when something else in the shadows catches my eye: a cardboard box. I pause. I'd almost forgotten about it.

Almost. But not quite. Like Flea, it's been in hiding.

I feel my chest tighten. I know I should leave it there. Ignore it. Get back up and watch TV as if I never saw it.

But then, doing what's right for me has never been something I'm very good at. Pulling it out from underneath the bed, I sit cross-legged on my sheepskin rug in front of the fire and place it in front of me. From the outside it's nothing special. There's no *ta-daa-daah* moment. It's not like Harrison Ford and *Raiders of the Lost Ark*. I'm not going to lift off the lid and discover the key to human existence. It's just an old Nine West shoebox.

And yet . . .

And yet inside it holds something just as important to me. Something even more valuable. Because inside is my relationship with Seb.

Maybe it's just me being some silly, sentimental idiot, but I used to save things from when we were together. Not big stuff, like expensive jewellery or long flowery love letters – just little, random things. To anyone else the contents of this box would look like a jumble of nondescript items, nothing special, just a bunch of worthless junk. But to me it's a box full of memories, of special moments shared, of snapshots of our life together.

Like, for example:

A pair of cinema ticket stubs

These were to see the first film I ever watched with Seb. *Star Wars*. We saw it at the British Film Institute as part of some festival. We had such a lovely time snuggling up in the back row.

I start going through the contents one by one.

Driftwood

From West Wittering beach. It was a freezing cold day in January and on impulse we wrapped ourselves up in scarves and hats and drove down to the coast, and he went paddling in the frozen sea. I stood watching him from the shore while he called me a chicken.

Concert wristband

Seb was a huge fan of all these American indie bands that I'd never heard of. To me it sounded a bit like a load of shouting and clashing guitars, but it was fun to go to our first-ever concert together.

Wine cork

Still with the red wine stain on it, I angle it to the light and read the name on the top: Stanly Ranch Pinot Noir. It was from the bottle of wine we drank at his flat; it was the evening we first spent the night together; the first night we ever had sex . . .

Card with a picture of a snowbunny on the front

Seb adored snowboarding and wanted to take me away to the Alps for a weekend, but we never ended up going. That was my fault. I've never snowboarded in my life and I suggested a spa break instead . . .

Opening the card, I decipher his awful handwriting: '*Can't wait to see you on the slopes and enjoy some après-ski with you. Seb xx*'.

I feel a lump in my throat and hastily stick it back in the box and pull out:

Matches

Turning the small box over in my fingers, I trace the inscription on the front. *Mala*. Seb adored spicy food and this was his favourite restaurant. He took me there once as a surprise and ordered all these amazing dishes.

At the memory a tear unexpectedly spills down my cheek. Quickly I wipe it away with my sleeve. I wasn't going to cry, remember?

Plectrum

Seb played the guitar and he had dozens of plectrums scattered around his flat. He once joked I should keep one for when he was famous one day and I could sell it for a fortune on eBay.

Barack Obama's autobiography

This book is so thick it takes up most of the box and, picking it up, I thumb through the well-worn pages with the corners turned down. This is Seb's copy. He used to rave about it, told me reading it would change my life, yet I never got round to it. Feeling a thump of remorse I put it back, my eyes falling upon something else . . .

Scarlet satin ribbon

From the box of lingerie he bought me from New York for my birthday; inside was a frothy French lace G-string and sexy red satin bra with peepholes and push-up bits. It's still in my drawer, all wrapped up in tissue paper as I haven't yet worn it. Well, I couldn't admit I needed a larger size, could I? Instead I kept hoping my bottom might get smaller (or the knickers might magically get bigger!).

Photograph

Taken at a friend's wedding (before we had that silly argument). Him looking incredibly handsome in a morning suit, me wearing one of those silly fascinators. We make such a lovely couple . . . *made* such a lovely couple . . .

I stare at the black-and-white image, watching it slowly turn blurry, as the tears that have been threatening to fall begin streaming down my face. And this time I don't try to wipe them away. This time I bury my head in my hands and cry my bloody heart out.

I don't know how long I stay like that before I feel something soft brush against me and I glance up to see Flea, rubbing up against my leg. Wiping my puffy eyes, I scoop him up and hug him to me, feeling his soft warm body against mine. Regret stabs. There are so many things I wish I'd done differently, so many things I wish I'd said and hadn't said, so many mistakes I made . . . I heave a deep sigh . . . but it's all pointless now. It's happened and I just wish I could erase all the hurt and regret, make it all go away . . .

'Have you ever been heartbroken?' I ask Flea, tickling him under his chin. 'No, you're too smart for that. Well, let me tell you, it sucks.' I glance across at my mobile phone. It's lying silent on the bed. For a moment I think about calling Seb, sending him a text . . .

Which is just ridiculous. Pathetic even. You've broken up, remember? He's not your boyfriend any more. Plus, he's most likely out there partying right now, having a good time, goads a voice inside me. My hurt is replaced by a hot flash of anger and I take another glug of tequila. Come on Tess, pull yourself together. You can't let him know you're crying your eyes out over him. Where's your pride, girl? Sod Seb Fielding!

Grabbing a tissue, I blow my nose violently, making Flea jump off my lap. He steps on the remote, his paw turning up the volume.

'*Well the New Year is nearly here, we've got less than a minute to go!*' chirps the presenter cheerily. '*So, Andrew, of all the traditions, which is your favourite?*'

I watch as the camera cuts to Andrew. He's still wearing his spacehopper ears and grinning maniacally. '*Well, Kerrie, my favourite is an ancient ritual that involves taking a piece of paper and writing down all the things you want to rid yourself of, be it regrets or painful memories, hurt, or maybe a bad habit or addiction, and throwing the list into the fire at the stroke of midnight.*' He gives a little chuckle. '*Though obviously in ancient times there were no pens or paper, so instead people would choose objects or pictures that symbolised these things.*'

'*But why throw them on the fire?*' asks Kerrie, frowning.

'*Because many cultures believe that by burning these things you get rid of them. You're cleansed of them, and that way you don't carry them with you into next year.*'

'*Wow, fascinating stuff!*' wide-eyes Kerrie. '*That's incredible.*'

I take another defiant glug of tequila. You've got to be kidding me. Is she really believing this rubbish?

'*Indeed,*' Andrew is nodding feverishly, '*and what's more, as the flames burn away these things, sparks will well and truly fly. So make a wish! Because whatever you wish for will be carried on these sparks into the New Year . . .*'

'Huh, well, in that case, do you want to know what I wish?' I heckle drunkenly at Andrew and Kerrie.

On the TV, Big Ben starts chiming midnight and impulsively I grab the shoebox and, smarting with disappointment and anger, throw the whole damn lot on the fire.

'I wish I'd never met him!'

Immediately it catches light and, as I watch my relationship with Seb go up in flames, burning away all those painful memories, all that regret, all my heartache, I think I see a single spark released into the air.

But then it's gone, disappeared up the chimney, to be taken away on the wind . . .

5

Euurrrgghh.

The next thing I know I'm waking up and my head feels like a lump of concrete. A *pounding* lump of concrete. Opening a bleary eye, I wince as a shaft of winter light painfully stabs my pupil.

Where am I? What time is it? Why do I feel like something died in my mouth?

Gingerly, I squint through my eyelashes, trying to take in my swirling surroundings. Everything seems to be at a weird angle, and there's some sort of wet, furry thing squashed up against my face.

Which is when it dawns on me:

1. It's my sheepskin rug and I'm lying face down on it, drooling.

2. I'm still fully clothed – that is, if you can call my sexy kitten costume fully clothed.

3. Doing tequila shots by yourself on New Year's Eve is a *really* bad idea.

4. I think I'm going to be sick.

I can hear people talking in the background and, moving my eyes slowly across the room, I realise it's coming from the TV. I must have crashed out last night with it still on and fallen asleep right here on the rug. I didn't even make it to bed.

Unlike some, I realise, spotting Flea curled up on my duvet, snoozing blissfully. As if on cue, he rips open a yawn and stretches out diagonally, resting his paws on my pillow. Obviously someone's been enjoying having the bed to themselves, I muse, feeling a little slighted that even the cat prefers sleeping alone than with me.

Which I know is ridiculous but I have a hangover. I'm allowed to feel sorry for myself.

I try stirring my limbs. They're like dead weights and it takes a superhuman effort to haul myself up off the rug. *Whoa.* As I sit upright the whole room starts spinning on its axis and I'm engulfed by a wave of dizziness. Flinging out my arm I clutch onto the bedpost to steady myself. Oh dear. This is not good. This is not good at all.

Feeling as if I'm going to throw up at any moment, I take a deep breath and stagger to my feet. I need a hot shower, a strong coffee and a bumper-size pack of paracetamol. Groaning, I stumble, eyes closed, out of my bedroom, like an extra from a zombie film, and make my way on autopilot to the bathroom. Pushing open the bathroom door, I grab a towel from the rail and turn to the sink. Only instead of something cold, smooth and made of porcelain, I bump into something warm, squidgy *and alive.*

'*Argghh!*' I shriek.

Stumbling backwards I snap open my eyes. I get the shock of my life. There's a half-naked man in my bathroom! Standing right in front of me. On the towelling bathmat. Wearing nothing but his boxer shorts and a bemused grin.

'Happy New Year!' he chirps jovially, as if greeting me in the street.

For a moment I just stare, stunned into speechlessness, clutching my bath towel to my chest. I'm like a deer caught in headlights. Unable to say or do anything.

'Um, yeh, hi . . .' I finally manage to stammer, trying to avert my eyes from a very hairy torso which appears to be tucked into a very tight pair of white underpants. So tight you can see *everything*, if you know what I mean.

Arrggh. Look away Tess, *look away*.

I snatch my eyes away in mortification. This is not what I want to see first thing on New Year's Day. And with a raging hangover.

Oh my god, he's got moobs, I suddenly notice.

And are his nipples *pierced*?

'I didn't know anyone else lived here . . .'

I zone back to see him looking at me. *Staring at him.* My cheeks flush with embarrassment. Oh fuck, Tess, what are you doing? You're supposed to be looking away, not staring at his nipples! Dropping my gaze to my feet, I begin hurriedly backing out of the bathroom.

'Oh right . . . yes . . . they do, I mean, I do . . .'

Not that there's anything wrong with pierced nipples, I mean, I'm not a prude or anything, I can do piercings, and tattoos, and . . . I trip backwards over the bathroom scales and nearly go flying. I let out a strangled yelp.

'Hey, you OK?'

'Ouch, yes, fine,' I gabble, trying to ignore the pain that's now shooting up from my big toe. 'Perfectly fine, thanks.'

'Great, well, I'm finished, so the bathroom's all yours,' he grins and strides nonchalantly past me and into the hall. With one hand, I notice, stuck down the back of his boxer shorts, giving himself an enthusiastic scratch.

Shuddering, I lunge for the door and close it firmly behind me, then collapse against it. My heart is pumping. My toe is throbbing. My head is pounding. I mean, what the hell is some strange guy doing in our bathroom?

Like I have to ask.

Fiona.

She must have met him last night at the party and invited him back. Well, it wouldn't be the first time. Not that I'm saying she's 'a woman of loose morals', as my mother would call it, but put it this way, since moving in with Fiona I've taken to wearing earplugs when I go to bed.

And not the foam type, but the mega-strength industrial ones that are supposed to block out about a million decibels. Obviously the earplug testers have never heard Fiona having an orgasm.

Wedging the laundry basket behind the door so I don't get any more surprises, I turn to the sink.

And get an even bigger shock.

Forget about the strange half-naked man in the bathroom, what about the absolute horror in the mirror? Bird's-nest hair, bloodshot eyes, last night's make-up. Which is bad enough when it's just a few coats of mascara and some lip gloss, but quite something else when it's crayoned-on whiskers and a black nose which are now smudged all over my face.

Oh my god, and is that a spider on my cheek? My heart skips a beat. Nope, it's just one of my fake eyelashes, I realise, peeling it off.

Resting my hands on the sides of the sink for support, I peer at my reflection and let out a groan. I feel as bad as I look. Or should that be: look as bad as I feel? Whatever. It's the same thing. I look, and feel, dreadful. Not exactly the brand-spanking-new me I was hoping for, New Year and all that.

Turning on the shower attachment, I tug off my Lycra catsuit that seems to have vacuum-sealed itself to my body, climb into the bathtub and set about scrubbing off make-up, cleaning teeth and washing hair, until half an hour later I emerge bare-faced, clean-haired and wrapped in my dressing gown. At least now I feel half alive. Now onto the next stage in the reconstruction of Tess Connelly. Coffee.

Padding barefoot into the kitchen I get my second surprise. Gone is the mountain of washing-up and countertops cluttered with Fiona's overflowing ashtrays and lipstick-ringed wine glasses. Instead I'm greeted by pristine surfaces, a shining, stainless sink and Fiona in full make-up and her best kimono silk dressing gown, flitting around the showroom kitchen, buttering toast.

And – hang on a minute . . . I glance at the radio on the windowsill. Instead of the usual thumping Capital Radio, is that *classical music*?

'Morning,' she trills.

'Oh hi,' I reply, dazedly. I feel as if I've stepped into a parallel universe. Normally the morning after the night before, Fiona would be sitting in a zombie-like state at the kitchen table, nursing a hangover, a pot of tea, and a Marlboro light.

But instead, this morning, the half-naked man from the bathroom is sitting at the kitchen table, a display of speciality jams and herbal teas spread out before him.

Of course. So *he's* the reason for all this.

'This is Gareth,' continues Fiona, passing him the toast.

'We already met,' he grins, opening her prized cognac marmalade. 'Sorry about earlier, the lock on the bathroom door didn't work.'

'Yeh, I know, it needs fixing.' I shoot a look at Fiona but she's staring dreamily at Gareth. Mentally I add it to my list of things to do around the flat. Fiona might officially be the landlady, but in the whole time I've lived with her, I don't think I've ever seen her so much as replace a light bulb.

'Another cup of peppermint and hibiscus tea?' she coos.

'Great,' he replies through a mouthful of toast. 'Mmm, this marmalade stuff is delicious.'

She smiles proudly. 'Though you don't need very much as it's so sweet,' she adds, and I can see her looking slightly alarmed as he slathers another huge dollop on a piece of toast.

'Like its owner,' winks Gareth, holding out his teacup for a refill.

Fiona blushes like a schoolgirl. 'Now, now, flattery will get you everywhere,' she giggles flirtily.

Watching this scene of domestic bliss, I change my mind about the coffee. It's too much. I'll have to get my caffeine fix at Starbucks.

I turn to leave the kitchen.

'Oh Tess,' Fiona calls after me.

I pause in the doorway.

'You haven't seen The Diptyque, have you?'

'The Diptyque?' A memory flashes across my brain, like a streaker at a cricket match. 'Umm . . . no . . .' I say, as innocently as I can, but I feel a sort of icy dread trickling down the back of my neck.

'Huh, how weird.' She frowns, and for a moment I think I'm busted and I'm going to have to come clean and confess that I borrowed it. At least with Gareth as a witness she wouldn't be able to kill me with the butter knife. But then she flicks her hair and shrugs, 'Well, it must be somewhere', and goes back to making herbal tea.

Which is my chance to escape and seek refuge in my bedroom, where the first thing I spot is the stolen item in question, proudly displayed on my mantelpiece. I feel a bolt of relief – followed by horror as I realise all the wax has vanished. There's nothing left but an empty glass and the remnants of a wick.

Fuck. I must have fallen asleep and let it burn down! I stare at it, feeling a bit sick. Forget the safety issues. Forget the fact I could have burned the flat down. Forget that we could have both been charred to a crisp. That's about forty quid's worth of candle! Gone! While I was out cold on the sheepskin rug.

Quickly grabbing hold of the evidence, I stuff the empty glass holder in my sock drawer. There's nothing else for it, I'm going to have to replace it without her knowing, which isn't going to be easy – a scene from *The Thomas Crown Affair* flashes across my brain: the bit where Pierce Brosnan concocts that elaborate ruse in the art gallery to replace the stolen artwork without anyone noticing, and there're all those men running around in bowler hats like something from a Magritte painting.

I feel a seed of panic. Right now I can barely stand up straight, never mind think about men in bowler hats. I'll have to figure it out later, I decide, quickly throwing on my jeans and a jumper and stuffing my feet in a pair of old trainers. It's not a good look, but they're the first things I can find, and trying to plan an outfit is beyond me this morning. In fact, to be honest it's beyond me most mornings, I curse, sticking my wet hair under a woolly hat and grabbing my coat.

Outside it's one of those grey, freezing cold days. Even the trees look cold, with their branches devoid of leaves, stretching skeleton fingers into the white, frozen sky. Shoving my hands into my duvet coat to keep them warm, I start tramping down the street, my breath making white puffy clouds.

Fortunately Starbucks isn't far and it's only about ten minutes before I'm pushing open its familiar door and entering the espresso-scented warmth. Inside it's pretty quiet, just a few mums with their babies in pushchairs, and I walk straight up to the counter. Brilliant. Caffeine at last.

'I'll have a tall triple-shot latte.' I rattle off my order before the barista even has a chance to say 'hi'.

'Are you sure you want three shots in a tall size?' she asks dubiously. 'The tall size isn't very big, it will be very strong.'

'Perfect,' I smile. It's like music to my hungover ears.

Dubiously she scribbles my order on a cup. 'Anything else – any croissants or muffins or toasted sandwiches?'

'No, I'm fine thanks, just the caffeine . . . I mean coffee,' I add quickly, digging out my purse and handing over a fiver.

Collecting my change, I go and wait at the end of the counter for my latte. As the barista starts frothing the milk, I let my gaze idly wander around the café: at the bad artwork on the walls; the harassed mum in the corner with a toddler who seems intent on throwing his babyccino all over the floor; a guy near the window tapping away on his laptop . . .

A blast of cold air distracts me and I glance at the door, which is now being pushed open as someone else enters. Hurry up and close it behind you, it's freezing, I curse inwardly, watching as a blurry figure in a tracksuit emerges from behind the Starbucks logo on the glass and into clear view.

All at once my stomach goes into free-fall.

Oh my god, it can't be. It just can't be . . .

I stare in disbelief at the tall, broad figure walking towards me.

But it is.

Seb.

I feel as if I've just jumped out of a plane without a parachute and I'm hurtling towards the ground at a hundred miles an hour. My mind is racing. *What's he doing here? I look like crap. He's probably been for a run along the river. Has he spotted me? God, I still love him.* My heart twists up inside. Last night's anger vanishes into thin air as my drunken bravado is replaced by an urge to go over and throw my arms around him.

Tugging my woolly hat down even further, I stare at my feet and try to steady my breathing, but my thoughts are running around in a mad panic. *Why oh why didn't I put on some make-up? Cover the spot on my chin at least. And lip gloss – what I wouldn't give for lip gloss . . .* Frantically rummaging around in my pocket, I'm overjoyed to find a lip balm. This is how the prospectors must have felt when they discovered gold, I think, rubbing a blob into my lips with the desperation of a dumped woman who's just seen her ex.

For a split second I think about hiding in the loo. If I can get in there before he sees me – but my pride, however battered, won't let me. Instead it pins me to the spot, makes me swallow hard, and look up.

OK. Ready. I brace myself.

Nothing.

Absolutely nothing.

He looks right at me. *Correction*: He looks right *through* me, as if I'm not even here. His eyes just sweep over me; his face doesn't even flicker as he walks straight past me to the counter to order his coffee.

For a dazed moment I stand there in complete and utter bewilderment. Er, hang on a minute, what just happened? Can we just rewind that again? Reeling from our encounter, or lack of encounter, I stare at him in disbelief. The adrenalin is still pumping through my veins, ready for fight or flight.

What it's not ready for is nothing. Zilch. Nada.

That's it?

I was expecting an uncomfortable encounter, awkward questions, having to pin on a happy smile and feign 'everything's just great' responses.

What I wasn't expecting was to be totally ignored.

I watch as he casually does some stretching as he waits for his change. I know, maybe he didn't see me, or – hang on – maybe he just didn't recognise me in this woolly hat? Yes, that must be it, I tell myself firmly. He doesn't know it's me. That's why he ignored me.

Oh, who am I kidding? I'm wearing a woolly hat, not a balaclava.

'Tall triple-shot latte?'

I snap back to see the barista looking at me, eyebrows raised, and notice my coffee is waiting for me on the stand. God knows how long it's been there. 'Oh, right, thanks,' I mumble and, snatching it up, I get the hell out of there.

I can't believe it.

I simply *cannot* believe it.

In a daze I walk down the street, my memory replaying the scene as if I'm watching footage from a CCTV camera: *there I am, waiting for my coffee, in he walks, looks right at me, and completely ignores me . . .* Rewind, play. *Here he is again, walking in, and now he's looking right at me and . . .* I slow it down, frame by frame . . . *nope, there's no mistake, he totally, utterly, unequivocally blanks me.*

Hurt stabs painfully: *How could he do that? How could he act as if he doesn't even know me? After everything we meant to each other*. Followed by a flash of anger: *The bastard! Blanking me like that! Who does he think he is? OK, so we might have broken up, he might have fallen out of love with me, but that doesn't mean he has to just ignore me!*

All fired up, I take a slurp of my long-forgotten coffee. It's gone cold. Damn! He's even spoiled my coffee!

Fuelled by indignation, righteousness and lukewarm latte, I stomp the rest of the way home, not taking much notice of my surroundings. All I can think about is Seb. In fact, this time it barely even registers when I bump into Gareth on the stairs as he's leaving. Fully dressed this time, thank goodness. Though only after he's asked me where the nearest tube station is and I've given him directions do I realise he's wearing a Henry VIII costume, minus the ginger beard. So *that's* who he was.

Walking into the flat, I find things back to normal. The display of jams and teas has vanished, like a magic trick, and Fiona is back to her old self, collapsed on a chair in the kitchen, smoking a cigarette and flicking through last week's copy of *Grazia*.

Joining her, I slump onto the chair opposite, my mind still reeling. 'I just don't believe it,' I blurt after a moment, resting my coffee cup on the table.

'I know, I didn't think he was my type either,' replies Fiona, looking up from her magazine. 'I don't normally go for small men.'

'Huh?' I look across at her in confusion.

'But seriously, once you got beneath those ermine robes, it's true what they say.' She raises her eyebrows and throws me a knowing look.

'No, I'm not talking about Henry the Eighth,' I gasp in realisation. 'I'm talking about what just happened.'

'Why, what happened?'

'I just saw Seb and he blanked me!'

I wait for her reaction. Knowing Fiona, she'll have plenty to say about this. After all, she's been very vocal about my relationship in the past.

She frowns and there's a pause as she takes a drag of her cigarette. Then, quite unexpectedly, she says only two words. But they're enough to turn my whole world upside down.

'Seb *who*?'

6

The ground shifts beneath me and I grip onto the side of the table to steady myself.

What did she just say?

For a moment I stare at her in bewilderment, not sure what to say or how to react.

Then suddenly I get it.

'Oh ha ha, very funny,' I grin, my body relaxing. 'You had me going there for a minute.' Feeling a flush of foolishness, I let go of the table. Of course, now I remember, I'm not supposed to talk about Seb any more or even think about him. According to Fiona, this is the only way I'll forget about him.

Though, to be honest, I'm not sure I actually *want* to forget about him.

'I have to pretend like he doesn't exist, right?'

Fiona looks at me uncertainly. 'Who doesn't exist?' she says slowly.

'I know, I know,' I nod, playing along, 'but can we stop pretending for just a minute?'

'Pretending?' She looks at me in confusion, as if she doesn't know what I'm talking about.

I have to say I'm impressed. I didn't know Fiona was this good an actress.

'Look, I won't talk about him after this, I promise,' I say, pulling up a chair next to her. I'm bursting with my news. Fiona and I share everything about our relationships, apart from the men themselves. 'But I have to tell you . . . I just saw him, at Starbucks, and he ignored me!'

With a flourish I throw my hands up in the air and wait for her reaction.

But instead of leaning forwards and going 'no way!', and launching into a detailed analysis of the situation, Fiona blows smoke down her nostrils and frowns. 'What *are* you going on about? I'm not pretending anything!'

I pause. I feel a slight wobble. Wow, she's *really* good at this acting malarkey. She's got that indignant thing down to a tee.

'Oh Fiona, come on . . .' I try pleading, but she lets out a gasp of impatience.

'Come on, what? I don't have a clue what you're talking about.'

'I'm talking about Seb!' I gasp. Now it's my turn to get impatient. It's time to stop fooling around with this 'never existed' stuff. After all, this isn't some one-night stand I'm talking about. *This is Seb!* This is the man I was – I still am – in love with. A man I'm heartbroken over. A man whose texts she used to painstakingly analyse for hours in the beginning, and whom she called every rude name you could think of and then some in the end.

'I mean seriously, how can you pretend not to know a man you called . . . what was it again?' I pause, trying to remember her exact words, '"*A bloody stupid idiot with shit for brains*"?'

Fiona reaches for her mug of tea and sighs. 'Sorry Tess, but you've lost me.'

I suddenly get a very weird feeling. Fiona might be a decent actress when it comes to feigning a wrist sprain so she gets out of her turn to do the dishes, but this is more than that. She's so adamant, so calm, *so sure*, it's like she really *doesn't* know who Seb is.

'But what about the time we all got drunk on toffee vodka and did karaoke?' I try jogging her memory but it's met with a blank stare.

'Six foot, short blond hair, American accent?'

Another blank stare.

'Really handsome?' I can't help adding.

Nothing.

'*My boyfriend for nearly a year?*' I gasp finally.

Her forehead furrows and she peers at me with a worried expression. 'Tess, have you been doing drugs?'

'Me? *Drugs?* Of course not!' I protest hotly. 'Well, unless you count paracetamol . . .'

Reaching over, I grab the family-size bottle that sits permanently in the middle of the kitchen table. Where most people would have a vase of flowers to make them feel better, we have painkillers.

'Are you sure you didn't have any of that fruit punch that was going around last night?' she continues, raising an eyebrow as I down two more tablets. 'I heard a rumour from Pippa that it had been laced with some hallucinogenics; apparently her friend Tarquin had just come back from visiting this tribe in the Amazon—'

'No, I didn't have any fruit punch!' I can't help snapping.

'So what the hell is wrong with you?' she says exasperatedly.

'Wrong with *me*? You're the one who can't remember Seb, my ex-boyfriend.'

'That's because you've never had a boyfriend called Seb,' she fires back.

That shuts me up. I open my mouth to say something but no words come out. Instead I just stare at her in astonishment. For like a second, then I get a stab of annoyance. 'This isn't funny you know.'

'Do you see me laughing?' Hugging her knees to her chest, she balances her mug on them and frowns. 'You're the one with the imaginary boyfriend,' she adds sulkily.

For a moment there's a standoff and neither of us speaks. I can't believe I'm arguing with Fiona over this. What is it with her? Why is she being like this?

'Look, I don't know what's going on here, but I for one am not in the habit of making up boyfriends,' I reply calmly. 'I mean, *hello*? If I never went out with Seb, then why is there a photograph of us together stuck on the fridge then, huh?' I glance self-righteously across the kitchen.

Only there is no photograph. Just a space where it used to be.

I meet Fiona's eye. She gives me an 'I-told-you-so' look.

'Oh . . . of course, I took it down when we broke up and threw it away,' I fluster, remembering. 'Well, I didn't want to be constantly reminded, did I?'

'Whatever,' she sighs, as if she doesn't believe me, then looks back down at *Grazia*.

My annoyance ratchets up a notch. Right, that's it. I've had enough of this ridiculous messing around. I don't know what she's playing at, or why, but I'm going to prove it, and *then* let's see what she has to say. Stomping into the bedroom, I snatch up my laptop from my bedside cabinet, then march back into the kitchen.

'What are you doing?' She looks up curiously as I plonk it down on the table in front of her.

'I've got hundreds more photos on my laptop,' I explain simply.

Ha. That told her.

Flicking open my computer, I click on the little icon for my photo library and wait for the application to open. I've got so many photos on here it takes a while to load . . . though not usually this long . . . Suddenly the little rainbow wheel pops up and starts turning. Oh no, it's the Wheel of Doom. I hate it when that happens; still, it should be OK in a minute . . .

I watch it for a few seconds, turning around, then all at once there's a funny high-pitched whining noise and abruptly the screen goes blank.

I feel a twinge of alarm.

'Oh no, what's happening?' I start jabbing at the keyboard in the vain hope that it might spring back to life, but nothing. The black screen stares back at me. 'I know, it must be the battery!' Triumphantly I rush back into my bedroom to grab my charger. Of course, that's what it is. Durr, I'm such a dummy. Dashing back into the kitchen, I plug it in and turn it back on.

Nothing. No lights come on. No familiar blue screen. No Johnny Depp screensaver.

My heart plummets. 'Oh god,' I groan, staring at the lifeless laptop with a feeling of dread. Desperately I click the on/off button a few more times, but it's no good. 'My laptop's crashed!'

The whole time Fiona has been watching me wordlessly.

'No photos then?' she says at last.

'No, they were all on my computer . . .' I trail off.

She pauses, a worried expression on her face, then leans over and squeezes my arm. 'Oh well, never mind, that's the end of that then, isn't it?' she says brightly, but in a way that's more a statement not to be argued with than a question. 'Now why don't you sit down and I'll make us both a nice cup of tea' and, passing me her beloved copy of *Grazia*, she hits a button on her BlackBerry and goes to fill the kettle. '*Pippa sweetie*,' I hear her hiss, '*what the fuck was in that fruit punch . . . ?*'

OK, now let's not panic. Like it says on my mug: Keep Calm and Carry On. You've just got a hangover, that's all. A really *bad* hangover. The kind of hangover that makes your flatmate seem to lose all memory of your ex-boyfriend.

Or something like that anyway.

After a cup of tea and several pages of Peter Andre, I leave Fiona on the phone and go back into my bedroom. I need to lie down. My head is pounding and I can't think straight. Being blanked by Seb was bad enough, but Fiona acting all weird has freaked me out even more. And now, on top of all that, my laptop has gone and died on me. Can today *get* any worse?

Maybe I need to just rest for a little while, try to get some sleep even? I'm actually pretty tired. Kicking off my trainers I climb back under the duvet. It's still warm in the middle where Flea has been sleeping. I sink into the pillow and close my eyes. Gosh, this is nice. I feel better already. In fact I'm sure when I wake up, things will be all back to normal . . .

I don't move again. Cocooned within my soft feather walls, I spend the rest of the weekend sleeping off my hangover by watching old black-and-white movies, cuddling Flea, and sleeping some more. Occasionally I venture out to make tea and toast, which I bring back to bed so I don't have to break the cycle. At some point I hear Fiona yell 'bye' and the door slamming, but it barely registers. Lost in time and duvet, I snuggle further into the depths as *It's a Wonderful Life* washes over me, lulling me back to sleep again.

By the time Monday morning rolls around, I feel so much better. It's a Bank Holiday, so I don't have to go to work, plus my hangover's gone, there are no strangers in tighty-whities lurking in the bathroom, and when I pad into the kitchen I'm not greeted by a Stepford Wife. Everything's back to normal. In fact, the weekend seems like such a distant, blurry memory, it's almost as if it never happened, I think with relief, banging on Fiona's door to see if she wants a cup of coffee.

Getting no answer, I pop my head inside and discover she's still fast asleep. She never gets up early. In fact, the only time she's ever been sighted before noon was when she was flying to Spain on a family holiday last summer. 'Being freelance means never having to set an alarm,' is one of her favourite sayings.

Unfortunately for Fiona, it isn't one of easyJet's. When she turned up late at Gatwick, they refused to let her on her flight, and she was forced to kill three hours in Accessorize waiting for the next one. Apparently, to this day, she's never been able to look at another pair of glittery flip-flops again.

She's still not awake when I'm ready to leave the flat, which also means I don't get a chance to speak to her again about

Seb. Not that I need to, I tell myself firmly, running to catch the bus which is indicating to pull out from the stop. Like I said, I'm sure it was all a misunderstanding.

Touching in with my Oyster card, I jump on board and make my way to a free seat at the back. Relishing the stuffy warmth after the bitterness outside, I rest my head against the glass and gaze out of the window. After all, what else could it be?

After twenty minutes the bus reaches a leafy suburb and I get off outside Hemmingway House, a shiny redbrick building that looks as though it's been made out of Lego and plonked in the middle of a car park. According to its colourful brochure, filled with cartoon drawings of Doris and Bert with their curly grey hair and denture smiles, it describes itself as a 'retirement community that offers assisted living for those who need it'.

'Assisted living, my arse, it's like bloody Big Brother', is how my granddad chooses to describe it. But then Granddad Connelly never did like anyone telling him what to do. Not even my nan when she was alive. Once, when she told him not to smoke his pipe inside, he rigged up the portable TV in his garden shed, moved in his armchair and refused to come out for weeks. Nan said he would probably have stayed in there forever, if hadn't been for the great British winter which drove him back indoors to the warmth. 'Stubborn he might be, stupid he's not,' she used to laugh.

Pushing open the double doors, I walk into the reception filled with houseplants and the type of cane furniture you find in conservatories. On the walls are hung framed photographs of jolly old-aged pensioners doing activities. I have a sneaking suspicion they are pictures 'posed by models' and not actual residents of Hemmingway House, as I've never seen any evidence of anyone sharing a bottle of rosé on a sun-drenched patio. Usually it's more a case of Scrabble in the stuffy games room.

'Hi Tess.' Walking towards the main desk, I bump into Melanie, one of the younger members of the nursing staff.

Mel's got bright pink dreadlocks and a nose-stud and is a hit with all the residents as she treats them like friends instead of nuisances to be bossed around. Arm in arm with one of them, she flashes me a huge grin. 'Looking for your grandpa?'

'Hi Mel,' I smile, pulling off my gloves and scarf. Gosh, they always have it so hot in here. No wonder all the residents are always nodding off in their armchairs: this heat makes you want to lie down and take a siesta. 'How is he?'

'Busy leading others astray,' answers the sour-faced staff manager, Miss Temple, from behind the front desk. Glancing up from her paperwork, she removes her reading glasses and gives me a hard stare.

Uh-oh. I feel a beat of trepidation. *What's he done this time?*

'Really?' I reply innocently, as if I have no idea what she's talking about. But I'm not fooling anyone, least of all Miss Temple. Since my parents flew to Australia and left me responsible for Granddad, she's called me three times to complain about his bad behaviour.

The first time was because he was playing his jazz records too loudly and refusing to turn down the volume; the second time was for breaking into the kitchen in the middle of the night and making pancakes; and the third time was for smoking his pipe inside. 'Hemmingway House is a non-smoking establishment, Miss Connelly,' she'd intoned down the phone, 'and your grandfather is deliberately breaking the rules.'

'He's in his room,' interrupts Melanie, and as I glance across at her she gives me a little wink. 'Last time I checked he was playing poker.'

'Right, thanks,' I smile and, avoiding Miss Temple's steely gaze, I quickly scoot off down the corridor.

'And will you kindly remind your grandfather that gambling is strictly not allowed,' Miss Temple calls after me, but thankfully I'm already through the fire doors and I can pretend not to hear.

7

I discover Granddad's door firmly closed. Locked actually, I realise, trying the handle. I give a little knock.

'Go away,' bawls a voice from inside. 'I'm busy.'

Granddad, it seems, isn't that eager to adopt the 'Open Door' community spirit talked about so much in the Hemmingway House brochure.

I knock again gently. 'It's Tess,' I hiss.

There's a pause, I can hear rustling inside, then the door is flung open to reveal a man with snow-white hair and crinkly blue eyes. Dressed impeccably in a grey pinstriped suit, complete with silk handkerchief in his top pocket, gold watch hanging on a chain from his neatly buttoned waistcoat, and highly polished brogues, he cuts an immaculate figure. Not surprisingly. This is Sidney Archibald Connelly, who for nearly fifty years was renowned as one of Savile Row's finest tailors.

But to me he's just Gramps.

'Hello beautiful.' His whole face lights up. 'What a lovely surprise.'

'Happy New Year,' I grin, breathing in his familiar scent of pipe smoke and cologne as I go to hug him. He ushers me inside. He's alone, but there's evidence of a recent poker game: playing cards stacked neatly on the table, four empty tumblers, a half-empty bottle of Blackstock & White whisky.

'Apparently I've to tell you that gambling isn't allowed,' I begin, but he snorts derisively.

'Pah, says who?' he demands, leaning heavily on his cane as

he makes his way across to the Chesterfield sofa that's shoehorned into the corner. It's far too big for the room, but he insisted on bringing it from his shop. Along with a tailor's dummy, a framed picture of the Queen at her Silver Jubilee in 1977, and his beloved sewing machine, which has pride of place on the wooden sideboard.

Easing himself down into the well-worn cushions which, according to Granddad, have seen many a famous man's bottom – 'I've had all the Bonds: Sean Connery, Roger Moore, even that Craig fellow' – he pats the cushion next to him for me to join him. 'Life itself is a gamble,' he says, clicking his tongue.

'I know, but if you keep getting into trouble—'

'What're they going to do? Kick me out?' He looks delighted at the very thought. Granddad has made no secret of the fact that he resents being in a care home, and the fiercely independent streak that runs right through him, like the letters in a stick of Blackpool rock, rebels against everything it stands for.

But after Nan died he just couldn't cope on his own. With two hip replacements and a habit of leaving the gas hob on ('But I could have sworn I turned it off!'), he was becoming a danger to himself, and his neighbours, and last year he moved grudgingly to Hemmingway House.

'I can just imagine that Temple woman's face now,' he chuckles, reaching for a bag of Jelly Babies and rattling them at me. 'She always looks to me like she's sucking a lemon. Either that or she's sat on something sharp—'

'Gramps, can I ask you a favour?' Quickly changing the subject away from Miss Temple's derriere, I sit down beside him and dig my hand in the bag.

'Go on then, how much?' he grumbles affectionately, putting down the Jelly Babies and pulling out his wallet.

'Oh, no, I don't need any money,' I protest quickly. 'I got a Christmas bonus.'

Granddad raises his eyebrows approvingly. 'Well, aren't you a clever girl?'

I feel my cheeks colour slightly. Clever hasn't got anything to do with it. It's more a case of having a kind boss who took pity on me and turned a blind eye all year to my appalling PA skills.

'No, the thing is, I wanted to ask if I could borrow your sewing machine? You see, I found this . . .' Digging into my ancient rucksack that has seen better days, I pull out a length of patterned material, all folded up, that I recently discovered in a charity shop. I can never resist popping into charity shops: you can find all kinds of weird and wonderful things. 'I thought I might make a bag out of it, as this one of mine is ready for the dustbin and bags are so expensive these days . . .'

Reaching for his half-moon spectacles, Granddad props them on the end of his nose and unfolds the material. 'Hmmm—' he nods, turning it over in his hands, examining it – 'well, it's possible, but this fabric is a very thick cotton, almost like a loomed hemp, and it appears to be some kind of *sack* . . .' Frowning, he looks up. 'I have made thousands of bespoke suits in my time, my dear, but they were made from the finest fabrics, not sacks,' he says, a little sniffily. 'Now, if you were talking a nice silk or Italian cashmere—'

'I want to use this,' I say stubbornly. 'And yes, OK, you're right, it is an old sack. The woman in the charity shop said an old lady brought it in with some clothes inside. Apparently it's from the 1950s and they used it to store flour when she lived on a farm in France—'

'And you want to make a bag out of it?' He looks bewildered.

'Absolutely,' I smile. 'I just loved the design on it and I thought if I lined it with some pretty fabric and then I sew these ribbons along the edges—' I pull out a piece of ribbon I saved from a Christmas present – 'so that it gathers up like this . . .'

I'm always going round to Granddad's so that he can help me with some new project or other. I'm forever making things, partly because I don't earn much money, but mostly because I get such a buzz from thinking up ideas and recycling someone's charity cast-offs into something new and interesting.

Bending both of our heads together, we pore over it for a few moments. 'So, what do you think?' I ask, turning sideways to glance at him.

Pushing up his glasses onto the bridge of his nose, Granddad peers at me intently, as if deep in thought. 'You've got the gift,' he says quietly after a moment, a smile playing on his lips.

'The gift?' I frown.

'I've never told you this before, but I always knew it,' he nods, looking very pleased with himself. 'I used to say to your mother: Tess will be the one to take after me . . .'

'Oh Gramps,' I laugh, 'you were one of the finest tailors on Savile Row. I wouldn't have a clue how to make a suit!'

'That bit's easy: anyone can learn how to measure an inside leg,' he pooh-poohs. 'What you can't learn is the vision.'

'Well, I don't know about that . . .' I smile, a bit embarrassed by his compliment. I'm not used to compliments, except of course from Gramps. For some reason, he thinks I'm the best at everything. 'I just like making things, that's all,' I shrug.

'You don't just make things, Tess, you *create* things,' he corrects, looking every inch the proud grandparent.

I blush, memories flashing back of Gramps coming to see me in the Nativity play at school. I played the donkey and had no lines, and he spent the whole time loudly applauding me whenever I came on stage, much to the annoyance of the other bemused relatives in the audience. To this day he still insists the donkey stole the show.

'So, you think it can work?' I ask, looking across at him.

'Well now, let's see . . .' Opening a drawer, he pulls out his fabric tape measure and, easing himself up from the sofa, moves over to his sewing machine. 'If we cut along this edge and do a double seam here . . .' As he begins explaining, I scoot across and pull up a little footstool next to him, watching as his pale, papery fingers come to life and begin expertly turning dials and levers on his sewing machine.

'Cooeee . . .'

We're interrupted by the high-pitched sound of a woman's voice and a lavender-permed head pops itself around the door.

'I saw the door was ajar and heard voices . . .'

'Oh hi Phyllis,' I smile.

Considering I made sure to close the door firmly behind me, and Phyllis is hard of hearing, I'm not that sure I believe her, but it doesn't matter. I love Phyllis. A widow in her eighties, her room's down the corridor and she's always popping in to see Granddad with her Scrabble set and gifts of shortbread. 'Do you know your Grandpa is a natural? I've never seen so many seven-letter words!'

Personally I have a sneaking suspicion she has a crush on Gramps, but when I mentioned it to him he told me to stop being so ridiculous. 'At our age we don't have crushes, we have angina,' he said firmly.

'Happy New Year, how are you?' I ask, giving her tiny frame a hug.

'Still alive,' she chuckles. 'How are you? Courting yet?'

I can't help but smile at her use of the word 'courting'. It's so wonderfully old-fashioned and conjures up all these lovely images of tea dances and walks along the promenade. So much better than our modern-day 'dating', I reflect, thinking about Fiona hunched over her computer, going through profiles on KindredSpiritsRUs.com, looking at a thousand photos of men snowboarding, scuba-diving, bungee-jumping. It would seem that every single man in London is an extreme sports fanatic.

'I was . . . but we broke up a few months ago,' I say, trying to make light of it and shrug it off.

She clucks sympathetically. 'Well, don't worry, at your age there're plenty more fish in the sea. Now, when you get to my age, the sea's pretty much empty; all that's left are a few old barnacles . . .' She grins a pink denture smile and gestures towards my granddad.

'Who you calling a barnacle?' he grumbles, before turning to me and demanding, 'What's all this about a chap?' like he's some kind of scary Sicilian godfather protecting the family honour, and not my eighty-seven-year-old granddad.

Phyllis tuts loudly. 'She doesn't need your permission, you know.'

'I know that,' he retorts hotly, digging out his pipe from his pocket and vigorously knocking the ash from the bowl. 'I just didn't know anything about a chap.'

'You remember Sebastian, I brought him to see you once,' I remind him, although part of me doesn't want to.

It's traditional for the first meeting between your *father* and your boyfriend to be a little nerve-wracking. After all, you're his little girl and now you're all grown-up and having mind-blowing sex with the guy sitting on the edge of his sofa, trying to make polite conversation about tractors. (Don't ask me why my dad brought up the subject of tractors. My dad's not a farmer, he's a retired biology teacher. But then applying logic to my dad would be a bit like applying it to Lady Gaga's wardrobe. Utterly pointless.)

But meetings between your boyfriend and your granddad are supposed to be cosy, genial affairs, with your grandfather reminiscing about the good old days and offering cups of stewed tea and Bakewell slices. They are *not* supposed to involve a scene where your granddad challenges him to a game of poker, interrogates him about 'his intentions' and warns him against cheating by waving his antique pistol around.

'But of course not, Mr Connelly, I would never do that to Tess,' Seb had stammered in alarm.

'I wasn't talking about my granddaughter, I was talking about cards,' my granddad had replied with a glare.

It was all very stressful. Made worse when the nurses came in and confiscated the pistol for being a dangerous firearm, and Seb went on to win two hands. I'm not sure which was worse, losing the pistol, or the poker game, but either way Granddad was not a happy bunny. Hence I haven't mentioned it again as I thought it best if it could all be forgotten.

Now, apparently, it is. *Completely*.

'Sebastian? I've never met a Sebastian!' booms my granddad, jabbing a pipe cleaner backwards and forwards into his pipe as if it's a lethal weapon.

I feel a seed of anxiety. Hoping he'd forget the card game is one thing, forgetting he's ever met Seb is quite another. But then Granddad's memory has been getting worse lately. At first we all just assumed it was his age, but then a few weeks before Mum and Dad left for Australia, they came in to visit and one of the nurses took them aside. Apparently a few of the nursing staff had noticed it was more than him just growing increasingly forgetful, he'd also been getting confused, and there was concern it might be the early signs of Alzheimer's. There was even talk about him seeing a doctor.

When Mum told me, I got really defensive and refused to believe it. Like I said to her, it's not that he doesn't know who I am, he just can't remember my name sometimes. It's no big deal. Loads of people are bad with names.

But now I'm beginning to wonder if there might be some truth in it. If it is something more sinister, and I've just been in denial.

'Yes you have, he was American, remember?' I prod gently. Except, in this instance, it's not just his memory that's worrying me; I've just had a flash of déjà vu to yesterday and Fiona.

'Oooh, an American?' pipes up Phyllis. 'I went out with an American in the war. Johnny James was his name: big tall fellow with bright red hair and a smile the size of Texas. He used to give me stockings so I didn't have to draw the seams up my legs . . .' She trails off, reminiscing.

Granddad shoots her a look that says he doesn't want to be hearing about Johnny James and his stockings.

Surprisingly, Phyllis gets the hint. 'Well, best be off,' she says quickly, 'I've got a pillowcase to embroider,' and, giving me a wink, she squeezes my hand and promptly leaves.

I turn back to Granddad. 'You played poker . . . he won.' I try again. My seed of anxiety is beginning to sprout.

Granddad Connelly looks aghast. 'Now my memory might not be as sharp as it used to be,' he concedes, 'but that I *would* remember.' He passes me the used pipe cleaner, and wordlessly I take a fresh one from the packet on the table and hand it to him. I'm like the nurse in the operating room, handing the surgeon his implements. 'Now, have you come to cheer me up or finish me off by casting aspersions on my poker game?' He peers at me over the top of his glasses, like he used to do when I was naughty, and I suddenly feel about five years old.

'I've come to see you, of course,' I protest.

'That's my girl,' he winks, and I smile despite myself.

'And, for the record, it would take a lot more than that to finish you off,' I tease.

'That's what the nurses say,' he laughs, reaching inside his breast pocket and taking out a pouch of tobacco. He begins packing the bowl of his pipe with it. I've seen him do this a million times, but it's still fascinating to watch. He's so methodical and precise the way he does it. When I was a child he told me that I had to think of him filling up his pipe like a family of three . . .

A memory begins playing in my mind like a QuickTime movie: me as a little girl sitting on his knee and him saying, 'First you pat the tobacco gently like a child would, see?' and taking my finger he gently taps it on the soft, springy flakes.

'Next you fill it up again and press it more firmly, like a mother would,' and holding my finger he pushes it down harder. 'And then finally you fill it up one last time and press it down very hard, like a father would,' and, wrapping his huge hand around my tiny finger, he squashes it firmly against the tobacco.

'Now pass me those matches,' he's saying now, and I snap back to see him gesturing towards a little bowl filled with various packets of all different shapes and sizes.

'Gramps!' I hiss, giving him a disapproving stare. 'You can't smoke that in here, you'll get thrown out!'

'Chance'd be a fine thing,' he grumbles.

I surrender. 'Well, OK, just this once, but I'll have to open a window.' Walking over to the window I push it open, then reach for a box of matches. I glance at the inscription: *The Savoy*. Abruptly I feel a beat of sadness. Granddad used to go to all those places when he worked in Savile Row. It must be hard being here.

'Here, let me do that for you,' I offer, lighting up a match. Sod Hemmingway House and their rules.

Granddad looks at me in surprise, then leans his pipe forwards. He takes a few deep puffs then blows out a cloud of sweet-smelling smoke. 'Now, about this jacket you want to make,' he says, turning back to the sewing machine.

'No, it was a bag, remember?'

A crease etches down his forehead and it's obvious he's struggling to remember.

'Of course,' he nods vigorously. 'I just got a bit muddled.' Briskly he grabs the material. 'Righty-ho, well, come along, let's get cracking.'

I sit down next to him and immediately I feel myself relax. I need to stop worrying. There's nothing weird going on. It's just Gramps's bad memory. That's why he doesn't remember Seb. And I'm sure that's just an age thing.

Dismissing the thought, I press my cheek against my

granddad's shoulder as he fires up the machine. I love this bit. Love seeing my ideas come to life. Love the transformation of something old into something new. It's like magic.

And, feeling a tingle of excitement, I watch as the needle begins to fly over the fabric.

8

After a couple of hours at the sewing machine, it's time for me to leave. Gathering up the fabric, which is already beginning to take shape, I promise to pop back soon for my second lesson. 'And in the meantime, try not to get into any more trouble,' I chide, giving him a kiss on his sandpapery cheek.

'I'll try,' he says cheerfully, and quite blatantly with no intention whatsoever of doing so, 'and don't forget the ribbons for next time . . . oh, and you need to decide whether you want a zip or buttons . . .' He frowns in concentration. 'I think buttons would be better, some gilt perhaps, or a nice mother-of-pearl. In fact I think I have some somewhere . . .'

'OK, great,' I grin, turning to leave, but he pins me in the doorway.

'. . . and the lining material, that's very important, it makes all the difference. I think a nice shot silk – none of this nasty polyester you get nowadays . . .'

I haven't seen Granddad this animated for a long time and his enthusiasm is infectious. 'Silk sounds perfect,' I agree. 'I know, what about a lovely raspberry colour? Like your handkerchief? In fact' – a thought strikes me as I look at it – 'we could use your handkerchief!'

He glances down for a moment in surprise, then pulls it out of his breast pocket and shakes it out with a flourish. His face lights up. 'Splendid idea, Tess! What did I tell you about the gift?'

I start laughing, and before he can come up with any more

suggestions, I leave him waving goodbye with his handkerchief and scoot off down the corridor.

Outside I jump on a bus and head to the big shopping centre nearby. Even though it's a Bank Holiday all the stores are open, keen to take advantage of everyone being off work and eager to spend their Christmas money. I've brought my laptop with me to take into the big computer store there. Fingers crossed, they're going to be able to fix it.

Arriving, I glide up the escalators and start making my way through the crowds. My eyes flit over the windows of all the designer stores: Tiffany's, Gucci, Prada. I glance inside one. A clutch of blonde women are cooing over the display of handbags, taking it in turns to try them on their shoulders and do twirls in front of the mirror. I slow down to watch in fascination. I've never understood why women spend so much money on handbags. It doesn't make sense to me.

Not that I'm anti-designer. I can see the appeal of a pair of expensive shoes – after all, who doesn't covet a pair of beautifully made stilettos that make your ankles look super-skinny and your legs look as if they go on forever? Or an exquisitely cut dress, made of gorgeous fabric that hugs and flatters and gives you a waist and boobs.

But a designer handbag? I just don't get it. A six-thousand-pound Birkin is never going to make you look a size smaller. Or five inches taller. Plus, it's not like they're even unique. Every time I open a magazine I see all these celebrities lugging around the same one, I mean, imagine if they were all photographed wearing the same dress? Even Fiona covets them. In fact, she's the reason I even *know* there's a bag named after a sixties actress that is the price of a small car. And that apparently she'd give her life for it. 'I'd die for a Birkin! Seriously, I'd die!' she once gasped, poring over a picture of Posh.

At least I think it was Posh – the bag was so ridiculously big she was practically hidden behind it. All I could think was, What the *hell* has she got in there?

David?

But then, what on earth do I know? I'm making a bag out of recycled flour sacks and my granddad's handkerchief.

Striding quickly past, I head up another set of escalators and finally reach the computer store. Inside it's heaving with shoppers and lots of friendly staff in brightly coloured T-shirts asking if you want any help.

'My laptop's broken,' I explain dolefully as one swoops upon me.

'No worries,' beams the assistant. 'We'll get one of our technicians to take a look at it. If you want to give me your name and take a seat' – he gestures to a row of chairs where other people are waiting – 'it shouldn't be too long.'

'Oh OK, thanks,' I nod, giving him my details and sitting down on a spare seat.

I'm just dumping my bags on the floor next to me when my phone rings. It's an Australian number. It must be my parents. Despite my brother having been in Sydney now for nearly six months, I've not heard from him once, apart from a text to say, 'Who won the football?' My mother, on the other hand, has no such communication problems.

'Tess? Is that you?'

This is how my mum starts every phone conversation. I've never actually asked her who she thinks I might be, considering it's my number she's dialled.

'Hi Mum, yes, it's me,' I reply, playing along. Though I keep thinking that one day I'm going to put on an accent and pretend to be someone else. Like the Queen maybe. Or maybe an alien from outer space who's invaded the body of her daughter and stolen her mobile phone.

'It's so hot and sunny here!' she says, diving straight into a weather report. She's in Australia. It's their summer. It's hard to mirror her surprise, but I do my best.

'Gosh, really?' I say.

'Ninety degrees yesterday.'

'Wow.' I know what's coming next.

'What's the weather like there?'

'Oh, you know, pretty cold.'

Maybe I'm missing something here, but my parents have lived in England their entire lives. Since when has January been anything other than cold? And yes, I know all about climate change, but did it used to be tropical before I was born? Balmy and hot even?

'Tell Dad I just saw Gramps,' I say, changing the subject away from the weather.

'How is he? Has he been behaving himself?'

'Yes, of course,' I say, immediately coming to his defence. 'It's Miss Temple, she just doesn't like him . . .'

'Well your grandfather has to be nicer to her then. You know, he's very lucky to be at Hemmingway House; there's a long waiting list to get a place there—'

'I know, but it can't be easy for him.'

'It's not easy for any of us, Tess,' replies Mum, a little tersely. 'We all have to put up with things we don't like . . .'

There's the sound of my dad and brother in the background, yelling at sport on the TV, and Mum tells them to shush.

'Anyway, he was in really good spirits. He's showing me how to use his sewing machine.'

'Right, yes,' she says distractedly, and I can tell she's not really listening. But then Mum never really listens to me. It's as if she's already formulated her answer, regardless of what I might have to say. It's always been like that, which is partly why I'm so close to Gramps. When I was growing up he'd always listen to me; it didn't matter what I had to say, how stupid or silly it sounded, he'd never pass judgement, just listen. Sometimes that's all you need: someone to listen.

'But his memory does seem to be getting worse,' I add.

'Why, what happened?' Abruptly she snaps back.

I feel a bit guilty for bringing it up when she's away, but I've been thinking about it on the bus, and although I'm *sure* it's nothing, just his age, I admit I am starting to get a bit worried.

'Well, I was talking about Seb, and he didn't know who he was. It was like he had no recollection of him at all.'

There's a pause on the other end of the line, and I think Mum is going to bring up the topic of Alzheimer's again, but instead she replies, 'Oh, is that Fiona's new chap?'

I feel my heart thud loudly and I feel a slight panic. Not Mum as well.

'Fiona?' I try stalling, in the hope the conversation won't continue towards its seemingly inevitable outcome.

'Is that short for Sebastian?' continues Mum.

But it's no good. I can't stop it. It's happening all over again

'Um . . . yes,' I manage. I suddenly feel very light-headed.

'You've never mentioned him before,' she continues blithely, 'Is he nice?' *This* from a woman who was over the moon when I met Seb and had to be physically restrained from buying a new hat when we celebrated our six-month anniversary.

'Um . . . yes,' I say again. My mind is beginning to swirl and I'm trying to hang on for dear life but it's as if everything is receding. None of this is making any sense. Either the whole world's gone mad or—

I freeze the thought and start frantically running around in my head like someone trapped in a maze and trying to find a way out.

Or I have.

I manage to get off the phone with Mum, which isn't easy, as she's intent on telling me all about how she took a recipe for Brussels sprouts from the new Jamie Oliver cookbook she received for Christmas and how 'quite frankly it wasn't a patch on how your nan used to make them', followed by her recommendations on how Jamie could improve his: 'sprinkle on my secret ingredient, coffee, and brown them under the grill'.

Right yes, Mum, I'm sure a mega-successful, millionaire chef will be just *dying* to take on your suggestions for his Brussels sprouts. Furthermore, no offence, but Brussels sprouts – be they yours, my deceased nan's, or Jamie's – aren't really at the top of my priority list right now, *because I think I'm going crazy.*

Feeling as though I'm about to have a full-blown panic attack, I take a couple of deep breaths.

OK, focus. *Focus.*

I close my eyes, pinch the bridge of my nose and try to relax. There's no point panicking and getting all stressed out, it's not going to help. I need to think calmly and clearly. Calmly and clearly. Yes, that's it, I think, repeating it over in my head. After all, there has to be a rational explanation for all this. There just has to be.

I concentrate. It takes a few seconds, and then . . .

I know! Perhaps there's some weird type of selective amnesia going round, a bit like swine flu, and everyone's caught it but me. And it's not me that's losing my mind, just everyone else that's losing their memory. These viruses are everywhere in winter. And maybe all that's needed is a course of antibiotics or a vaccination or something and . . .

And what, Tess? Everyone will suddenly remember who Seb is? Realising how ridiculous I'm being, I keep wracking my brains.

Hang on, I've got another idea! Maybe this is Fiona's idea of a joke and everyone's in on it, like April Fool's Day, only instead it's January. And maybe in a few hours she'll confess she was just winding me up and ha ha, wasn't it funny?

I feel a flash of triumph: that's a much better idea! Swiftly followed by niggling doubts. Yes, it *could* be true but the more I think about it, it's unlikely. For starters Fiona doesn't really *do* jokes. Only recently we were at the pub with a bunch of friends, swapping jokes, and when it came to her turn she deadpanned, 'The only joke I know is my last boyfriend Lawrence.'

Then there's my mum. She can't be in on anything for longer than two seconds without letting something slip. In fact, she's single-handedly ruined at least half a dozen surprise parties by unwittingly calling up the person in question to wish them a happy birthday and finished off with a cheery, 'See you tonight at the party!'

Plus that doesn't explain my granddad either.

Anxiety quickly ratchets back up a dozen notches.

Plus why? *Why* would Fiona want to joke that I never went out with Seb? It's not exactly hilarious, is it? And *why* would she get my mum involved? Or Gramps, for that matter? It just doesn't make sense. None of it makes sense.

I try grappling with it like you see people grappling with umbrellas in the wind, trying to find an answer, but it's futile. I give up. I'll just have to add this to my list of things that I'll never understand – like the Dow Jones index, the appeal of Russell Brand, or why men always feel compelled to ask if they'll need a coat before they go out.

There *is* no explanation.

'Tess Connelly?'

Hearing my name being called, I see it's my turn for the helpdesk. Getting up, I walk over to the counter, where I'm greeted by a chubby-faced technician wearing glasses with the thickest lenses I've ever seen. He introduces himself as Ali.

'So what seems to be the problem?' he asks cheerfully.

How long have you got? I think ruefully.

'Excuse me?' Ali's smile wavers ever so slightly.

Oh crap, did I just say that out loud?

'Oh, er, sorry, ignore me . . . one of those days.' Feeling my cheeks go hot, I quickly pull out my laptop and plonk it in front of him. 'It crashed, I can't get it to do anything,' I say quickly.

'Right OK,' he nods briskly. 'Let's have a look at it, shall we?'

Of course there's no 'we' about it. Pushing his glasses onto the bridge of his nose, he cat-cradles his fingers to limber them up, then dives on the keyboard. I watch as his fingers start flying all over the keys, like some kind of magician, and try not to think about my own two-finger typing.

'Well, we've managed to get the machine to turn on,' he says brightly, as a screensaver of Johnny Depp flashes up on the screen.

'Brilliant,' I say, feeling a surge of happy relief. At last something is going right. Feeling myself relax into Ali's capable hands, I watch as he starts dexterously tapping away, his face a mask of concentration.

'Okey-dokey, what have we here?'

See: jokey, fun words. Everything is going to be just fine. Well, not *everything*, but at least I'll be able to read my horoscopes online, Google completely random things and look up ex-boyfriends from school on Facebook and see how badly they've aged – all completely necessary ways to try to mend a broken heart.

'Oh dear . . .'

I zone back. Hang on. That didn't sound fun, or jokey. 'Oh dear' is not 'okey-dokey'. 'Oh dear' is what you never want to hear your dentist say when looking in your mouth. Or your computer technician when staring at your laptop.

'I'm afraid there's a bit of a problem with your hard drive.'

Now I don't know much about computers, but putting the words 'hard drive' and 'problem' in the same sentence sounds deeply worrying.

'But you can fix problems, right?' I ask hopefully. Actually, change that to *plead.*

'Well, we do try to fix most things, but once the hard drive has gone, it's pretty much the nerve centre of the computer . . .'

He pauses and, seeing my face fall, adds quickly, 'But the good news is your laptop is still under warranty, so we can replace your hard drive free of charge.' He beams widely.

'You can?' I beam back. See, I knew I could trust Ali. He looks like one of the super-brainy types you always wanted to sit next to in Maths.

'It does means that you'll lose all your data, but that shouldn't be a problem. When did you last back it up?'

'Back it up?' I repeat tentatively.

'Yes, we can transfer the backed-up data,' he says matter-of-factly. 'Do you use an external drive, or a remote data-storage facility online?' He stops typing and looks up.

It's as if he's speaking gobbledegook. Somewhere, in the recesses of my mind, lurks a memory of me thinking I must learn all about this kind of stuff.

'Erm, no,' I admit, reluctantly. 'Neither.'

Followed by another memory of me thinking I'd get around to it later and watching *Strictly Come Dancing* instead with Fiona.

Ali's cheerful smile freezes slightly. He falls silent and studies me for a moment, eyes unblinking behind his glasses, like a Maths student focused on trying to figure out a really tricky algebra equation he's never seen before. 'Oh, I see,' he says finally, a sharp crease appearing down his forehead. 'Well, in that case I'm afraid you've lost pretty much everything that was on this computer.'

'Everything?' I look at him with horror.

'Everything that was stored on your hard drive, yes. So any documents, files, music—'

'Even all my photos?' My voice trembles. I think about all the photos I took over the past year with Seb. All gone.

'I'm afraid so,' he nods.

Unexpectedly my eyes start watering. It's not the photos – after all, I threw most of them away. It's just . . . well, everything. The last few weeks have been tough, breaking up with Seb, getting through Christmas and New Year, bumping into him again and being blanked – and now this. It's all too much. A tear escapes and rolls down my cheek.

'Are you OK?'

I catch Ali looking at me with concern. 'Sorry,' I sniffle. 'I broke up with my boyfriend and, well . . .' I get a lump in my throat and feeling my eyes welling up. I break off and roughly rub my eyes with my coat sleeve.

'Look, there might be another way.' Taking pity on me he hands me a screen wipe. 'In nearly all hard-drive recovery cases, data can be recovered by a trained specialist technician. It's only when there's really bad platter damage, magnetic degradation or a file overwrite that the data is impossible to recover.'

He waits for me to say something.

'I'm sorry, you lost me at hard drive,' I confess, blowing my nose.

'Well, it's like this: your computer stores everything on the hard drive, every keystroke, every site you've visited, every email you've sent . . . If that crashes, it's like a plane, everything goes down with it – you lose everything.' He pauses, then leaning forwards, lowers his voice and adds darkly, 'Unless you know where to look.'

He gives me a pointed glance and I break off from blowing my nose to stare back wide-eyed. Gosh, it all sounds very cloak and dagger.

'The workings of a computer are extremely complex. It's like a rabbit warren of tunnels, and computers can hide things deep, deep inside. That's why you have people involved in criminal activity who try to erase their hard drive and browsing history, but there's still a record of it somewhere.'

'There is?' I have a flashback to me on Facebook looking at the pages of Seb's ex-girlfriends and going through their photo albums.

'Yes,' he nods gravely. 'You can try to delete everything, try wiping them clean, but if you dig deep enough and know how to use the right software, you can still find things lurking. It's virtually impossible to erase everything from a computer. In fact, I'd say it was impossible.'

'How do you know all this?' I gape, dabbing my eyes.

'I used to work for a data-recovery company in my spare time when I was at university in Delhi.'

'Wow, you really *are* a genius.'

'Oh, I don't know about that. I'm just a bit of a geek. At least that's what my ex used to tell me.' He gives an embarrassed shrug.

'Well then your ex was an idiot,' I say supportively.

'So was yours,' he replies kindly.

We exchange sympathetic looks. Then, glancing around to make sure no one is listening, he adds, 'Look, I really shouldn't do this, but I've got a fifteen-minute break – I'll see what I can retrieve for you, if anything, OK?'

'Really?' I sniff gratefully.

'Leave it with me,' he says and, passing me another screen wipe, he leaves the counter.

Feeling slightly cheered up, I go and sit back down. I dig out my hand-mirror, and I'm wiping away my smudged eyeliner and streaked mascara when I'm interrupted by a voice.

'Excuse me, is this seat taken?'

It has an American accent and I stiffen. Hang on, I recognise that voice.

I look up.

It's like a bowling ball in my chest.

'*Seb?*'

9

At the sound of his name he turns to look at me.

My breath catches in the back of my throat and I hold it tight inside of me, waiting to exhale.

His eyes search mine out and there's the longest pause. It seems to stretch out like chewing gum. Everything around me seems to disappear, people, chatter, noise . . . All gone. It's as if someone's just turned off the volume; all I can hear is my heart beating a drum roll in my chest. Last time he totally ignored me, but this time there's no way he can pretend he hasn't seen me. I mean, I'm right here. Sitting right in front of him.

I wait for him to say something. *Anything*.

'I'm sorry,' he says finally, his face void of all recognition. 'Have we met?

But not that.

I stare at him in disbelief. You've got to be kidding, right?

Except the spooky thing is, he doesn't seem like he's kidding. Whenever Seb used to fool around there were always telltale signs. But today there's no twitching of his lips, no nervous scratching of his head, no shifty not meeting of the eyes.

Indignation suddenly hits me around the head like a frying pan.

Well, come on, this is crazy. Not to mention fucking rude. OK, I know everyone deals with break-ups differently; going out and getting drunk, sleeping around, lying in bed with their cat eating Jaffa Cakes and watching *Desperate Housewives* on a loop (I've gone for the last option).

But pretending you've never met that person? Like they've never seen you naked? *And on the loo?* A flashback of Seb sitting on the toilet, with no clothes on, reading the Proust questionnaire from the back of *Vanity Fair* and shouting to me that there's no loo roll. I mean, come on, this is *me* you're talking to, I think hotly. The girl who came to your rescue with more Andrex.

'Are you seriously trying to tell me you don't know who I am?' I blurt out.

He looks abashed. 'You have to forgive me, I'm terrible with faces. Sometimes I look in the mirror and don't even recognise myself.' He smiles ruefully. 'Then again, I'm pretty sure I'd remember you if we had met.'

Oh my god, is he *flirting* with me?

I stare at him aghast. I honestly don't know what to say. Or how to react. It was bizarre before but now . . .

'So . . . is it OK?' He gestures to the free seat next to me.

'Erm, yeh,' I nod dumbly. My mind is all over the place, trying to find a logical answer for what's going on. Maybe Seb got the same advice as I got from Fiona. Pretend like I don't exist. Forget about me.

Even so, isn't this a bit *extreme*?

'So, was I nice?' he says, sitting down.

I look at him in confusion. 'Excuse me?'

'When we met?'

I have a sudden urge to grab him by the shoulders and shake him, tell him to act normal. Like once when I was little and Dad was fooling around, pretending to be a scary monster, and I started crying and begged him to be himself again.

'Er . . .' I grope around for something to say, but now I'm lost for words.

Only he's still looking at me, waiting for an answer. As if we're two strangers making chitchat, not a couple who've just broken up.

'I . . . er . . . can't really remember, it was a while ago.' Caught in some bizarre, dream-like scenario, I struggle to form a sentence.

Seb, on the other hand, seems to be having no such problem.

'Well I hope I was,' he smiles cheerfully and, sitting down next to me, starts looking at his iPhone.

Conversation over, I sit back in my seat, stunned. I can't believe what just happened. *What is still happening*, I remind myself, sneaking a look at him out of the corner of my eye. Maybe I got it wrong. Maybe it's a case of mistaken identity. After all, isn't everyone supposed to have a doppelgänger? Maybe this is Seb's.

I peer at him from under my eyelashes. He's still looking down at his iPhone and I trace the familiar outline of his face: same golden tan from his frequent skiing trips; same thick blond hair and neatly trimmed sideburns; same strong jaw and sexy cleft in his chin; same habit of distractedly pulling at his eyebrows when he's concentrating . . .

My heart thumps. The same name is one thing. Same physical appearance is another thing. *But the same characteristics?*

'I broke the screen.' He tuts loudly and turns to look at me, catching me staring.

Startled, I jump. 'Excuse me?' I say quickly, grabbing my fringe and trying to hide beneath it.

'Snowboarding,' he shrugs, gesturing to the glass on his iPhone that's shattered. 'I tried to get an appointment at their store in Regent Street, but they were booked solid till next week. So I raced over here instead.'

He's talking to me as if everything is completely normal, as if he hasn't noticed my discomfort. As if he hasn't noticed it's *me. Tess. The girl he used to spoon before he fell asleep at night.* I stare at him in bewilderment. What the hell is going on?

'Hi, Miss Connelly?'

I look up to see Ali, the technician, standing over me.

'Oh, hi,' I try to focus.

'I think I might have found something,' he whispers urgently. 'Everything else was completely erased, but this was buried deep inside your hard drive, I almost didn't find it . . .' He looks furtively from side to side to make sure no one is watching, then sticks his hand in his pocket. 'It's a Word file, I've put it on here.' He quickly stuffs a disk in my hand as if he's handing over stolen goods. 'I'm afraid it's not much . . .'

'Oh, thanks,' I smile gratefully. 'That's really kind of you . . .'

I break off as I catch Seb glancing over curiously. Or is it? Maybe it's his double.

Double of what, Tess? *Some guy you dreamed up?*

Shit. I need to get out of here. And fast.

Saying goodbye to Ali, I shove the disk in my pocket and quickly rush out of the store.

I go home in a daze. I don't know what to think so I try not to think anything by jamming in my earphones and turning up my iPod to full volume. The bass rattles my eardrums. Normally whenever I see those people on the tube with music thumping loudly from their ears, I tut and think, what are they doing? They're going to go deaf!

Now I am that person and I don't care. So what if I go deaf? By the looks of things I've already gone completely bloody loopy.

I walk into the flat to find Fiona at the kitchen table in her fluffy dressing gown, hair all over the place, the phone wedged under her chin and a cigarette hanging from the corner of her mouth. Not quite how one would imagine a health and beauty journalist. And certainly not what the readers of her magazine column would picture. The column that has a photo of her sitting cross-legged on a yoga mat, dressed in Lycra and drinking fresh orange juice.

'I don't care if it's a Bank Holiday. Don't you realise my deadline's tomorrow?' she's yelling down the handset. 'Well, fine then, you can stick your new Botox face cream!' She gives a snort and hangs up. 'Stupid PR woman,' she tuts, taking a furious drag of her cigarette and pouncing on her keyboard.

Dumping my bag on the table, I flop into a chair.

'Good day?' she asks distractedly from behind her laptop screen.

'Good and bad,' I reply, heaving a sigh. 'Gramps is good, but my laptop's broken. Apparently it needs a new hard drive.'

'Oh dear,' she tuts, not looking up from her keyboard. 'Did you back up?'

Why is it that you can go your whole life never hearing about something, and then when it's too late, that's all people talk about?

'No, I didn't. I lost everything. Including my mind,' I can't help adding, but she's not really listening as she's already furiously typing away, no doubt sending an angry email to the poor PR.

'Oh, except this . . .' Wiggling out of my coat, I remember the disk in my pocket and put it on the table.

'What's that?' Fiona stops typing and her head appears from behind her laptop.

'I dunno,' I shrug wearily. 'The man at the store says he managed to save a file or something.' I hoist myself out of the chair and flick on the kettle. I desperately need a cup of tea. Actually, I need something stronger, but I'm not sure starting on the tequila is a good idea. Look where that got me last time.

'Let's have a look . . .'

I turn around to see Fiona snatch up the disk and pop it into her laptop.

'Tea?' I ask, reaching for the PG tips.

She doesn't hear me. She's too preoccupied. 'Um . . . it looks like loads of writing . . .'

I make her a cup anyway. Fiona's not the kind of person to turn down anything. I've witnessed some of her online dates . . .

'Oh hang on, I think it's a diary . . .'

'*Diary?*'

'That's what it looks like.' She glances up at me. 'I didn't know you kept a diary!'

I feel my cheeks colour. 'Well, I haven't for a while—'

I'm interrupted as the microwave suddenly pings. 'My Tom Yum soup's ready.' She jumps up from her chair. 'I had some left so I thought I might as well finish it off – in for a penny, in for a pound and all that . . . *well, nearly five pounds now, actually*,' she mutters under her breath.

As she heads across the kitchen, I abandon the tea and scoot over to her computer. Sure enough, on her screen I see a diary entry from 4 January 2011:

Dear Diary,

Had my first date with Seb! We went for a drink in Chelsea . . .

I see his name and break off, the words spinning before my eyes.

What the . . . ?

Suddenly I go hot and cold. For a split second there's a pause, then my thoughts begin crashing over each other, tossing my mind around like a boat on stormy seas. Yet above the din, one thought is loud and clear: So I'm not crazy. I didn't make him up. I haven't imagined it all.

I feel a flash of vindication.

'See, I told you!' I say triumphantly to Fiona, suddenly finding my voice.

'Told me what?' She turns around, a bowl of soup in her hands.

I'm about to drag her over to show her the evidence when halfway down the page my eyes come into focus and I see:

. . . and Fiona bought a dress for her online date next week. It's super-tight and super-short and this sort of funny pale pink colour

which makes her look a bit like a sausage. She asked me if it made her look fat. I lied and said no . . .

'Um, nothing,' I say, quickly pressing eject. 'It's just a load of old nonsense, nothing important.'

And, snatching up the disk, I leave her eating her soup and beat a hasty exit from the kitchen.

I close my bedroom door and sit down on the edge of my bed. Flea lets out a disgruntled squeak at being disturbed on my eiderdown, but I'm too distracted to scoop him up. Instead I remain motionless. I'm vaguely aware of the hot cup of tea burning the palms of my hands, but I can't move.

I can't do anything. It's like every bit of energy is diverted to my mind, which is racing around and around, just like that little rainbow-coloured wheel I got on my computer, furiously trying to process all the weird, unexplained events from the last few days: being blanked by Seb in Starbucks, Fiona's reaction, everyone's reactions . . . Like a tape recording in my head, I hear a cacophony of voices. Fiona: '*Seb who?*' Gramps: '*I've never met a Sebastian.*' Mum: '*You've never mentioned him before.*' They're all blurring into stereo, into one single voice . . . and then I see Seb again: he's sitting next to me, talking to me, and I'm looking into his eyes and there's not a flicker of recognition; it's as though he doesn't know who I am.

But that's impossible! What about my diary? demands a voice in my head. And this time it's my own voice, bringing me up short.

I place my cup of tea on the bedside cabinet and start rummaging around inside. There must be more evidence of our relationship, something more tangible than words on a computer disk. An old photograph, a card that he wrote me, *something* . . . My fingers scrabble around desperately. There's so much junk thrown in here: old lipsticks, my stash of earplugs, those spare buttons that come with new tops and I never know where to put . . . Yet nothing that links me to Seb. No pictures of us together, no cards he sent me, nothing.

But of course I'm not going to find anything, I remind myself quickly. I threw it all away, remember? I wanted to try and forget about him. That's why I deleted all his texts, his emails, his Facebook page. That's why I burned all the mementos from our relationship in the fire on New Year's Eve.

As the thought strikes, a blurry memory stirs – an image flashes up of the man on TV. He was wearing spacehopper ears. What was his name? He was talking about rituals. I grope back through the tequila-sodden memories, trying to recollect . . .

'. . . *an ancient ritual . . . all the things you want to rid yourself of, be it . . . painful memories, hurt . . . throwing them into the fire at the stroke of midnight.*' I strain harder, thinking back: '. . . *many cultures believe that by burning these things you get rid of them . . . and that way you don't carry them with you into next year . . .*'

I suddenly go hot and cold.

I stop myself. Oh come on, he was wearing glittery spacehopper ears on his head, for Christ's sakes. As if I'm going to believe anything he says. It's superstitious rubbish. I'd have to be completely bananas.

And yet . . .

A chink of possibility is opening up in my brain. It's completely ridiculous. Impossible. Utterly unfeasible. And I can hardly believe I'm even *thinking* it, but . . . but it would make sense, in a completely bonkers kind of way. That by throwing the stuff on the fire I magically got rid of all the memories, all the dates, all the time we spent together. I totally erased the relationship. I totally erased *us*.

Except for my diary – the one shred of evidence that managed to survive through some technical blip and that prevented him from being erased from my mind and my heart – *it's like it never happened.*

I hear the presenter's voice again in my head: '*. . . as the flames burn away these things, sparks will well and truly fly . . . whatever you wish for will be carried on these sparks into the New Year . . .*'

My mind flashes back to that night. To the spark I glimpsed escaping up the chimney when I threw everything onto the fire. To my wish.

My heart hammers in my chest as I suddenly remember.

I wished I'd never met him.

And now it's come true. I haven't.

My thoughts are interrupted by a loud buzzing. It's the intercom in the hallway. Vaguely I hear the murmur of voices, then Fiona calling, 'Tess, it's for you.'

'Who is it?' I call back, finding my voice.

But there's no answer. I feel a twinge of frustration. Whoever it is, I don't want to see them. I don't want to see anyone. I remain motionless for a moment, part of me hoping that if I ignore them they'll just go away.

'Tess!'

It's Fiona again. Resisting the urge to yell back 'Go away', I get up. I check my reflection in the mirror, attempt to do something with my hair, then give up and walk through into the hallway. I can see the back of Fiona, her bathrobe-clad figure blocking someone in the doorway.

She's talking to them, but as I approach she turns. 'There you are!' she reprimands in her Sunday-best voice. 'Apparently you left your bag at the store.'

'My bag?' I had to take two bags with me today as I couldn't fit my laptop and everything else in just my leather rucksack. Now it suddenly dawns on me I only brought one home. I must have left the other one. God, I'm such an idiot . . .

'Honestly, Tess, what are you like?' She gives a tinkly little laugh, the kind of laugh she always adopts when there are men around. 'Luckily for you, this very nice man found it.' Aha, I knew it.

Beaming brightly, she gestures at the figure in the doorway.

'Oh, gosh, thanks . . .' As I reach the door, Fiona steps to one side so I can thank the stranger.

Only it's not a stranger.

My voice stalls in my throat. Oh my god, what's *Seb* doing here?

'You left this.' He smiles awkwardly and holds out my bag.

Blankly I look at him, then it registers. In the computer store. I was sitting next to him. I rushed off quickly . . .

I realise I'm just standing there, gawking.

'Um . . . yes, thanks,' I nod, quickly taking it from him.

'I hope you don't mind, I had to look inside to find your address.'

'No, no of course not,' I fluster, hugging it to my chest tightly and feeling light-headed. I've got to hang onto something. Anything.

There's a pause and I'm vaguely aware that Fiona has disappeared and it's just me and Seb. I swallow hard. I have to say something. I can't just ignore what's happened. *What's happening?*

'I just want to say . . .' I manage to gulp. He looks at me expectantly with his pale blue eyes. I struggle inwardly, trying to find the right words. 'Um, I just wanted to say . . .' I repeat again, then break off. Oh, who am I kidding? It's pointless: there are *no* right words. How can I explain it to him when I can't explain it to myself? He'll think I'm a lunatic. 'Thanks again,' I stammer.

For a split second I think I see disappointment flash across his face, but then it's gone and he's smiling again. 'No problem,' he says, batting away my thanks. 'Well, I've probably taken up too much of your time . . .' As he turns to leave, I'm gripped with a sudden panic. 'I should go . . .'

He's leaving. I have to stop him.

'OK,' I nod dumbly. Is that it? I'm never going to see him again and that's all I'm going to say?

'But before I do, I was going to ask you something,' he says, turning back, and I feel a rush of relief.

'Yes?'

His hands are shoved deep into his pockets and he's got a nervous look on his face. My chest tightens. 'Well, I was just wondering . . . if maybe . . . you'd like to go out for a drink with me sometime . . .'

As he trails off, his eyes meet mine, and for a split second I'm right back to that moment when we first met. The moment a year ago when, standing in a crowded bar, I turned and caught his eye and he spoke to me, offered to buy me a drink and proceeded to ask me on a date. A moment in my life when everything changed.

Only this time we're standing in the hallway of my flat. Different time, different place. But it's still the same Seb. It's still the same me. Everything's changed and yet nothing's changed. I'm right back to where we began. Where it all started.

Except this time I can stop it from ever happening.

I can stop us before we even start.

Relief bursts like a firework. Just think, no more heartache. No more tears on my pillow. No more walking down the street and suddenly, without warning, being hit with such an intense longing to see him again it takes my breath away. I need to forget I ever met him and now, for all intents and purposes, I haven't, have I?

It's so simple. So easy. Why on earth would I put myself through all the heartache again? Why repeat it, when all I have to do is politely say no, close the door and never look back? I know how this story ends, and it's not happily ever after.

'Well?' asks Seb uncertainly.

I open my mouth ready to turn him down; I'm already rehearsing the lines in my head, but as I look into his familiar, faded-blue eyes, all the old feelings come rushing back. They never went away, I just tried to bury them deep inside of me.

And something stops me. A realisation: I might have erased an entire relationship, but I haven't erased my feelings towards Seb. I still love him.

Well, you don't just unlove someone, do you?

And suddenly, out of the blue, a shiver of possibility runs up my spine. An idea starts to form, grow, take hold . . . It seems crazy and yet this whole thing is crazy.

What if I can make us have a different ending?

What if I can do all the things I wish I'd done? Have the time again to make right all the regrets? They say no one ever gets a second chance at their relationship; no one gets to give it a rehearsal, to do it second time around. *But I do*. Until now I never believed in rituals, or superstitions, but somehow, by some strange, incredible, magical twist of fate, I've got a second chance to get it right. With the gift of hindsight I can make it work out . . .

My mind spools backwards through our relationship, rummages through the shoebox of memories, all the mistakes I made, the things I didn't do, all the silly things I wish I could change: accidentally making fun of his favourite movie, the snowboarding trip we never went on, the book he gave me that I didn't bother reading, having that stupid argument after I caught the bouquet at the wedding. Seriously, what was I thinking? Why the hell didn't I throw the bouquet back?

But this time I can.

This time I can change everything.

Teetering on the edge of that moment, like a diver on the high board, I take a deep breath. And smiling at Seb, I jump right back in.

'A drink sounds great.'

Dear Diary,

Had my first date with Seb! We went for a drink in Chelsea and I was so nervous I knocked a glass of red wine all over him. God, it was SO embarrassing! He was really nice about it but still, why can't I be cool for once in my life? Why am I such a clumsy idiot!!!???

10

It's the next evening and I'm supposed to be getting ready to go out, but instead I'm sitting on my bed in my dressing gown reading my diary. I've printed it out from the disk and this is the entry from my first date with Seb last year.

And now I'm about to go on it all over again.

At the thought, a cage of butterflies is opened in my stomach.

I'm meeting him at the same bar I met him first time around – Seb suggested it and I couldn't very well tell him the reason why I'd like to go somewhere different – but this time I'm going to make sure it *is* different. This time I'm not going to make the same mistakes twice; instead I'm going to be super-careful. No spilling red wine. In fact, I know, I won't even *drink* red wine. I'll order white instead.

Or vodka.

Maybe even gin. No. Gin's supposed to be a depressant. I can't drink gin on a first date . . .

I stop myself before I work my way through the entire drinks cabinet. Whatever, as long it's clear and won't stain.

Just in case, of course.

For the past twenty-four hours, since Seb asked me out, I haven't been able to think of anything else. I still can't quite believe it's happening. It's so surreal I've spent the whole day walking around in a daze. Every so often I've had to stop and remind myself: *I'm going on a first date with Seb again.* A couple of times I might have even said it out loud, as the lady in the corner shop gave me the most peculiar look when I popped in there to buy loo roll earlier and commented, 'I'm sure that will be nice.' Which at the time I thought was a bit of a forward thing to say, even if it *was* Andrex super-quilted.

I glance at the clock on my beside cabinet. Gosh, is that the time already? We've arranged to meet in just over an hour, at 8 p.m., and I'm still not dressed. Feeling all excited and jittery about seeing him again, my eyes sweep over the various outfits that I've tried on and discarded on the bed. I just can't decide what to wear. None of them seems right and it's really important I make a good impression.

Which is ridiculous considering Seb's seen me in a scruffy old T-shirt and leggings. Except he hasn't, has he? I have to quickly remind myself.

God, this is all very confusing

I look again at my tiny wardrobe, a find in a second-hand shop that *looks* lovely, all 1930s walnut curves and delicate inlay, but is completely impractical as it's too narrow for my modern-day coat hangers and everything's squished in at an angle.

Meaning everything I pull out of there is a crumpled mess.

I stare gloomily at a blue silk dress that now resembles an old dish rag, trying to calculate how long it will take me to iron it: finding ironing board (5 mins), struggling to put it up (5 mins), giving up and putting towel on bedroom floor (2 mins), filling iron with water and waiting for it to heat up (4 mins), dribbling water all over dress because I haven't waited long enough and steam function isn't working properly yet (3 mins), turning up iron even hotter (2 mins), having another go with iron and discovering it's now too hot and has stuck like chewing gum to the silk (2 mins), staring at horrible burn mark on dress and wondering if I can hide it with a brooch (1 min), trying it on and realising instead of the sexy vibe I was going for I now look like someone's granny (3 mins).

Shit. I'm crap at maths, but that's a lot of minutes, and I *still* won't have anything to wear.

For a moment I stare, paralysed, at my wardrobe, feeling the pressure of time tick-tocking away, when I'm suddenly hit by an idea. Hang on, wait a minute. I snatch up the pages of my old diary and quickly scan down the entry:

> *. . . wore my jeans and a pink chiffon top I found in a charity shop. It was a bit frumpy, so I shortened the sleeves and sewed these tiny mother-of-pearl buttons down the front (with the help of Gramps of course). Seb said I looked lovely. Though my new high-heeled boots were a BIG mistake. I could barely walk in them and the bar was miles from the tube station. I turned up really late, all red-faced from rushing, with toes full of blisters . . .*

Brilliant! That's my outfit decided then.

Rummaging in my wardrobe, I find the chiffon top and pull out my trusty jeans. Well, I don't have to do *everything* differently, not if it was a hit the first time around. Just change the stuff that wasn't. Like, for example, those dratted boots, I decide. Shoving my heels back in the shoe hanger, I dig out my flat ankle ones instead.

Twenty minutes later and I've finished drying my hair, doing my make-up, and pulling on my blouse and jeans. OK, I'm good to go. Just need to check out my reflection. I don't have a full-length mirror, just one propped on the top of my fireplace, so I do my usual trick of standing on my bed and twisting and bending myself like a pretzel, trying to check out the different parts of my body.

Well they all look OK. *Separately*. I bob down to see the neckline of my blouse, then jump up and, balancing on one leg, lift up the other and waggle it at the mirror . . . It's just I'm not quite sure what they look like put *together*. After all, it's been a while since I wore this outfit and second-helpings of mince pies have come between me and this pair of jeans since then.

Not to mention Fiona's family-size tin of Quality Street.

I feel a pinch of regret. My particular weakness are the pink fudges. Saying that, I'm not responsible for all the rest of them disappearing. Ever since her grandparents sent them to her, there have been tiny screwed-up balls of glittery foil mysteriously scattered all over the flat. I say *mysteriously*, as Fiona is on another one of her crazy diets and insists it's not her. Denial, it seems, is not just a river in Egypt.

Speaking of Fiona, I don't need a full-length mirror when she's at home. She's a bit like the speaking clock, only instead of telling me the exact time, she'll tell me exactly what I look like. Hopping off the bed, I shove my diary in my bag and head into the kitchen, where I find her hunched over the stove, stirring a saucepan.

'Ooh you look nice,' she says, glancing up as I walk in. 'Great combo.' She gestures at my jeans and top with her wooden spoon and nods approvingly. 'Give us a twirl.'

I duly twirl.

'Wow Tess, you look amazing, you're going to knock him dead . . .' She suddenly pauses and fixes her gaze on my feet, an expression of confusion on her face.

'What?'

'You're wearing flats,' she says in disbelief.

'I know,' I nod.

'You're not wearing heels.'

'Uh-huh.'

'And you're going on a date.'

She looks utterly bewildered. And well she might do because, to Fiona, I'm doing the unthinkable. Going on a date without heels is like going on a date without clothes. In fact, if she had the choice, she'd probably rather be naked than without her stilettos.

'I thought my flat boots would be more comfortable,' I offer in explanation.

She looks aghast. 'Tess, you're going on a first date! You're not *supposed* to be comfortable. You're supposed to look as tall and skinny as possible. Don't you know a pair of heels adds five inches and takes off five pounds?'

She says this as if she's asking me if I didn't know the earth was round.

'Um . . . maybe,' I say vaguely. I have to admit, I like the sound of losing five pounds, but I can hardly tell her the real reason I'm wearing them. 'So, what are you cooking?' I ask, quickly changing the subject.

'Kidney beans,' she replies, turning back to the saucepan.

'That's it?'

'Oh no, I'm having them with tomatoes, red cabbage and radishes,' she says cheerfully.

'That's . . . er . . . an unusual combination,' I say uncertainly.

'I'm on this new rainbow diet,' she explains. 'Each day you can only eat foods that are all the same colour.' She peers into her saucepan. 'Today's red.'

'And tomorrow?'

'Um . . .' She pauses, then sings a little song under her breath, '*Red and yellow and pink and blue* . . .' She breaks off. 'Blue,' she says decisively. 'It should be yellow but what the hell, be a rebel, mix it up a little.' She gives a throaty laugh.

'There are blue foods?' I ask in amazement.

'Of course,' she replies, and snatches up her diet sheet. 'There're blueberries,' she says, reading off the list, 'and aubergines—'

'Aren't they purple?'

She frowns, then, ignoring my comment, continues. 'Anyway, the main thing is it's supposed to be amazing for flushing away all those nasty toxins like salts, refined sugars—'

'Oh look, there's another one!' I interrupt, spotting a flash of orange tinfoil under the kitchen table.

Fiona stiffens. 'Golly, how strange,' she wide-eyes, all theatrically.

It's so obvious she's fibbing. Fiona is not the kind of person who says golly. She says fuck and bollocks and sometimes even *fuck-bollocks*. Golly is strictly reserved for Pippa and her posh friends.

'I wonder what that's doing there?' she continues stiffly.

'Hmm, I wonder,' I muse, playing along. I bend down – damn these jeans are tight – and scoop up the tiny ball of tinfoil.

'Maybe it's Flea?' she muses, avoiding my gaze and turning pointedly back to her saucepan.

'Flea!' I gasp, glancing across at him curled up on the sofa. 'Flea doesn't eat chocolate – he's a cat.'

'How do you know he doesn't?' she argues, a touch defensively. 'Maybe he likes chocolate. Maybe he gets down like all the rest of us and needs cheering up.' She starts stirring more vigorously.

'With a hazelnut whirl?' I stifle a giggle.

'Well why not?' she protests, looking a little affronted. 'You know, just because Flea likes sleeping on your bed more than mine, it doesn't mean you know his innermost thoughts.'

'Well, for starters, chocolate is bad for cats . . .' I begin.

'It's actually a good source of iron,' counters Fiona sagely, turning to me and giving me her serious journalist look. 'I once wrote a thousand-word article about it for *Saturday Speaks*.'

'Yes, but animals aren't supposed to eat chocolate.'

'Well, none of us are *really*,' she acquiesces, looking down at her thighs and frowning.

'Aren't you forgetting something?' I say, raising an eyebrow.

'Oh bollocks,' she jolts upright, her face stricken. 'I knew there was something I needed to remember . . .' She darts over to the kitchen table and starts rummaging through the piles of face creams and hair masks that PR companies are always sending her in the hope that she'll write about them in her column. And which are taking on mountainous proportions. I'm worried I'm going to come home from work one day and discover Fiona trapped under an avalanche of beauty products.

I can see the headlines now:

HEALTH & BEAUTY WRITER FOUND BURIED ALIVE UNDER COLLAGEN-BOOSTING MOISTURISERS

Emergency services fought for hours to dig her out, but the sheer size and scale of the pile of hair-conditioning masks was just too much. Her devastated flatmate, Tess Connelly, was quoted as saying, 'It was a disaster waiting to happen.'

'Happy Birthday,' she gasps, reappearing with a luxury seaweed body scrub and thrusting it at me.

'Thanks,' I smile bemusedly, 'but it's not my birthday.'

'It's not? Phew,' she sags with relief, then frowns. 'Well, what then?'

'The lid,' I gesture to the tin of Quality Street. 'Flea might be smart for a cat, but he's not smart enough to open an airtight cover . . .'

Two spots of colour appear high on her cheeks, and just when I think she might come clean and confess, we're both distracted by the smell of something burning. 'Fuck, my beans!' she yelps, diving back to the stove. She lets out a loud groan. 'Bollocks! They're all black, and it's supposed to be a red day!'

'I don't think black's in the rainbow,' I reply, amused. 'It must be a sign.'

'A sign?'

'That you should give up these fad diets,' I nag. 'They never work, plus you don't need them. You look great as you are.'

'Aren't you going to be late?' she replies, ignoring me.

I know she'll never listen and, taking the hint, I grab my thick duvet coat. 'Bye,' I wave, and turn to leave. 'See you later.'

'Have a fab time.' She waves her wooden spoon after me, then winks. 'I reckon he's a keeper.'

It's incredible. Only a few days ago Fiona was calling Seb every name under the sun and telling me to forget he even existed. Now I can't believe the change. But then a lot has changed in the past few days, hasn't it? And an awful lot more is about to, I think, a tingle flurrying up my spine.

'Don't you?'

I snap back. 'Yes,' I say quietly. 'He's definitely a keeper.'

And, crossing my fingers, I hurry out of the flat. Because this time I don't want to lose him. This time I hope it *is* for keeps.

11

The tube ride from Hammersmith is only four stops, but it's still almost eight o'clock by the time I arrive at Gloucester Road. As I leave the station I have a flashback to me on my last first date, trying to rush in those high heels, twisting over on my ankle as I hurried along the slippery pavement, wincing as I felt blisters the size of marbles forming, looking at my watch and panicking that I was going to be horribly late.

But not this time. Oh no. Now I stride out in my comfy flat boots, overtaking girls in their stilettos who are tottering along cautiously, trying not to slip on the patches of sheer ice that have turned the paving stones into a skating rink. Gosh, this is so great! I could walk for miles in these boots, I think with satisfaction, relishing their crepe nonslip soles as I advance effortlessly along the street, breathing out clouds into the wintry air.

In what feels like no time at all I see the pub ahead on the corner. A large Victorian building with huge curved, etched windows and, outside, a few tables and chairs around which a brave few are huddled, smoking cigarettes. Approaching, I suddenly feel a jangle of nerves at the thought of seeing Seb again.

Which is mad as I went out with him for nearly a year, I remind myself firmly. It's not like he's a stranger. Well, not to me anyway. Still, I suppose it's a bit like actors when they're about to go out on stage for the first time. It doesn't matter how many rehearsals they've had, once the curtain goes up, that's it. There's no more room for mistakes; this time they have to get it right.

This time *I* have to get it right.

I pause at the door and take a deep breath. OK, just relax. Remember, nothing can go wrong because I've done it all before. I glance at my watch. See! Last time I was late, and now look, perfect timing!

And, for the first time since Seb asked me out, the nerves disappear and I feel a burst of excitement. Reassurance. Hope. Because, although I'll never understand how this can be happening, it *is* happening. Some incredible bit of magic got into my corner of the universe, and I have to trust in the universe that it's happening for a reason.

Curling my woollen fingers around the handle, I push open the door.

This is going to be a perfect first date.

Entering the pub I'm hit by the beery warmth and noise of chatter. It's one of those gastropubs, with stripped floorboards, lots of wooden tables and chairs, and a big chalkboard menu featuring things like overpriced fishcakes and *moules-frites*. Gastropubs, for some reason I've never worked out, like to write their menus in French.

I scan the crowds for Seb. Last time he was sitting near the open fire, on the old leather sofa, reading a book and waiting for me. I glance across towards it, and sure enough, there he is. He's wearing jeans and a pale blue shirt that matches his eyes. My heart skips a beat; he looks as gorgeous as ever. Pulling off my scarf and gloves I make my way over.

'Hi,' I say as I reach him.

He looks up and a big white smile breaks over his face. God, Americans have such great teeth. 'Hey,' he greets me in his easy drawl and jumps up to give me a hug. He has none of that English awkwardness when you first meet someone, the clumsy kiss on the cheek, the not-quite-sure-what-to-do-with-your-hands dance where you hover around each other like teenagers at a school disco.

Instead he confidently puts his arms around me, pulling me close in a friendly embrace. As he does, my cheek brushes against his freshly shaved one and I inhale his familiar scent. I feel a warm glow inside. It's the same kind of feeling you get when you come home after a long journey.

'You look great,' he smiles, breaking apart, his eyes sweeping over me.

'Thanks,' I smile back. 'You too.'

For a brief moment we stand opposite each other, drinking each other in, then he seems to remember himself and starts clearing space on the sofa, 'Sorry, for some reason I thought you might be late . . .'

'What? You think all girls keep men waiting?' I tease, sitting down next to him.

I feel a beat of pleasure. I'm off to a really good start, thanks to my diary and knowing to wear my flat boots. Otherwise I would have still been puffing and panting down the street like a steam train.

And not sitting next to him while he smiles at me sheepishly.

'Sorry, I should have known you'd be different,' he says, his eyes searching out mine.

'I hate being late,' I say, meeting his gaze. Which is true, I *do* hate it. Unfortunately, however hard I try, I usually am. It's as if my keys hide themselves down the sofa on purpose. Or tube trains intentionally sit in tunnels.

'Well that's one thing we've already got in common,' he grins. 'I can't be late if I try. It must be something to do with my dad being in the military. I think I must have inherited his punctuality gene,' he laughs.

Right, that's it. From now on I'm going to make a serious effort to *always* be on time. Early even.

'Though usually it means I'm the poor dude who's always waiting for everyone else,' he continues with a wry smile. 'That's why I always carry something to read. I've got nearly half a library in there.' He gestures to his bulging backpack on the floor, and a book sticking out of the side pocket. 'I'm halfway through the second one by Obama.'

'Oh, is it good?' I ask politely. 'I always see those types of political autobiographies on the bestseller list and think they must be really fascinating to read.'

Then I go and buy the latest chick-lit novel because I know I'll enjoy it so much more, I think sheepishly.

'It's amazing, though I actually thought his first one was better. You should read it! Hang on, I think I've got a copy in here . . .' Bending down, he rummages around in his backpack and pulls out a big chunky paperback. 'Here it is! What was I saying about carrying a library in here?' He laughs. 'It's a brand-new copy as I can't find my original one. I think I must have lent it to someone.'

Yes, to me, I think, recognising the book in his hand. It's the same one he gave me before but I never got around to reading.

However, like I said, this time I plan to do things very differently.

'Wow thanks,' I say as he hands it to me. 'I can't wait to read it!' I have a quick flick through. Gosh, I don't remember it being this long – almost five hundred pages.

'It's awesome. Believe me, it totally changed my life. It'll change yours too,' he enthuses.

'Brilliant!' And quite heavy, I realise, resting it in my lap.

We smile at each other, bonded by Obama, and for a moment I get this lovely image of us discussing the great man himself, his social reforms, his famous speech: *Yes We Can!*

'So what's your trick?' he asks.

I blink.

'*Trick?*'

'Yeh, for passing the time when you're waiting for everyone else.'

'Oh . . . um . . .' Caught off-guard, I grope around for a way out, then see it – my earphones trailing from my pocket. 'My iPod,' I blurt, grabbing hold of them and waggling them as evidence. 'I'm surprised I've got any eardrums left,' I quip in a ha-ha sort of way.

He laughs and I feel a flush of relief.

'So, next question . . .'

Gosh, another? I brace myself.

'What would you like to drink?'

The embarrassing memory of me spilling a glass of Merlot all over his crotch and me diving on it with a fistful of paper towels fires across my brain. Ah, now this bit I do know. Feeling on firmer ground, I pretend to think for a moment.

Remember Tess, nothing red, nothing that will stain, just in case.

'Um . . . I'll have a white wine, please,' I smile.

'Any particular type?'

'Oh no . . . anything, I don't mind,' I shrug casually. 'Just as long as it's not red.'

'Red?' He's evidently only half listening, and throws me a puzzled look. 'I thought you just said white?'

'Oh . . . um . . . yes, I did,' I fluster, realising. '*Durr*, I meant any kind of white.'

He laughs. 'OK, cool, coming right up,' he says, throwing me a smile.

'Great!' I reply, throwing him a wide smile back. I watch as he turns and heads to the bar. Then exhale. Actually, this might not be as easy as I thought.

But any doubts I may have soon disappear as he returns with the drinks and settles himself back down on the sofa. Only this time he sits a little closer and, as his thigh brushes against mine, I feel a delicious tingle.

'How's your wine?' he asks, giving me one of his stomach-flipping smiles.

I take a sip. 'Mmm, it's delicious.'

And it is, really chilled and delicious. Perfect for a summer's day.

Though probably not really ideal for a freezing January evening like tonight, I notice, cradling the icy glass in my fingers. It's actually making me rather chilly. In fact, if I'm honest, I'd much rather have had a glass of red; after all, there's nothing nicer in front of an open fire, is there?

But of course it doesn't matter. This is still lovely, I think, trying not to shiver as the ice-cold wine weaves its way down to my stomach.

Introductions over, we start chatting. Seb asks me all about myself, my family, what I do. I gloss over that bit – as I remember Seb was never really that interested in my job, which is understandable as he's this big high-flyer in the City and on about a million times my salary – and chat about my granddad instead.

'He sounds like a real character, I'd love to meet him,' he grins as we start on our second round of drinks.

'I'm sure he'd love to meet you.' I have a sudden flashback to their last first meeting and Gramps suddenly turning into Tony Soprano. 'But anyway, enough about me, what about you?' I say, quickly getting off the topic.

'What do you want to know?' he laughs.

'Everything,' I enthuse, even though of course I know all the answers.

'OK . . .' He takes a deep breath as if gearing himself up. 'I grew up in Chicago, the youngest of four brothers.' He rolls his eyes. 'As a kid I learned the guitar and wanted to be the next Eddie Van Halen, but sadly it wasn't to be,' he pulls a comic frown, 'and so after I left college I put on a suit and went to work for one of the big financial services companies in New York, then a couple of years ago I got transferred to their London office.' He pauses to take a thirsty sip of beer. 'Hmm, what else? Good sense of humour, kind to animals, hobbies include helping little old ladies across the street.' He grins and I start laughing. 'Oh, and I love all kinds of sports and exercise . . . I like to work out, try to keep myself in shape, you know.' He laughs modestly and pats an imaginary spare tyre.

'I know,' I nod, reminded of being woken at the crack of dawn by his alarm so he could go for a run *before the gym*.

'You do?'

'Um . . . I mean, I can tell,' I correct myself quickly. 'You look very fit.'

Fit? Did I just say the word fit? I feel myself blush.

'I'll take that as a compliment,' he says, his mouth twitching in amusement. 'What about you?'

My mind splits in two. In one half I think about the application form for gym membership that is languishing in my drawer at work, my ill-fated attempt at jogging along the river that ended in blisters, a stitch and a near heart attack, and the years at school spent sitting on the reserve bench because of my two left feet.

That's the real me.

In the other half I think about Seb being sports- and exercise-mad. When he wasn't in the office he was on the treadmill or playing tennis, and he would always disapprove of me for lying in bed at the weekend, saying he wished I was more sporty.

'Oh, um, yeh, I love exercising,' I nod. Out of the corner of my eye I spot a flyer pinned on the noticeboard behind his head. 'I do military fitness classes,' I blurt.

Seb looks galvanised.

'Wow, really? Impressive.' He seems to look at me with a new-found respect. 'Those guys are tough.'

'I know, tell me about it,' I groan. 'All those bench presses!'

Bench presses? Hearing myself, I flinch. I've never done a bench press in my life. In fact I'm not even sure I know what a bench press is.

'I could do with some of that military fitness. I went snowboarding for a few days over the holidays and I was so out of shape it was embarrassing.'

He rolls his eyes and I indulge him with a smile. 'Yeh right,' I laugh.

'It's true,' he protests with mock indignation, as only someone who knows it plainly isn't true can. Like skinny girls who complain they're fat. Or supermodels who say they're ugly, like the one who was recently on the front cover of Fiona's magazine with cheekbones to die for and those pillow-lips that make you want to throw away your lipstick in defeat. Inside was an interview with her going on about how she 'hated' looking in the mirror as she had a face like a duck and lips that were too big. I mean *please*, who is she trying to kid? *Lips that are too big?*

'Do you snowboard? Or ski?' he adds, taking a sip of his beer.

I falter. The nearest I've got to ski are the yoghurts in the supermarket.

'No, but I've always wanted to learn,' I reply, blocking out thoughts of my two left feet. 'Though I'm sure I'd be a natural at après-ski,' I quip, waving my wine glass.

He laughs. 'Wish I was. Too many beers after and *wham*. That's how I broke my phone. Still, I'm glad I did.'

I look at him quizzically.

'Well, if it hadn't broken, we wouldn't have met,' he explains, his expression softening.

'Oh . . . right, yes.' I say quickly, taking a sip of wine.

'Though, if I remember, you thought you'd met me before, right?'

I nearly choke as it goes down the wrong way.

'Hey, you OK?'

'Yeh fine,' I splutter, putting down my glass. Only I'm coughing so hard I misjudge the edge of the table and the glass tips forward. As if in slow motion I see the wine slosh towards the edge of the glass, Seb's lap only inches away . . . oh fuck, I wasn't supposed to spill it this time . . . this time I was supposed to do it differently.

Lurching forwards I grab it just at the last second.

'Wow, amazing reflexes,' he says, impressed.

For someone who's never been able to catch a ball, so am I.

'Thanks,' I laugh, but it's more from relief. *Phew.* Accident averted.

'So Tess . . .' Leaning back on the sofa, he seems to move his body closer to me and I feel a tingle of anticipation. 'I was wondering what your plans are this week?'

'Nothing much, just work and military fitness,' I say, trying to sound all casual and trying not to think about the fact that I'm now going to have to sign up for real. Still that's not a bad thing; in fact it's a very good thing. New Year's resolution to get fit and all that.

'Because I wondered if you'd like to go see a movie, maybe?'

My stomach flutters. 'That sounds great,' I say, trying not to sound too eager.

'Awesome,' he looks pleased. 'There's that new 3D thriller coming out, I could get tickets . . .'

'Yeh, that sounds interesting—' I break off as a thought stirs. Hang on a minute. 'Though actually I'm not really in the mood for a thriller.'

'Oh, no worries, we can see something else. What do you feel like?'

My mind throws up an image of the shoebox that I threw in the fire, and that pair of ticket stubs to the first movie I ever saw with Seb: *Star Wars*.

'Something totally different,' I say, suddenly struck by an idea. 'To be honest, I know this probably sounds a bit silly, but what I'm really in the mood for is some classic sci-fi.'

'You like sci-fi?' Seb suddenly becomes all animated. 'No kidding? Me too!'

'Really? What a coincidence,' I say, trying to sound surprised.

'Totally,' he grins, then, leaning closer, fixes me with those big blue eyes of his. 'So tell me, which is your favourite movie?'

'Well that's easy,' I say, feeling my insides go all gooey. 'It's got to be *Star Wars*.'

Seb looks as if he's just died and gone to heaven. 'Wow, a girl after my own heart,' he beams. 'I must have seen that movie a hundred times!'

I know, I remember you raving on and on about it afterwards and me not being able to understand what all the fuss was about.

'Maybe we can go see that instead? It's probably on at some art-house cinema somewhere—' He breaks off, suddenly looking unsure. 'That's if you want to, of course.'

'I'd love to,' I smile widely. Any nerves I might have had at the start of the evening have vanished. This date has been such a success, I can't wait for our second.

'So it's a plan,' he grins, and meeting my eyes he chinks his glass against mine. 'Here's to our movie night!'

12

Except there's a slight problem.

Early the next morning I go to Blockbusters on my way to work to rent myself a copy of the movie in preparation for our second date. It's ages since I saw it and I've forgotten most of it, but not to worry, I've got it all worked out. I'm going to do my homework and watch it a couple of times so that when I see Seb again, I'll know it off by heart. He'll be so impressed! It will be fantastic.

Only when I get there I discover it's not open. And when I hammer on the door, a grumpy-looking sales assistant curtly informs me they are closed for refurbishment. 'Try our online store,' she barks at me through the glass before yanking down the blind.

So I do.

And yes, they have it, only it will take a few days to arrive in the post. Except I don't have a few days, as Seb has already texted to say what a great time he had last night and:

Guess what? Our favorite movie is playing at a theater in the West End and I've gotten us tickets for tomorrow evening.

To which I text back:

Gr8, can't wait.

Before nearly having an anxiety attack.

Fuck. What am I going to do? It's supposed to be my all-time favourite film and yet I can barely remember anything about it. Except that I couldn't understand what all the fuss was about and got so bored I nodded off before the end. Now, in less than thirty-six hours, I have to become an expert. I have to be able to discuss my favourite scenes, offer insights, *quote dialogue.*

OK, don't panic.

It's nearly lunchtime and I'm sitting at my desk furiously Googling '*emergency DVD rental*'. Because of the refurb, today is the first day the whole office is back after the festivities and I really should be concentrating on tackling the emails that keep pinging into my inbox. Not to mention the pink and yellow wallpaper of Post-it notes framing my computer screen that have been there so long they're now starting to get a bit dusty, I notice, worryingly, trying to brush them clean with my sleeve.

But right now there are more urgent matters at hand. My second date with Seb is tomorrow night and despite dozens of desperate phone calls I've got absolutely sodding nowhere. I need a plan of action. One that doesn't involve throwing myself off Hammersmith Bridge.

'Hi Kym, have you ever watched *Star Wars*?' I call out across the foyer to Kym-with-a-'y', our receptionist, who's perched behind her desk like a brightly coloured parrot. Winter has no effect on Kym. Whilst everyone else is hiding their pale limbs beneath opaque tights and Zara cardis, she looks as if she's in Ibiza in August, with her pumpkin-orange fake tan, shimmery eyeshadow and cropped bleached hair that's teased and perched on the top of her head like a fascinator.

She looks up from reading Missed Connections. Despite going out with Wayne, our driver, Kym is addicted to the website where people post ads trying to track down strangers who caught their eye but they were too shy to talk to. 'Because I'm a hopeless romantic,' she always sighs wistfully in explanation.

Which I've no doubt is true. But I also think she's hopelessly sick of Wayne who, after eight years, still hasn't proposed, and is secretly hoping one of the ads will be about her so she can find the courage to leave him.

'Oh, is that that new reality show on Channel Four?' she asks eagerly. 'The one with celebrities falling out and having really big rows?'

Admittedly it was a long shot.

'*Celebrities?*' barks a shrill voice, and we both swivel our heads to see a short, pinch-faced woman thundering down the corridor towards us. My heart sinks. Wendy Montgomery, one of our managing directors. Otherwise known as The Witch, and not just because she always wears black. She works on the floor above us, in an office filled with silver-framed pictures of her cats, and her collection of cacti, which sit along her windowsills like prickly, misshapen soldiers.

It's been rumoured she's applied for Sir Richard's job, but I'm hoping it's exactly that, *a rumour*. Along with the one that she tried to seduce Gary in Accounts at the Christmas party, by pinning him behind the water-cooler and sticking her tongue down his throat. Apparently he rang in sick this morning so no one's been able to find out if there's any truth in it or not.

Though if you listen to the office gossip mill, *which of course I don't*, he's suffering from post-traumatic stress. Quite frankly, if the rumours are true, who would blame him?

'What's all this talk about celebrities?' accuses Wendy, glaring at us both. 'Kym, I hope those are invoices you're so engrossed in reading.' She glances at her computer screen with a scowl. 'Your lunch break isn't for another five minutes.'

Poor Kym jumps a mile and there's a frantic shuffling on her desk as she logs off Missed Connections and onto Excel.

'And what about you, Tess? Sir Richard keeping you busy?' She casts a beady eye over my desk as she sweeps past in her Hush Puppies. Someone once told me she wears them as the crepe soles make no noise on the carpet so she can creep up on people.

'Yes, absolutely,' I say brightly. 'Just sorting out the visas for

India,' I add, spotting the Post-it note on my computer. Shit. I really must remember to do that.

'Well make the most of it, as this will be his last trip as CEO. Very soon you'll have a new boss . . .' She gives a knowing smile, her scarlet lipstick looking like a gash across her white face. That's another thing about Wendy: she always wears so much pan-stick foundation and red lipstick that her face looks like a Japanese Kabuki mask. 'And I'm sure there's going to be lots of changes around here—'

'And what kind of changes might those be?' asks Sir Richard, poking a tousled head out of his office. Together with his new green policies, he decided the company needed to 'break down barriers and get rid of the old hierarchy', so he recently moved his office down to the ground floor. Most of the senior management said, 'What a brilliant idea', while clinging steadfastly to their plush corner offices on the upper floors. Including Wendy, who was overhead calling him an old hippy and shrieking, 'Over my dead body!' Which sadly, turned out to be only a threat.

Startled by his appearance, Wendy opens and closes her mouth like a goldfish. 'Ah, Sir Richard, I didn't realise you were in today,' she splutters.

For some people, having the boss on the ground floor has taken a bit of getting used to.

'Why shouldn't I be in? I'm still the CEO,' he says, an edge in his voice that I've never heard before. Emerging from his doorway in his shiny brown suit, which seems to look even more crumpled than ever, he eyes Wendy critically.

'Well yes, of course, of course,' she nods, looking very uncomfortable. 'I was referring to all the huge changes that would be needed to try and compensate for the loss of your expertise and leadership . . .' She swallows hard, her beady eyes blinking rapidly, 'And . . . um, your valuable experience, *Sir*.'

'Is that so?' Sir Richard raises a bushy eyebrow. 'Well in that case it's going to be very difficult to fill my shoes then, isn't it?'

'Well I'm sure I . . . I mean, *whoever* the successful applicant is will have to be truly outstanding . . .' Drawing herself up to her full five foot four, she lifts her chin and strikes a pose that she obviously thinks makes her look outstanding. It's the same pose she struck for the company catalogue. Rumour is she copied it from a photograph of Hillary Clinton.

'Indeed,' murmurs Sir Richard. To tell the truth he doesn't look impressed.

I look across at Wendy, still with her chest puffed out, and I can't help feeling a bit sorry for her. She thinks she's this super businesswoman – what she doesn't realise is that everyone just thinks she's really sad.

But Wendy is oblivious and, mistakenly believing she's made a good impression, is trying to make small talk. 'So what are you planning to do when you retire? I'm sure you and Lady Blackstock must have lots of plans.'

At the mention of Lady Blackstock, Sir Richard suddenly looks uncomfortable and attempts to smooth down his comb-over. It rebels like a teenager and pings back up again. 'Well . . . um, I'm not quite sure,' he says awkwardly.

'You should go on one of those round-the-world cruises,' hoots Kym, who's been eavesdropping the whole time. 'That's what my nan and granddad did when he finished at the council.'

Wendy throws her a scowl. 'Thank you, Kym. If you don't mind, this is a conversation between senior personnel.'

'Well I was only saying—'

As the commotion continues between these two, I glance back at my boss. He looks unusually nervous and I notice he's carrying his briefcase.

'Well I must go, I have a meeting,' he interrupts.

I frown. That's odd; there's nothing in the diary.

'If you'd be so kind as to take any messages, Tess,' he says, turning towards me, then adds in a low voice, 'I'll be out for most of the afternoon and I'll have my mobile turned off.'

'Of course, no worries.' For a moment I wonder if I've missed something and do a quick sweep of the scribbled Post-it notes, but there's nothing. I might not be the best PA in the world, but wherever Sir Richard is going, he obviously doesn't want anyone to know.

He smiles gratefully. 'And don't you be working through lunch,' he reprimands good-naturedly before striding off towards the lift.

I smile to myself. He really is the best boss in the whole wide world.

'Lots of changes,' repeats Wendy sharply.

I look over to see her glaring at both me and Kym, who blanches beneath her tan, before turning on her crepe soles. She continues her march up the corridor, accompanied by the rustling sound of her flesh-coloured tights rubbing together. What with the nylon carpets, I'm surprised she's not constantly getting electric shocks from all the static.

Though that's probably just wishful thinking.

I turn back to my computer to continue my search, but after a few minutes I'm ready to give up. This is ridiculous. I'm never going to get a copy of *Star Wars*, I think, despairingly trawling through endless websites without any luck. I stab the delete button on the keyboard.

'Hey, how's it going?'

'*Shit, bugger, bollocks!*'

'That good, eh?'

I pop my head out from behind my laptop screen to see a pair of bright green eyes peering at me quizzically.

They belong to Fergus, the bicycle courier.

'Oh god, did I say that out loud?'

'Don't worry, I'm the only one in earshot,' he grins with amusement, and I glance over to reception to see Kym's desk is empty. She must have made a break for it when The Witch disappeared.

'Sorry.' Turning back I throw him an apologetic look and let go of my mouse to sign for his delivery. As I do, I realise my fingers have gone stiff as I've been gripping it so hard. 'I'm just trying to find a DVD and no one has it,' I explain, wriggling my fingers to get the circulation going again.

'Have you tried that little rental place near the station?' he suggests helpfully.

'It closed down ages ago,' I reply.

'It did?' He looks surprised. 'Tower Records?'

'Ditto.'

'Blockbusters?'

'Closed for refurbishment.'

'Crikey, you've really done your research,' he says in admiration. Unfastening his helmet he shakes out his flattened hair. 'I know, what about just buying it?'

'Everyone I've tried is out of stock and buying it online takes a few days.' I pull a face.

'And you can't wait?'

'No,' I sigh, shaking my head. 'I have to watch it before I go to see it.'

He scratches his head. 'Sorry, can you run that bit by me again?'

I feel my cheeks colour. 'I just need it sooner, that's all.'

He beetles his eyebrows together. 'Hmm . . . there must be somewhere . . .' he mutters, thinking hard.

'It's hopeless, I've tried everything,' I sigh resignedly.

That's it then. My plan of being the perfect girlfriend and Seb falling madly in love with me this time around has failed before I've barely even started. Well done, Tess. Another one of your huge, groundbreaking successes in life.

'I know!' Fergus suddenly slams his fist on my desk and I jump. 'The library!'

'The library?' I repeat in astonishment.

'Yes, you know, they have them in most towns—'

'I know what a library is,' I gasp. 'It's just . . .'

'Just what? You think they're full of musty old books and homeless people?'

'No, I did not think that!' I protest.

Well, maybe a little bit, I think guiltily.

'When did you last go into a library?' he challenges. 'These days they're amazing. It's not just books, you can get CDs, video games, e-books, DVDs . . . I'm always using my local one, it saves me a fortune,' he enthuses, his eyes flashing. 'You should try yours and soon, before the council tries to close it down, what with all these government cuts . . .'

But as Fergus starts on a rant I've already Googled my local one and am ringing them. A librarian picks up and for the umpteenth time today I gabble my request down the phone, only this time, 'They have it!' I hiss, putting my hand over the mouthpiece. 'OK, brilliant, thanks, I'll pick it up later.' I put down the phone with a wave of relief.

He breaks off from his tirade against the government. 'Grand,' he grins, looking pleased. 'What did I tell you? You see, it's like I was saying about the government—'

But before he can start up again, I interrupt. 'Have you had lunch?' I ask. I suddenly realise I've been so distracted I haven't eaten anything all morning and I'm starving. 'There's a great little café across the street that does the most amazing baked potatoes. None of the usual microwaved rubbish; these are baked in the oven so their skins are all crispy and they have all these delicious toppings . . .'

'Mmm, sounds good, but I should probably get going,' he says reluctantly as his radio springs to life and starts crackling.

'My treat, for coming to my rescue,' I tempt.

He hesitates, then flicks off his radio. 'OK, sold,' he grins.

'Great,' I smile. 'Let me just grab my coat.'

13

Being lunchtime, the tiny café is crammed with diners, but we manage to find a wobbly table in a nook by the window.

'So, how was your New Year's Eve party?' he asks, folding his long frame into one of the small plastic chairs.

'Great!' I fib, sitting down opposite. Until now I hadn't realised how tall he was and I watch as he has to scrunch himself up like a concertina to fit his knees underneath the table. 'How was yours?' I ask politely.

Now we're out of the office and alone in the café together I'm wondering if this was such a good idea. I suddenly feel a bit awkward. After all, I barely know him. What are we going to talk about?

'Pretty shite,' he grins cheerfully.

His answer catches me by surprise.

'It's the same every year,' he shrugs matter-of-factly. 'Everyone else always seems to have a great time, but I just don't enjoy it. In fact, I don't even bother to go out. This year I spent it like I always do, by myself on the sofa, watching bad TV and wishing it would hurry up and be over with.' He laughs. 'I know, I probably sound like a weirdo . . .'

'No . . . not at all,' I protest, feeling a sudden affection towards him. 'I'm the same.'

'You are?' He frowns and peers at me across the table. 'Well, then it's a date. Next New Year's Eve. My sofa or yours?'

I laugh, feeling myself relaxing.

'So what's good here?' he asks. 'I'm bloody starving.'

'Oh . . . all the different fillings are on here,' I say hurriedly, passing him one of the small plastic menus.

Screwing up his eyes, he squints at the writing. 'Hang on a mo . . .' He fumbles around in the top pocket of his jacket and digs out a pair of wire-framed glasses. 'Ah, that's better, now I can actually see what I'm going to eat,' he says, shoving them up his nose.

'I didn't know you wore glasses,' I say, taking in this new bespectacled Fergus.

'I ran out of contacts,' he explains, 'used the last pair for an audition.'

'An audition?' I repeat, looking at him in surprise for the second time in five minutes. Fergus, I'm fast realising, is full of surprises.

'Ready to order?'

We're interrupted by a frazzled-looking waitress.

'Oh, um, just the goat's cheese and sundried tomato,' I say quickly, choosing my usual.

'And I'll have the black bean chilli,' chimes in Fergus.

She scribbles it on her pad and disappears. I turn back to him. 'What kind of audition?'

'It was for some TV show,' he shrugs, then, seeing my confused expression, explains, 'I'm an actor.'

'You mean like Johnny Depp?' I say stupidly, before I can stop myself. I wince with embarrassment. Honestly Tess, sometimes you should try putting that brain of yours into gear before you open your big mouth.

But if Fergus thinks I'm an idiot, he doesn't show it. 'Not quite,' he says evenly. 'I don't think Johnny Depp doubles as a bicycle courier to pay the bills. Captain Jack Sparrow on a push-bike? Maybe I'm wrong but I don't think so . . .' There's a flash of amusement in his eyes.

'No, I suppose not,' I nod, smiling despite myself. 'So have you been in anything?'

'I did a bit of theatre when I was at drama school,' he shrugs, 'and I've done a few commercials.'

'Ooh, which ones?' I look at him agog across the table. Well, I can't help it. It all sounds so exciting and glamorous.

Now it's his turn to look embarrassed. 'Well, I recently played the dad in a toilet-roll commercial,' he confesses. Avoiding my gaze, he starts fiddling with the condiments.

'No way!'

'Now who's the one acting?' He raises a thick black eyebrow.

I look at him nonplussed.

'Well c'mon, don't tell me you're actually impressed?'

'But I am!' I protest. 'You're on the TV!'

'Selling bog roll,' he reminds me with a glum smile. 'Not exactly an Academy Award-winning performance.'

'Everyone has to start somewhere. Look at Colin Firth!' I say encouragingly.

'Why, how did he start out?' he asks, perking up.

'Well . . . um . . . I'm not sure *exactly*,' I add hastily, 'but I'm sure it was something terrible.'

'Are you saying a bog-roll commercial is terrible?' he demands, looking offended.

Fuck.

'No, I didn't mean—'

'I'm just fooling with you,' he winks.

'You bastard,' I stab him playfully with my fork. 'Anyway, I'm sure you were amazing in it,' I grin.

'Oscar-winning,' he laughs, rolling his eyes.

The waitress returns with our food and for a few moments we stop talking as Fergus dives hungrily into his potato. 'Crikey, you weren't wrong,' he groans through a mouthful. 'This black bean chilli is the dog's bollocks.'

'I take it that's a compliment,' I reply with amusement, watching him devour his food with alarming speed.

'So what about you?' He looks up from his plate and waggles a fork in my direction.

'What about me?' I ask.

'What is it exactly that you do in there?' He gestures towards my office block across the street.

'I'm the boss's PA,' I explain, eating a forkful of potato.

'Right,' he nods slowly. 'Well, don't take offence, but it doesn't seem like your true talent lies in being a PA.' His eyes meet mine and I blush.

'Is it that obvious?'

'Well, I'm no expert, but aren't you supposed to answer the phone if it's ringing?'

'I do!' I protest indignantly.

'And not to pretend you're the answering machine?' he adds, his mouth twitching.

I'm stung with mortification. 'Oh my god, you saw that?'

'I was in reception, I happened to glance over.' He pauses to clear his throat, then does his impression of a robot, '*I'm sorry, but no one is here right now so please call back later—*'

I shriek and cover my face with my hands in embarrassment. In my defence, it happened once. I had all these urgent invoices to file and the phone was ringing off the hook, so I picked up and tried to make my voice sound like one of those automated messages.

'I know I'm rubbish,' I admit, reappearing shamefaced from behind my hands.

'I thought you were very good actually – you could have fooled me,' teases Fergus good-naturedly.

Despite myself, my face breaks into a helpless grin. 'Well, I'm glad you find me so funny,' I smile, 'but I don't think anyone else does. In fact the only reason I have a job is because of Sir Richard, my boss. He's so sweet but he's retiring soon.'

'And then what?' Fergus stops laughing and looks at me evenly.

'Back to temping I suppose,' I shrug, trying to keep the worry out of my voice. 'Though to be honest, I'm not much good at that either.'

'What are you good at?'

His question throws me slightly. No one's ever asked me that before. All my school reports told me what I *wasn't* good at. 'Um, I dunno, nothing really,' I mumble, feeling suddenly self-conscious. 'I don't have some big mega-talent like you.'

'Hey, don't get too excited, you haven't seen me act yet,' he quips with a grin.

'You know what I mean,' I smile. 'Some people are naturally really brainy, or talented at sport, or have an ear for music – it's like they were born good at something, they don't even have to think about what they're going to do in life, they just know. But I'm just not one of those people,' I shrug.

He studies me for a moment, as if weighing me up, then, propping his elbows on the table, leans closer.

'You're telling me you don't have a dream?' And he looks at me so intently, it's as if he's seeing right inside of me. 'Everyone has a dream, Tess. What's yours?'

For a split second my mind flashes back to me sitting next to my granddad at the sewing machine a few days ago, the excitement I felt as I watched the needle flying over the material, the thrill I always feel when I see my ideas start taking shape.

Imagine if one day I could—

I stop myself right there, before I even let the thought form in my head.

'Nope, not me,' I say quickly, shrugging his question off. 'Though if you'd have asked me earlier, I'd have said my dream was finding that DVD.' I give a little laugh, trying to make a joke of it, and turn back to my potato. Though for some reason my appetite seems to have disappeared and I realise I'm not really that hungry any more.

There's a gap in the conversation, and for a moment Fergus doesn't say anything. He doesn't look convinced and for a brief moment I think he's going to challenge me, and I feel my defences rising. But then he seems to think better of it and, taking my cue, he turns back to his lunch with renewed vigour. 'Well, in that case, glad I could be of service,' he says cheerfully, 'though to be honest, I wouldn't have thought it was your kind of film. Johnny Depp isn't in it, you know?' He looks up from his potato and flashes me a mischievous smile.

I reach over and swipe him with my paper napkin. 'It's not my favourite,' I confess. 'In fact I think sci-fi films are boring, but it's my boyfriend's—' I break off. Can I call Seb my boyfriend yet? We've only had one date. Well, *officially*.

'Oh, right,' nods Fergus, without missing a beat. But I feel the intimacy shift. As if, by mentioning I have a boyfriend, Seb's pulled up a chair at the table and suddenly it's not just the two of us any more.

'What about you?' I ask, ignoring it and throwing the focus back on him. It's always like this when you make a friend of the opposite sex. I once read an article about it called 'Establishing the Platonic Boundaries'. Apparently this is all perfectly normal.

'You mean have I seen *Star Wars*?' He pulls a face and scoops up the last of his potato. 'Once, ages ago, when I was a kid. To be honest, I never really got what all the fuss was about.'

Resisting the urge to agree, I shake my head. 'No, I mean do you have a girlfriend?'

'Oh, right, gotcha.' He finishes chewing and shakes his head. 'Nope, 'fraid not.' He suddenly freezes mid-chew and sits up like a meerkat. 'Saying that, I think I've just fallen in love.'

'*In love?*' I repeat. Hang on, have I just missed a step?

But he doesn't answer, just stares over my shoulder like a shop dummy.

Twirling around in my seat, I look across the café and see

the object of his affections: a girl sitting by herself, engrossed in a book. Looking up, she catches Fergus gazing at her, and for a brief moment they make eye contact, before she smiles blushingly and quickly glances back at her page.

I swear, it's like I'm invisible.

'She's pretty,' I note, and am surprised to realise I feel a little miffed. It must be those platonic boundaries I was talking about.

'Pretty? She's Venus herself,' he waxes lyrical, a misty glaze in his eyes.

I watch her self-consciously playing with her pale blonde hair. She knows we're talking about her.

'So go over, say hello,' I suggest encouragingly. 'I think she likes you.'

He looks at me as though I've just told him to take off all his clothes and run naked down the high street. 'No way!' he hisses, visibly recoiling into his waterproof neon jacket. 'She's never going to want to go out with me.'

'Don't be ridiculous, why not?' I ask, suddenly not recognising the man sitting before me as the one who's usually flirting with all the girls in reception. Hang on a minute, where's the Irish charm gone? The roguish smile? The winks and gift of the gab? It's all disappeared.

'How long have you got?' he replies.

And been replaced by a man who's now curled up in the plastic chair like a five-year-old on their first day at school, I think, watching him nervously chewing his fingers.

'Don't tell me you're shy?' I tease, playfully poking him in the ribs.

'No, of course not,' he counters hotly.

'Well then?' I persist.

Heaving a sigh, he takes a deep breath. 'OK, well for starters I'm an out-of-work actor whose most recent job was an ad for bog roll and who's resting as a bike courier to pay the rent on a poky little bedsit at the wrong end of Shepherd's Bush—'

'You know you've got to stop talking yourself up like that,' I interrupt.

'And by the time I've paid my rent I'm usually broke and have to survive on beans on toast.'

'Lot of fibre,' I say supportively.

He looks unconvinced. 'And, last but not least, I'm losing my hair.'

For a moment I gaze speechlessly at his head of thick black hair, then burst out laughing.

'It's not funny,' he pouts, 'I keep finding it in the plughole.' Leaning across the table he sweeps it off his forehead. 'Look, it's receding!'

I stare at his straight black hairline.

'I'm going to go bald.'

'When? In thirty years?' I gasp, finally finding my voice.

'For an actor, going bald is the kiss of death,' he counters solemnly.

'Fergus, stop worrying, you're not going bald,' I say reassuringly. Now I know what Seb must have felt like when I used to go on about a nonexistent spot on my chin and wail that I had acne. 'And anyway, I'm sure there are lots of successful bald actors.'

'Like who?' he demands.

'Um . . . well, I don't know, but I'm sure I can think of some.'

There's a scraping of a chair, and we both turn to see the girl getting up from the table and leaving the café. As soon as she's out of the door, Fergus lets out a loud groan.

'And now she's gone. Damn. Why didn't I say something?'

'I don't know, why didn't you?'

I'm still trying to figure out what's caused the sudden transformation. Fergus is like a changed man. His confidence has evaporated and now he's like a six-foot-five ornament that doesn't know where to put himself.

'Maybe because we were too busy arguing about you *not*

being bald,' I suggest, trying to joke him back to his earlier good humour.

But he refuses to raise a smile. 'Maybe I just don't want another rejection,' he shrugs. 'I've had enough of that in my so-called acting career.'

Oh, so *this* is what it's all about.

'But you're not auditioning for a role,' I try to persuade him.

'Aren't I?' he raises his eyebrows. 'So when a guy asks you out, you don't look at him and think: Possible date? Boyfriend material? Could be The One?'

Actually, he's got a point.

'But maybe you'd have got the part?' I smile ruefully. 'If you don't try . . .'

'Yeh, maybe,' he acquiesces. 'But she was Beauty to my Beast, a princess to my frog . . .' He starts waxing all lyrical on me again.

'From what I remember, the princess kisses the frog,' I point out.

'That's the stuff of fairy tales,' he counters, 'not real life.' Spearing a forkful of my unfinished potato, he falls silent, and together we look out of the window, watching as her figure recedes down the high street and disappears into the crowd.

I stay late at the office to catch up on the backlog of work, then pop into the library on the way home to pick up the movie. Letting myself into the flat, I dump my bag in the hallway and walk into the kitchen, where as usual I find Fiona, barricaded behind her laptop in a swirl of cigarette smoke, with the radio playing loudly.

'Gosh it's smoky in here,' I say, going to open a window.

'Is it? I hadn't noticed,' she says, looking up from the screen. 'I've been trying to write my column all day and it's just not coming.' She tuts loudly and takes a drag of her cigarette.

'Oh, what's it about?'

'Piranha pedicures,' she says, breathing out a cloud of smoke.

I look at her blankly.

'Well, they're not piranhas *exactly*, but you put your feet in tanks full of these tiny little flesh-eating fish and they nibble off all the dead skin,' she explains.

'Ouch, that sounds painful,' I cringe, flicking on the kettle and starting to make tea.

'It's all the rage in Japan; apparently they leave your feet feeling really soft.'

'But what if they get really hungry and nibble off a toe or something?'

Fiona suddenly looks worried. 'Oh my god, you don't think that can happen, do you?'

'Well, don't you remember that James Bond film on Boxing Day?'

We exchange looks, both remembering that scene from *You Only Live Twice* where Blofeld feeds a piece of meat to his piranhas and within seconds it's reduced to a bone.

'So anyway, how was your date last night?' she asks briskly, changing the topic. 'I was dying to ask you this morning, but you'd already left by the time my alarm went off.'

Fiona says this as if it's a first and not an everyday occurrence.

'Really good,' I smile happily, grabbing the milk from the fridge.

'So when are you seeing him again?' she asks excitedly.

'Tomorrow,' I say, feeling a tingle of anticipation. Seb's already sent me about half a dozen flirty texts about how much he's looking forward to our second date and I can't wait.

'Wow Tess, that's so great,' she grins, then adds, 'Does he have any friends?'

I look at her in surprise. 'What happened to Henry VIII?'

'He hasn't called.' She tries to sound nonchalant, but the hurt in her voice is audible.

'It's only been a few days, he still might,' I encourage her, passing her a mug of tea.

'I don't think so. Pippa says he only ever goes out with really skinny girls. Apparently his last girlfriend was a size zero,' she says dolefully, taking a sip.

I didn't think it was possible to dislike Pippa more than I do already but, seeing Fiona's expression, I realise that actually, yes, it is possible.

'She was also probably only about four foot tall,' I say supportively. 'He was tiny.'

'Not in the bedroom,' sighs Fiona, putting down her mug and reaching for the bowl of half-eaten food next to her computer. In times of distress, Fiona always turns to food for comfort. Though in this case, I'm not sure how much comfort it's going to be.

'What are you eating?' I ask, quickly getting off the topic of the size of Henry VIII's *you-know-what* and trying to identify the strange-looking concoction.

'Aubergine mixed with prunes – it's part of the rainbow diet,' she says, eating a large mouthful. 'Today's blue, remember?' she explains, visibly wincing. 'Want to try some? There's loads left.'

'Um . . . no, thanks, I'm still stuffed from lunch,' I say quickly, backing away from the scary purple gunge. 'I think I'm just going to lie on my bed and watch a DVD I rented.'

'Oooh, what did you get?' asks Fiona, perking up. 'Is it that new Johnny Depp one you've been dying to see?'

'Um, no, not exactly,' I say, feeling a bit awkward. 'I thought I'd try something a bit different from usual.' For some reason I realise I don't want to admit the truth to Fiona.

'But you love Johnny Depp.'

'Yes, but he doesn't have to be in *every* film I watch.' I see Fiona looking at me dubiously and I try to brush it off. 'Anyway, want to join me?'

'Yeh, why not,' she shrugs, standing up. 'I could do with a good movie, it's probably just what I need, clear this writer's block.' Carrying her bowl of purple food and mug of tea she follows me into the bedroom and plops herself onto the beanbag in the corner as I slide the DVD into the player.

Pressing play, I join Flea on the bed and settle back as the music starts. Oh, I nearly forgot. I grab a pad and pencil from my bedside table to make notes.

'What are you doing?' asks Fiona, glancing over.

'Oh, um, nothing, just doodling,' I say nonchalantly.

'I thought you wanted to watch this movie,' she frowns.

'Oh, you know me, I like to doodle when I watch movies.' I pretend to do a squiggle on my notebook.

'*You do?*' Fiona peers at me for a moment, as if not quite sure what to make of me, then turns back to the TV.

I start to relax. I feel a bit guilty. I don't like pretending to Fiona, but I can't tell her the truth now, can I? Where on earth would I start?

Settling back against my pillows, I look at the screen. It's totally black and a bit of text appears about it being in some faraway galaxy; then the unmistakable theme music starts.

'Wait a moment – this is *Star Wars*,' gasps Fiona in astonishment.

'It's actually called *Episode IV: A New Hope*,' I correct, authoritatively.

She looks aghast. 'Tess, have you rented this *on purpose*?'

'It's supposed to be a classic,' I protest, as a space battleship shoots across the screen firing missiles.

She stares at me as if I've gone bananas. 'Hang on, is this the same woman who will only ever watch a movie if it's got Johnny Depp in it?'

'I don't think there's anything wrong with broadening our horizons,' I say defensively.

Fiona gapes at me, as if not quite believing what she's

hearing, then gives a little shrug. 'Fair enough,' she nods, 'but in that case I'm going to leave you to broaden your own horizons, I'm going to get an early night,' and, hoisting herself up from the beanbag, she flashes me a smile. 'Enjoy!'

And then she's gone, leaving me on my own with Flea and this stupid movie. Correction: *A classic*, I remind myself firmly. And, more importantly, it's Seb's favourite film, remember?

Taking a sip of tea, I enthusiastically concentrate on the screen again. Though after a few minutes I can feel my eyelids going. I'm actually rather tired and I could do with an early night myself. In fact, what would be perfect would be a lovely long bath beforehand with some of that nice scented bubble bath Gramps got me for Christmas . . . and I could put on that seaweed face-mask Fiona gave me . . .

Shit! What's happening? There's been an explosion!

A loud bang from the TV makes me snap back and I suddenly realise I've completely zoned out. Oh crap, I'm going to have to rewind . . . Grabbing the remote, I start whizzing back. Honestly, at this rate I'm never going to get to bed.

Going right back to the beginning, I press play and start all over. Right yes, lots of spaceships . . . girl with funny earmuff hair . . . strange little robot thing . . . a man in what looks like a Yeti costume . . . gosh, it's a bit too much like fancy dress, isn't it? You'd think they'd be a bit more realistic – oh, and there's lots of shooting . . . and now there's another battle in space. *Again.*

I let out another yawn. It might be a classic but the plot is a bit silly. Still, at least it will be over soon. I pick up the cover and glance at the box. I wonder how long it is. My heart plummets – *over two hours*? For a moment I'm tempted to fast-forward, when I check the time on my mobile and see Seb's text about the movies tomorrow night. My heart leaps. And I suddenly remember why I'm doing this.

Because I love Seb. And because I've been given a second

chance! This magic happened for a reason. Seb and I are meant for each other, otherwise why would this amazing, miracle twist of fate have happened? Why would it have brought us back together? No, I mustn't waste this opportunity. So many other people enjoy these movies, it's not just Seb. There must be something wrong with me.

And now I've got a chance to put it right. How lucky am I?

With a superhuman effort I stare back at the screen with renewed interest. If Seb loves this film, I can learn to love it too! I watch as two men start fighting with fluorescent lights like the ones we have on our kitchen ceiling. Oh dear. But this film is *terrible*. Even worse than I thought! What the hell am I going to say?

Dear Diary,

My second date with Seb!! He took me to see Star Wars *and we sat on the back row which was really romantic. I didn't think much of the film though and fell asleep before the end. Afterwards I laughed about how stupid and boring it was, but he didn't laugh along. In fact he got a bit grumpy. Only then did I find out it was actually his all-time favourite film . . .*

Honestly, me and my big mouth!

14

'It was amazing! That has to be the best film ever made in the history of cinema!'

It's the next evening and Seb and I have just been on our second date to see *Star Wars* at a little art-house theatre in Soho, and we're making our way out through the red velvet foyer, along with the rest of the audience.

'Wow, you really love that movie, huh?' He flashes me a delighted grin.

'Absolutely!' I gush, nodding vigorously to stifle a yawn. If I couldn't learn to love it, I was still going to appear to. 'I've lost count of the number of times I've watched it.'

Three.

Actually, make that three and a bit times if you include the first time I watched it last night, when I fell asleep halfway through, and trust me I can remember them all. Every single galactic battle is ingrained on my memory, like scratches on vinyl. Last night I stayed up till gone 3 a.m., drinking black coffee to keep myself awake. At one point I nearly had to put matchsticks in my eyes to prop them open, but what kept me awake was knowing I'd been given this once-in-a-lifetime chance. Then today I skipped lunch and spent it at my desk doing research about it on the internet.

To be honest, I'm exhausted. I'm also flabbergasted. I had no idea how many websites, conventions – not to mention all the merchandise, even theme parks – there are dedicated to this film. I knew it was popular but people are *obsessed*! A

Google search brought up over three million fan sites, all full of devoted followers. There was even an entire forum devoted to discussing how Chewbacca (believe it or not, the Yeti has a name) goes to the loo!

'Did you know that the word Jedi is derived from the Japanese words "*Jidai Geki*", which translates as "period adventure drama"?'

Thanks to Annie in Texas, for making that point.

'Wow, you really are a true fan, aren't you?' he says in admiration.

My conscience pricks and for a split second I feel slightly guilty. Is it wrong to pretend like this? Should I instead be coming clean and telling the truth? But then it's no different to when Seb used to fib and say he loved the dress I was wearing, just to get me out of the door when we were running late. Or when I reassure Fiona that no, of course her bum doesn't look big in her new jeggings. Or when Dad pretends to Mum that he's a huge fan of her terrible cooking and asks for seconds. It's not hurting anyone.

On the contrary, it's doing the opposite, I muse, looking at Seb and seeing his face all lit up. He looks so happy. I mean, seriously, how can that be wrong?

'Sorry, I tend to get a bit carried away,' I say, and give a little embarrassed laugh. 'Stop me if I'm boring you.'

'Boring me?' he exclaims, gesticulating excitedly with the programme. 'Are you kidding me? I could talk about Luke Skywalker and Jedi knights for hours. You're the first girl I've ever met who loves the movies as much as I do and it's awesome . . .' He breaks off as we exit through the main doors, and as we empty onto the street he turns to me, his face softening. '*You're* awesome,' he adds quietly.

Despite the subzero temperature outside I feel a warm flush of happiness. Who cares if I had to stay up late and skip lunch? Feeling his fingers brushing against mine, he gently, but firmly, interlaces them. It was all worth it to have him look at me the way he just did. It's like that saying, 'No pain no gain.'

Plus, it's not as though I'm ever going to have to sit through that movie again, I remind myself, as we set off walking hand in hand to escape the crowds.

After a few minutes we turn down a side street and our pace slows.

'So . . .' he says, glancing sideways to look at me. All wrapped up in a slate-grey overcoat and a beanie pulled down low over his hair, he looks more adorable than ever. We pass underneath a streetlamp and I see his white teeth against his tan. I swear, Seb's the only person I've ever met who can still manage to look sexy in a British winter. The rest of us have gone all pale and chapped lipped, with noses that turn bright red as soon the temperature drops below freezing.

'So . . .' I reply, trying to be all enigmatic and not think about my own nose, which looks like one of those ones that people wear for Comic Relief.

'What happens now?' He raises an eyebrow and gives me a little smile.

Well, last time we said goodbye and I caught the tube home and kicked myself all the way back for opening my big mouth and saying all the wrong things.

'We could get a drink, maybe?' I suggest. 'There are lots of nice bars around here.'

His smile widens. 'I've got a better idea. Why don't we go back to mine? My apartment's only five minutes away and I've got an awesome bottle of red I haven't opened yet . . .' He breaks off, his eyes searching out mine in the darkness. 'What do you say?'

I say there's nothing in the whole world I'd rather do right now than go to back to your flat and share a bottle of wine, I think, my stomach fluttering.

But of course I have to at least *try* to play it cool. Officially this is only our second date.

'Hmm . . .' I pretend to think for a moment, as if I'm actually *mulling over* his invitation.

'You're safe with me, I promise,' he says, crossing his heart with his free hand.

'Damn,' I curse jokingly.

He laughs. 'So do you want to join me? Or do I have to drink all that bottle by myself?'

Like he really has to ask.

'Well now you put it like that,' I say at last, all thoughts of cool flying out of the window, 'that sounds lovely.'

I've been to Seb's apartment so many times I could do the route with my eyes closed, and I have to keep stopping myself from automatically turning a corner, or crossing a street. At one point I almost blurt out, 'No, it's quicker this way,' and lead him down a little alley I always used as a shortcut.

Before I was forever telling him it was quicker this way, and he was forever telling me it wasn't. Once we got into such a disagreement about it that we each went our separate ways and Seb insisted on timing us both to see who was quickest – he could be really competitive like that – and he said his way was six-tenths of a second faster. (He has one of those super-chunky top-of-the-range sports watches, so I couldn't disagree.) Saying that, I could have *sworn* he was a little flushed, as if he'd been running, but he was adamant he'd walked the whole way and it was just the wine we'd been drinking.

But then this was nothing unusual. Seb and I always used to squabble about directions. It didn't matter where we went, we'd always end up disagreeing and it would often deteriorate into a full-scale row, with him grabbing the map from me and declaring I'd taken us 'the wrong way!' Which I don't think is very fair. I mean, I'm not one of those people who have an inbuilt compass, but I can navigate my way around H&M *even in the sale*, and believe me, that's saying something.

In the end I bought him a Sat Nav for his birthday. Brilliant. Problem sorted! But that didn't work either, as he just disagreed with that as well. And it was Stephen Fry giving the directions. I mean, who disagrees with Stephen Fry, for goodness' sake?

Now, however, I let him lead the way and we arrive at his address without any squabbles. Not so much as a cross word (though I do still think my way is quicker) and, after he punches in his security code, we step inside the carpeted foyer. Seb lives in one of those prestigious portered blocks, with shiny brass name-plates and a lift with a sliding grille to whisk you up to his flat on the second floor. It's a whole world away from Arminta Mansions with its Tipp-Ex-ed buzzers and lung-busting flights of stairs.

'So here we are,' says Seb, as we walk out of the lift and down the corridor to his flat. Sliding his key in the door, he pushes it open. 'Welcome to my humble abode.'

That's just Seb being modest. Trust me, there's nothing humble about his apartment. It's twice the size of mine and Fiona's, and is all open-plan with these big lovely windows and polished parquet floors. It reminds me of a New York apartment – not that I've ever been in a New York apartment, but you know what I mean. The colour scheme is all muted greys and white with cool abstract paintings on the walls, and he's got this huge grey sofa that could seat about twenty people and a glass coffee table with three legs by some designer whose name he told me once but I can't remember.

'This place is amazing,' I say, looking around and feeling wowed all over again.

'Thanks,' he smiles, 'but I'm afraid I can't take all the credit.'

'You can't?' I stop gawping at a pair of fancy modern lamps, and turn to him.

He shakes his head. 'No, when I moved in I had an interior designer come in to decorate. She chose all the furniture, even the artwork,' he explains. 'I was too busy at work.'

'Oh . . .' He had never told me he didn't decorate it himself. I turn back to look at the apartment, but instead of feeling impressed, now I can't help feeling disappointed. 'What a shame,' I console. 'I've always imagined the best bit about getting your own place would be buying those little tester pots and painting patches of walls all kinds of weird and wonderful colours until you work out what looks amazing.' I turn back and catch his expression, only instead of nodding in agreement he's looking at me as if he doesn't understand what I'm saying.

'Seriously?' He frowns in surprise. 'Wow, not me. I'd rather have a professional choose my colour scheme for me.'

'But that's half the fun,' I protest.

'Maybe for you, but I'm pretty colour blind,' he laughs. 'I'd probably end up with purple walls.'

'Well what about all the other stuff?' I laugh. 'Like spending weekends rummaging around the markets, like Spitalfields and Portobello, hunting out all the weird bits and pieces and junk you can transform. Like a ratty old armchair you could cover with some vintage fabric, or even a whole sofa – and what about a lamp that you could make a new shade for?' Getting carried away with ideas, I start gesticulating enthusiastically.

'Like I said, I don't have time for any of that,' shrugs Seb.

I get the distinct feeling he's not sharing my enthusiasm, and I feel a bit silly for even suggesting it. It's true: he's far too busy to be rummaging around markets. He's got this high-flying career and he's always at the office. Saying that, he does spend a lot of time at the gym or doing sport. Still, I guess it's just priorities, that's all.

'Well, it's still really lovely,' I say, rather lamely.

'Thanks,' smiles Seb, throwing his keys on the table and taking off his coat.

Meanwhile I look around me. It all seems to be exactly the same as before. Nothing has changed, and yet everything has changed. My eyes sweep across a shelf of photographs. There used to be one of us two at a party, but it's gone now. Sadness flickers, and for a moment I feel a sense of loss, of bittersweet nostalgia for all the times we spent together that have now never happened. Like Sunday afternoons spent reading the papers. Like the dinner party we threw last summer where we all got drunk on toffee vodka, and did karoake.

Like when we broke up, I remind myself sharply.

Suddenly it hits me – that was the last time I was here – and out of nowhere an old hurt rises up inside. Rewind a couple of months ago and I was sitting right there . . . I glance across at that big grey sofa and it's like *Sliding Doors* . . . there I am, hugging a cushion and trying not to cry, and sitting opposite on the armchair is Seb, staring at his trainers, the atmosphere strained and awful.

'Everything OK?'

I snap back to see Seb looking at me, concern in his face.

But that's all gone now. Deleted. Erased forever. Like a tape that's been wiped clean. And now we're recording over it again, only this time with something different. And I'm not sorry, I'm glad. The good times might have gone, but so have all the bad times. The last time I was here was the ending, but now we're right back at the beginning. A new beginning.

'Yeh, everything's great,' I smile, delighted by the thought. I still can't believe this is really happening, that I'm getting to do it all over again. I almost want to pinch myself.

'Good.' His face relaxes. 'You're still wearing your coat, I was worried you were thinking of leaving . . .'

I suddenly realise I haven't taken it off. 'Oh, sorry,' I laugh, and start unzipping it and tugging my arms out of the sleeves. 'It just takes me a little time to warm up.' Making excuses, I pass it to him.

'Well in that case let me get that wine. A good bottle of red will warm you up in no time,' he grins, taking my coat and hanging it on the stand in the corner, before walking into the open-plan kitchen.

There's a wine rack next to the fridge and I watch as he expertly selects a bottle and grabs a corkscrew and two glasses, then turns to me. For a moment I think he's going to say something, but instead he angles his body towards mine and kisses me gently on the lips.

It's the first time he's tried to kiss me and it's so casual and relaxed that for a split second it barely registers what's happening.

Until his lips brush against mine.

The effect is immediate and all at once a familiar ache ripples through my body. God, I've missed him so much. And for a heady, breathless, urgent moment, all I want to do is pull him closer, wrap my arms around him, and snog the living daylights out of him—

I slam on the brakes and my mind screeches to a halt.

Tess, no! You can't. You've only just met him, remember? Plus you've barely been in the flat five minutes – you can't just jump on him in the kitchen. What will you look like? You're aiming for perfect girlfriend, not complete slapper.

Fighting the urge, I give him a quick peck on the lips.

And I thought giving up chocolate for Lent last year was hard. Believe me, that kiss took *serious* willpower.

We break apart and he holds my gaze for just long enough to make my legs go all wobbly, then says, 'Let's go make ourselves comfortable,' and gestures towards the sofa area.

'OK,' I reply, in what I hope is a husky voice. But instead it comes out all squeaky and high-pitched, like the time I went to an engagement party with Fiona and we got drunk and inhaled the helium balloons and spent the whole evening talking like Pinky and Perky.

Only this time there's no helium balloons. Just me and Seb. Alone in his apartment with a bottle of red wine and a whole night ahead of us. My lips are still tingling and, feeling a flutter of anticipation, I follow him towards the sofa.

As for all that other stuff, there's plenty of time for that later.

15

Picture the scene:

Soft lighting, the kind you get from nice, expensive lamps placed strategically around the room; ambient chill-out music wafting from concealed speakers, and me and Seb snuggled up together on the big, squidgy sofa.

Two glasses, forty minutes and quite a lot of kissing later, and I'm in heaven. As second dates go, it can't get much better than this, I muse, nuzzling into his neck and inhaling his familiar aroma of faded aftershave and deodorant. I breathe it in deeply. Forget all those fancy expensive perfumes, this has to be my favourite scent.

'Want some more wine?' murmurs Seb into my ear.

'Mmm, yes please.' Emerging from my dreamy reverie, I sit up tipsily. I feel all fuzzy around the edges, like a pencil drawing that's been smudged with an eraser, rubbing out all the hard lines.

'I love this vintage,' says Seb, reaching for the bottle and pouring me another glass.

'Mmm, yes, it's delicious.' I take a sip. 'What is it?'

'A Pinot Noir, from one of my favourite vineyards back in the States.'

Somewhere in the back of my mind a vague bell starts ringing, and as he turns to pour himself a glass, I reach over and pick up the corkscrew that's lying on the table. I glance absently at the cork, at its red-wine-stained bottom and, unscrewing it, turn it over in my fingers to see the embossing on the top: 'Stanly Ranch Pinot Noir 2002'.

I recognise that name.

My mind flashes back to the shoebox I threw on the fire. To its contents. To the wine cork that I kept as a memento. It's the same wine as the bottle we shared the first time we got drunk together. The first time we spent the night together.

The first time we had sex.

'It's getting late . . .'

I tune back in.

'. . . and I was wondering . . .' He pauses, and somewhere deep inside of me I can feel a pulse beating. I know what he's going to say and yet it doesn't make it any less exciting. In fact, it makes it even *more* exciting. 'Do you want to stay?'

My groin answers for me. It must be telepathic.

'Or I can call you a cab,' he adds quickly, looking unsure.

I once read one of those books about dating, and it had all these rules in it about how to make a man fall in love with you. One of them was that you have to wait until the third date to have sex. Apparently, those are the rules.

I hesitate. This time I want to do it all properly; this time I want to do everything by the book.

Saying that, there are *some* rules that are made to be broken . . .

Slipping the cork into my pocket, I flash him a smile. 'Do you have a spare toothbrush?'

A new relationship is always a bit nerve-wracking, but there's nothing worse than reaching that tantalising moment when you might sleep together . . . only to realise you're not ready. And I don't mean as in 'things are moving a little too fast and you want to get to know him more first'. I'm talking 'not ready' as in you haven't had a bikini wax since last summer and the regrowth is so bad you'd give Bob Marley a run for his dreadlocks.

Or you're wearing your comfy T-shirt bra and knickers that come in packs of three and are flesh-coloured so you can't see them under your clothes. And *not*, as is obviously crucial the first time you have sex with a man you are crazy about, the kind of underwear that is *supposed* to be seen, i.e. little expensive, uncomfortable scraps of frothy lace that get right up your *you-know-what* and have you wriggling around on the tube like you're dancing the Salsa.

Underwear like the expensive lingerie that Seb bought me last year, I note, doing a little wriggle as I get up from the sofa and follow Seb towards the bedroom. It's too small but I squeezed into it just in case. I admit I also waxed my legs and did all my naughty bits. I even did an all-over body scrub and applied a fake tan. The whole process took hours. I had to set my alarm and get up super-early so I could do the full makeover before I left for work this morning.

And trust me, applying hot wax to your nether regions at 6 a.m. when you've only had a couple of hours' sleep because you've been watching Luke Skywalker take on Darth Vader till gone 3 a.m. is very dangerous. I was so bleary-eyed the wax mistakenly went in some *very* painful places.

Still, I needed to be prepared this time. I didn't know exactly when sex might strike, but this time I was going to make sure I was primed and ready. Like the Angels, when Charlie gets on the telephone. Last time, our first time wasn't planned at all. It was all very spur of the moment, which was exciting and spontaneous, but I do also remember wishing I'd worn a sexier bra as he fumbled to undo it. And when he pulled off my jeans, all I could think about were my pale, hairy legs, which I'd kept hidden under opaques all winter, and hoped he wouldn't notice them.

And don't even get me *started* on my bikini line.

But now I've got the benefit of hindsight *and* a full bikini wax. Not to mention a few condoms that I popped into my bag, I think, with a slight blush of excitement. OK, so I know it's cheating a bit, but I've got a second chance to wow him in the bedroom and I can't wait to make the most of it!

Entering the bedroom, Seb pulls me towards him and,

wrapping his arms around me, gives me a long, lingering kiss. I kiss him back, relishing the anticipation of what's about to happen next. Surprises are nice, but sometimes it's even *nicer* to know what's in store.

'I'll just go freshen up,' I say flirtily, breaking away finally.

'Sure,' he gives me an easy smile. 'The en-suite's just through here.' He pads across the thick carpet and pushes open the door to a limestone bathroom. 'There are fresh towels on the shelf next to the sink.'

'Great,' I smile back, shimmying past him.

'And here's a spare toothbrush.' Pulling open a drawer, he hands me one of those travel ones you get when you fly transatlantic. Seb's always going away on business and has dozens of them, along with eye masks and all these lovely toiletries they give you for free when you fly club class and stay in five-star hotels. Not that I know personally, of course – the only travelling I do for work is with my Oyster card, I reflect, reminded of my own rubbish career and quickly batting it away.

'Thanks,' I say, taking it from him. 'Won't be a min.'

Shooing him out in a teasing way, I close the door and lean against it. I feel a bit woozy from all that red wine and for a moment I remain there, letting the events of the evening sink in . . . the movie . . . the wine . . . and now here I am. Back here again. About to have sex with Seb for the first time. *Again.*

How fantastic is that?

Feeling the frisson of excitement building, I wipe away smudged eyeliner and pull out my lip gloss. So far the evening has been awesome, as Seb puts it, and I want tonight to be perfect, faultless, like a gold-medal Olympic athlete. In my head I get an image of judges holding up score cards . . . only instead of perfect sixes they have big fat zeros as my performance is terrible.

Hang on, what's all that about? Quickly I scrub that image from my brain. It must be just nerves talking. Seb and I always had a good sex life. At least I *thought* we did. Saying that, since we broke up I confess there've been times I've wondered if I could have done a few things differently. Like, for example, what if the times he wanted to have sex and I said I was tired and had to get up early for work I'd been all ripe and up for it and reaching for the massage oil? And not setting the alarm and reaching for my earplugs.

Or what if I'd worn sexy lingerie all the time, even those nipple tassels he once bought me? And not thought they were a joke and hooted with laughter when I unwrapped them, and which Flea thought were little black mice and promptly tried to eat.

And then there was that time once in the middle of foreplay, Seb told me I needed to let go, so I did and promptly fell off the bed. Which, looking back now, wasn't what he meant, I don't think.

Unexpectedly I feel a bit anxious. Maybe that was the reason we broke up but he never told me? Maybe I wasn't sexy enough. Maybe I didn't satisfy him sexually? Maybe – my stomach knots – *I was bad in bed.* Hurriedly I force myself to dismiss the thought. No, that's rubbish. We had a great time together in the bedroom. Admittedly, like most couples, it took a little while for us to find our groove, to experiment, to discover what each other liked and didn't like, but that's normal.

But this time around there's not going to be any fumbling or nervousness, I remind myself firmly. We're going to have mind-blowing sex right from the start as – *and this is the brilliant bit about getting to date Seb again* – I already know what turns him on. I've already learned all the tricks!

Applying my lip gloss, I pout at myself in the mirror. For instance, I know that Seb really likes it when I . . . I trail off, unable to finish the thought. I frown. That's funny, my mind's gone all fuzzy. Must be all that red wine, I'm always hopeless after a few glasses. Giving myself a little sobering shake, I blot my lips with a bit of loo roll (well, I don't want to *look* like I'm wearing make-up) and think about the thing I do with my . . . Crikey, I really must be drunk. I can't even remember that either!

I swear, it's that third glass of wine. Once, after sharing a bottle of Pinot Grigio with Fiona, I forgot where we'd parked the car. We spent ages looking, until one of us sobered up enough to remember that we don't actually *have* a car.

I know, maybe if I just imagine having sex with Seb *generally* it will come flooding back. It usually does, I muse, thinking about the nights I've spent alone in my bed since we broke up. Well, a single girl's got to have a *little* bit of light relief. Closing my eyes, I visualise Seb with no clothes (this is how I always start the fantasy), then brace myself for all the X-rated memories to come surging back . . . except, that's weird, nothing's happening . . .

Suddenly I freeze. My mind's gone blank! I can't remember anything. Panicked, I scrabble around for even a single X-rated memory but I can't find one. My anxiety increases. I can't have drunk *that* much. It's as though I've suddenly got amnesia. *Sex amnesia.*

Abruptly a thought strikes. Oh my god, that's it! I haven't just erased our past.

I've erased our sex life!

I snap my eyes wide open. Fuck, what am I going to do?

Then it hits me. *My diary.*

Diving into my bag, I rummage around inside. I've been carrying it around with me all week, ever since our first date, and grabbing the dog-eared pages I pull it out and plonk myself on the loo to read it. Right, OK. I start flicking through the pages. *Come on, come on, I must have written about sex somewhere. I must have.*

'Hey, are you OK in there?'

Seb's voice makes me jump. Shit. He can probably hear the pages rustling and is wondering what the hell I'm doing in here.

Hastily I turn on the taps.

'Um . . . yes, fine . . .' I call out, trying to sound all light and breezy, and not pinned to the loo with panic that I'm about to have sex with Seb for the first time, and I can't remember the last time, I think, my mind tangling itself in knots.

Oh hang on, what's this . . .

Dear Diary,

Slept with Seb for the first time!!!! I was really nervous but it was amazing, though I wish I'd known we were going to do it as I'd have shaved my legs! And done a fake tan. I spent the whole time feeling self-conscious and hiding underneath the duvet, which spoiled things a bit as it can be very hot underneath a duvet. And very dark. There was a lot of fumbling around and at one point we got all tangled up and bumped our heads together and nearly knocked each other out.

I feel a beat of relief. Well, at least I don't have to worry about that happening. This time I'm going to prance naked around the bedroom with the lights on. I'm going to be confident, proactive.

A seductress.

Well, that was the idea, I think with a stab of panic as I feel the entire evening I've rehearsed in my head beginning to quickly unravel into a disaster. I keep reading.

. . . and it was a bit embarrassing as I wore the ring that Fiona bought me for my birthday last year, the one with the big blue stone, and it got caught on his you-know-what . . .

I glance down at my finger. The big blue ring stares back at me. Shit. I'd better take that off. I try to pull it off but it's stuck. Soaping it up I try and squeeze it over the knuckle. Abruptly it flies off across the bathroom and rattles around on the floor. Damn! Where's it gone?

But I don't have time to look for it just now, I'll have to find it later. I need to crack on. I need to read up on some tricks. Find out what he likes, and doesn't like, what turns him on. *And turns him off*. Panic grips. What if I start talking dirty and he tells me to shut up? What if he's a bum man not a boobs man and I get it the wrong way round?

Snatching up the diary, I flick much further on.

We've been seeing each other three months now and the sex just gets better and better! Tonight when we were in bed I drove Seb wild when I . . .

I break off, blushing.

Golly, I can't remember writing that. It's like something from a Jackie Collins bonkbuster! Feeling my face go all hot, I turn the page to keep reading.

Abruptly my right mind comes flying in through the window. Tess, what are you doing? There's a hot, sexy man out there! The man you're in love with. The man you've spent the last few months missing so much you even resorted to wrapping one of his old T-shirts around your pillow. One that he'd taken off after the gym *and was unwashed*.

And now he's here. On the other side of the door. All ripe and ready to jump on you, a*nd you're sitting on the loo reading your old diary?* You're not cramming for an exam! You're about to have sex with Seb, which you've done hundreds of times. Stop worrying, it's just nerves. It'll be like riding a bike, you've just got to get back on. *So to speak*.

Brought to my senses I jump up from the loo and, stuffing the diary in my bag, quickly clean my teeth, flick my hair, and adjust my bra so the lacy bits show and go back into the bedroom.

Seb is sitting on the edge of the bed in just his jeans, waiting for me. My stomach does a cartwheel. I'd forgotten how good he looks with no top on.

'Hey, I missed you,' he drawls lazily, his eyes sweeping over me.

Me too, answers my groin. Trust me, ten weeks has felt like a very long time.

'So . . . um, do you want to use the bathroom?' I say, hovering in the doorway. But before I can finish, he loops his arms around my waist, pulls me down onto the bed and runs his hands underneath my top.

'Mmm, your skin is so soft,' he murmurs.

'Is it?' I reply, trying to sound surprised and not think about all those hours spent salt-scrubbing and moisturising.

'. . . and so tanned, have you been away?'

'No, nowhere,' I say innocently.

Well, Boots doesn't count, does it?

He starts kissing my neck and unbuttoning my shirt. 'Wow,' he says approvingly when he sees my peek-a-boo bra, 'sexy.'

'Oh it's nothing special, just something I threw on,' I say nonchalantly, as his tongue brushes my nipple and I feel a shiver of desire. God, how I've missed this. Lying tangled together on top of the duvet, our breathing quickens and I can feel the excitement building as we take it in turns to remove each other's clothing.

Until now I'm unbuttoning the fly of his jeans and, remembering my diary, I'm tracing my hands over his washboard stomach and expertly moving my mouth lower and lower . . .

He lets out a gasp of pleasure.

I pause, teasingly, and smile to myself. What was I worrying about?

Suddenly it's all coming back to me . . .

16

The next morning I'm woken by Seb kissing my face. All warm and snuggled up in bed, I feel soft feathery kisses on my eyelids, tracing a path across my cheeks, stirring me from the depths of sleep.

'Hey, sleepyhead,' he whispers in my ear.

Mmmm. Lovely. This is *my* kind of alarm clock.

I feel his teeth gently teasing my earlobe and a delicious shiver runs up my spine, sending little darts of joy all over my body.

'Time to wake up.'

I feel a pang of excitement. *He wants to do it again!* Anticipation tingles. It's true what they say, sex is like riding a bike. Once you get back on . . .

Stretching out a hand underneath the duvet, I feel for his warm naked body next to mine. Except – hang on a minute, *where is it*?

I snap my eyes open to see the blinds suddenly shoot upwards to reveal Seb, out of bed and wearing a tracksuit.

'Time to go for a run.'

'Huh?'

'I thought you'd want to join me,' he grins, grabbing his baseball cap and putting it on backwards. 'You told me how much you love exercising.'

Blinking at him in the stark winter light that is coming through the window, I feel as if I've just been plunged into an icy cold shower.

'I did?' I squeak, a flashback of that night at the pub suddenly coming back to me. 'Um . . . yes, I did . . . I mean I do,' I correct myself quickly, hoisting myself up on the pillow with my elbows and rubbing the sleep from my eyes.

'Though you military-fitness types are super-fit – you'll probably outrun me,' he laughs.

Outrun him? I look at him dazedly. Before he used to leave me in bed snoozing when he went for a run, but not now. Now he thinks I'm a fitness fanatic. Now he thinks I'm one of those lunatics who run around the park in the freezing cold wearing a coloured bib while some bloke in camouflage army trousers yells at them.

'Afterwards you can show me those bench presses you were talking about,' he winks flirtily.

Bench presses? 'Um . . . I'd love to but . . .' I start grappling around for an excuse in my groggy brain, which is still half asleep, then it comes to me. 'I don't have my trainers.'

Which is absolutely true. And of course if I had them I would go. Honestly.

'Maybe you can borrow a pair of mine,' he suggests brightly. 'What size are you?'

'Tiny,' I say quickly, knowing full well Seb is a size nine.

His face falls in dismay. 'Bummer.'

'I know, bummer.' I pull a disappointed face.

'Oh well, next time.' Doing a calf stretch, he bends over and gives me a kiss. 'I'll be back soon, you stay there right there.'

'OK, if you insist.' I give a little smile.

'I insist,' he murmurs, kissing me deeper. 'Last night was so amazing, *you* were amazing, that thing you did . . .' He slips his hand underneath the duvet and pulls me towards him. 'How did you know . . . ?'

'Now that would be telling,' I whisper, unzipping his tracksuit and tracing my fingers downwards.

His breathing deepens. 'You know what, maybe I'll skip my run this morning . . .'

* * *

I float into the office on a sex cloud. A white fluffy orgasmic sex cloud that transports me all the way from Seb's flat, onto the tube, into Starbucks, and through the revolving doors of Blackstock & White as if I'm on some magical flying carpet.

Nothing can pierce my good mood. Not the train carriage that's crammed with commuters and the bloke in a suit who keeps treading on my toe. Or the huge queue in Starbucks. Or the hail cloud that decides to follow me up the high street, shooting little hard pellets of ice at me.

Not even the fact that Seb had to fly to Geneva this morning on business and is gone all weekend.

Instead I waft along with a huge smile on my face, my mind drifting back over the past few days. It's been such a whirlwind, I've barely had a chance to stop and draw breath. When we haven't been seeing each other we've been calling, texting, emailing . . . It's incredible. We've only been on two dates but it's almost as if we're closer than we were before. More connected, somehow. It's funny, before I used to hear people talk about how it feels to be on the same page as their partner, and I never knew what they meant.

But now I do.

Sitting at my desk I gaze dreamily at my computer screen and think about Seb. I'm not seeing him until Monday and it seems like aeons away. Still, at least I'll be able to put on some comfy knickers, I console myself, wriggling around in my chair and trying to free my *vajayjay* from the stranglehold of my lacy G-string. And only making it worse.

Ouch.

I wince as it pinches.

Actually, I think I might just have to go commando, I realise, as a series of little shockwaves shoot up inside me. Only this time it's got nothing to do with Seb and that thing he does with his . . .

I feel myself blush and quickly glance around to see if

anyone's looking. That's the thing with morning sex, I always feel like everyone must be able to tell. Like the whole office must be able to read my mind and it says: *I've just done IT with my boyfriend.* But there's only Kym sitting at her desk and as usual she's engrossed in her daily helping of Missed Connections.

'Oooh, look at this one,' she says, reading out loud, '"I doubt you remember me but I was visiting London and I saw you on the London Eye. You were in the next pod and we stared at each other through the glass. A year later I still think about it."' Resting her chin on her elbows, she heaves a loud sigh. 'Isn't that just the most romantic thing you've ever read?'

'Nah, the most romantic thing I've ever read is "dinner's in the oven",' chortles Wayne, her long-term boyfriend who at that moment walks into the foyer, dressed in his chauffeur's uniform. He throws her a wink.

Kym throws him back a scowl.

'What do you think, Tess?' she asks, deliberately ignoring him and turning to me.

'Um . . . me?' Caught unawares trying to free my G-string, which is now cutting into me like cheese wire, I go bright red. 'I . . . um . . . think I just need to pop to the Ladies.'

Leaving Wayne and Kym having a domestic, I dash into the loos and lock myself in a cubicle. Once inside I quickly wriggle off my G-string. *Ah, the relief.* Who would have thought a scrap of Chantilly lace could turn into a torture device? Shoving the offending item in my bag, I pull on my trousers and emerge from the cubicle.

And bump into The Witch.

What did I say about those crepe soles of hers? I never heard her come in. Standing in front of the mirrors, she's applying more scarlet lipstick and practising her Hillary Clinton pose.

Spotting my reflection behind her, she turns to me with a beady expression. 'Ah Tess, I noticed your desk was empty, I was wondering where you'd absconded to.'

My heart sinks. If there's one person who can cloud my good mood, it's her.

'Morning Wendy,' I nod, briefly wondering if I can make a quick exit, but she blocks my path. Despite her diminutive frame, she's like an American quarterback. There's no getting past her.

'You haven't forgotten you're taking the minutes at the meeting this morning, have you?' she reminds me with a fake smile.

'No, of course not,' I say, trying to sound casual, but my hand cramps up at the thought of it. I hadn't so much forgotten, as blocked it out. Taking minutes is probably my least favourite part of my job. I'm never sure what exactly you're supposed to leave out and what you need to write down and I spend the whole time madly scribbling everything down, until my hand's gone into cramp and my notepad is so indecipherable it would take a handwriting expert to crack the code.

But it's not for want of trying. When I first started I went out and bought all these books with titles like *How To Record Really Useful Minutes!* and *Minutes Made Easy!*, which are full of lots of jaunty bullet points about recording the 'Date and Time of Meeting' (well, that bit's easy), 'A List of Attendees' (yup, can manage that), 'Assigned Action Items' (this is where it gets slightly trickier. What does this mean *exactly*?), and 'Decisions Made' (which sounds great *in theory*, but to be frank, there never appear to be any real decisions made. Just about three hours of everyone sitting around the mahogany conference table talking vaguely about reports and strategies whilst drinking coffee and eating lots of those 'extremely chocolatey biscuits' that Kym has been sent out to buy from Marks & Spencer).

Then, of course, there's the final whammy, 'Type up minutes and hand out copies to attendees' (OK, now it's time to *really* panic).

'You know, I never received my copy of the minutes to the last meeting,' she continues pointedly.

'Oh, didn't you?' I feign an innocent expression. 'That's odd, they must have got lost in the internal post. Or something.' That 'something' being me deliberately leaving her off the mailing list. Well, it's hard enough without her picking them apart.

'Can you resend them?' She raises a thin, pencilled-on eyebrow. For some bizarre reason she appears to have plucked away her real eyebrows, then crayoned them back on in harsh black arches. 'Sooner rather than later. If you don't mind.' She switches on that fake smile again.

'Um . . . yes, of course,' I nod, crossing my fingers behind my back. Oh crap, now I'm going to have to think of another excuse. 'OK, well, I must dash,' I say, carefully side-stepping her. 'Don't want to be late for the meeting!'

Lunging for the door, I make my escape and hurry back into the office. Anyway, it's not like I have time to think about getting minutes to Wendy right now, I need to get to Sir Richard. He usually likes to brief me before we go in to a meeting as he knows I find them – how does he put it? – ah, yes, that's right: C*hallenging.* Which probably isn't the word I would choose, but then mine's unprintable.

Passing the kitchen, I grab his usual morning cup of coffee – black, three sugars – and go over to his office. That's odd. Normally his door is wide open – part of his 'no barriers' approach to the company – but today it's firmly closed. I knock on it. There's no answer. Confused, I wait for a moment, then balancing the coffee in one hand, I turn the handle and push it open.

The office is in darkness, the Venetian blinds pulled down, and as I step inside it appears empty. Then I hear something. A faint rattling noise. What on earth's that? Feeling a slight tremor, I look around, my eyes trying to adjust, but it's difficult to see anything. And I'm not sure where the light switch is. Oh my god, there's that noise again! What the hell is it? Maybe an animal's got trapped in here overnight, like a stray cat, *or maybe a fox*! Suddenly all those newspaper headlines come flooding back about people being ripped to shreds in savage attacks . . . no, don't be ridiculous. That's just newspaper hype. Foxes are lovely creatures.

There's a loud rustle.

Fuck.

Dumping the coffee on the desk, I quickly yank up the blinds.

Sharp, wintry sunlight streams in, flooding the office, and I hear a loud splutter behind me. '*What the heavens . . . ?*'

I twirl around to see a figure lying on the sofa, covered in an old blanket.

'Sir Richard!' I gasp in shock.

Grappling around for his glasses on the coffee table, he shoves them on. 'Oh Tess, it's you . . .' Vacuuming his throat, he quickly throws off the blanket and sits upright. I notice he's slept in his suit. So that explains why it's been looking even more crumpled than usual.

'Is everything OK?' Quickly I shut the door behind me. My eyes take in everything: an overflowing holdall on the floor, a toothbrush . . . how long has he been sleeping here?

'I'm terribly sorry, you shouldn't have had to see me like this.' He begins apologising profusely and trying to tame the fronds of hair that look like a dead spider plant perched on the top of his head.

'Oh don't worry, I've seen much worse – you should meet my flatmate,' I try joking, passing him his cup of coffee.

He takes it from me gratefully and takes a thirsty gulp.

For a moment nobody speaks.

'OK, well, perhaps I should just wait outside . . .' I make a move towards the door.

'Lady Blackstock and I are getting divorced. I've moved out.'

I turn to look at him in astonishment. 'Oh I'm so sorry, I had no idea . . .'

'No, don't be,' he says, shaking his head. 'Our marriage has been over for a long time, it's for the best.'

'But where are you going to go? You can't stay here.' I look at his large frame perched on the tiny sofa. It looks terribly uncomfortable; he can't have got much sleep.

'This was just a temporary measure, until I sorted myself out . . . I'd normally stay at my club but I didn't want everyone there knowing my business . . .' He trails off awkwardly. 'Anyway, I went to view some flats in town yesterday.'

So that's where he sneaked off to yesterday, I realise. No wonder it wasn't in the diary.

'I move into one this weekend.'

We're interrupted by the shrill ringing of the telephone on his desk and, quickly gathering himself up from the sofa, he answers it. 'Thanks, we'll be right there.' Replacing the receiver he turns to me. 'That was Wendy, kindly reminding us that everyone is assembled in the conference room,' he says, a slight note of irritation in his voice. Tucking in a shirt flap, he goes to fasten his crumpled jacket, then tuts loudly. 'Oh bugger, the button must have fallen off.'

I glance across at him and feel a trace of alarm. He might be the CEO but he looks a complete shambles. As his PA I can't let him go into the meeting like this.

'Hang on, take your jacket off a minute,' I say quickly.

Confusion flashes across his face. 'But . . . ?'

'Your jacket. Take it off,' I instruct, holding out my hand impatiently. He hesitates – and I realise too late I really shouldn't be bossing my boss around – before dutifully taking it off and handing it to me. Quickly I turn it inside out. 'Yup, I thought so. Look, there's a spare button on the inside,' I say triumphantly, showing him.

'Why you clever girl, how did you know that?'

'Tailors always put them there,' I explain, 'my granddad taught me that.' Grabbing my bag, I rummage in it and pull out my little sewing kit that I always carry around. 'I'll quickly sew it on for you.'

'You can do that?' Sir Richard looks incredulous.

'It will only take a minute,' I say, already threading the needle. 'Why don't you have a quick shave in the meantime?' I gesture to his electric razor that I see on the side of his desk.

'Oh yes . . . of course!' Sir Richard snatches a hand up to his whiskery chin in sudden realisation. Grabbing his razor he flicks it on. 'What would I do without you, hey Tess?' he exclaims over the electric buzz, and shooting me a grateful smile, he begins energetically shaving over the wastepaper basket.

'Oh it's nothing, honestly,' I protest, but inside I feel a faint tinge of pride. OK, so I might be useless at taking minutes, but when it comes to sewing on buttons . . . I bite off the cotton and admire my handiwork. Gramps taught me well. Still a bit crumpled, but other than that, as good as new.

17

A few minutes later we ride up in the lift to the third floor. The doors ping open and we start to hurry down the corridor when Sir Richard slaps his forehead. 'Goodness me, I completely forgot to brief you on the meeting.'

With everything that's been going on, it had totally slipped my mind as well, but now, reminded, anxiety starts to knot in my stomach.

'Don't worry,' he reassures me, seeing my expression. 'It will all be splendid, just follow my lead.' And, pulling open the door to the boardroom, he sweeps me inside. 'Ah, good morning everyone, how wonderful to see you could all make it,' and, without missing a beat, he begins his round of greetings like a true professional, shaking hands, trading jokes, making small talk.

We take our seats, Sir Richard at the head of the table, and me – oh shit . . . my heart sinks as I see the only free seat left is next to Wendy the Witch. There's bad luck and then there's *really bad luck*.

Ignoring her glares, I quickly sit down and get out my notepad and pen. I can feel her eyes on me, trying to crane over my shoulder to see what I'm writing, and I'm tempted to doodle a witch on her broomstick. But of course I'm far too mature for that. *Sadly*. Instead I write MINUTES in block capitals and underline it twice.

OK, so far so good.

Thirty minutes later and I've finished noting down the time and place of meeting and making a list of attendants, like they tell you to do in my books, and am now trying to think what other bullet points I can make.

'So this next graph shows the recent analysis of effective branding strategies,' drones Kevin from Accounts, who's up at the front doing a PowerPoint presentation that seems to consist of one identical-looking slide after another of graphs and pie charts, none of which I can make head or tail of.

Sneaking a glance around the table, I remember a point in my *Minutes Made Easy!* book: 'Avoid personal or inflammatory observations'.

So in that case, it's probably best not putting:

1. Wendy has scoffed that entire first packet of chocolate biscuits and is now making a start on the second.
2. Adam, one of the directors, has his fly undone.
3. John from Marketing is picking his nose . . .

I watch as he has a good root around and then inspects what's on the end of his finger. There's a pause . . . oh god, he's not going to do what I think he's going to . . .

. . . *and eating it.*

Looking away sharply, I stare back at Kevin and try to concentrate on what he's saying, but my mind's like a kite. No matter how hard I try to tether it to the boardroom, it keeps drifting away – far far away from pie charts and Excel sheets – to sequins and buttons and an idea for a new, smaller type of clutch bag. I love my original bag, but this would be perfect for a night out, just big enough to hold a lip gloss, keys and a mobile phone. I could make a wrist strap out of some of that gorgeous velvet ribbon I have; it's a dark plum colour and if you looped it over your hand . . .

And what about if I sewed peacock feathers all over the bag? I'm always finding those in charity shops, the bright green and blue of the feathers with the deep plum velvet of the ribbon . . . gosh, yes, that would look amazing . . .

'Thank you Kevin, fascinating stuff,' enthuses Wendy. 'Don't we all agree?'

I zone back to see her staring at my pad and I suddenly realise that I've been doodling the whole time. Instead of taking notes I've been absently sketching designs for my new bag and the pages are filled with scribbles and drawings.

Fuck. Hurriedly turning over the page, I try to focus back on Kevin, but he's finished and is returning to his seat. Fuck, fuck, fuck, now I'm totally lost. I'll never be able to even *attempt* to write up the notes now. I can feel witchy eyes boring into the side of my face. Oh god, she's never going to let me hear the end of this.

Feeling doomed, I glance across at Sir Richard, who's started talking. 'So, just to clarify, Kevin, the main points when simplified are . . . ?' He catches my eye and throws me a wink.

It takes a moment to register, but as Kevin proceeds to recap in words I can understand, I feel a rush of relief, and shooting Sir Richard back a grateful smile, I quickly start jotting them down.

The rest of the meeting passes without a hitch, thanks to Sir Richard and his constant need for clarification, and afterwards I quickly scoot back to my desk and spend the rest of the morning typing up my notes and sending the minutes out. It's a personal first. I'm even tempted to hand-deliver them to Wendy. Though, on second thoughts, perhaps I don't need to go *that* far.

Anyway, I'm feeling pretty good about everything by the time lunchtime swings around and I walk across the road to grab a baked potato to take back to the office. Putting in my order I lean against the counter to wait, which is when I notice a figure sitting in the corner. He's half hidden behind a copy of *Metro*, and my eyes almost pass over him, but for the familiar-looking tufts of black hair springing over the headlines.

Hang on, is that . . . ?

'*Fergus?*'

His face appears from behind the paper, looking a little startled.

'Hey, fancy seeing you here!' I smile.

'Um . . . yeh, fancy that,' he nods, his eyes darting around the café.

'Couldn't resist, hey?'

He looks back at me, sort of frozen.

'The baked potatoes,' I prompt.

'Ah yes, of course, the spuds!' he enthuses, making a big show of smacking his lips and patting his stomach. 'Couldn't keep me away from those spuds!'

I glance at his table. It's empty, but for a Coke.

There's a pause, and then . . .

'OK, I'm busted,' he confesses, following my gaze. 'I'm not here for the spuds, I came to see if that girl was here again.'

'And was she?'

'Nope,' he shakes his head.

'How long have you been waiting?'

He pulls a face. 'Put it this way, I'm on my fifth Coke.'

We exchange looks.

'So, what about you? How did the movie go?' he says, changing the subject.

'Oh great,' I nod, my mind flicking back to last night and feeling a delicious shiver running up my spine.

'You liked it?' He looks surprised and, putting on a voice booms, '*May the Force Be With You.*'

'Well no, not the *actual* movie,' I confess, laughing, 'but my boyfriend did, and afterwards . . .' I trail off, realising I'm in danger of offering too much information.

But I needed haven't worried, Fergus isn't even listening. Instead he's focused on the door as someone's just walked in. Only it's a builder with a shaved head and tattoos.

Disappointment flashes across his face. 'Sorry, you were saying?' he says, turning back to me.

In fact, for the next five minutes I don't think he really hears a word I'm saying as we continue a conversation of sorts. Every time the café entrance bell pings he twirls around and glances at the door, his body inflating with excitement, before realising it's not her and deflating like a days-old balloon.

Until finally my takeaway potato's ready and, as he walks me back to the office, I turn to him. 'And you'll never guess what! A tiger came into the office and bit off my boss's head!'

'Um, really . . .' he replies absently.

'Fergus!' I exclaim.

He snaps out of his trance. 'What? Did I do something?' He looks stricken.

I feel a beat of sympathy. I know how he feels. I've been that dreamy way about Seb. Hell, I still *am* that way, I muse, thinking about the fluffy white orgasmic cloud that transported me into work this morning.

'Do you want to talk about her?' I encourage.

'What's there to talk about?' he shrugs, holding the door open for me. 'I'm never going to see her again. It was a long shot. '

'Hi Fergus.' We're interrupted by Kym as we walk into reception. 'How are you?' She smiles flirtily and pats her hair to check it hasn't moved out of place. Which, considering it's sprayed rock-solid to her head with the can of Elnett hairspray she carries with her at all times, is unlikely, unless you took to it with a sledgehammer. Even then it's questionable.

'Better for seeing you,' he grins, flicking his charm back on like a switch.

She giggles, delighted by the attention, then turns to me. 'Hey Tess, wait till you hear this Missed Connection, you're going to love it!'

Suddenly I'm hit by an idea. 'I know! I've got a great idea! Why don't you post one of those ads?' I suggest, turning to Fergus.

'Ooh, have you had a Missed Connection?' exclaims Kym, overhearing. 'How exciting!'

'Well, I don't know about that—' he begins, but she cuts him off.

'What do you want to put in the ad? I'll post it online for you right now.'

'You would?' Fergus looks taken aback.

'Of course! I've always wanted to post one of these; you know, they're so romantic, you read these amazing stories where people get married and live happily ever after . . .'

'Is that so?' Intrigued, Fergus draws closer.

'Absolutely!' cries Kym, thrilled to have a captive audience.

I feel a beat of concern. Kym is getting completely carried away, and she's taking Fergus with her. 'Actually, on second thoughts, I'm not sure it is such a good idea,' I try reasoning, but it's too late.

'You know, maybe I should,' Fergus is saying now. 'Why not? I mean, it can't hurt, can it?'

'Cool!' grins Kym. 'OK, so first we have to put it in the boy meets girl section—' Abruptly she breaks off. 'Unless of course it's *boy meetsboy*.' She gives him a look.

Fergus flushes. 'Crikey, what do you take me for? It's a girl,' he gasps indignantly.

'Well you can't make assumptions these days, you know,' trills Kym, her fingernails clackety-clacking on the keys. 'OK, so what do you want to put?'

'Hmm . . .' He rakes his fingers through his messy black hair, his brow creased deep in thought.

'If you want I can help with some suggestions,' she advises.

'Maybe he needs to give it a bit more thought,' I say, shooting Kym a look. 'I mean there's no rush.'

We're both interrupted by Fergus who, suddenly galvanised, finds his tongue and launches into a monologue.

'*You were the beautiful girl with blonde hair in Café Lux on Wednesday at lunchtime . . . I was the guy in the red T-shirt and neon jacket who was too shy to say hello . . .*'

It's like he's on stage playing the Dane himself, slapping his hand against his chest, imploring the audience to heed his plight. I glance across at Kym, whose fingers are flying over the keyboard.

'*. . . So I'm saying it now: Hello. I'd like to buy you a cup of coffee some time—*'

'Oh come on, if you're going to ask a girl out, you've got to ask her out for dinner,' I interrupt, 'or at least a drink.'

Well, if I can't stop him posting the ad, I can at least help him write it.

He breaks off from his soliloquy and turns to me. 'I don't drink on first dates. Not after Suzy and the Malibu and pineapple incident.'

I look at him blankly.

'Aged fifteen. My school disco.' He shakes his head and makes a face as if he's just eaten something sour.

I don't need to ask him to explain. His expression is enough.

'OK,' I shrug. 'Coffee's good.'

'Righty-ho, so all I need now is your email address,' Kym is chirping, and as Fergus tells her it, she quickly types it in. 'OK, so that's it. Post!' With a flourish of her mouse, she leans back in her chair. 'All done!' She flashes him an overexcited grin and holds out her hand to high-five him. 'Good luck!'

'Thanks,' he smiles, high-fiving her back.

We're interrupted by the shrill ring of Kym's phone, and as she picks up I glance back across at Fergus. Only his smile's slipped and he's suddenly looking a bit nervous. Almost as though he's not quite sure what he's done.

'So now what?' I ask him.

Turning to me, he shrugs and throws me a hopeful look. 'I guess I just have to wait.'

18

At the end of the day I leave the office and catch the bus to Kensington where I've arranged to meet Fiona after work. She called earlier, offering me the chance of a free pedicure if I went with her to Oceano, a new Japanese nail salon that's just opened.

There was only one catch:

'It's not a regular pedicure, it's of the fishy variety,' she confessed down the phone.

'Nuh-huh,' I replied, 'I happen to like my toes.'

'Oh c'mon, it's for my column,' she pleaded.

'You're scared, aren't you?' I said, unable to keep the amusement out of my voice.

'Scared? Don't be silly! Of course I'm not scared!' she protested hotly. 'I just thought it might be fun if we go together.'

'You mean like safety in numbers?'

There's a sulky pause.

'By the way, you know I still can't find my Diptyque candle . . .'

Oh fuck. With everything going on I'd totally forgotten about that.

'Actually, on second thoughts, you're right, that does sound like fun. What's the address again?'

Despite detailed directions, I still get lost, and it's only after circling the block a few times that I eventually find it, tucked away on a cobbled side street. From the outside it looks like any other nail salon, but pushing open the door I'm greeted by a row of tanks, all lined up, full of fish ready to feast on strangers' feet.

I try not to cringe.

'Tess!'

I look up to see Fiona, trousers rolled up to her knees, being led barefoot towards one of the fish tanks by one of the kimono-clad assistants, a look of fear on her face. It's like that scene from the Bond film with Helga Brandt when she's fed to the piranhas.

'Sorry, I got lost—' I begin, but she cuts me off.

'No worries, I'll wait for you.' She hastily signals to the assistant.

'It's OK, you go ahead,' I say, tugging off my winter boots.

She turns pale underneath the spotlights. 'No, it's fine, honestly . . . In fact, guess what? I must dash to the loo . . .' and making her excuses, she disappears behind a curtain at the back. It's like the time we were at school and accidentally broke the headmistress's window with a rounders ball, and Fiona ran off and left me to face the music.

Only this time it's hundreds of tiny little fish. I wince as I'm shown to my chair a few moments later and tentatively lower my feet into a tank. Immediately they dive upon my toes and I brace myself as they start nibbling. Oh my god, this is going to hurt, this is going to be painful . . .

I let out an unexpected giggle.

Oh my gosh, it's so ticklish!

'How is it?' asks Fiona, re-emerging from the Ladies and sliding onto the seat next to me. For a split second I'm about to tell her how nice it feels. Then I change my mind. Well, I still owe her payback for that broken window.

I stifle the giggle rising up inside me and force my face into a grimace. 'Agony,' I gasp.

'Oh my god, you're serious?' Fiona pales.

I nod mutely, doing my best to suppress my laughter.

'Argh,' I let out a yell.

'What?' Startled, Fiona jumps a mile.

'My toe!' I gasp. 'I think they've chewed off my toe!'

'Fuck! You're kidding!' she gasps back, a terrified expression on her face.

It's too much. I can't pretend any longer and I burst out laughing. 'Of course I'm kidding,' I snort, trying to catch my breath.

It takes a moment to register and then, 'Tess!' she yelps indignantly, bashing me on the shoulder. 'That's so mean!'

'Well you deserve it,' I reply, wiping the tears of mirth from my eyes.

'That's so unfair! I was really worried!'

'So worried you ran away and left me to face the fish alone?' I say, still grinning.

She pouts and does that thing where she pretends she hasn't heard me. Like when I mention it's her turn to do the washing-up, or there's no loo roll left. I call it selective hearing, as all I have to do is *whisper* the words 'chocolate' or 'he's handsome' and her ears prick up like a bat and she's all, 'What? Where?'

Steeling herself, she slowly lowers her feet into the tank. For a second there's a look of surprise on her face, then, 'Oooh, it's tingly . . .' she exclaims, as the fish begin nibbling hungrily. 'I like it.'

'Me too,' I grin, settling back into my chair. Bizarre as it sounds, it's actually very relaxing, like having a mini-massage on your feet.

'And it's nothing like that James Bond film,' she reprimands, giving me *that* look.

'Well I wasn't to know,' I reply innocently.

She narrows her eyes and stares at me for a moment, as if not quite sure whether to believe me or not, then gives up and shoots me a furtive smile. 'By the way, I noticed you didn't come home last night.'

'I stayed at Seb's,' I admit, feeling all tingly again, and this time it's got nothing to do with the Garra Rufa fish.

She leans closer, excitedly. 'So how was it?'

'Oh Fiona, it was amazing,' I grin, barely able to contain my delight.

'The sex was that good, huh?'

I feel myself blush. 'Well yes, but it's not just the sex, it's everything. We're getting on so brilliantly . . . and he's so smart and successful . . . and handsome,' I add with a blissful smile. 'And he seems to really *really* like me . . .'

'And so he should,' replies Fiona loyally. 'What's not to like?'

I smile bashfully. 'You would say that, you're my best friend.'

'No, I'm just being truthful,' she says evenly. 'You're such a gorgeous, funny, interesting person, Tess: why shouldn't he think you're amazing?'

I feel myself colouring up at her effusiveness and I don't know what to say – after all, I know she's only being kind, and I'm glad when the assistant reappears with green tea and a stack of magazines for us to read.

'Oooh fab!' exclaims Fiona, ignoring the green tea and diving on the magazines with delight. 'Here, which one do you want? Brad and Angelina, or Peter Andre?' She holds up two covers.

'No it's OK, I've got a book,' I say, reaching into my bag and pulling out my Obama biography. I've been carrying it around since Seb gave it to me and it weighs a ton.

Fiona frowns. 'What? You don't want to read all about celebrity cellulite?'

She flashes open the magazine and I catch a glimpse of a bikini special.

For a moment I'm tempted, but I resist.

'No thanks,' I say, feeling a little pious and turning over the page.

She peers at me doubtfully for a moment, then shrugs. 'OK, suit yourself.'

We both fall silent and start reading, but after a few minutes I'm distracted by Fiona gasping.

'Oh gosh, you should see this!' she exclaims, and I look up. 'Oops sorry, I forgot you're not interested in celebrity gossip any more,' she says, putting a finger over her mouth to sshh herself.

'It's OK,' I say, turning back to my book. I can hear Fiona flicking over the pages as I continue reading and then—

'I can't believe it!'

'What?' I jerk my head up.

'Oh, nothing,' she shrugs, shaking her head.

Curiosity itches. What *is* she looking at? Jennifer Aniston in a minidress at a premiere? Topless pictures of Peter Andre? Some drunk celebrity falling out of a club?

Not that I care, *of course*, I'm just wondering.

Firmly bending back the spine of my book I stare down at my page. Now, where was I? Finding my paragraph I continue reading. Only for some reason I seem to be having problems concentrating. The words are swimming in front of my eyes and I'm reading the same sentence over and over . . .

'Mmmm, he's gorgeous,' murmurs Fiona.

OK, that's it. I've cracked. Sorry Obama. You might be the most powerful man in the world but the lure of celebrity gossip is too much. Furtively I crane my neck, trying to catch a glimpse of Fiona's magazine pages.

Oooh look, it's an at-home spread with that handsome actor from Grey's Anatomy*!*

'Is that book good?'

I snatch my head back, almost cricking my neck, to see Fiona staring at me with a raised-eyebrow look.

'Um yes . . . really *really* good,' I nod vigorously. 'Seb says it completely changed his life.'

'You haven't got very far,' she frowns, and I look down to realise I'm still on page two.

Page two?

As in, I've only read two pages?

I stare at it in astonishment. I already feel as though I've been reading this for days. 'Well . . . um . . . it takes a while to absorb everything, you know,' I say, hurriedly, 'so you have to read it slowly and . . . um . . . sort of think deeply about all his views on life and . . . um . . . stuff.'

'What are his views on life?'

'Er, well, I haven't got to that bit yet.'

'Hmm.' Fiona looks at me silently for a few moments, as if she's about to say something, but is distracted by the ping of an email on her BlackBerry. 'Ooh, look I've been sent some soul mates,' she says, glancing at her screen. 'I joined a new dating site, Sassy Soul Mates,' she explains, seeing my blank look.

'You have?' I say, relieved to be off the subject of my Obama book.

'Yup,' she nods. 'Well, after Henry the Eighth didn't work out I thought I'd widen the net – plenty more fish in the sea and all that,' she finishes resolutely.

That's one of the things I like about Fiona. She gets knocked down but she always gets back up again. I know she was hurt by what happened, but she refuses to show it.

'So who are your soul mates?' I ask curiously.

'Hang on, it's loading . . .' She peers at the screen of her BlackBerry. 'Oh dear,' she says, frowning.

'What's wrong?'

'None are my type,' she says, scrolling down, 'and one of them needs a serious makeover.' Peering closely at her screen, she tuts. 'What on earth is he wearing?'

'Who? Let me see . . .'

But Fiona's not listening, she's already replying.

'I was just sent your profile but I don't think I'm your sassy soul mate,' she taps furiously away at her BlackBerry. 'However . . .' She frowns again at her screen and shakes her head. '. . . I had to get in touch as I don't think you will have much success with your photograph. I'm sure you're a very nice man but I think you could benefit greatly from a makeover. Do you have any female friends that could help with fashion and styling advice? If not, as a health and beauty writer, I would be happy to give you some tips. Best wishes . . .' She presses send with a flourish of satisfaction. 'There. Done.' She pops her BlackBerry back in her bag. 'You know, I think if I wasn't a health and beauty columnist I could be an agony aunt,' she says, turning to me and looking very pleased with herself.

For a brief moment I think about pointing out that most men doing online dating are more likely after a legover than a makeover, but we're interrupted by one of the assistants.

'Excuse me, but the fish have finished your pedicure.'

'Oh really?' I glance into the tank and notice that whereas before the fish were clustered around my toes, they're now lazily hanging around the edges.

'Can you see how they are no longer eating?' explains the assistant. 'That's because they are full.'

'Well I'm glad someone is,' grumbles Fiona, as her stomach makes a loud rumble. She slaps a hand over it to try and quieten it.

'Why don't we get a pizza on the way home?' I suggest, lifting my feet out of the tank. Gosh, it's amazing, it really does work. I've never felt them so soft.

'I can't, I'm still on the rainbow diet.' She pulls a face.

'What colour are you on now?'

'Yellow.'

'Well that's easy, you can have four cheeses, just hold the tomato,' I suggest cheerfully, drying my feet and putting my socks back on.

'True,' she nods, wriggling her feet into her obligatory stilettos, 'but I don't have time. I have to get back to the flat. Pippa and Grizzle are coming over with a few of the other girls.'

My heart sinks. 'Oh, that will be fun,' I say, trying to sound all jolly, which is hard when you're speaking through gritted teeth.

'Yes, I said we could do a beauty product party. You'll be pleased to hear I'm going to give away the big pile on the kitchen table—'

'I'll call off the emergency services,' I grin.

'And I'm going to get wine, and lots of nibbles . . . which obviously I can't eat . . .' she adds hastily, 'but I thought it would be a nice girlie evening. What about you? Seeing Seb?' She gives me a nudge-nudge-wink-wink kind of look.

I shake my head. 'No, he's gone to Geneva for the weekend on business.'

'Are you going to miss him?' Fiona reaches across and squeezes my arm sympathetically.

'It's only for a couple of days,' I smile ruefully. It's true, I am going to miss Seb but, to tell the truth, it will also be nice to have a little time by myself. This week has been pretty hectic. What with staying up till 3 a.m. watching *Star Wars* on a loop, bikini-waxing at the crack of dawn, not to mention last night and this morning, I'm actually pretty exhausted. Don't get me wrong, it's been amazing, but I need some time to recover. Plus my jaw is aching from all that . . .

Well, *you know*.

I don't want to get lockjaw, for Christ's sakes.

We thank the assistants and Fiona leaves her card, promising she'll send them a copy of her column with the article.

'To be honest I really fancy a night in,' I confess, as we push open the door and step into the wintry evening.

'You do?' asks Fiona delightedly. 'Brilliant! You can join our girlie night!' Linking her arm with mine, she beams at me. 'We'll have so much fun!'

'Great,' I smile and, ignoring my plummeting stomach, I fix a grin to my face like a ventriloquist dummy's. 'I can't wait.'

19

Arriving back at the flat, Fiona whips herself up into a frenzy of house-cleaning. With a screech of 'Pass me the Marigolds!', she dashes around the flat in her stilettos, a blur of yellow rubber, until, after twenty minutes, gone are the piles of paperwork, mouldy coffee cups and overflowing ashtrays that have taken over the kitchen table like a bunch of squatters.

In their place are artfully arranged bowls of nibbles, a vase of fresh flowers and a bottle of wine chilling in an ice bucket. And not just the usual £4.99 Chardonnay from the local off-licence, but an expensive bottle from a rather swanky wine merchant's in Kensington, where the salesman went on and on about gooseberry undertones and lemongrass aromas, until finally Fiona blurted, 'Yes, but will it taste *expensive*?'

As for the shampoo and moisturiser mountain, it's now been transformed into a display on the kitchen counters that would give Selfridges' beauty hall a run for its face creams.

Suddenly the buzzer goes.

'Oh my god, they're here!' gasps Fiona, yanking off the rubber gloves and lurching for her lip gloss. She's all jittery and nervous like she's going on a first date. 'How do I look?' she gasps, fiddling with her hair and pulling down her dress.

'You look great,' I reassure her. She's changed into a new dress which, like everything in Fiona's wardrobe, is a size too small 'for me to diet into' and is breathing in so hard she looks as if she might pop at any moment. 'Everything looks great, don't worry.'

'I know, but it's the first time Pippa's been to the flat. I've invited her over tons of times, but she's always been too busy before.'

'Hmmm, I bet,' I murmur. Funny how when there are lots of free beauty products up for grabs, she can manage to find the time in her packed schedule.

Grabbing the intercom, Fiona hastily buzzes them in. 'Hi darling, top floor,' she trills in her posh voice.

'Where's the lift?' crackles Pippa through the speaker.

Fiona looks stricken. 'Um . . . actually we don't have one,' she flusters.

'No lift!' exclaims Pippa in disbelief. 'Do you mean I have to carry my Birkin up all these stairs?'

I'm speechless. She cannot be serious.

'Oh dear, I'm sorry . . .' Fiona begins apologising profusely. 'If you want I can come down and carry it for you . . .'

I have to wrestle the intercom from her. 'It's flat number seven. See you in a few minutes!' I instruct, before hanging up and shoving the handset back on its cradle.

Fiona stares at me wordlessly, as if not quite sure what just happened.

'Well, don't you need to finish putting on mascara . . . or something?' I say innocently, quickly turning away before she can argue, and pretending to polish an already spotlessly clean wine glass.

A few minutes later there's the loud clattering of Louboutin heels and Pippa and her entourage appear, red-faced and breathless.

'You made it!' beams Fiona, greeting them like visiting royalty. I haven't seen Fiona this thrilled since she lost ten pounds the Christmas before last from a bad case of tonsillitis.

'Only just,' gasps Pippa, lurching into the hallway as if she's about to collapse. A troop of skinny blonde girls follow, grumbling loudly and panting like my parents' Labrador. 'I'm surprised I didn't have a heart attack.'

'Really? And there was me thinking you'd run up those stairs,' I interject with an air of surprise, 'what with all that working out you do with the personal trainer Fiona's been telling me all about.' I smile sweetly.

'Er, right . . . yah,' Pippa smiles tightly and gives me the evils.

'Would you like any wine?' offers Fiona, shimmying across the kitchen like something from *Abigail's Party*, and starting to open the bottle that's been chilling.

She's completely ignored.

'Where are the products?' demands one of the blonde girls. I think it's Grizzle, then again it could be Lolly – to be truthful it's hard to tell them apart.

'Oh, they're over there on the—'

But before Fiona can finish she's pushed roughly aside as the pack of blondes rush past and dive on her display like shoppers on the first day of the Harrods sale. 'Ooh, look, wrinkle-smoothing serum . . . I want the Perfecting Fluid . . . give me the Protecting Complex Cream . . . No, I want it, you can have the mineral hair mask . . .'

As a scuffle breaks out over the beauty products, Fiona looks on with dismay.

'I'll have a glass,' I say supportively.

As she pours me one, her other hand trembles, and I realise she's nervous and am suddenly reminded of being back at school. Of how Fiona used to be so nervous around Susan Fletcher, the most popular girl in the class. She was actually a bit of a cow, but Fiona used to desperately want to be her friend. It was almost as if she hoped some of her confidence and popularity would rub off on her, as if by gaining her approval and being accepted as part of her gang, she would become one of them. Which, in return, meant she'd no longer have to be herself: a rather shy, frizzy-haired girl with puppy fat and a pushy mother.

'Would anyone like any nibbles?' Picking up a bowl of

wasabi peas, Fiona tries again, but it's as though she's invisible. It's a frenzy over there. I glance across at Pippa, who's dumped her Birkin bag on a kitchen chair, and now has her arms full of face creams. Glumly Fiona puts the bowl back on the table.

'Mmm, this is delicious wine,' I say, giving her an encouraging smile.

'Oh . . . good,' she replies gratefully, but after all the effort she made, I can tell she's horribly disappointed. This is not how she envisaged her evening going at all. I glare at Pippa & Co., and am just about to say something when I'm suddenly distracted by the Birkin bag.

Hang on a minute. Did that just *move*?

Which, of course, is ridiculous. Bags don't move.

I stare at it for a few moments, but it remains still on the chair, *of course*, and glancing away I take a sip of my wine. Honestly, I've only had two mouthfuls of wine and I'm already seeing things.

It just wriggled!

I see it out of the corner of my eye. And this time I'm definitely not mistaken. It's definitely wriggling! And sort of shaking. I stare at it, frozen, then suddenly a tiny pink nose appears and a pair of beady eyes, followed by a thin hairy body. As quick as a flash, it leaps into the bowl of wasabi peas.

'Oh my god, it's a rat!' I gasp.

'*A rat!* Where?' shrieks Fiona, jumping backwards on her stilettos and piercing Pippa's toe.

Who lets out an ear-splitting scream. 'Argghhh!'

Which sets off everyone else until the kitchen is filled with the sounds of girls screaming hysterically and moisturisers flying everywhere as they cling onto each other in terror. 'Oh my god a rat! It's a rat! It's—'

'Tallulah!' wails Pippa, suddenly breaking free and flinging herself across the table. 'Darling Tallulah!'

Tallulah?

Abruptly everyone falls silent as she pounces on the rat and clutches it to her chest, stroking its little head and trilling and cooing in its ear as if it's a baby.

She has a rat called Tallulah?

'Don't worry baby, Mummy's here,' she gushes, before looking up and glaring at me. 'A rat!' she snorts incredulously. 'Tallulah happens to be my new puppy.'

'That's a dog?' I stare at the tiny, rodent-like creature in amazement.

'It's not just a dog,' she says hotly. 'It's a miniature Chinese crested breed. But then, silly me, of course you wouldn't know anything about pedigrees, would you?' She looks pointedly across at Flea, who's sitting on the arm of the sofa, legs splayed. With perfect timing, he starts vigorously cleaning his bottom.

'Well, never mind, panic over,' interrupts Fiona, who's down on her hands and knees on the kitchen floor, picking up all the products everyone dropped in their panic. 'It was all a silly misunderstanding.' Pulling herself upright, she pats her hair and gives everyone a bright smile. 'I think we could all do with a lovely glass of wine, don't you?'

''Fraid we can't stay,' shrugs one of the blondes, lighting up a cigarette.

'It's no smoking inside,' I fib, annoyed that she didn't ask if we minded.

'Nonsense,' says Fiona, laughing lightly and immediately providing her with an ashtray. 'Please, everyone make themselves at home. I've got mushroom vol-au-vents in the oven.'

Pippa practically sneers. 'Vol-au-vents? Do people eat those any more?'

Fiona looks somewhat confused. 'Well, I got them from Waitrose—'

'Thanks, but we really can't stay.'

'You're leaving already?' Fiona looks crestfallen.

'I'm afraid so, sweetie. We're going away for the weekend.

Our friends Freddie and Bells have invited us to stay, only there's just one teeny-tiny problem.'

'What's that?' I demand, narrowing my eyes and peering at her suspiciously. I don't like the sound of this.

'Well, they've just had Zebedee, their adorable baby girl, which means I can't take Tallulah. Babies and puppies and all that.' She gives a tinkly little laugh.

'No,' I say firmly before she can ask. I know what's coming next.

'Tess,' hisses Fiona, shooting me a look.

'And so I was wondering if you'd look after Tallulah, just for a few days, while I'm gone . . .' Blanking me, she gives Fiona one of her brightest, shiniest smiles. 'You're so wonderful with animals and there's no one else I could trust with my beloved but you, Fifi . . .'

It works like a charm. In disbelief I watch Fiona's disappointment melting away as she swells up with pride. 'Well, if you're sure, she *is* super-cute.'

'What about Flea?' I say.

'Oh Tallulah is fine, she won't try and eat your cat,' says Pippa dismissively.

'Yes, but Flea might try and eat Tallulah,' I warn.

Pippa frowns and hugs her little rat-like dog tighter.

'She's only joking,' reassures Fiona quickly. 'Tess has got a very quirky sense of humour.'

'Yes, hasn't she?' grimaces Pippa, handing over Tallulah, who immediately snags Fiona's new dress with her diamanté collar.

'OK, well, we must go, otherwise we're going to miss our flight,' interrupts one of the blondes, glancing at her watch.

'Your flight?' repeats Fiona, looking bewildered. 'I thought Fred and Bells lived in Wiltshire?'

'No, that's Tiggy and Tarquin,' corrects one of the blondes.

'So where do they live, Pippa?' I ask directly, fixing her with a look.

Fastening up her coat, she looks all shifty. 'Oh, didn't I say? Silly me.' She gives a tinkly laugh. 'Bali.'

'*Bali?*' gasps Fiona in astonishment.

'You've got to be joking!' I snort. 'There is no way—'

But she doesn't let me finish. 'It's a flying visit, I'll be back before you know it,' she says, quickly air-kissing Fiona on both cheeks. '*Mwoah, mwoah*, thanks darling, have a fabulous weekend . . .'

Grabbing her Birkin, she pauses by the kitchen counter on her way out. 'Oh, mustn't forget,' she says lightly, and with a sweep of her hand clears the countertop and fills her bag with products, before continuing on her way. Followed by all the rest of the blondes, lugging bulging carrier bags, who march behind her into the hallway and out through the door.

Fiona hurries after them. 'Bye, have a safe trip,' she calls out from the doorway as they disappear into the communal stairwell.

Then I hear Pippa.

'Fuck, I forgot about all these stairs.'

Followed by Fiona: 'Do you want me to help you carry—'

I slam the door shut and give Fiona a look that says 'don't you dare'.

Wordlessly we both walk back into the kitchen. Grabbing the bottle of wine I fill my glass, then gesture to Fiona who, despite her rainbow diet, is making a start on the mushroom vol-au-vents. She nods gratefully and holds out her glass. I fill it up to the brim and she takes a grateful slug.

'It's a very sweet puppy,' she says sheepishly, glancing at Tallulah, who gives a little growl and tries to nip Flea. Arching his back, Flea lets out a loud, terrifying hiss and Tallulah scurries under the sofa.

We both look at each other. Fiona holds out the tray of vol-au-vents and I take one. We both chew silently.

Something tells me it's going to be a very long weekend.

20

I wake up on Saturday morning and lie dozing for a few moments, thinking lovely warm woozy thoughts about Seb. Wishing I was waking up next to him. Imagining him here lying next to me.

Except he wouldn't be, would he? I think abruptly. He'd already be up in his tracksuit and going for a run. *And I'd be going with him.*

I snuggle further down into the sleepy depths of my duvet. Actually, thinking about it, it's actually a good thing to miss someone, isn't it? Makes the heart grow fonder and all that. Plus, this way I get to lie in. And hugging my feather-pillow boyfriend, I try to ignore the worrying thought; though I don't know for how much longer – pretty soon a lie-in is going to be a thing of the past.

For a while I lie there, drifting in and out of sleep, before finally I drag myself out of bed and into the kitchen to make myself a cup of coffee. I reach for my espresso pot, then freeze.

'Um . . . Fiona,' I call out.

'Wha . . .' comes back a muffled grunt from her bedroom.

'There's . . . er . . . been a bit of an accident.'

'Huh?' There's a lot of thumping around and Fiona appears, bleary-eyed, hair all mussed up, wearing her animal slippers and coffee-stained dressing gown. I swear, it never ceases to amaze me how she can go from looking like this in the morning – which I call 'normal Fiona' – to the kimono-clad, blow-dried, lip-glossed version known as 'man-spent-the-night' Fiona. It's as though they're two completely different people.

Letting out a giant yawn, normal Fiona looks at me, then at the kitchen floor.

'Oh shit.'

'Exactly,' I nod, pleased that she took the words right out of my mouth and now I don't have to explain.

Tallulah, it appears, isn't yet toilet-trained and has had an accident in the night. In fact, several, I notice, looking at the piles dotted across the lino as if there's been a mole in here.

'Where is she?'

'Hmm, judging by the trail, I think she must have gone that way.' I gesture behind the sofa.

Sleepily she starts shuffling across the kitchen, when suddenly I notice – 'Watch out!' – a hidden pile behind the yucca plant.

It's too late.

'Fuck!' she curses, as her furry animal slipper steps right in it. 'That fucking dog!'

'I thought you said to Pippa she was super-cute?' I reply, my mouth twitching with amusement.

Standing in a pile of dog shit, Fiona's jaw clenches. I can see her loyalties wavering, and for a moment I think she's finally had enough of Pippa. That she's finally seen what she's really like. But then, 'Well yes, Tallulah is super-cute, of *course*,' she says, doing a U-turn and forcing her grimace into a smile. 'Tallulah, sweetie . . .' she calls out, balancing on one leg whilst gingerly trying to slide her other foot out of the offending slipper. 'Come to Mummy's friend.'

There's the sound of scuffling, then a loud meow, and Tallulah scuttles out from underneath the sofa, chased by Flea who also seems to have mistaken her for a tiny rat. 'Aww, look, she's so sweet,' coos Fiona, picking her up. She holds her awkwardly out at arm's length as Tallulah growls and bares her teeth. Fiona is not what you'd call an animal person. She's nervous around them. Not surprising, considering that at school she killed not one, not two, but three class gerbils by over-feeding them, until fearing she would soon have a gerbil massacre on her hands, Miss Douglas, the teacher, had to ban her from being the Gerbil Monitor. Of course it wasn't intentional; I think she was overcompensating for the fact that she was constantly hungry herself.

Still, let's just hope Pippa's puppy doesn't suffer the same fate as Flopsy, Topsy or Mitzy, I think, looking at her with a beat of worry as she feeds her a treat.

'See, she likes me,' she continues, throwing me a see-I'm-not-totally-useless-with-animals look.

'Um, yes, I can see that . . .' I gesture downwards.

Fiona looks at me blankly, then follows my gaze. 'Oh crap!' she wails.

'No, not this time.' I can't help laughing, and together we both watch helplessly as Tallulah pees all over her dressing gown.

Afterwards I feel a bit bad for laughing and offer to help clear up, but Fiona makes a big deal of 'showing me the hand' to silence me. 'Pippa is my friend, and Tallulah is my responsibility,' she says, sniffily. 'And by the way, Flopsy, Topsy and Mitzy were an accident,' she adds defensively. 'How was I to know they couldn't eat pizza? I was only eight.'

I leave her liberally squirting the kitchen with an expensive bottle of designer perfume she's been sent to review in her column – it was her turn to buy air-freshener and as usual she's forgotten and we've run out – and quickly go and get ready. Gramps called yesterday, all excited, to tell me he'd found the perfect buttons for the bag I'm making and I promised I'd go and visit him today. What with work and Seb, I haven't seen him all week.

But first I want to pop into the charity shop where I found the material I'm using.

'Oh, I remember you,' greets the woman behind the counter as I walk inside, 'you bought that old flour sack, didn't you?'

'Yes, that's me,' I smile.

'Thought so. I never forget a face. I remember thinking how funny it was you only wanted that and not any of the clothes that were inside it,' she laughs heartily, causing the glasses that are hanging on a chain around her neck to bounce up and down on her mohair chest. 'So what can I do for you?'

'I wondered if you had any more?' I ask hopefully.

'Well, it's funny you should ask, but the old lady just came by to drop off some more things,' she beams delightedly. 'You just missed her. She's lovely, from France you know . . .'

Damn, I would have liked to have met this mysterious French lady, I muse, glancing towards the pile of cardboard boxes she's left.

'Apparently her husband died not so long ago and she's having a clear-out.'

For the next fifteen minutes I rummage through the belongings of someone else's life: plates that someone has eaten dinners from with family and friends; a vase that's held flowers given by loved ones; a red silk dress no doubt bought for a special occasion, a party maybe . . . I imagine the old French lady wearing this when she was much younger, her husband twirling her around the dance floor in some wonderful hotel in Paris with a chandelier and a band playing, telling her how beautiful she looked . . .

My mind drifts off. That's the wonderful thing about charity shops: everything has a history; everything has a past and memories attached; everything has a story. It's fascinating to imagine what it was, to think about the stranger you're never going to meet, but how their life has touched yours simply through a vase that once belonged to them and is now sitting on your shelf, filled with spring flowers.

I end up finding a couple more brightly patterned flour

sacks and, removing the contents, quickly buy them, along with a pair of old dungarees with leather braces. Then, leaving my number in case the old French lady should drop by again, I go outside and jump on the bus.

For once there's hardly any traffic and, arriving at Hemmingway House, I walk into reception, where I spot Miss Temple talking to another member of staff. Lowering my head, I try to skulk by without her seeing me.

'Ah, Miss Connelly . . .'

But of course it's hopeless. Getting by Miss Temple is how I imagine getting through Checkpoint Charlie used to be. I look over and try to pin on a nonchalant smile.

'Miss Temple,' I nod.

'About your grandfather . . .'

Oh no, what now?

'Could you please remind him that the games room is meant for quiet relax—'

But I don't get to hear the rest of her sentence as it's drowned out by a loud commotion that blasts out from the double doors with the force of an explosion.

Two old ladies, making their way through reception, look startled and cling onto each other.

Oh shite. This time Gramps is going to be in big trouble.

'I'll tell him right away!' I yell, trying to make myself heard above the din and, leaving Miss Temple trying to calm down the old ladies who are saying something about the Blitz, I hurry towards the games room.

Once through the double doors the noise amplifies. And to think I used to assume retirement homes were filled with people quietly embroidering in button-back chairs, I think, heading towards the crowd clustered around a large table in the far corner of the room. As I approach, I can hear an argument going on.

'You can't have that!'

'Yes I bloody well can!'

'But it's disgusting!'

'So what? It's a word, isn't it?'

'*Gramps?*'

Excusing my way past a bald-headed man on a mobility scooter, I catch sight of Phyllis shouting at my granddad, who's thumping his fist on the table. Hearing my voice, he looks up and peers through his half-moon spectacles, his bright blue eyes flicking across faces until he finally spots mine. 'Tess, darling!' he booms, his face lighting up. 'What brings you here?'

'We spoke yesterday and I arranged to come and see you. We were going to work on my bag, remember?' I smile, trying to ignore the worrying thought that his memory seems to be getting even worse. 'Did you forget?'

'Not at all, not at all,' he protests cheerfully. 'I was just playing a game of Scrabble until you arrived.'

Scrabble? It's only then that I notice a Scrabble board on the table.

'This is what all the arguing's about?' I ask, in disbelief.

Forgive me, but there was me thinking Scrabble was a quiet, unassuming board game, and the nearest you got to any kind of excitement was getting a seven-letter word. Not the cause of a near riot.

'He used a rude word,' accuses Phyllis, from across the table.

'Gramps!' I say, shocked.

'It's not a rude word, it's—'

'Don't you repeat that again, Sidney Archibald Connelly,' warns Phyllis, stabbing a bony finger in his direction. 'Or I'll have your guts for garters.'

Crikey. I didn't realise Phyllis could be so scary. There was me thinking she was the nice old lady with the shortbread fingers and a crush on Gramps.

'Maybe we should go now,' I suggest tactfully, raising an eyebrow at him.

'What do you want to bet it's in the dictionary?' he demands, ignoring me and reaching for the thick red-leather-bound volume in the middle of the table.

That's the problem with Gramps. He can be so pig-headedly stubborn.

'Gramps,' I hiss, glaring at him.

'Aye go on, look it up,' jeers the bald-headed man on the scooter, and there's a ripple of dissent from the gathered crowd.

Oh Christ. It's fast turning into a mob mentality. At this rate he's definitely going to be kicked out. Miss Temple is on the warpath and he's on his last warning.

Taking a deep breath, I step into the fray. 'OK, that's it,' I say, doing my best to sound authoritative. 'Game over.' And reaching for the Scrabble board, I fold it firmly in half.

'Awwww.' There's a loud groan of disappointment.

'Sorry,' I say to the other players. 'But if you can't play quietly . . .'

I suddenly realise I'm sounding just like my mother when she used to tell me and my brother off. Which is OK when it's children and you're their parent, but slightly more embarrassing when they're adults with an average age of eighty.

Telling Granddad to 'say goodbye to your friends', I march him back to his room. 'Honestly Gramps,' I tut, plumping his cushions and easing him down on to his leather sofa, 'you're going to get yourself into big trouble one day.'

'I know, I know,' he nods sheepishly, reaching for a bag of Jelly Babies and offering me one. 'It was fun though, wasn't it?' he adds, his eyes twinkling mischievously.

I try not to smile. 'Phyllis was very angry,' I scold, sitting down next to him and sticking my hand in the bag.

'Pah, Phyllis. She likes a good argument, gets the juices

flowing.' He lets out a chuckle. 'Anyhow, it wasn't a rude word, it was—'

'I saw it on the Scrabble board,' I say quickly, cutting him off. Despite my resolve, a giggle rises up inside of me. That's the problem with Gramps: it's impossible to stay angry with him. 'You are terrible, you know,' I tease, elbowing him in the ribs.

He elbows me back, and we both look at each other and break out laughing.

'If Nan was alive she'd make you wash your mouth out with soap,' I giggle.

'She'd do more than that, all right,' he chuckles, but there's a glint of sadness in his eyes and he glances towards a black-and-white photograph on the side table. It's their wedding photograph, taken nearly fifty-seven years ago. They look so young – her in a simple white dress and him in an old-fashioned suit – and they're smiling excitedly at each other, their whole lives ahead of them.

'I do miss her, you know,' he says quietly.

'I know you do,' I nod, the understatement of his words causing a lump in my throat. Reaching out I clasp his worn hand in mine. 'We all do.'

For a moment we stay like that until, giving himself a little shake, as if to stir himself out of the past, he turns to me. 'Now then, young lady, about those buttons . . .' Hoisting himself up from the sofa, he grabs his cane and walks over to his sewing machine table. 'I had a good look through all my old ones I've kept, and I found these . . .' He reaches into a drawer, then falls silent.

'Gramps?' I look across at him. He's just standing very still, a confused look on his face. 'What's wrong?'

'They've gone!' He shakes his head.

'Oh, I'm sure they haven't, they must be there somewhere, you must have misplaced them . . .'

But he doesn't reply, rummaging around in the drawer with increasing frustration.

'Hey, let me help you . . .' I jump up from the sofa and cross the room, but he's already emptying it, the contents scattering on the floor.

'Someone must have stolen them!' He looks up at me, his blue eyes filled with panic.

'Gramps, please, let me help.' His distress is obvious and I feel a clutch of anxiety. This is the behaviour the nurses have been talking about. This isn't just a bad memory. It's more than that. 'No one will have stolen them,' I say reassuringly, trying to calm him down.

'It's not the first time, you know. Things keep going missing,' he accuses, turning back to the drawer.

'Here, are these them?' Out of the corner of my eye I suddenly spot a small bag of buttons on the mantelpiece, and snatching them up I hold them out.

Immediately he stops what he's doing and his face relaxes. 'That's them! You clever girl! Where were they? I didn't see them.'

'Oh . . . they'd fallen on the floor,' I fib. 'They must have slipped when you were emptying the drawer.' I don't want to tell him they were in a completely different place; it will only worry him and he's upset enough.

Or was. Because now he's found the buttons, it's like the storm has passed as quickly as it came, and his calm demeanour has returned. His old self is back and it's as if it never even happened. Like he's forgotten about it already.

'See, aren't they beauties?' he's saying now, emptying the bag's contents into his hand and holding them out for me to see. There, in the criss-crossed palm of his hand, are perfect flat discs. Made from mother-of-pearl that seems to glow and shimmer in the light.

'Gosh, they're perfect!' I break into a smile.

'Aren't they?' He nods, looking chuffed.

'And look, I found these . . .' Now it's my turn and, grabbing my carrier bag, I pull out my charity shop finds. 'Look, it's an old pair of men's dungarees, I thought we could use the leather braces as handles . . .'

'My, you're full of ideas, aren't you?' Taking them from me, Gramps turns them over in his hands, 'Aye, that might work, though we'll need to make sure the leather's stitched firmly into the seam . . .'

'Oh, and I found more vintage flour sacks to make more bags!' I say excitedly.

'Wonderful,' he nods, the corners of his mouth curling up in amusement, 'but perhaps we should finish this one first, hmm?' He lays a steadying hand on my shoulder.

'Oh, yes, of course,' I say quickly, realising I'm getting completely carried away. Familiar doubts prickle. Gramps is right, I need to finish this one first. After all, what if it doesn't work and ends up looking rubbish? Glancing across at my half-finished bag, I feel a sting of self-doubt. It's probably all a stupid idea in the first place anyway.

'Oh, and I wanted to ask you . . .'

I snap back to see Granddad looking at his pocket leather diary. 'I'm having a poker night a week on Friday. Interested?'

'Gramps, you know gambling's against the rules,' I begin, but he waves away my concerns with a flick of his hand.

'In or out?' he challenges.

'In.' I smile ruefully.

'Splendid,' he beams, scribbling down my name.

'Actually, can I bring someone?' I ask, suddenly having a thought. 'Seb, my boyfriend,' I add, waiting for his reaction.

It's as I expected.

'A new boyfriend?' His eyes light up. 'Well, yes, of course I must meet this new chap. See if he's worthy of my granddaughter.'

'Gramps.' I feel myself going red.

'Gramps nothing.' He clicks his tongue and scribbles down something in his diary, then tucks it back into his breast pocket and reaches for his tape measure. 'Righty-ho, let's get cracking,' he says, patting the seat next to him.

Getting up from the sofa, I slide my bottom next to his.

'Just one more thing.'

'What?' I ask, turning to him.

Leaning close, he presses his whiskery cheek to mine. 'This bag is going to be amazing, my dear,' he whispers and, before I can answer, he turns away and fires up his sewing machine.

21

A few hours later I wave goodbye and, telling Gramps to try to keep out of trouble until I see him next week, I head to the shopping centre. Ali, the computer technician, has left a message on my mobile saying my laptop is ready to pick up.

'It was as I thought,' he says gravely, placing my newly fixed computer on the counter in front of me. 'There was a catastrophic motherboard failure due to a head crash where the internal read-and-write head of the device touched a platter, though in this case it was a magnetic data-storage surface, which of course led to severe data loss.' He looks up and, seeing my glazed expression, grinds to a halt in his explanation. 'It works again,' he says simply.

'You're amazing,' I smile.

His mouth twitches. Ali, I've learned, when he's not in shop assistant mode, is not a natural when it comes to smiling. As a baby he probably skipped learning that bit and went straight onto logarithms. Pushing his thick glasses onto the bridge of his nose, he peers myopically at me. 'So, how are things? You seem in much better spirits.'

Reminded of how last time I burst into tears in front of him about Seb, embarrassment prickles. 'Um, yes, great,' I nod, feeling myself blush slightly. 'I got back with my boyfriend,' I confide, in explanation. Well, it's only fair, considering last time he was having to pass me screen wipes for me to blow my nose on.

'So he's not such an idiot after all,' he nods approvingly.

I smile ruefully. 'What about you?'

'Still single,' he shrugs.

'Well then, your ex-girlfriend is still an idiot,' I say firmly.

Unexpectedly, the ever-serious Ali starts laughing.

'What's so funny?' I ask in confusion.

'Boyfriend,' he corrects, his dark eyes flashing with amusement.

It takes a moment, then the penny drops. 'Oh gosh, I'm sorry, I didn't realise—'

'It's fine, don't worry, not many people do,' he says, cutting off my apology. 'It's not easy for an Indian man to be gay. My parents are still not speaking to me; they won't accept me how I am . . .' He shakes his head sadly. 'Still, I'm glad for you. I'm glad your boyfriend realised he made a mistake. It gives me hope that people can change.'

'Yes, they can,' I smile reassuringly, but inside I feel a bit uneasy. Because only now, hearing those words, does it occur to me that there's only one person that's changed.

And it's me.

But then change is a good thing, isn't it? I tell myself firmly as I wave goodbye to Ali. Fiona has a stack of self-help books on her shelf, and when I first broke up with Seb I started reading one and it was all about growing and changing. Admittedly I only got to about page twenty as *The X Factor* came on, but it made the point that we all need to evolve to survive. I mean, look what happened to the dinosaurs!

Leaving the computer shop, I glide down the escalators. The original plan was to pick up my laptop and head straight home, but now I'm here I might as well get a few things, I decide, pausing by a shop window displaying lots of silky lingerie. I desperately need some new underwear. The only sexy stuff I've got is the bra and knicker set that Seb bought me and I can't keep hand-washing it. Before, when it came to my choice of underwear, 'comfort' and 'support' were the key words. But not any more. Now the key words are sexy, plunging and . . .

How much?

Having gone inside, I've pulled a black satin G-string off the rack and am now staring open-mouthed at the price tag. Surely that must be a mistake. £75! For what amounts to pieces of string and a triangle the size of a postage stamp? And as for comfort and support . . . trust me, those words have no place here. In fact, I saw more comfort and support in a medieval torture museum I once visited, I wince, fingering a 'rhinestone playsuit' with a certain trepidation.

Still, it will all be worth it, I tell myself firmly, imagining Seb's reaction when he sees me in it. Plus, I won't be wearing it for very long if the last time in bed is anything to go by, I think naughtily to myself as I scoop one up. Along with several pairs of French knickers, barely there G-strings, peek-a-boo bras and a basque that laces up at the back and is fully boned . . . Gosh, I wouldn't like to wear that after eating a baked potato . . .

Momentarily I feel a wistful twinge for my comfy old T-shirt bras and big knickers. This stuff might look sexy, but it's all so much *effort*. But then, dating Seb first time around I didn't make *enough* of an effort. I wasn't sexy enough. This time it's all going to be different. *I'm* going to be different. This is the new sexy me, remember?

Handing over my credit card to the sales assistant, I try not to look at the total on the machine as I punch in my PIN, but I can't help glimpsing a few noughts. My stomach does that churning thing it always does whenever I press 'check balance' on the ATM, but I try to ignore it. After all, it's not as if I'm *spending* money: I'm *investing* it in my future. Forget cash ISAs, this is like a relationship ISA.

Pleased by my financial brainwave, I leave the shop with my big bag swinging over my shoulder. OK, speaking of investing, what other investments do I need? Ah yes, of course, something a lot less glamorous, but just as necessary. Trying not to give a little shudder, I walk next door into a sports shop. I always find these places really intimidating. All those bouncy, ponytailed assistants in tracksuits, trainers and Madonna-style headsets, ready to pounce on you and make you feel like a total moron for not knowing your Nike Airs from your Asics Gel.

Speaking of . . .

'Hi, can I help you?' chirps an assistant, bouncing over as I stare at the vast display of trainers on the wall, feeling completely overwhelmed.

I take a deep breath. This isn't just the new sexy me, it's also the new sporty me. The one who does all that military fitness. I've signed up for my first class on Monday so I need to get kitted out.

'I need some new trainers,' I say, trying to sound confident and resisting the urge to ask which are the cheapest.

'How long have you had your last pair?'

I think about my old pair that are falling apart and buried in the back of a cupboard and try to remember. 'Um, about five years,' I say vaguely.

The bouncy ponytailed shop assistant's smile slides from her face. 'Five years?' she gapes in horror. 'They need to be replaced every twelve months, six months if you're exercising regularly.' She gives me an accusing look and I can feel my inner thighs wobble.

'Do you overpronate?'

I have no idea what she's talking about, but it sounds painful. 'Um, I'm not sure—'

'And what kind of exercise will you be doing? High impact? Running? Aerobics? Or are we talking more cross-training?'

'Er . . .'

Twenty intimidating minutes later, I leave with new top-of-the range trainers, along with a new gym kit, some leg weights, sweatbands and a gym ball. All this investing can get very expensive. I've completely maxed out my credit card. I don't even have enough money on my Oyster for the bus home and I have to walk back to the flat.

I arrive tired and broke to find Fiona at the kitchen table frowning at her computer screen.

'What's campanology?' she asks, bypassing the hi-how-are-you pleasantries and diving straight into a conversation without any explanation, as only your best friend who's known you for years can.

'Bell ringing,' I reply, dumping my shopping. See, there are advantages to growing up with a father who's addicted to the *Sunday Times* crossword. 'Why, you thinking of taking up a new hobby?'

'No, I got an email from someone on Sassy Soul Mates . . .' She starts reading: '*Hi, my name's Steve and I'm searching for that special someone for a committed loving relationship*—'

'Sounds promising,' I interject encouragingly. 'He mentioned the word "commitment".'

'Exactly,' nods Fiona. 'Unlike the men I've met who can't say it without coming out in a rash.'

'So are you going to go on a date with him?'

'Well here's the thing . . .' She glances back down at her computer screen and continues reading, '. . . *and to share my great passion in life: campanology* . . .' She breaks off and we exchange glances.

'Well, I suppose it's different,' I say, trying to sound positive.

'I'm widening the net, not looking for Quasimodo!' she protests, hitting delete firmly on her keyboard. Looking up, her gaze lands on my bags. 'Oooh, you've been shopping,' she says, diving on them excitedly. Nothing can distract Fiona like a shopping bag. 'Wow, very sexy,' she nods approvingly, pulling out my peek-a-boo bra and holding it up against her own large chest. Fiona is forever complaining that she can never find any nice bras as her boobs are too big and she has to resort to buying these huge, cantilevered things that leave deep red grooves in her shoulders and are deeply unflattering.

Seeing it's way too small, she lets out a little sigh of

disappointment and puts it back reluctantly. 'What else have you . . .' She breaks off as she peers inside the other bag. 'Hang on, who's all this sports gear for?'

'Me,' I say, trying to sound as nonchalant as possible, flicking on the kettle.

'*You?*' Her gaze flicks from the sweatbands and back to me in astonishment. 'But you hate sport!'

'I watched Wimbledon last year,' I say defensively.

'Only because you fancied Nadal,' she reminds me, and we exchange lustful looks. 'The last time you played any sport was netball at school, remember?'

Reminded, I have a flashback of me completely missing the net for the umpteenth time. In all the years I played, I never once scored a goal. 'OK, so maybe I need to work a little on my hand–eye coordination,' I admit, reaching for the teabags and chucking them into two mugs. 'But I'm not that bad.'

The teabags miss completely and land on the floor.

'Anyway, it's not about sport, it's about doing exercise and keeping fit,' I say quickly, avoiding Fiona's gaze and scooping them up. 'As you well know, being a *health* and beauty writer,' I add pointedly.

'I'll have you know I've taken Tallulah for two walks today already,' she boasts proudly.

'Wow, really?' Going to grab the milk from the fridge, I turn to her, impressed. 'Where did you walk, along the river?'

'No, to Primark. Have you seen their sale? It's amazing.'

I burst out laughing. 'You took Tallulah to Primark?' I don't know which is more funny: that Fiona thinks that constitutes taking a dog for a walk, or imagining Pippa's reaction if she knew her beloved puppy had been in Primark and not Prada.

'And Waterstones,' adds Fiona, looking a bit miffed by my reaction. 'I bought a book by the world-renowned dog expert Cesar Millan, *How to Raise the Perfect Dog*.'

'That's great,' I nod, trying to make my face serious. Fiona is obviously taking her dog duties very seriously.

'In fact I think I'll take her out again now,' she continues, shutting her computer and reaching for her coat. 'Tallulah, walkies!' Something stirs on the rug and I notice it's Tallulah. 'You have to establish leadership with your new dog,' says Fiona authoritatively, turning to me. 'It's all about showing who's the alpha.' Looking very pleased with herself, she turns back to Tallulah, who's still curled up on the rug, not moving. 'Walkies,' she repeats, only this time a little more shrilly. Tallulah lazily opens one eye, then promptly closes it, as if to say, *You're out of your mind, woman, it's goddamn freezing out there.*

'What does Cesar say to do if they ignore you?' I ask, trying to stifle a smile.

'Er, well, I haven't got to that bit yet . . .' Snatching up the book, Fiona starts flicking through, then gives up and closes it. 'But I'm sure there are always occasions when you need to take a more hands-on approach.' Clipping on Tallulah's diamanté lead, she tugs on her collar. 'See, I'm not completely useless with animals,' she adds, as Tallulah reluctantly gets up and follows her across the kitchen, dragging her paws. 'The gerbils were just an unfortunate accident.'

'Unfortunate,' I nod in agreement.

She colours up.

'Anyway, is it OK if I borrow your scarf? The red one with the glittery bits?'

'If you can find it,' I reply, kicking off my shoes and hanging up my coat. 'I haven't seen it since you borrowed it last time.' Fiona is always borrowing things and she never puts anything back. 'It could be anywhere . . .' I break off to see it's already tied around her neck.

'Brilliant, thanks,' she smiles brightly. 'Right, must dash.'

Hearing the door close, I flop on the sofa and flick on the TV.

Bliss. At home on Saturday night, slobbing out in front of the TV, just what I feel like. Flea curls up in my lap and, sipping my tea, I reach for the tin of Quality Street that's balanced on the side of the sofa, and dip my hand in it. Except, hang on . . . my fingers scrabble around and, dragging my eyes away from *The X Factor*, I peer inside . . . it's completely empty. Someone's eaten them all!

And of course it isn't Fiona, I think wryly, remembering her vehement denial and how she tried to pin the blame on Flea. I tickle him protectively under his chin and he purrs loudly, oblivious to the fact that he was very nearly the fall guy. 'It's a mystery, isn't it?' I coo, grinning to myself – a complete and utter mystery.

I'm distracted by the shrill ring of my phone. I snatch it up and glance at the screen. It's Seb. I feel a flash of surprise. He's calling me from Geneva!

'Hi,' I say, picking up with delight.

'Hey there,' says Seb with his distinctive American drawl. 'How's it going?'

'Great,' I smile. 'What about you?'

'Great now I'm talking to you,' he replies, and I feel a beat of happiness. It's only been a week but there's no playing games. We can just be totally honest with each other.

'So what are you doing?' he continues cheerfully.

For a split second I think of Seb staying in some five-star hotel in Geneva, about to spend the evening in some swanky restaurant with all his expensively suited business buddies, and suddenly I don't want to admit I'm lying slobbed out on the sofa, watching some random reality show with my cat on a Saturday night.

'I just got back from a military fitness class and a run,' I say, quick as a flash.

Well, honesty isn't *always* the best policy, is it?

'Wow, on a Saturday evening? That's dedication,' he says approvingly.

Plus where's the harm? He'll never know.

'So how far did you run?'

'Oh . . . er . . . not far, about ten miles,' I say, plucking a number out of the air.

'Wow, that's far!' He sounds impressed.

'Yes, isn't it?' I agree. God, why did I go and say ten miles? Three would have done it.

'You must be all sweaty,' he continues wickedly.

'Very,' I reply, playing along. What am I worrying about? I could have said I'd run a marathon, Seb will never know, he's in Geneva. Plus my exercise regime starts on Monday as I've signed up for my first military fitness class, so it's not like I'm *completely* making it up. I'm just getting a bit ahead of myself. I fully *intend* to run ten miles. I just need a bit of practice first, that's all.

'So you'll be needing to get in the shower, won't you?' he continues.

'Well, first I've got to take all my clothes off,' I say flirtily.

'Get all naked you mean?'

'Completely starkers. Just me and a bar of soap.'

'Mmm, sexy,' he says and I laugh.

'So, how did your meeting go?' I ask, steering the conversation back before it gets totally X-rated.

'Awesome,' he enthuses. 'We brokered the deal.'

'Gosh, that's great,' I say, feeling proud of him. I'll never understand Seb's job in the mind-boggling world of finance, but I do know he's incredibly good at it. 'So what are you doing to celebrate?'

'Taking you out for dinner,' he quips.

'Ha ha, very funny,' I quip back.

'Why is it funny?' he asks.

'Well in case you hadn't noticed, I'm not in Geneva.'

'Neither am I.'

'You're not?' I feel a jolt of surprise.

'No, I flew back early to see you.'

'You did?' I sit bolt upright on the sofa, dislodging Flea from my lap. He lets out a disgruntled meow.

'Yeh, I'm just driving back from the airport now and heading over to yours. It's number twenty-seven, right?'

The surprises are coming thick and fast; I'm momentarily lost for words. 'Um . . . yeh,' I manage to croak. 'So whereabouts exactly are you?' Which sounds like a innocuous question, but is really me desperately trying to gauge how much time I have. An hour and I can get in the shower, wash and blow-dry my hair *and* iron my dress. Forty-five and it's a choice between wet hair or a crumpled dress. Less than half an hour and it's both. Fifteen and—

'I'm outside.'

I'm screwed.

Suddenly the buzzer goes and I nearly jump off the sofa with fright.

Fuck!

'Yes, er, that's right,' I say, swallowing hard and trying to keep my voice even when inside another voice is shrieking: you just told him you'd been to military fitness! You told him you'd run ten miles! You told him you were all hot and sweaty and needed a shower! I glance down at myself, sprawled on the sofa in a pair of jeans and sheepskin slippers, with a cup of tea balanced in my lap. I couldn't look less like someone who's just run ten miles if I tried.

'Come right up. Top floor. Flat seven.'

But I have to. *And in less than three minutes!*

Argggh. Putting down my phone, I leap up from the sofa and, tugging off my clothes, race naked around my flat, hiding all traces of cups of tea, shopping bags and aforementioned clothes and tugging on my new leggings, sports bra and sweatbands. Lacing up my trainers, I dash to the mirror in the hallway and glance at my reflection. Only there's something missing . . .

Dashing into the bathroom, I dive into the airing cupboard and grab the spray bottle we keep by the ironing board. I start frantically spritzing my face and chest – I need to look like I'm all sweaty.

In the middle of spritzing I hear a knock. Oh my god, he's here!

By the time I dash to the door and pull it open, I'm genuinely breathless.

'Hey, look at you, all sweaty,' he grins.

'Yes, I know, sorry.' I pull a face.

Wrapping his arms around me he draws me to him for a kiss. 'Mmm . . .'

It's like magic. Suddenly all that panic is forgotten and I feel myself melting into his kiss. Feeling his tongue, I close my eyes as we start kissing deeper and deeper and . . . *That's funny, my face is starting to feel a bit weird.*

In the middle of snogging, the thought zips through my brain, then out again. After all, it's probably because his five o'clock stubble is rubbing against my skin . . . I focus back on the kissing . . . mmm, Seb is such a great kisser.

Like it's going really tight.

Shut up! I'm having a sexy reunion with my boyfriend. I feel Seb's hands wandering across my sports bra . . .

Actually, the word I'm looking for is stiff.

Suddenly I have a flashback to the spray bottle, to Fiona ironing that guy's shirt for work, starching his collar . . .

And suddenly I realise.

Oh my god! I've starched my face!

'I'll just jump in the shower,' I blurt, hastily breaking away.

Panic is shooting through my body. Any minute now and my face is going to set like concrete.

'Oh . . . uh . . . OK,' says Seb, visibly taken aback by my abruptness, I notice, glancing down at his trousers.

'Make yourself at home,' I say hurriedly.

'Sure you don't want me to join you?' he asks, recovering and throwing me a sexy smile.

I try to smile sexily back but my face is having trouble creasing. 'Um no, you stay here, relax, watch TV, I'll be back in a jiffy.' I turn to go.

'Oh, hey, Tess?'

'Yes?' I turn back.

'You've left the sales tags on.' He gestures to my sports bra.

'I have?' I freeze. 'Oh . . . um . . . they must have been on for ages and I didn't notice,' I fluster, trying to twist my arm around to pull them off and nearly dislocating my shoulder.

'Here, I'll do it,' he offers, moving towards me.

'No!' I shriek. 'I mean, it's fine, thanks,' I say quickly, tugging them off with such violence I make a hole.

'Oh, OK,' he shrugs, looking at me as if I'm acting really weird.

Probably because I am acting really weird, I think helplessly.

'Well, wear something nice, I'm taking you to a fancy restaurant,' he says, changing the subject.

'Great!'

'Oh, and don't forget to bring your sneakers this time. We can go for that run we didn't get around to the other morning, work off some of those carbs we're going to consume tonight . . .' He shoots me a smile. 'And it'll be a chance for you to kick my ass,' he jokes, pretending to kick my bottom.

'Ha ha . . . yes,' I laugh, pretending to kick him back but losing my balance and nearly toppling over. 'Just you wait!' And turning back I dash towards the bathroom.

Kick your ass.

Ha ha.

Oh god.

Dear Diary,

Tonight Seb took me to Mala, a super-posh restaurant in Mayfair. It was very romantic though I barely ate anything as I can't eat spicy food. Which was a shame as it all looked really delicious and Seb seemed a bit disappointed. He made some joke about going to Pizza Hut next time. Though, to be honest, I'm not sure if he was joking . . .

22

Fifteen minutes later we're speeding along in Seb's sports car that he's just got back from the garage. 'I had a little accident, smashed my wing mirror,' he grins, as we zip through the streets of London. Despite the freezing cold weather, he's got the roof down and the heaters blasting and I snuggle against the soft, heated leather seats, feeling all warm and snug as he expertly navigates the traffic, the radio tuned to some club music.

I sneak a peek across at him. At his broad shoulders clad in expensive cashmere, the softest kind you can only get from some exclusive shop in Knightsbridge, and not the machine-washable jumpers you find in Gap. He's still sporting that tan, and he's got the kind of strong, square jaw any leading man would kill for. He senses me looking and glances across at me, his mouth breaking into a smile and showing off his perfect, gleaming-white smile.

'So what do you think of the car?'

'It's lovely,' I nod.

'You don't seem very impressed,' he jokes, but I get a sense that he's a little miffed that I haven't raved on about it. When we dated before, I don't remember him bragging about his car, but then I probably didn't notice. Funny, how you often don't notice things first time around, isn't it?

'So where are we going?' I ask, getting off the subject. A list of the restaurants we used to go to zip through my mind. Gosh, I hope it's that Italian in Soho. I really feel like a big plate of pasta.

'One of my favourite restaurants,' he grins as we turn into a cobbled side street.

Hang on, this looks familiar . . .

We pull up outside a large, glass-paned building and a valet parker rushes out to greet us.

Mala. One of the best restaurants in London. Famed for its award-winning, spicy food.

'This looks great,' I enthuse, but my heart plummets. Now I remember. We've been here before and it was a disaster as I couldn't eat anything. It's not that I'm a fussy eater, I just can't eat spicy food; I have no tolerance for it.

For a split second I think about suggesting a different restaurant. But I can't. I was given a second chance for a reason: this time I *have* to get it right.

'The food's delicious,' continues Seb. 'Do you like spicy food?'

'Love it!' I reply emphatically.

I'll just have to eat rice. Or maybe I can do that thing models do where they just move the food around their plates to pretend they're eating. One thing's for certain, I'm not going to mess it up this time.

'Awesome,' he grins. 'You're gonna love this place!'

We walk through the glass doors into the Stygian depths of the lobby. What is it with expensive restaurants and hotels being so dark? Surely they can afford more light bulbs? But then I read somewhere that dim lighting is supposed to equal sophistication.

Although there's nothing sophisticated about fumbling down the staircase, clinging onto the handrail for dear life as I can't see where one step ends and another one starts. Gingerly I put one high heel in front of the other. Unlike Fiona, stilettos are not my footwear of choice.

I follow Seb's lead and we make our way towards the bar, where he orders us both the house cocktail, a lychee martini.

After a few minutes a waiter comes and, taking our drinks, asks to show us to our table. I smile graciously. *Unlike last time.* I cringe at the memory. Well, how was I to know he wasn't trying to clear away my martini before I'd finished it?

A tussle had ensued as I'd tried to cling onto it (well, at fifteen quid a drink those last few dregs were worth at least a fiver) and Seb had had to quickly jump in, like a referee at a boxing match, before I'd release my grip. God, it was so embarrassing.

Still, this time I'm determined everything is going to be *very* different, and as we're led to a discreet booth in the corner of the restaurant, and I slip into my seat as the waiter fluffs out my napkin, I get one of those lovely, rare feelings where, right now, at this precise moment, everything is exactly how I want it to be. At a romantic restaurant, with my boyfriend, who's gazing adoringly at me across the table.

'So, did you miss me while I was gone?' asks Seb, reaching across the table for my hand.

'Of course,' I reply as he interlaces his fingers with mine. I feel a lovely warm glow inside and it's got nothing to do with the martini.

'So what did you get up to while I was away brokering deals?'

I root around for a funny anecdote to tell him. Oh I know! I lean forwards, Seb is going to love this. 'Well, you'll never guess what I did last night,' I enthuse, already giggling as I think about mine and Fiona's fish pedicures. I pause for him to play along and guess, but instead he seems suddenly distracted. I feel a funny vibration. 'What's that?'

'My iPhone,' he replies, snatching it up from the table and glancing at the screen. 'It's an email from the Geneva office.'

Until now I'd forgotten about Seb's iPhone. Ever since we broke up, I've been too busy missing all the good bits to think about all the other bits. It's as if your memory purposefully edits out any annoying habits or things you didn't like about a relationship, and gives you the rose-tinted version instead. A bit like when you throw away all the crap photographs of yourself and just leave the ones where you look nice. So that when you look back on that holiday to Greece last year you have this distorted view that you were a size thinner, had no cellulite, and every day was a good hair day. When, in actual fact, half the time you looked bloody awful, with hair that had gone yellow from the chlorine in the pool, a spare tyre from when you'd forgotten to breathe in – and as for when the sun was shining directly on the backs of your thighs . . . *Ouch!*

But of course those photos are long deleted, and with them your bad memories.

Except now I'm being reminded, I note, as I glance back at Seb, who's tapping away at his screen, and feel a familiar twinge of irritation. This time, however, I'm just going to ignore it. Pretend I don't even notice. I am not, repeat *not*, going to lose my temper and start throwing iPhones out of car windows (in my defence it was to stop him from driving and texting at the same time, which everyone knows is *really* dangerous). Instead, if it happens again, I'm just going to calmly ask him to stop the car and get out and walk.

'Is everything OK?' I ask, as I hear the familiar whooshing sound of an email being sent.

'Fine, just tying up some loose ends,' he nods, putting down his iPhone. 'You were saying?'

Except my earlier enthusiasm has waned now and somehow the story doesn't seem that funny any more. 'Oh, nothing.' I give a little shake of my head.

'Hey Seb!'

A loud American accent causes us to look up to see a rather chubby man in a suit has paused by our table.

'Hey Chris,' beams Seb, jumping up, and there ensues a lot of high-fiving. 'How you doing?'

'Awesome,' beams Chris.

I remember Chris. He's one of Seb's work colleagues. I only met him a few times, but to be honest I was never that keen on him; he always seemed a bit fake. Whenever I saw him, he could never remember my name and seemed more interested in showcasing a new Porsche and a new blonde.

'I saw you just as we were leaving.' He gestures to an attractive blonde in a cocktail dress.

See, some things never change.

'Anna, I didn't see you there,' smiles Seb, leaning in to give her a kiss. 'Hey Tess, meet two really good friends of mine,' he says, turning to me. 'Guys, this is Tess. *My girlfriend*,' he adds emphatically, and I feel a flicker of delight.

'Hi,' I smile widely. This time around I'm going to try to make more of an effort. After all, he is one of Seb's colleagues.

'Wow, great to meet you.' Chris kisses me enthusiastically on both cheeks; meanwhile Anna is a lot more tight-lipped. Her eyes do the classic 'once-over' to see if I'm any competition. Obviously deciding I'm not, she proffers a hand.

'Hi,' she says tightly. Anna, it would seem, is not as friendly as her American boyfriend, but hails from somewhere near Chelsea and is a fully paid-up member of the Pippa brigade.

'Well, look, we don't want to keep you from your dinner,' Chris is saying. 'Let's catch up later.' He claps Seb vigorously on the back, like you would if you were trying to stop someone choking and, slipping his hand around Anna's tiny waist, strides off through the restaurant.

'Awesome couple, aren't they?' comments Seb as we sit back down.

I look at him in astonishment. That's what he thinks is a great relationship? Two fake people with zero love between them?

'Um, yes, awesome,' I fib in agreement. I don't want to offend him about his friends, but it does make me wonder: is that what he's hoping for *our* relationship to be like?

'So, where were we?' smiles Seb, as we sit back down and he picks up a menu.

Well, you were on your iPhone and I was resolving that it wasn't going to annoy me any more, I can't help thinking, but instead I say, 'My granddad's having a poker night soon and I was wondering if you wanted to come. I'd like you to meet him . . .'

'Mmm, sure . . .' he nods, focused on the menu. 'How about the spicy shrimp to start with?'

I break off as I realise that Seb isn't actually listening to a word I'm saying.

'Um, yes, that sounds good,' I say flatly.

Seb looks up and, catching my expression, creases his face into an apology. 'Sorry, I got distracted. The food here's amazing.'

'It's OK,' I smile. 'It wasn't important.'

'Of course it was,' he protests, putting his hand over mine and squeezing it against the white linen tablecloth. 'Everything you say is important.'

'Well, I was just talking about my granddad,' I say, emboldened. 'He wanted to invite you to one of his poker evenings – not this Friday but the next.'

'Hey, count me in, poker's my game,' he enthuses.

'You sure you can come?'

'Try and stop me,' he grins, and I feel a wave of happiness. It's really important to me that Seb and Gramps like each other, and this time I'm certain they're going to hit it off. I just know it.

I'm still feeling all happy when the waiter reappears to take our order. 'Would you like to hear the specials?' he asks cheerfully.

Seb looks thrilled. 'Sure,' he nods, throwing me a smile across the table as if to say 'Isn't this great?', while I listen anxiously as the waiter reels off a huge list of dishes, each one sounding hotter and spicier than the next.

'Do you do prawn crackers?' I ask hopefully, after he's finished.

The waiter almost visibly curls his lip. 'No, we don't do *prawn crackers*,' he says, repeating the words as if they're beneath him.

'We're not in your local Chinese now,' laughs Seb, and I feel myself colour up.

'I know – I just thought maybe to snack on . . .'

'Don't worry, we'll order plenty,' he smiles, 'you won't be hungry,' and he expertly reels off a long list of dishes: pan-fried dumplings with chilli oil, firecracker beef, Kung Pao chicken, spicy Szechuan noodles . . .

With every dish I feel my stomach blanching. Crikey, that's a ton of food.

Finally he breaks off and looks at me across the table. 'What do you feel like, Tess? Anything special? I've ordered some of my favourites for us to share.'

I glance nervously at the menu. There's little illustrations of chillies next to each dish, signifying how hot they are. Most of them seem to be either very hot or incendiary.

'Gosh, I don't know; to be honest I'm not *that* hungry.'

'After all that exercise?' protests Seb. 'Come on, you must be starving! A ten-mile run burns off a ton of calories. You're going to need to eat a lot of food to replenish your fuel reserves.'

'I am?' I squeak.

'Totally,' he says, serious-faced.

'Well, if that's everything,' interrupts the waiter.

'Actually, there is one more thing,' I say, turning to him. 'Could I order a bottle of water? A very large one.'

I brace myself. By the looks of things, I'm going to need it.

The rest of the evening slips away in an eye-watering blur of sizzling hot plates, tongue-scorching noodle dishes and more red-hot chilli peppers than you could shake Anthony Kiedis at.

Each dish is hotter than the next and I have to keep dabbing my face with my napkin to stop the sweat from pouring down. At one point Seb is feeding me with chopsticks and I actually remember a story I once read about someone who died from eating a chilli.

But I'm resolute. By some amazing miracle I've been given a second chance at making Seb fall in love with me. I can't waste that! I'm going to do this date differently if it kills me so, screwing up my courage and my taste buds, I try each and every dish. Thankfully I manage to survive and am relieved to make it back to Seb's apartment where we cuddle up on the sofa.

Now this is more like it, I think, snuggling up to him.

'Can I try the nook?' I ask, tilting my face to his as he wraps his arm around me.

'The what?' Seb peers at me, his brow crumpling questioningly.

'You know, *the nook*,' I repeat, then seeing his blank expression, reprimand teasingly, 'Don't you know what the nook is?'

'Erm, no,' he replies, looking vaguely amused. 'Should I?'

'Absolutely,' I admonish.

'I'm a fast learner,' he smiles, a glimmer in his eyes.

'Well, in that case . . .' I twist my body around and nudge my shoulder underneath his armpit, wriggling my body into the gap between his ribcage and the crook of his arm. I used to love lying in the nook with Seb. It's one of the million things I missed so much when we broke up. 'It's this space right here, you see, a little hidden spot that you can fit right into – that's why it's called the nook.'

Only for some reason, now it doesn't seem to quite fit. Which is really odd, I think, feeling slightly disconcerted.

'Are you sure about this?' he laughs. 'Maybe we need a cushion,'

'No, you don't need a cushion,' I say, wriggling a bit more.

'Ow, I hurt my shoulder at the gym,' he winces.

'Oh sorry,' I apologise, quickly adjusting my position. 'Is this OK?'

He fidgets for a bit. 'Yeh, it's fine now,' he says. 'You?'

'Yeh, fine,' I nod.

Though to be honest it's not as comfy as I remember. In fact, to tell the truth my neck's now twisted at a funny angle and my arm's a bit squashed. A bit like after you've had sex and you're lying curled up together and your arm goes numb but you don't want to say anything.

Anyway, it doesn't matter, as I soon forget all about the pins and needles tingling in my arm as Seb starts kissing the side of my face. 'You know, I find a girl who can eat hot spicy food like you can very, very sexy . . .'

'Really?' I feel a thrill.

'Totally,' he murmurs as he runs his fingers underneath my dress. 'Wow, what's this?' he says approvingly, as he discovers my new basque.

'Do you like it?' I smile flirtily.

'Like it? I *lurvve* it . . .' He trails off, his breath hot and ragged in my ear.

'Mmmm.' I lie back, happy with anticipation and pleased at the effort I've made. His hands move up my thighs and I feel a shiver of anticipation. God, I love this bit.

He starts kissing me, and it's all getting hot and heavy when suddenly my stomach makes a growl.

'Ooh, sorry,' I giggle with embarrassment, but he shushes me with his lips and starts kissing me deeper.

The excitement heightens, and he starts kissing those delicious erogenous zones behind my ears. I let out an involuntary moan.

And a loud burp.

Oh my god, I'm so embarrassed.

I quickly cover my mouth, but thankfully he's so engrossed

he doesn't appear to have noticed and I abandon myself to the feeling of his lips on my breasts as he starts to unlace my basque. I can feel him hard beneath my inner thigh. I can feel his urgency.

Then I feel something else. A sort of rumbling.

Oh no.

Please, no.

I can hardly bear to think the thought. One way of putting it would be that I'm a little gassy. Another would be that *I need to fart.*

Horror flashes through my body as I desperately try to hold it in, but now I can feel another rumble brewing. It's all that spicy food. I knew I shouldn't have eaten it. I can't eat spicy food. My stomach hates it.

And now it's payback time. I flinch with terror as Seb reaches for my French knickers and tries to peel them off.

I cling onto them desperately.

'Playing hard to get?' he grins, tugging them harder.

'Um, something like that . . .' I try to giggle in a nonchalant, sexy way, while clenching my buttock muscles tightly. My stomach gives another rumble. Louder this time.

Somewhere in the recesses of my brain, I remember a bit of mindless information about how a volcano rumbles for approximately five minutes as a warning before it erupts.

Oh Christ. I'm going to erupt. *Like a volcano.*

For a few moments more, I try to focus back on having sex with Seb. I'm a seductress, remember! I need to prance around in my basque! Jumping up from the sofa, I get up to do a bit of prancing while Seb settles back on the sofa, arms behind his head. 'Mmm, sexy,' he murmurs approvingly.

I give a little appreciative wiggle. Then I realise something else. Something much *much* more terrifying than any volcano.

It's not just gas.

'Sorry, I won't be a moment, I've just got to—' I don't even get to finish my sentence, or register Seb's surprised face as with my legs crossed I make an awkward dash across the living room.

Argh. I need the loo. Quick!

23

'That's so strange, I must have caught a bug from somewhere.'

Fast-forward to Sunday morning, and I've just crawled back into bed after spending the last twelve hours doing a relay between the bedroom and the bathroom. Last night my stomach staged a revolt from all that spicy food and I was held hostage on the loo for hours at a time. At one point I actually fell asleep with my head in the sink.

But of course I can't admit the truth to Seb, can I?

'There's probably a virus going around,' he nods sympathetically, passing me a glass of water and two aspirin. 'It's that time of year. Here, take this.'

'Thanks,' I say gratefully, giving him a little smile and taking a sip. There's an ominous growl from my abdomen, rather like when a dog bares its teeth to warn you it's going to attack. I brace myself. Oh no, please god no. I know I wanted to do things differently, but I think maybe this time I went a bit too far. Making Seb happy is one thing, but making myself ill is something else.

Still, he is being very sweet, playing nursemaid and looking after me. I'm a very lucky girl to have such a caring boyfriend.

'OK, well I better dash,' he says, checking his watch.

I feel a beat of surprise. *He's leaving?* 'Where are you going?' I ask as he pads quickly across the bedroom floor and disappears inside his walk-in wardrobe.

'For my run,' he replies, his voice muffled, before

reappearing a few seconds later in his tracksuit. 'I know we were going to go together, but now you're sick . . .' He trails off.

'Of course, you go ahead.' I force a bright smile. The only running I'm doing now is in the direction of the loo. 'So when will you be back?'

'Probably later this afternoon. I'm going to hit the gym afterwards, do some weights, have a sauna. I like to do a proper workout at the weekends.'

'Oh, I see.' For some reason I was assuming he'd only be gone an hour. 'Well, have fun, and don't worry about me,' I set about reassuring him, along with myself. So what if Seb isn't going to stay home today and keep me company? I'm not disappointed, I totally understand. OK, I admit, if the tables were turned I wouldn't leave him, but girls are different, aren't they?

'You should just stay in bed, watch TV.' He gestures to the giant flat screen pinned on the wall of the bedroom.

'Yes, I will,' I nod. Actually, maybe it will be nice to be home alone. Watch TV. Rest. I still feel physically weak and want to stay near the loo. I don't want to be caught out like last night.

As my memory flicks back, I give a little shudder. I can still barely think about my expensive sexy new lingerie. It's lying ruined, hidden in the bottom of my handbag as I wasn't, how shall I put this delicately, *quick enough*. I swear, spicy food should come with a government health warning: 'Could seriously damage your sex life *and* your underwear.'

'Oh, before I forget, I've got a friend's wedding coming up and I wondered if you'd be my guest,' he asks casually, doing a hamstring stretch.

'*A wedding?*' At the mention of the word, all thoughts of my ruined underwear are forgotten and I feel a rush of delight. He's asking me to accompany him to his friend's wedding. *Already.*

'Well not really a friend,' he qualifies, 'more a colleague.'

My mind is racing ahead. Who cares whose wedding it is? Everyone knows a guy has to be really serious about you before he invites you to a wedding. It's an unspoken rule. You don't take your girlfriend to see another couple waltz up the aisle unless you want to follow them up there. It's like a public declaration – you might as well put an announcement in *The Times* which says, 'Here she is, everyone, my future wife!'

'When is it?' I ask, trying not to look too excited. Gosh, I wonder what I should wear? I'll need to get a new dress. And some new shoes.

'A week from Wednesday, but it's just a lunchtime thing at a register office. They're both lawyers and have afternoon meetings scheduled . . .' He lets go of an ankle and bends his body in a side stretch. 'What do you say?'

Oh wow, yes, I'd be delighted, what time shall we meet, do I need to get a gift . . . ?

The words are stacked up on the runway like aeroplanes about to fly out of my mouth when suddenly I remember the last time we went to a wedding. The bouquet. The row. Seb telling me he didn't believe in marriage.

Actually, on second thoughts . . .

'No, I don't think so,' I say, slamming on the brakes and promptly doing a U-turn.

Seb pops back up from his side stretch and looks at me in surprise. Obviously that wasn't the response he was expecting.

'You don't have to take time off work. It's just a quick "I do", a glass of champagne, and then back to the office,' he justifies quickly.

'It's not that,' I say, shaking my head.

'It's not?' He crumples up his forehead. 'Then what is it?'

I swallow hard and cross my fingers underneath a cushion. 'I don't believe in marriage.'

'You don't?' He looks at me in astonishment. To be fair, I'm probably the first girl that's ever said this to him.

'And . . . er . . . I think it would be hypocritical of me to go to a wedding when I feel this way,' I continue firmly. Put like that, I actually feel quite proud of myself for sticking by my principles. Even if they don't happen to be real. 'I hope you understand.'

Seb is still looking at me in amazement. Like he can't quite believe his ears. 'Oh wow, totally,' he says, finding his voice. 'I'm exactly the same. I don't believe in it either. I'm like, why get married? It's such an outdated institution and a total waste of money.'

'I know, right?' I agree, and roll my eyes. 'All that expense for just one day!'

I'm actually getting into this; in fact I'm starting to convince myself. I mean, maybe Seb is right. Maybe marriage has no place in the modern world and all this time I've just been really old-fashioned. After all, isn't this what feminists have been going on about for years? Isn't this what my mother burned her bra for? Well, not my mother *personally*.

'I just don't get all these girls that are obsessed with the dress and the big white wedding and the honeymoon on safari!' I snort.

OK, I confess, going on a safari for my honeymoon has always been a fantasy of mine. It just seems so romantic: floating in a hot-air balloon above the Serengeti with your new husband; driving out into the bush at daybreak to spot lions and elephants with the man you're going to spend the rest of your life with; sipping gin and tonics by the campfire at sunset, making plans for your future together . . .

But then who's to say you can't just go on a safari anyway? You don't have to be married.

'I mean *honeymoon schmoneymoon*,' I huff dismissively.

Seb is nodding away vigorously like he's really identifying.

'Seriously, what's the big deal about a piece of paper?' I continue emphatically. 'Why can't two people just live together?'

'Totally,' he enthuses, gazing at me as if he's just found a kindred soul.

'It's like I always say . . .'

'*If it ain't broke, don't fix it,*' we both say in unison.

There's a pause as we both look at each other, marvelling at this new bond between us. It's as though we're suddenly closer than ever.

'It's just with them being colleagues, I feel like I have to go,' says Seb sheepishly. 'Would you mind coming with me? It will only be like an hour. Ninety minutes max.' He looks at me beseechingly. 'I'd be really grateful.'

I take a few moments to think it over – though, let's be frank, I only really need a second. 'Well . . . OK,' I sigh magnanimously, while making a note to self: No catching the bouquet this time.

'Awesome!' grins Seb, his face lighting up and revealing his perfect white teeth. My stomach flips over and this time it's got nothing to do with the spicy szechuan noodles. Gosh, he really is handsome. 'I owe you big time.'

'Don't mention it,' I smile, but inside I feel a happy glow.

'In fact I know how I can repay you . . .'

'You do?' I smile, but I feel a slight twitch of anxiety. Oh god, I hope he's not going to get all fruity; after last night I'm really not feeling up to doing any tricks.

But instead of moving closer, he strides over to some shelves that are filled with DVDs. 'Wow, why didn't I think of this before?' he's saying excitedly. 'You're gonna be stoked!'

'Great,' I smile bemusedly. Seb is so cute when he gets all animated about something.

'*Ta-daah!*' Triumphantly he pulls out a large box. 'Here it is!'

'Here's what?' I laugh.

'Only the special digitally re-mastered edition boxed set of *Star Wars: The Complete Saga Episodes I to VI*.' His face is flushed with exhilaration. 'The entire series!'

Abruptly I feel a sinking dread.

'All six movies,' he continues enthusiastically. 'And in Blu-ray!'

I stare at him, my brain slowly registering. Oh my god, this cannot be happening. What happened to spending Sunday lazing in bed watching *EastEnders*?

Suddenly an entire day of never-ending galactic battles is stretching out in front of me . . . All digitally re-mastered and in high definition.

'It's the director's cut, so it's got all the extra behind-the-scenes footage, and special interviews, and there's even some never-seen-before special effects that were deleted . . .'

My smile is frozen. There are no words.

'I knew that would cheer you up and put a smile on your face,' grins Seb, misinterpreting my horrified silence for one of delight. 'Just think, you can lie here all day and watch it, you don't have to move.' He's already sliding out the silver discs.

That's exactly what I *am* thinking, and it's terrifying me. One *Star Wars* film was bad enough. But now I've got to watch *six*? *Back to back*? It's like a life sentence.

'Actually, you know, maybe I'll just watch TV – these DVD controls seem really complicated,' I say, finally managing to find my voice. I wave the remote and pull an 'I'm-such-an-idiot-when-it-comes-to-anything-technical' face.

'No, not at all, they're super-easy,' enthuses Seb, steamrollering me. 'I've got this new DVD recorder, it can load six discs at a time so you don't even have to do anything.' He presses a button and a holder pops out, and he starts merrily inserting discs. 'It'll run for hours. Just press play.'

'Brilliant,' I croak.

'Isn't it?' he grins, pressing play on the remote for me.

'In that case, why don't you skip the gym and stay and watch them with me?' I try vainly. Well, if I've got to watch them, I might as well have the fun of cuddling up to Seb.

But it's no good. 'Sorry, I gotta run.' He pulls a face. 'Enjoy!'

'Oh . . . OK, you too.'

It's as though he's almost desperate to leave.

Then, with a quick peck on my forehead, he's out of the bedroom. I hear the door of the flat close behind him and theme music starts blasting:

'*A long time ago in a galaxy far, far away . . .*'

My stomach growls loudly. Oh no, not again . . .

24

By the time Monday rolls around, I've finally managed to get off the loo long enough to make it to the office. Briefly I toyed with the idea of taking a sickie, but I didn't want to let Sir Richard down, plus there's no way I could stomach any more sci-fi movies. Mala's chilli beef hotpot *nearly* killed me, but Seb's entire DVD collection might just have finished me off.

Still, there is a bright side: not only are Seb and I growing closer than ever, I've lost those five pounds I haven't been able to shift since Christmas. Sitting at my desk, I take a sip of Pepto-Bismol (sadly I had to forgo my usual triple latte this morning in favour of the pink stuff). Maybe I should suggest it to Fiona as an alternative to one of her fad diets.

An image flashes across my brain of Fiona ingesting raw chillies – she's never one to do things by halves – followed by another image of our shared bathroom being out of bounds for the next week.

Then again, on second thoughts, perhaps not . . .

Focusing back on the paperwork on my desk, I start making a pile of invoices. I'm busy sorting out the arrangements for Sir Richard's retirement party, which is happening at some swanky private members' club in Mayfair next month. *Next month!* At the thought I'm seized by a clutch of worry. I've been trying to block the reality of Sir Richard leaving out of my mind, brush it away as some fuzzy, blurry event that's going to happen in some way-off distant future. Except I can't put off the reality forever. It *is* happening, and I *do* have to think about it.

OK, so this is what I know so far:

1) They've been interviewing several candidates for his job.

2) Much to everyone's dismay, it turned out the rumours were true and one of them was Wendy (a collective groan went around the office when she went in for her interview with the board).

3) As yet there's still been no announcement about who's going to replace him.

4) But I do know that whoever they choose, I'll have to reapply for my job as it was only ever a temporary contract.

My stomach knots at the prospect. Sir Richard said he'd write me a wonderful reference, but who am I kidding? I'm never going to make PA of the Year. In fact, it's probably pointless me even applying. Even if by some fluke I did get the job, my new boss is never going to be like Sir Richard. And it could even be Wendy, I remind myself with a shudder. Which leaves me . . . where exactly? Out of work? On the dole? PA to a boss who hates me?

Heaving a sigh, I make a mental note to call up some temping agencies this afternoon. Maybe I can find another contract. One that requires someone who can type with only two fingers, create Excel spreadsheets with too many cells that crash for no reason and can do a really good impression of the answering machine.

Exactly. I'm sure there's heaps of jobs like that just waiting for me.

Collecting up the pile of papers that need Sir Richard's signature, I make my way to his office. His door is ajar and when I poke my head around the corner I see he's not there. He's probably doing what he calls his 'walkabout'. Sir Richard has a policy of being friendly with all his staff and on Monday he tends to do the rounds after the weekend, catching up with everyone, seeing how everyone is. As a CEO he really is one in a million.

Oh well, never mind, I'll just leave him a note, I decide, entering anyway. I make my way across his office towards his desk and am just popping the papers next to his laptop when he comes back in.

'Good morning Sir Rich—'

I'm stopped in mid-greeting as he charges towards me and almost flings himself on top of his laptop, snapping closed the lid under his weight. 'Ah, Tess, yes, good morning,' he puffs, trying to appear nonchalant as he lies prostrate over his desk.

Startled, I stare at him for a moment before quickly recovering. 'Is . . . um . . . everything OK?'

'Yes, fine, fine,' he nods, smoothing down his comb-over and pushing his glasses up his nose.

I wait for him to move. Except he doesn't. He remains lying there, head resting on his elbow, as if in some bizarre bikini pose.

'And you?' he says chirpily, as if everything is perfectly normal.

'Um . . . yes,' I say unsurely. His behaviour is off the wall, even for Sir Richard. Out of the corner of my eye I notice there's one of those little webcams on the desk. What on earth is he up to?

'Well, unless you need me for anything . . .' he trails off, and I suddenly remember the papers.

'Oh, yes, sorry. I need your signatures on these.' I gesture to the pile of invoices and forms. 'If I just leave them here . . .'

'I'll get them signed and straight back to you,' he finishes, still not moving.

'OK, great,' I smile brightly and, leaving him still lying there, I turn and walk out of his office.

What on earth was all *that* about?

I'm still thinking about it when I get back to my desk to find my phone ringing. I snatch it up. 'Hello, Blackstock and White, Sir Richard's PA speaking.'

'You dirty stop-out!'

It's Fiona.

'Where were you all weekend?' she demands teasingly. 'I nearly sent out the search and rescue services.'

'I'm sorry, I meant to text,' I smile, winding the telephone cord around my hand and sinking back into my chair.

'But you got distracted with all that love stuff,' she finishes, inhaling loudly on a cigarette.

'Something like that,' I say, feeling myself blush. 'So how are you? How's Tallulah?' I ask, focusing back on her before I get all gooey.

As if on cue there's a sharp barking in the background and I hear scuffling.

'Oh, coming along. I'm taking her to an obedience training class tonight,' she replies airily, but her voice rises sharply. 'So, things are really hotting up between you and Seb, then?' she says, swiftly changing the subject.

'Yes . . . I think so,' I reply, reaching for my bottle of Pepto-Bismol. 'Hotting' quite literally being the operative word, I grimace, taking a hefty sip.

'Well, if a guy wants to spend all weekend with you, it sounds like he's really serious,' she reasons.

I nod wordlessly, but doubt prickles. It's not that I don't think Seb is serious. He invited me to a wedding, remember? But is spending all day Sunday by myself watching *Star Wars* films while Seb is at the gym, the same as spending all weekend together? I'm distracted by the sight of Sir Richard emerging from his office and heading towards my desk. 'Hang on a mo,' I hiss, quickly covering the receiver with my hand.

'Here you go.' He waves the pile of papers at me. 'All signed,' he says cheerfully.

'Oh, thanks,' I reply, taking them from him.

'Who was that?' demands Fiona as he strides away.

'Sir Richard, my boss,' I answer, taking my hand off the receiver. 'I went into his office earlier and asked him to sign these invoices for his retirement party—'

'Uh . . . mmm . . .'

I can tell Fiona has already lost interest and zoned out. Individually the words 'office', 'invoices' or 'retirement' are enough to send her to sleep; strung together in a sentence and I'm amazed she's not already comatose.

' – and he was acting really weird.'

She snaps back. 'Weird? How?'

Now someone acting weirdly is a different matter altogether.

I pause and surreptitiously glance around to make sure no one is listening. There's only Kym nearby and as usual she's engrossed in her Missed Connections. I slink down further behind my computer. 'Well, you know he's getting divorced,' I whisper into the mouthpiece.

'Hmmm, do I?' she says vaguely.

Admittedly I don't take my work home with me so maybe I haven't mentioned it. My mantra's always been, 'What happens in the office, stays in the office'.

'Well, anyway, I was just in his office, and when he saw me in there he slammed his laptop shut and looked really secretive. It was like he was up to something.'

'Well of course he's up to something,' she snorts, as if it's obvious.

'*He is?*' I say in surprise, then quickly lower my voice again. 'What?'

'Internet porn,' she replies matter-of-factly.

I gasp in horror. 'No, not Sir Richard!' I protest.

'Divorced, lonely . . .' she continues.

At that moment an email pings through to Sir Richard's email account, to which I have access. It's from an 'undisclosed website' and tells me that his '*credit card payment for the subscription fee has been processed and you now have full member access, including all videos and live webcams.*'

I stare at it, frozen. Oh my god. Fiona's right!

'Trust me, we did an article on it at *Saturday Speaks*, one of those real-life stories . . .'

But I'm no longer listening. I'm trying to imagine Sir Richard—

I slam on the cerebral brakes. *Argh, no!* Stop it, Tess. Scrub that image from your brain right this minute. Giving myself a little shake, I quickly compose myself. I'm being immature. After all, there's nothing wrong with a grown man using such a . . . *an online resource.* I mean it's perfectly normal. Everyone has needs. Even Sir Richard—

Oh god, I'm doing it again. Stop it.

'Fiona, I need to get back to work,' I say abruptly.

In full flow about someone who was addicted to internet porn and ran up thousands in credit card debt, she breaks off. 'Oh, OK,' she says cheerfully. 'No worries, see you later.'

'Yeh, bye.'

'Bye.'

Putting the phone down, I stare at the email for a second more, chewing my thumbnail, then with a flick of my mouse I quickly hit delete.

For the rest of the morning I get on with work and try to put all thoughts of Sir Richard out of my mind. Like I said, he's a grown man – it's his business what he gets up to. But still I try to avoid him, and when I need a signature on a letter, I have a flashback to the email reference to 'live webcams' and initial it myself, rather than go to his office. Well, I don't want to interrupt anything, do I?

So I'm quite relieved when it gets to lunchtime and I can escape to the café across the street to meet Fergus. He left a message with Kym earlier that he needed to speak to me urgently.

'What's up?' I ask, squeezing between the tables and plopping myself down opposite him. He looks as if he hasn't shaved all weekend and is almost sporting a beard, while his thick black hair is sticking out in crazy tufts all over his head.

'Two days twenty-three hours and eight minutes,' he deadpans.

''Scuse me?' I look at him blankly. I know I'm late as I had to send an urgent fax, but I'm not that late.

'And I'm still waiting.'

'Sorry Fergus, you've lost me.'

'My Missed Connection!' he gasps, as if it's obvious.

Suddenly the penny drops. 'Is this what was so urgent?'

He looks at me as if to say how could I ask such a question. 'She hasn't replied!' he says pointedly.

'*Yet*,' I add, equally pointedly.

A waitress appears and puts a large baked potato down in front of him, heaped high with sour cream, cheese and black beans. 'Can I get you anything?' she asks, turning to me.

'Just a plain potato, thanks,' I reply, looking at Fergus's plate warily. Sadly I'm zero topping. I daren't risk it. Not after Mala.

'She's not going to, I just know it,' continues Fergus, as the waitress disappears. He eyeballs his smartphone, which sits silently on the table between us. 'It was a stupid idea, I'm an *eejit*.'

'She probably didn't even see it,' I argue. 'How do you even know she reads Missed Connections?'

'Hmmm.' He looks unconvinced and opens his mouth to say something, then seems to change his mind. 'So what are you up to this week? Anything fun?' he asks, digging into his potato.

I run though my diary in my head. Last week I signed up for military fitness and tonight's my first class. Earlier I was a bit worried I wasn't going to make it because of my stomach, but now I'm feeling back to normal. Still, I'm not sure it's exactly what I'd call fun. Then there's the wedding Seb invited me to, but that's not till next week anyway, plus I know enough about men to know it's unlikely Fergus would class that as fun either.

'Seb's taking me to a concert tomorrow night,' I proffer instead. He managed to get two tickets on eBay for one of his favourite bands and he just texted earlier to tell me the good news.

'Ah yes, I forget, some of us have a love life,' he says glumly.

Which reminds me . . . Ignoring Fergus, I grab a pen out of my bag and scribble on my hand.

'What does that say?' he asks, trying to read my terrible handwriting.

'Earplugs,' I say, turning my hand around to show him the black scrawl.

'Am I that boring?' he frowns sulkily.

'No, silly, they're for the concert.'

'You're wearing earplugs at the concert?' Fergus looks bewildered. 'Forgive me if I'm getting this wrong here, but don't you usually go to concerts to actually *listen* to the music?'

My cheeks grow pink. 'Well usually, yes, but it's not my kind of music.'

'Who's playing?'

'Some indie band I've never heard of,' I say, wrinkling my nose.

'You don't like indie music?'

I look at Fergus in his torn Ramones T-shirt and feel slightly defensive. 'Nope. I'm afraid I'm a lot more naff than that.'

'How naff?' he grins.

'Very naff,' I smile ruefully.

'The Nolans?'

I burst out laughing.

'What's wrong?' he says with a straight face. 'They happen to be a highly successful Irish band, I'll have you know.'

I stop laughing and look at him curiously. He is joking, right?

'"I'm in the Mood for Dancing" was a number one hit.'

'It was?' I look at him in surprise. Gosh, no, I don't think he is joking; in fact he seems deadly serious.

'In Japan,' he adds solemnly.

'Japan, wow, that's amazing,' I enthuse. Gosh, I hope I haven't offended him. He's probably really proud of them because they're Irish. In fact, maybe they're a national treasure, like the Queen is for us Brits.

'I know, right?' he nods earnestly. 'But then it's a brilliant song, isn't it?'

'Brilliant,' I agree fervently, 'really catchy.'

'And the harmonising . . .' Shaking his head in deference, he says in a low voice. 'Respect.'

'Respect,' I nod, trying to look suitably reverential.

He pauses, then clears his throat. I feel a stab of alarm. Oh no, he's not going to do what I think he's going to start doing. Not here in the middle of the café—

But he is. And he does.

His voice is loud and baritone and I stare at him, frozen, as he starts singing 'I'm in the Mood for Dancing'. I'm not sure which is more startling, the fact that he's broken into a Nolans song in the middle of a busy café and people are staring, or that he's actually got quite a good voice. 'Come on, harmonise,' he cajoles.

'Um, no, I don't think so,' I start to protest, but he nags louder.

'*Come on . . .*'

Oh fuck. You know when you *just know* you're not going to be able to get out of something. My heart sinks. I'm a terrible singer. And yet I don't want to offend him.

Swallowing hard, I join in.

'*Atta* girl,' he grins.

And after a few seconds I realise that actually, I'm not that bad and I'm really quite enjoying it and I'm closing my eyes and doing the chorus and . . .

Hang on, what happened to Fergus?

Realising I can't hear his voice, I snap open my eyes to see him keeled over the table, killing himself laughing.

'You bastard!' I gasp.

'I'm sorry, I couldn't resist,' he cracks up. 'That was classic.'

'*Harmonising?*' I cry, bashing him with my hand.

'Ouch.' He clutches his stomach.

Despite myself, I can't help breaking into laughter. 'So anyway, what are you up to this week?' I ask a few moments later, after I've wiped my eyes with a paper napkin and sworn I'm going to get him back.

'Probably what I've been doing all weekend,' he shrugs.

'What's that?' I ask curiously.

He gestures to his phone, lying silent on the table. 'Staying in, checking my emails.'

25

At exactly six o'clock I turn off my computer and race out of the office to catch the tube to Wimbledon for my first-ever military fitness class. I don't want to be late. I already filled in the form online and got ready in the Ladies loos at work. I'm wearing my new sports gear: black Lycra leggings, with these little go-faster stripes down my legs, and a matching sports vest; bouncy, top-of-the-range trainers, plus lots of sweatbands.

It's amazing, but just wearing it makes me feel much fitter already and I keep getting these little glances of approval from people on the tube, as if they think I'm a real athlete. So much so that by the time we cross Putney Bridge I'm starting to feel like one. In fact, I even catch myself looking disapprovingly at someone sitting opposite me eating a big bag of Maltesers and reading the *Metro*. I mean, honestly, some people!

So I'm feeling quite positive as I set off at my stop and start springing jauntily down the road towards the park, swinging my arms and blowing out clouds of white air like a steam train. Gosh, it really is quite chilly, I realise, pulling up my pink woolly scarf around my ears. Still, soon I'm sure I'll be all warmed up and rosy-cheeked with exercise.

I smile to myself. Believe it or not, I'm actually looking forward to this class. In fact, maybe dating Seb again has helped me discover something about myself that I didn't know. All this time I thought that I didn't like sports or exercise, but perhaps I do. Perhaps I'll be really good at it and it was just my school's fault. Perhaps they made me think I was rubbish at sport, like they made me think I hated rice pudding. It was only years later, when Nan died and left me all her own recipes, that I discovered it wasn't necessarily lukewarm with a horrible skin on the top, but hot and creamy and utterly delicious.

Turning the corner I see the floodlit park ahead. According to the instructions I read online, we all meet in the car park where I'll be introduced to the instructors. I feel a beat of anticipation. Gosh, this is actually quite exciting. I mean I love Seb, *obviously*, but still, what girl doesn't go a bit fluttery at the thought of meeting lots of super-hunky fitness instructors. All that testosterone and army fatigues. I should bring Fiona along . . . in fact, yes! What a fantastic idea! Why didn't I think of it earlier? She can get fit *and* meet someone! Forget all that online dating business – military fitness is where she needs to be . . .

Making a mental note to bring her along next time, I stride enthusiastically across the tarmac. Ahead of me I can see a military van parked up, and lots of people milling around in coloured vests. Amongst them are several large muscular men in army fatigues, holding clipboards and issuing instructions.

'You're late!'

One of them gives a loud bark and I look around to see who he's shouting at.

'Girl with the pink scarf!'

His voice is like a round of gunfire. What girl with the pink scarf? I can't see anyone – *ooer*, hang on – *I'm* wearing a pink scarf.

Oh shit.

'Yes, you! Got something in your ears, have you?'

Filled with trepidation I turn back around to see this very scary hulk of a man, with biceps the size of butcher's hams, glaring at me.

'Erm . . . it's only five past,' I stammer, glancing at my watch. Then promptly jump out of my skin.

'Five past! Five past!' he rants, charging towards me with his clipboard. 'You were supposed to be here at eighteen hundred hours! On! The! Dot!'

Oh shitty shit shit.

My heart starts clanging hard in my chest. Lately I've tried so hard with my timekeeping. Ever since I told Seb I was never late, I've been setting alarm clocks, wearing a watch, leaving early. I've made a major effort, and yet it's like it's my default setting. It's as if I wasn't made to be on time. Even my mum said I was three weeks late being born and had to be induced.

Yet somehow I don't think this is going to wash with Mr Angry Sergeant Major.

'Where's your form?' he thunders, bearing down upon me like the Incredible Hulk. Only he's not green. His face is more a kind of purple, and the veins are bulging in his forehead like wiggly worms.

'Oh . . . here,' I fluster, pulling it out of my backpack and ripping it in the process.

He grabs it from me and runs his eyes across it. I don't think I've ever felt more nervous. 'OK then, Tess Connelly,' he continues, looking up after a moment, 'my name's Woody and I'm going to be one of your instructors.'

'Hi Woody,' I smile with relief. Oh, thank god, he seems to have softened up. Maybe he's one of those 'bark's worse than his bite' types.

'So you think you're fit?' he asks, raising an eyebrow.

'Well, I won't say fit *exactly*, but I do walk to work every day and my flat's on the fourth floor and we don't have a lift . . .'

Well I don't want him to think I'm totally hopeless.

'Go on then, show us five press-ups, right now.'

I look at him unsurely – he's got to be kidding? *Right?*

'What? You mean, like, *right now*?' I stammer nervously, looking around me to gauge the reaction of everyone else, but no one else is listening, they're all forming groups and being led out onto the grass by the other instructors.

'What do you think?' he fires back like ammunition.

What do I think? I think I can't even do one press-up, let alone five, that's what I think.

'I . . . um . . .' I've been reduced to gibberish.

'No worries, we'll let you warm up first,' he interrupts before I can formulate an answer, and I feel a rush of relief. Thank god – for a moment there I had visions of me face down on the tarmac being bawled at by a drill sergeant, like in *Private Benjamin.*

'OK, so you need to choose a bib,' he continues swiftly. 'There's three different colours, all based on levels of fitness. If you're not sure of your fitness, go for the blue. If it's decent and can hack hard exercise, take the red. Only take the green if you think you're a serious athlete.'

'Right, OK,' I nod. Crikey, I wonder which one I should choose? I glance across at the Blues doing warm-up exercises and some are struggling to touch their toes. Well, I'm not *that* bad. So I should probably go for the red.

Then again . . .

'Well, we haven't got all day,' he barks impatiently. 'Come on, move it! MOVE IT!'

Sod it. I grab the green. I know it will be tough, but I need to get in shape fast. Seb thinks I'm super-fit and ran ten miles the other night, remember? I don't have time to be in the Reds, I need to go for the more intensive approach.

Plus, c'mon, how unfit can I be?

For a moment I'm sure I see a flash of surprise across the instructor's face, but then it's gone again and he's yelling, 'OK, that way!' and gesturing in the direction of the Greens that are already sprinting off towards the end of the park.

Throwing my coat and rucksack in the minivan, I pull on my bright green bib with a number thirty-four on the back and set off running across the grass. It's freezing, and I feel the icy cold blasting into my lungs as I suck in deep, hungry breaths.

'Get a move on! Don't let your team mates down,' he yells after me as I race, stumbling across the park, towards the Greens.

Only instead of getting closer, they seem to be moving even further away. It's like a mirage. Or a rainbow. Only there's no pot of gold at the end of this – just sit-ups, squats and something called burpies. Which sounded fun and interesting from the warm, ergonomic comforts of my office chair, but now seem a lot less so in the cold darkness of Wimbledon Park.

Finally, when my lungs feel as if they're going to explode out of my chest, I reach them, and that's only because they've stopped running and are lined up on the grass doing press-ups. Spotting the instructor, I raise my hand in a sort of Native American 'how' greeting. I can't speak. My body's gone into shock at this sudden, unexpected blast of exercise, and I double over, trying to catch my breath.

'Enjoy your little stroll?' roars the instructor right in my ear, as he bounds up behind me.

I nearly jump out of my skin. Except I don't have the energy.

'Sorry . . . I was trying to catch up . . .' I manage to gasp, but he cuts me off.

'Fifty sit-ups!' he commands gruffly.

And I thought Woody was tough.

Dropping to the grass, I flop onto my back. It's barely been five minutes and I'm already exhausted. All I want to do is lie here, but I can't. I have a very scary instructor standing right above me already counting:

'One . . . two . . . three . . .'

OK, I can do this. It's only fifty sit-ups. It's not like it's going to kill me. Putting my hands behind my head, I take a deep breath and start crunching . . .

* * *

I take that back. I think *it is* killing me.

Twenty torturous minutes later and I'm going to throw up. And this time it's got nothing to do with spicy food, but because it didn't stop at fifty sit-ups. Oh no. I've been doing relay sprints, press-ups, burpies – which involve squatting down, kicking your legs back and standing up again, and which are, quite frankly, excruciatingly painful. Not to mention jumping jacks, lunges and crawling around the edge of the park on my elbows.

No, I'm not kidding.

And yes, I did pay good money to do this.

I've never been so exhausted. If you fall behind you're only made to do more, so I try my hardest to keep up, but there's fitness *and there's fitness*. The rest of the Greens are like Olympic athletes. At one point we have to partner up and act as if we're soldiers and one of our squadron has been wounded in a bomb attack and we have to carry them to safety. I get Gary, a six-foot IT expert who competes in triathlons 'for fun'. Suffice to say, when I have to give him a piggyback to our 'bunker' I nearly keel over.

Which is why I'm now hiding behind a tree. Well, I'm sorry, but I had no choice. Our instructor told us to do laps around the park and my legs are like dead weights. I can barely walk, let alone sprint. And to think I could be at home watching the TV. Or having a glass of wine. Or lying in the bath. Or even doing my hand-washing. Do people really do this for pleasure? Of their own free will? *Several times a week?*

Peering around the trunk, I watch as several green vests go whizzing by. They'll never notice I'm gone. I'll just stay here for a few minutes, have a rest, get my breath back, then just slip back out and join them when they go past again. What a brilliant plan! Closing my eyes, I sit on the damp grass and lean back against the tree.

'Number thirty-four! Where the hell are you?'

I snap my eyes open. *Oh fuck.*

'Number thirty-four! I want to see you! Right. Now!'

Fuckity-fuck.

My chest tightens. I should have known I wouldn't get away with it. Even in the dark, those instructors have eyes in the back of their shaven heads. Nothing gets past them.

'Number thirty-four!'

He's really yelling now and I peek out round the side of the trunk and see him standing a hundred yards away. A huge rectangle of a man in army fatigues, like a large fridge-freezer painted in camouflage colours. Oh crap. I'm never going to be able to escape from my hiding place. He's going to catch me slacking and punish me with about a million burpies. I'm doomed. I'm just going to have to come clean. I'm—

A loud barking interrupts my spiralling thoughts and I see a big golden retriever bouncing towards the instructor. Briefly he turns to pat it.

I'm making a break for it.

Seizing my chance, I charge out from behind the tree and start sprinting across the grass. Only within seconds I suddenly feel the most intense pain in the back of my leg. 'Ouch!' I shriek, clutching it and hopping on the other leg.

Hearing a scream, the instructor twirls around and, seeing me, races over. 'Are you all right? What's happened? Let me see.'

If I wasn't in so much pain, I'd be impressed by how swiftly he scoops me up and carries me to a bench, where he sets about inspecting my leg. 'Looks like your hamstring,' he says knowledgably. 'I think you might have torn it.'

'Torn it?' I repeat, alarmed.

'Either that, or you've just pulled it. I'm not sure, but you're going to need to go home and put some ice on it.'

'What? Right now? *Without finishing the class?*' Forget the fact that I might have a serious injury, I'm almost heady with relief at the thought of being able to go home.

'Yes, right now,' he nods gruffly. 'I'd take a couple of ibuprofen as well; it will help with the swelling.'

'OK,' I nod obediently, feeling suitably chastised. Easing myself up from the bench, I start hobbling over to the van to collect my things.

'Oh, and there's one more thing . . .'

Mid-hobble, I turn to see the instructor watching me, his arms folded.

'Next time, I think we should get you into the blue bibs. Beginners,' he adds, raising a tufty eyebrow and giving me a pointed look.

Damn. So there goes my brilliant plan.

'Um, sure . . .'

Well I'm not going to disagree with a burly six-foot-something instructor with guns the size of mini-tanks, am I? Only I know something he doesn't.

There isn't going to be a next time.

Dear Diary,

Haven't had a chance to write in my diary as I've been so busy, what with the wedding (and that row!), the trip to the beach and the concert (remind me next time to take earplugs!!) – it's been manic! And then of course there was the meeting between Seb and Gramps!! EEK!! That was a bit nerve-wracking, and didn't go exactly as I'd hoped . . .

But anyway, I have to write as I have big news . . . drum roll please . . .

I'm in LOVE!!!

26

Luckily my torn hamstring turns out to be just a pulled muscle, and the next couple of weeks whiz by in a nonstop montage of successful dates with Seb.

For example, there's the night we go to the concert. Like I said, it's one of his favourite indie bands and, just like before, it's lots of shouting and clashing guitars. Only this time, instead of spending the whole time with my fingers in my ears for fear of tinnitus, I'm prepared, with my extra-strength Fiona-orgasm-proof earplugs, and merrily join Seb in the mosh pit, pogo-ing around by the speakers with the best of them. It was brilliant; I couldn't hear a thing!

Including Seb talking to me afterwards, as I'd wedged them in so far they got stuck and I had to spend the whole journey home in the car trying to lip-read. Which was quite stressful as he was driving and kept looking forwards so it was difficult to see his mouth moving. At one point I nearly got busted when I thought he was accusing me of being lazy and I got all defensive, before realising he actually said the band were *crazy*. I swear it was like a bad game of Chinese Whispers.

Then there's the wedding. Usually I love a good wedding, but this time I go as a marriage sceptic and do my best to have a terrible time. The bride looks beautiful, but instead of oohing and aahing over her dress, I bite my lip. I even remain dry-eyed when they say their vows (which is *a lot* harder than I thought as I always cry at weddings, but thinking about my Visa bill really helped). As for the bouquet . . . this time when I catch it, I throw it straight back.

Admittedly I feel a total killjoy, as weddings are supposed to be a joyous occasion. Still, at least Seb and I are on the same page this time around, and instead of rowing, we get along like a house on fire, sharing little digs about how people must be crazy to get married, and rolling our eyes at each other during the ceremony. It works a treat, even if I've never been so miserable at a wedding before!

Then when Seb declared he missed the ocean, we drove down to the coast after work one evening, back to the same beach we went to the first time we dated, where he found me the piece of driftwood and went paddling in the frozen sea. Except this time, instead of staying on dry land, I rolled up my jeans and joined him. See, I'm not a chicken!

'*Achoo!*'

Fast-forward to Friday and I've caught a cold. Moonlight paddling on the Sussex coast might seem romantic, but have you any idea how cold the English Channel is in January? *It was freezing!* I nearly died of hypothermia. In fact I think I've still got frostbite in my toes.

'Bless you!'

I look up from my desk to see Sir Richard walking through the office with his red setter, Monty. Apparently he and the soon-to-be-ex-Lady Blackstock have agreed to share custody and, as it's his weekend, their driver has dropped him off.

'Oh thanks,' I sniffle, looking up and blowing my nose. Since his bizarre behaviour with the computer I've barely seen Sir Richard, as he's had lots of meetings out of the office, but he seems to have really perked up. In fact, I'd go as far as to say he's undergone a bit of a transformation.

Gone is the old, shiny brown crumpled suit, scuffed ancient

brogues and his alma-mater tie from his college days at Oxford. In their place is a brand-new charcoal grey suit that looks suspiciously designer, with the only creases being the ones down the front of his trousers; a pair of loafers which Kym swears are Paul Smith, as apparently there was a photo of Jude Law wearing a pair in *Grazia*, and – get this – no tie! Instead he's wearing his shirts open-necked.

Open-necked! Sir Richard? What next? A T-shirt? An earring? *Stubble?*

'Well, have a wonderful weekend,' he beams, striding past my desk, Monty at his heels.

'Yes, you too,' I call after him as he walks out through reception with a visible spring in his step. Obviously his 'online hobby' has worked wonders in restoring his mojo. Which is brilliant, and I'm not feeling in the least bit prudey about it or anything, I remind myself firmly.

I watch as he walks out through the doors, passing Fergus, who enters carrying a large box with 'PartyTime' in bold lettering down the side. It's probably the balloons I ordered for the party. I know it's in a super-posh private members' club, but even so, you can't have a party without balloons.

'So c'mon, spill the beans, tell me what's been going on!' demands Kym before Fergus is barely through the door. She's been off sick with a cold and now she's back with a vengeance. 'I'm dying to know what happened. Did she get in touch? Have you been on a date? Are you in love?'

As she fires off questions without pausing for breath, Fergus shoots me a desperate look. I throw him an encouraging one back. We've only seen each other briefly since our heart-to-heart in the café but I know there's been no more news.

'Not yet,' he says, borrowing my line. 'Now, if you just want to sign here,' he continues chirpily, putting the package on the counter.

But Kym's not having any of it. Pursing her

frosted-lipsticked mouth, she frowns. 'Not yet as in you're not yet in love, or not yet as in she didn't reply?'

'The second one,' he says, colouring slightly and passing her his electronic pad for her signature.

'Who didn't reply?' barks a voice, and Wendy appears thundering down the corridor in her duffel coat, on her way home.

'Fergus posted a Missed Connection,' says Kym.

I quickly turn and glare at her. Honestly, talk about a betrayal.

'What?' says Kym of my look. 'Wasn't I supposed to tell anyone?'

'A Missed Connection?' chime in a few people from Accounts who are leaving and are now milling around in reception.

Fergus goes even redder.

'You? *No way!*' One of the guys, a chubby bloke with a paunch whose name I can never remember, lets out a little snort and looks secretly thrilled that this handsome Irishman has had to resort to posting a small ad. 'What, and she never replied?' he whoops.

'Well, he wouldn't know yet as he's still working through all the replies from the girls who did,' I announce loudly, grabbing my coat and marching over to Fergus. 'There're hundreds of them, it's taking him forever, isn't it?' I roll my eyes at Fergus who grins back gratefully.

That silences the chubby bloke and, linking my arm through Fergus's, I steer him quickly out of the office. 'Just ignore them,' I hiss in his ear as we walk out through the automatic doors and into the chilly evening.

'Hey, I'm an actor, I'm used to rejection. It comes with the territory.' Unchaining his bicycle, he starts wheeling it down the road as he walks alongside me down the street. 'In fact, I don't know why I'm even bothering with this audition.'

My ears prick up. 'What audition?' I ask, rounding on him.

'For a TV drama.'

'Fergus, that's fantastic!' I gasp. 'Why didn't you tell me?'

'My agent only just called me,' he shrugs, trying to sound casual. 'It's all very last-minute.'

'When's the audition?'

'Tomorrow. I've got to learn my lines tonight.'

'Wow that's great!' I grin excitedly.

He allows himself a small smile. I can tell he's secretly really excited, but desperately trying not to be. 'What about you?' he asks.

'Going to see my granddad, it's his big poker night.' I'm interrupted by the shrill ring of my mobile. 'Sorry, hang on a sec,' I say, pulling it out of my pocket and answering. It's Seb, wanting to know where I am. 'I'm just walking to the bus stop. I should be at Hemmingway House in about half an hour,' I answer happily. I've been really looking forward to tonight all week. I can't wait for the opportunity to introduce Seb and Granddad to each other again.

'Cool,' he replies.

'So as long as you arrive before seven when the game starts—'

'Well that's the thing, there's been a bit of a problem.'

'*Problem?*' My good mood suddenly stalls, like a car engine. 'What kind of problem?'

'I totally forgot I had a squash game already arranged.'

I don't want to believe what I'm hearing.

'But can't you just cancel? It's only squash . . .'

At the word 'only' I can almost hear him bristle on the other end of the line. 'It's been in the diary for ages, I can't just cancel at the last minute,' he says impatiently.

'But I really wanted you to meet Gramps,' I say redundantly. The first time they met it was a disaster, and I so wanted it to be different this time. I was even planning to hide my granddad's antique pistol to be on the safe side.

'I'm sorry, babe,' he says, softening, 'I made a mistake with the dates.' But he still doesn't change his mind. 'Another time, huh?'

Disappointment kicks hard and flat in the stomach. I've spent the last few weeks doing things that Seb wanted to do, and yet the one thing that was important to me . . . Unexpectedly tears prickle. I feel upset. Let down. *Pissed off.* Because this isn't just about me, it's about Gramps. He lives for his poker nights and will have been looking forward to this game for days. I can't upset the numbers. I can't let him down. I *won't* let him down.

Putting down the phone I turn to Fergus. 'How's your poker face?'

We end up doing a deal. Fergus is to come with me to the poker night, and afterwards I'm going to help him learn his lines. 'Let's shake on it,' he grins, jumping on his bike and promising to meet me there.

'Hang on, I haven't given you directions,' I yell after him.

But he just laughs. 'Don't worry, I'm a courier, I'll find it,' he replies, before disappearing into the traffic.

Sure enough, as my bus pulls up outside Hemmingway House, he's already waiting for me, and together we walk through the automatic doors.

'Ah, Ms Connelly,' cries Miss Temple, pouncing on me as soon as we enter reception.

'Oh, hi,' I force a smile. I swear she lies in wait for me.

'Who's that?' hisses Fergus in my ear.

'The dragon who hates Gramps,' I hiss back.

'And you are?' she demands sternly, turning to Fergus.

'Fergus O'Flanagan,' he replies, throwing on his charm like an overcoat. Smiling broadly, he fixes her with a twinkling gaze. 'And who do I have the pleasure of meeting?'

The effect is incredible. Miss Temple visibly melts before

my eyes and suddenly goes all girlie. 'Please, call me Catherine,' she blushes.

Catherine? I stare in disbelief.

'Like our future queen herself,' he flatters, reaching for her hand and kissing it. 'In fact, I can see quite a similarity.'

'You can?' she giggles flirtily, the blush rising even higher on her cheeks.

A similarity? Between the Duchess of Cambridge and Miss Temple? That's like saying there's a similarity between a newborn kitten and a Rottweiler.

I clear my throat loudly and both of them turn to me. 'We should go, Gramps is expecting us.'

'Of course, I'm sorry, will you excuse us?' Fergus turns back to Miss Temple – correction – *Catherine*.

'Oh, no, not at all, don't mind me.' Reluctantly letting go of his hand, she starts fanning herself with a sheaf of papers. 'Enjoy yourselves, and give my regards to your grandfather,' she smiles giddily. 'A charming gentleman . . . you must visit again soon.'

'We will,' smiles Fergus, flashing me a wink as I link arms with him and propel him through the fire doors.

'*Like our future queen!*' I gasp, as they swing shut behind us.

'Hey, I didn't have my glasses on,' he protests, smirking.

For a moment we don't say anything and continue down the corridor until, unable to hold it in any longer, we both turn to each other and burst out laughing.

We're still laughing by the time we reach Granddad's room and I knock on his door. Three fast raps, followed by three slow ones. Fergus glances at me quizzically.

'It's a special knock . . . poker nights are against the rules,' I whisper.

'Crikey,' murmurs Fergus, looking suddenly nervous at all this subterfuge.

There's a pause, then the sound of a lock turning, and the

door opens to reveal Gramps looking dapper in his pinstriped suit, an emerald green silk handkerchief spilling from his top pocket. His face lights up when he sees it's me, and without saying a word he checks the coast is clear before ushering us both inside.

Once the door is closed he embraces me in a whiskery hug. 'Tess darling,' he beams, 'I'm so glad you could make it.'

'I wouldn't miss it for the world,' I grin, waving at all the familiar faces, all residents of Hemmingway House, who are already sitting around a fold-up table. There's a ripple of cheery hellos. 'I brought my friend Fergus.' I gesture towards Fergus; he's already being accosted by Phyllis, who's trying to get him to sit next to her.

'Phyllis, let go of the poor chap,' chastises Gramps sternly.

Caught in the act, Phyllis tuts loudly. 'What? I'm not doing anything,' she protests innocently.

Breaking free to join us, Fergus smiles gratefully. 'Thanks for that,' he says under his breath as he extends his hand.

'You be careful there my son,' grins Gramps, shaking it vigorously. 'She'll be trying to steal you from under Tess's nose.'

'Oh no, Fergus isn't my boyfriend,' I begin explaining hastily, but I'm interrupted by Phyllis.

'Did I hear the word "*boyfriend*"?' she says loudly, rounding on me.

I feel my face go bright red and can't look at Fergus. Maybe this wasn't such a good idea.

'Yes, that's right,' replies Fergus, before I've got a chance to answer.

What the . . . ? I round sharply on him to see a big grin plastered all over his face.

'You can't let me get hit on all night by Phyllis,' he hisses through gritted teeth like a ventriloquist.

Out of the corner of my eye I see Phyllis poised on the edge of her chair, her beady eyes magnified beneath her glasses. She might be nudging eighty, but she's a man-eater.

'Um, yes,' I nod, playing along. 'This is my boyfriend.'

I feel a bit guilty pretending to Gramps, but I'll just have to explain later.

'Splendid! Splendid!' he cheers, looking thrilled. Throwing his arms around Fergus he gives him a fatherly embrace. 'At last!'

Er, all right, Gramps, you don't have to go that far, I muse, catching Fergus's look of amusement. 'OK, so shall we start?' I say briskly. 'Everyone's waiting.'

'Yes, yes, indeed,' he nods, and there's a ripple of agreement as everyone starts shuffling up to make room for me and Fergus.

We sit down at the table on which is a deck of cards and a bottle of Blackstock & White whisky. And is that . . .

'Gramps, are you burning incense?' I ask, suddenly noticing the small smouldering cone in the middle of the table.

'Nag Champa,' he corrects with amazing clarity, considering his memory is failing. 'That nice nurse Melanie gave it to me. Said it would help with the pipe,' he winks, sticking it in the corner of his mouth and lighting a match.

'But Gramps, the rules,' I protest anxiously, but I'm silenced by Fergus who pours me a large tot of whisky. I give up and take a grateful glug.

'Now then, people . . .' As Gramps calls for everyone's attention, the chattering falls silent around the table. Puffing merrily away on his pipe, he reaches for the deck of cards. 'Let's get this show on the road.' And, with a flourish, he starts dealing.

Two hours, a bottle of whisky and a serious amount of gambling later, I've lost all my money, along with most of the other players. Gramps, however, is on a winning streak. Despite only betting with coins, he's up over fifty pounds and is winning every hand. Now it's down to just him and Fergus.

'Well that's me out,' he announces, laying down his hand. 'I'm no match for you.'

'Nonsense!' refutes Gramps, but his chest swells up with pride.

'Your granddad should be doing this professionally,' says Fergus, winking at me.

'Hey, don't you be giving him any ideas,' I protest.

Gramps chuckles delightedly and puffs on his pipe. 'Oh come along, one more game,' he cajoles.

But Fergus shakes his head. 'That would be grand, but I'm afraid I have to get home. I've got an audition tomorrow.'

'Ooh, are you an actor?' pipes up Phyllis, who was out a long time ago and has been nodding off on the sofa for the past hour.

'For my sins,' he grins.

'I once courted an actor, you know. He trod the boards at the Variety Hall, handsome chap he was.'

'Right, yes, Phyllis,' says Gramps sternly, before turning to me and muttering, 'Who hasn't she courted?'

I try not to laugh and elbow him to stop it.

'Are you leaving too?' he asks.

'I promised I'd help Fergus learn his lines,' I smile ruefully, expecting him to grumble, but instead he looks pleased. 'Good girl,' he nods approvingly, giving my knee a little pat.

'I'll just get our coats,' says Fergus, walking over to the stool next to the sewing machine where they've been piled. Reaching for them, he pauses. 'Is this one of your projects, Mr Connelly?' he asks. 'Tess told me you worked as a tailor.'

Glancing over, I realise he's holding up the bag I'm making. My chest tightens. It's as if he's uncovered my secret.

'A tailor?'

But I'm distracted by the blank expression on Granddad's face. For a split second he looks as if he can't remember.

'On Savile Row, Gramps,' I prompt. 'He worked there for fifty years,' I continue, for his benefit as much as Fergus's.

'Ah yes, I did,' he nods, suddenly registering, 'but I'm afraid I can't take the credit. That's one of Tess's designs that we've been working on together. Isn't she talented? I keep telling her she's got the gift but she doesn't listen—'

'It's just a little project,' I cut in, cringing with embarrassment and silencing Granddad with a hug. 'Bye, I'll be back soon.'

'Bye my dear.'

'Have fun,' waves Phyllis from the sofa, 'and don't do anything I wouldn't do,' she winks.

By the sounds of it I'm not sure there is anything Phyllis wouldn't do, I conclude, catching Fergus's eye and reddening. Honestly, this is so embarrassing. When I said I wanted the first time Gramps met my boyfriend to be different this time, I meant *the evening* to be different, not the actual *boyfriend.* At the first opportunity, I'm going to have to explain there's been a big misunderstanding. Fergus is just a friend, that's all.

And, giving Gramps a hug, I wave goodbye. The sooner I clear that up the better.

27

'I've got a confession to make: I'm totally in love with you.'

'You are?' I look deep into Fergus's eyes.

'Yes,' he nods, fixing me with a loving gaze. 'Ever since that first moment when I was performing emergency open-heart surgery and you passed me the scalpel.'

'Doctor Lawrence . . .' I swoon.

'Nurse Kathy . . .' he replies huskily.

Back at Fergus's flat in Shepherd's Bush, we're practising his lines for his audition tomorrow. He lives in a tiny studio, high under the eaves of a large Victorian terraced house, with sloping ceilings that mean he's forever having to duck down so he doesn't bang his head as he paces up and down, script in hand.

'It's Nurse Kelly,' I correct.

'Crikey, so it is!' he curses, scraping his fingers through his scalp and tugging at his hair. 'I keep getting that wrong.'

'It's fine, don't worry,' I try to soothe. 'Kathy, Kelly, what's the difference?'

'Probably whether I get the part or not,' he replies gloomily, a deep frown etched down the middle of his forehead.

Chucking his script onto a tea chest, he flops himself down on an old velvet chaise longue. Forget modern minimalism, Fergus's flat is a bit like Aladdin's cave. It's decorated with an eclectic mix of vintage maps, a large Indian wall hanging, piles of leather books – the type with gold lettering on the spines – and old-fashioned tasselled lamps over which are hung silk scarves to emit a soft, rosy glow.

Everything, I learn, has a story attached, and none of them has anything to do with a trip to IKEA. Instead Fergus found most things either on his travels or outside on the street.

'People throw away all this wonderful stuff. I found this chaise longue chucked in a skip,' he told me proudly when I first walked in. 'I showed it to a friend who works in an antique shop and he told me it was turn of the century, can you believe it? It just needed re-covering . . .' and then pointing to his lamps, 'They were left out with the recycling; they only needed shades and they were as good as new . . .' I listened, fascinated. For someone with a charity shop habit, this was even better. This stuff was free!

'So anyway, thanks for letting Gramps win,' I smile gratefully, plopping down next to him on the chaise longue and trying to distract him from his pre-audition nerves. 'We're all a bit worried about him; we think he's starting with Alzheimer's.' Hearing myself say those words, I realise it's the first time I've admitted it out loud, either to myself or someone else.

'My gran had that,' he says quietly, 'it can get pretty tough. On them and the rest of the family.'

'I know,' I nod, my insides twisting up as I think about Gramps. I can barely think about the future, about what's going to happen. I'm too scared to think of losing him.

'But by the way, I didn't,' he continues.

I break off from my thoughts and look up, confused.

'I didn't let him win,' explains Fergus with a smile. 'He's a great player.'

I know he's fibbing. At one point I snuck a glance over his shoulder and saw he had a royal flush, but he quickly switched out his cards to deliberately lose.

'And I'm sure he'll be a great player for a while yet,' he reassures me.

I know it's his way of trying to comfort me. 'Thanks,' I smile appreciatively, 'and thanks for coming.'

'Thanks for inviting me, I had a lot of fun,' he smiles, 'but all that gambling's worked up an appetite. You hungry?'

'Starving,' I nod. I've barely eaten anything today and I'm ravenous.

Unfolding his frame, Fergus gets up and walks across to the tiny kitchenette, where there follows the sound of lots of rummaging around and opening and closing of cupboards.

'Well, I'm afraid it looks like I'm out of the fresh lobster,' he says after a few moments, his head reappearing from behind a cupboard door, 'but I can offer you baked beans on toast.'

'That's lucky,' I reply with a straight face. 'I don't like fresh lobster.'

He laughs and starts busying himself with popping bread in the toaster, beans in a pan, and within a few minutes he's serving up two steaming plates of beans on toast.

'Mmm, this is delicious,' I rave, through a mouthful of hot buttery toast. 'Compliments to the chef.'

'It's one of my favourite recipes,' nods Fergus with mock seriousness. 'I find the flavours are really brought out by a full-bodied can of Guinness.'

I laugh as he opens a can and pours the black, foamy liquid into two glasses, then passes me one. He's cleared a little space and we're sitting cross-legged on cushions on the floor, balancing our plates on the old tea chest, which is doubling as a makeshift table. For a moment my mind flashes back to the meal with Seb at Mala, with its exotic dishes and expensive prices, and I can't help thinking how much more I'm enjoying this one.

But of course that's only because I don't like spicy food, I remind myself quickly, and not for any other reason.

For a few moments we eat in comfortable silence until, scooping a forkful of beans, Fergus pauses and asks, 'So I thought you told me you didn't have a dream?'

I look at him, not understanding.

'That bag I saw back there,' he prompts.

Comprehending, my face floods with self-consciousness. I was hoping he wasn't going to mention that. Apart from to Granddad, I've never admitted it to anyone, never been brave enough to lay myself wide open to ridicule, but now my secret's out. 'Oh, that?' I give a nonchalant shrug. I'll just brush it off, dismiss it jokingly as nothing important.

But there's something about Fergus's steadying gaze that makes my dream seem suddenly possible. I don't want to deny it. I *want* to talk about it.

'Well, I've always loved making things and I had this idea . . .' I've always thought I'd find it hard to express myself if I tried to explain my plan, but as I start speaking, the words come tumbling out. 'You know how women spend a fortune on bags – well actually, you probably don't, as you're a guy,' I correct myself quickly. 'But anyway, I wanted to make a bag that was pretty and stylish but that didn't cost a fortune and wasn't made in some sweatshop in India or China. A bag that's handmade from vintage flour sacks from France, so it's also recycled and recyclable . . .'

'So you're also doing your bit for the environment,' interjects Fergus.

'Exactly,' I enthuse. 'And for this one we're using my granddad's silk handkerchief as the lining and some old ribbon and buttons, and I found these old leather braces for handles that are just perfect. So you see it's also got a history, a past – a bit like all the things you found for your flat . . .' Energetically I throw my hands out, gesturing around me, before turning to face Fergus. Who's studying me with a thoughtful look on his face.

'Oh god, sorry, I got completely carried away, didn't I?' I say, blushing with embarrassment.

'So you should,' he protests, 'If it's something you're passionate about, you should get carried away.'

Passionate about. I turn his words over in my head. I've never thought of it like that before, but he's right. I am passionate about what I'm doing.

'I think it's really great,' he continues, his face serious.

'Really?'

'Well, not that I know much about women's handbags,' he confesses with a rueful smile, 'but I love the whole concept, and from what I saw it looked pretty good to me. I mean, I'd use one. If I was a girl that is,' he adds quickly. 'You need to make some that are unisex – why restrict yourself to just one half of the market?'

'Hey, that's a good idea,' I nod, the cogs in my brain already turning.

'I'm not just a pretty face you know,' he quips.

I smile, then hesitate before asking, 'And you don't think I'm stupid?'

'Well, *now* you're asking . . .'

'I don't mean *in general*,' I say, pulling a face. 'I mean stupid for thinking I could design bags and somebody might want to buy one . . .' The hope is audible in my voice and I nervously meet his eyes.

'Well, not any more stupid than me wanting to be an actor . . .'

I smile appreciatively, and for a moment we exchange a look of mutual understanding.

'I've never asked you, but why *did* you want to become an actor?' I ask curiously.

'Oh, it's probably because I'm an attention seeker,' he laughs self-deprecatingly. 'Growing up in that great big family of mine, I was always wanting attention, for someone to notice me, and they never did . . . my mum and dad always had their hands full with one nipper or another. And then I discovered drama at school, and being on stage, and the feeling I got . . . it just went from there . . .' He breaks off, as if thinking back.

'And of course I thought it would be a great way to meet women,' he adds wickedly. 'Leading man and all that. Not that it's quite worked out that way.'

'Oh, I don't know, I think Dr Lawrence could change all that,' I laugh, then pause, and try to ask as casually as possible: 'So, have you ever fallen in love with any of your leading ladies?'

'Lots,' he nods.

'*Lots?*' I repeat. For some reason that wasn't the answer I was expecting.

'Hell yeh,' he grins. 'When I first started acting I was always falling in love, but nothing ever lasted for more than a few months; nothing ever turned out to be anything serious. It was mostly just sex . . .'

'Fergus!' I pretend to chastise, and he laughs.

'I'm kidding,' he says. 'Well, a little bit.' He pauses, then looks more thoughtful. 'None of them were ever based on anything solid, like a real friendship . . .'

He breaks off and looks at me, and for a second I feel the atmosphere change, before he suddenly looks over my shoulder.

'Hey look,' he exclaims, breaking into a huge smile and pointing out of the window. *'It's snowing!'*

Twirling around, I look out of the French windows, and sure enough he's right.

'Oh wow,' I gasp, watching white snow flurries swirling around in the inky darkness.

'Come on, grab your coat.' He jumps up and unlocks the French windows, pushing them open to reveal a huge roof terrace, which is bigger than his entire flat. 'This is why I took the place,' he says, leading me outside.

It's incredible. Stepping outside is like stepping into another world. Now I know how the children must have felt walking through that wardrobe and into Narnia. With amazement I look out across the rooftops, at the snowflakes whirling and dancing around our heads, like tiny pieces of white glitter, lighting up the darkness. It feels magical. Exhilarating. As if we're cocooned inside one of those snow globes, and someone has picked it up and shaken it.

There's a small wooden bench tucked away to one side, amongst the potted plants that have lost their leaves, and we both sit down.

'You know, every snowflake is totally unique, like people,' he says, sticking out his tongue and catching one. 'I always thought that was incredible when I was a kid.'

I smile and turn my face up to the sky, letting them land on my face. Tiny frozen flecks that instantly melt. Up high among the chimneypots, it feels a million miles away from real life. London is so manic. Even after living here for five years, I'm still not fully used to its constant noise and clamour, the crowded pavements, the never-ending buzz of traffic.

Most days I love it. I love the energy of the people; the way you can walk down a street and find an eclectic mix of Indian sari shops, Moroccan restaurants, Thai cafés and greasy spoons, all jostling up next to one another; how you can wake up in the middle of the night and look out of your window and see the city still lit up from across the rooftops.

But sometimes I can't help wishing the city had an 'off' switch. A button I could press that would bring everything to a halt, like a merry-go-round ride at the fair, and allow you to get off and draw breath.

Like now.

Up here with Fergus I feel as if I've found that off switch. Everything is so still, so quiet . . .

A gust of wind blows and I give an involuntary shiver.

'Are you cold?' he frowns.

'No, I'm fine,' I fib, tugging my coat tighter around myself, but my chattering teeth give me away.

'Yeh, right,' he tuts, 'come here,' and, wrapping his arm

around my shoulder, he pulls me towards him. He's so tall, I fit easily underneath his woolly armpit, and for a few moments I remain there, cosy and warm, watching the snowflakes dancing around us. Tucked into the snug warmth of the gap between his ribcage and his arm.

In the nook.

The shrill ring of my mobile interrupts my thoughts and I fumble for it in my pocket. 'Hello?'

'Babe, look, I'm sorry about earlier . . .'

It's Seb, apologising about not being able to come tonight, and hearing his voice I feel suddenly guilty. As if I've been caught doing something wrong. I jump up from the bench. Which of course is ridiculous; I was just keeping warm.

'It's OK, Seb, don't worry,' I say quickly, walking across the terrace. It's almost as though he's intruding. I catch Fergus making a gesture that he's going back inside, and as I watch he gets up, his figure disappearing through the French windows, and regret stabs.

'Listen, I feel I should call your granddad and apologise—'

I focus back in on the phone call. 'No!' I cry. 'I mean, that's not necessary, it was fine,' I jabber.

'Well if you're sure . . .'

'Positive,' I say firmly. In my head I get a marker pen and twice underline that mental note to call Gramps at the first opportunity to explain.

'OK, I'm going to make it up to you,' he continues. 'I'm taking you away for the weekend.'

'You are?' I'm caught by surprise.

'I'll pick you up tomorrow at 6 a.m. Bring your passport.'

Passport? We're going abroad?

'Where are we going?' is all I can manage. This is all happening so fast I'm having trouble keeping up.

'That's for me to know and for you to find out,' he teases.

'But how will I know what to pack?'

He laughs. 'Don't worry about anything. I've got everything sorted,' he soothes, then there's a pause and he adds softly, 'You know I really missed you tonight.'

'I missed you too,' I reply, but it's automatic rather than heartfelt because it's only now, hearing those words, that I realise I haven't missed him. In fact, until he rang I haven't thought about him at all. But that's only because I've been so busy with Gramps's poker night and helping Fergus learn his lines and . . . well, everything else.

We say bye and he rings off, and for a moment I remain motionless, feeling slightly dazed at this sudden turn of events, before going back inside.

I find Fergus bent over his script, a deep cleft running down his brow. 'Everything OK?' he asks, looking up.

'Um . . . yes,' I nod, feeling a strange mix of emotions. 'That was Seb,' I add, rather redundantly.

'Yeh, I heard,' he nods.

The mood has been broken and now suddenly it feels strangely awkward between us.

'He's taking me away for the weekend,' I explain, though I'm not sure why.

'Great.' Fergus smiles. 'A mini-break, huh?'

'Yeh,' I smile back.

The conversation drops and there's an uncomfortable pause, then, 'Well, I should go,' I say brightly.

'You OK to get back?'

'Yeh, it's not that late, and Granddad gave me money for a cab.' Though 'forced it into my pocket' might be a better description.

'Hang on, I'll walk you outside,' he says, grabbing his keys. Leaving the door on the latch, we clatter down the stairs to the main door of the building, which thuds behind us as we step out onto the street.

It's still snowing but the ground is so wet it's refusing to settle, and instead it's melting into little grey slushy piles. I glance across at the yellow neon sign of the kebab shop across the road, the gangs clustered outside, the traffic as it rumbles by. The rooftop seems like another world, a magical place far away from down here where reality bites.

A cab pulls up, and we jump back to avoid being sprayed.

'Well, have a great mini-break,' he cheers, kissing me goodbye on the cheek.

'Thanks,' I smile, pulling open the door and climbing inside, 'and good luck tomorrow with the audition. I know you're going to get it. I've got a good feeling.'

'Was that the same good feeling you had when you suggested posting a Missed Connection?' he jokes half-heartedly. 'She never did email you know.'

I feel a knot of guilt. 'No, this is completely different,' I say determinedly. 'Completely.'

He gives a little resigned smile. 'Don't worry, I'll be fine. Like I said, I'm used to rejection – it comes with the territory,' and, closing the door behind me, he throws me a wave as I pull away into the night.

Later, back at home, I pack a few things for the weekend and get ready for bed. The flat is empty. Fiona's not back yet. In fact, I've barely seen her the past few weeks as I've been staying most nights at Seb's and she's out every night with Tallulah. Apparently they've been on some intensive doggy obedience course, but the times I *have* stayed at the flat she's never been back before midnight and, although I admire her dedication, surely even dogs need an early night once in a while?

Anyway, I sent her a text telling her about my surprise weekend away and making sure she could look after Flea and she immediately replied:

Wow!!!! Yes!!!! Call me tomz!!!!

Which, to be honest, made me feel a bit guilty as her reaction was a lot more excited than mine had been. Not that I'm *not* excited. Of course I am! What girl wouldn't be? It just came as a bit of a surprise, that's all . . . Spying another jumper, I shove it into my already bursting holdall. I have no clue what to take, so I'm doing my usual and taking everything.

Zipping up my bag, I climb into bed with Flea. OK, now I'll just do a bit of reading before I turn out the light. I reach for the book on my bedside cabinet, open it, then promptly close it again. Try as I might, I just can't seem to get into it. Obama might be the most fascinating man to millions of people, and I know I should be gripped, but . . . well, I'm just not.

Shoving it back on the bedside cabinet, I lie back on my pillows and tickle Flea behind his ears. I'm tired but my brain's still buzzing, and my mind starts throwing up snapshots of this evening, Gramps's poker night, Fergus rehearsing his lines, Seb's phone call . . . I really should try to get to sleep. Seb's picking me up at 6 a.m. Anticipation flutters. I wonder where he's taking me? Maybe it's Paris, or New York . . . no, that's too far for just one night.

'*She never did email you know.*'

Fergus. My mind flicks back. To the soft lilt of his Irish accent. To the little resigned smile he gave me as I wished him luck.

That guilty feeling returns. If only I hadn't suggested he post that stupid ad. It's all my fault. He's so talented but it really knocked his confidence and I'm responsible. He's never going to get the part by being so negative. All this talk of rejection, it's as if he's talking himself into not getting the part before he even goes for the audition.

Thumping my pillow with my fist to make it more comfortable, I turn over. I wish I could give him a confidence boost, make him a bit more positive, show him that he is great, but how?

How?

And then suddenly I hit the seed of an idea, which grows, takes hold, comes together. Of course! Why didn't I think of it before?

Leaping out of bed I grab my laptop and flick it open. As the screen lights up I log onto my email account and quickly set up a new address. There's nothing else for it. Balanced on the edge of my bed I start typing. I caused this mess, so I'm going to fix it.

I'm going to be his Missed Connection.

Dear Diary,

Seb sent me a card with a picture of a snowbunny on the front. Inside he'd written,

'Can't wait to see you on the slopes and enjoy some après-ski with you. Seb xx'

Which is so sweet of him. Seb adores snowboarding and wants to take me away to the Alps for a weekend, but to be honest I've never learnt how to ski or snowboard and I don't really want to start now. Freezing cold weather, falling over, bruises, possible broken limbs . . . doesn't really sound like much fun.

I rang him up and thanked him tons, but then suggested a spa break instead.

Funny, but he didn't seem that enthusiastic . . .

28

Who doesn't dream of their boyfriend whisking them away for the weekend? And not just that, but *as a surprise*. It's the stuff of romantic fiction, of movies starring Julia Roberts, of wishful thinking. Not real life. And certainly not *my* life.

Until now.

I, Tess Connelly, am being taken away on a mini-break! It's so exciting! I'm constantly reading about them in Fiona's glossy magazines: boutique B&Bs, hip hotels, urban boltholes, spa retreats . . . Every time I flick through the pages I find myself daydreaming; heaving long, deep sighs as I stare longingly at photo-spreads of four-poster beds, kidney-shaped swimming-pools, exotic-looking cocktails . . .

So you can imagine the build-up of anticipation as we drive to the airport, me begging Seb to tell me, Seb laughing and refusing. By the time we reach the short-stay car park at Heathrow I can barely contain my excitement. Another minute and I'm going to burst.

Until finally, *finally* he can't keep me in suspense any more and lets me in on the surprise.

'So what do you think?' he asks excitedly, waiting for my reaction.

There's a split-second pause as I digest this information, then:

'*Snowboarding?*' I repeat. My voice comes out a bit shriller than I intended.

'I knew you'd be stoked,' he enthuses, his face breaking into a huge white smile. 'I remembered you telling me how much you'd love to learn on our first date.'

'Yes, me too,' I smile dazedly. Oh crap, me and my big mouth. Images of being cosied up in some hip hotel in Paris are fast disappearing. 'But I haven't packed anything to snowboard in,' I interject.

You never know. Maybe there's still time to swap our snowboarding trip for Paris. To drink cosmos at the Costes. To float around in a fluffy bathrobe having spa treatments.

'Don't worry, we can get it all there,' he appeases.

Or maybe not.

As he finishes unloading his luggage from the boot onto an airport trolley, he turns and wraps his arms around me, pulling me close. 'Trust me, it's going to be awesome,' he grins.

Deep in his embrace, I look into his pale blue eyes and have a flashback to the card I burned in the fire on New Year's Eve, the one with the snowbunny on the front, and his invitation to take me snowboarding inside. And I remember my regret at never having gone, remember wishing I'd done things differently.

And now I can.

I grab hold of myself. Tess, what are you doing? This is what you dreamed about all those nights you fell asleep on a tear-stained pillow and woke up with puffy eyes from crying. This is your second chance. This time you can go snowboarding! Tons of people do and they love it, why should you be any different? You're only reluctant because you've never been – I bet it will be fab! You can show him what a quick learner you are, how much you love the slopes, how much fun you're having. *You can show him just how perfect you are for each other.*

'Awesome,' I grin back, copying him. 'I can't wait.'

We're going to Chamonix. Seb's arranged everything – or rather his super-organised secretary has – and we're flying direct to Geneva in business class; yes, that's right! *Business class!* Then transferring to the ski resort on a shuttle bus where we're staying at a chalet owned by one of Seb's friends.

As the woman behind the check-in counter politely directs us to the executive club lounge, I think how different this is to my usual travelling experience: a cheap budget airline, ungodly flight times, trooping around Stansted with a Pret sandwich looking for a spare plastic seat, being herded onto the plane like cattle because I didn't pay the extra for early boarding . . .

This time we relax in the club lounge, watching TV and drinking champagne. At seven in the morning! It feels like Christmas, only without the repeats. Then, just before the flight's about to depart, we're whisked on board, shown into comfy, wide leather seats and offered even more champagne. Normally I'm a nervous flyer, but as the plane lifts into the sky, I feel a surge of excitement. If this is a snowboarding trip, then *bring it on*!

Just a couple of hours later and we're there.

'Welcome to Chamonix,' says the driver of the shuttle bus, as the automatic doors swoosh open and we disembark.

The first thing that hits me is the dazzling brightness. After the grey dullness of London, it's almost blinding, and I scramble for the cheap pair of sunnies I bought at Heathrow. As I push them onto my nose I take a deep lungful of clear Alpine air and just stand for a moment, taking in this winter wonderland. The scenery is, quite literally, breathtaking. Pristine white snow like icing on a cake, a freshly laundered sky the colour of forget-me-nots, brilliant sunshine and . . .

'Look, there it is!' I gasp.

'What?' asks Seb, without glancing up from his iPhone.

He hasn't looked up from it once during the whole journey from the airport – 'sorry, work crap' – but for once I haven't minded at all. I've been far too distracted between gazing out of the window at the stunning scenery and reading the tourist guide that I enthusiastically bought at the airport.

'Mont Blanc,' I exclaim, looking up from its pages and gazing at it stretching up above, towering majestically into the sky, the white-capped peak. 'Do you know it rises fifteen thousand seven hundred and eighty-two feet above sea level?'

'Yeh, I know,' he nods, looking up, his face splitting into a smile. 'Awesome, huh?'

'And did you know Chamonix's full name is actually Chamonix-Mont-Blanc and it was the site of the first Winter Olympics in 1924?'

Well, no point doing anything by halves is my motto. If I'm going to do something, I like to throw myself into it. Though perhaps sometimes rather too much, I reflect, as my hamstring gives a little twinge and I'm reminded of the military fitness fiasco.

I catch Seb looking at me, with a big smile on his face. 'What did I tell you? I knew you were gonna love it here.'

I laugh, because despite my initial reluctance, I have to agree. I can't believe how mistaken I was about snowboarding! I admit, I totally got it wrong! I shoot him a big smile. It's like finally we're a proper couple, doing what proper couples do, having fun together on a weekend away. He shoots me an even bigger grin back and I feel a burst of gratitude. Wow, I'm so lucky this happened to me, that I got this amazing chance to correct all my mistakes and get it right this time. Seriously, I must be the luckiest girl in the world.

All happy and enthusiastic, I link my arm through his and together we set off walking. Seb looks the part in his ski jacket and snow boots with thick rubber grips that remind me of tractor tyres, but my own boots are designed for British winters – i.e. slushy London pavements, not powdery snow and ice – and I immediately start slipping all over the place.

'Whoops!' I slide sideways, and Seb catches me, laughing.

'Hang on to me,' he grins. 'It's not far.'

With Seb leading the way, his feet crunching steadily

through the snow, we make our way past numerous ski chalets, each looking more luxurious than the last. Until finally we reach an amazing wooden A-frame set high on a slope, with panoramic windows, a huge deck and . . . my heart leaps with excitement . . . *is that an outdoor hot tub?*

'Well this is it,' announces Seb, coming to a halt. 'Our home for the weekend.'

'Wow,' I gasp, staring at it in delight. It really is like something from a glossy magazine. Wait till I tell Fiona!

Standing at the entrance, he bends down to kiss me. His mouth is soft and warm in the icy air and I feel as though I've been dipped in melted happiness. Could it be any more perfect?

Suddenly there's a commotion inside the chalet and I jump back, startled, as I hear a man's voice.

'Dude! You're here!'

A very loud American voice. A voice that sounds exactly like . . .

'Chris,' grins Seb, as the door is flung open to reveal Seb's friend from the restaurant. Leaping upon him with a high-five, there's lots of punching of shoulders and back-slapping.

I watch, as frozen as the landscape around me. I can't believe what I'm seeing. Chris is here? In our ski chalet? *What the . . . ?*

Oh no. This is the friend.

My heart plummets. I can barely dare to think it. But as the words peg out in front of each other, I force myself to string the words together.

It's. His. Chalet.

Abruptly I feel my earlier enthusiasm melting faster than the polar ice caps.

'And Tina!' booms Chris, turning to me. 'Great to see you!'

'It's Tess,' I try to correct, but he's already lassoed his huge arms around our shoulders and is corralling us inside like an overexcitable cowboy.

And just when I thought it couldn't get any worse . . .

'Hey Anna, look who's here!' he yells.

As we enter the open-plan living room-cum-kitchen, the Ice Queen herself emerges from behind the fridge door. Dressed in white jeans and a white polo neck, she reminds me of a skinny white icicle, and has about as much warmth.

'Guys, hi,' she says in clipped Chelsea tones, the ones that Fiona is forever trying to master. 'How was your trip?' She holds out two beers.

'Cool,' grins Seb, dumping the bags and grabbing one. Chris grabs the other. I watch them taking thirsty glugs. I'm actually quite parched myself, I realise, glancing back at Anna, but it's as if I'm invisible.

Something tells me that Anna and I aren't going to get along.

'So, you ready, powder monkey?' whoops Chris.

'Totally!' enthuses Seb.

I glance between them. I have no idea what they're talking about.

'What's a powder monkey?' I ask, tentatively.

Anna lets out a derisive little snort of laughter.

'It's what we call crazy snowboarders like us, babe,' explains Seb, sliding his arm around my waist. 'But don't worry, I've sorted you out some lessons.'

'You don't ski?' exclaims Anna.

'No,' I reply tightly, shaking my head.

'Golly,' she gasps, wide-eyed.

She looks so incredulous you'd think I'd just informed her I can't spell my own name.

'Skiing's for old ladies,' quips Seb, flashing me a smile. 'Tess is gonna learn how to snowboard.'

Anna looks as though she's just sucked on a lemon, and I smile gratefully back at Seb.

'OK, well, what are we waiting for? Let's hit the slopes!'

whoops Chris, slamming his empty beer bottle down on the countertop. 'You ready?' he looks at Seb.

'You bet,' Seb grins. Turning to me, he raises his brow questioningly. 'Tess?'

Nerves flutter, but I briskly push them away. 'As ready as I'll ever be,' I smile. I'm going to be fine. There's nothing to be worried about. This is going to be so much fun.

Right?

Er no, well no, not exactly.

Standing on the slopes for my very first time, listening to my instructor, I glance at my reflection in the window of the ski school. There are many words I could choose right now, but fun is not one of them.

For starters, I look like the Michelin Man. Whereas everyone else is wafting around looking sexy in their cargo pants and skinny thermal tops, goggles perched casually on their foreheads like sunglasses in St Tropez, I'm padded up to the nines like a comedian in one of those fat suits. Believe me, this brings a whole new meaning to 'layering'. In fact I have so many layers I can barely walk, let alone snowboard.

First off there're thermals and base layers. Followed by fleeces and mid-layers. Followed by a bright puffy jacket and waterproof trousers. Then kneepads, wrist pads and elbow pads. A pair of what are like waterproof oven gloves. A helmet. And just to make sure I don't harbour any hope of trying to look *in any way at all* attractive, a pair of reflective goggles that not only squash my nose down so it looks as if I've done too many rounds in a boxing ring, but also leave a big red mark around my face.

It was Seb who took me to the shop and got me kitted out. He was super-generous and paid for everything, then safely deposited me at the ski school for my first lesson. Which was really sweet and thoughtful of him, but if I'm truthful it's not really the romantic weekend away with my boyfriend that I was hoping for. In fact, as he waved me off on his way to the cable car to meet the others, wishing me luck and arranging to meet me back at the chalet later, I felt as though I was a four-year-old being dropped off at school on her first day, rather than his girlfriend.

But hey, I don't want to sound ungrateful. I'm sure it's just because it's all new to me, that's all. A couple of lessons and I'll soon be snuggled up to Seb on the cable car and whizzing down the slopes with him. Just think, we can be powder monkeys together!

'So, theez is 'ow you 'old your feet.'

I turn back to focus on the instructor. His name is François and he's handsome in that cool, eighteen-year-old French ski instructor way. All suntan, mirrored Ray-Bans and long blond hair pulled back into a ponytail, he's swishing around on his snowboard as if he came out of the birth canal on it.

In comparison I feel like his mother. This is not helped by the fact that I am indeed the oldest here. *By quite a few years*, I realise, looking around me and noticing that most of the other pupils in the class barely come up to my kneepads. Now I know why they call these the nursery slopes, because most of them are literally *still in nursery*. Even more embarrassing, whereas I'm struggling to stay upright, they seemingly have no fear and have picked it up in no time.

And are already whizzing past me like cannonballs. I shriek, hastily jumping out of the pathway of one before I get mown down.

'*Superb*, Freddy! *Bien*, Henri,' applauds the instructor, whizzing around on his snowboard to join them.

Actually, on second thoughts, I might need more than just a couple of lessons, I muse, wobbling over and landing flat in the snow.

It's not until a few moments later, after I've managed to

hoist myself back up on my board, that François appears to notice me again and whizzes over. 'No, not like that, like theez,' he instructs impatiently.

I try to balance. I really do. But it's impossible. Yet again the board shoots from underneath me and I fall over for what must be the umpteenth time. 'Ouch,' I yell, landing hard on my bum. Wincing, I rub it with my gloved hand and pick myself up again. It's only a few bruises, I tell myself cheerfully. Practice makes perfect and all that.

Trying to ignore the fact I'm growing increasingly cold and wet, I go to grab my snowboard, then falter. Unexpectedly my eyes start to water. Oh god, how embarrassing, why am I crying? I'm being silly. It's only a few bruises. Except that's not true – as much as I'm ashamed to admit it, it's more than a few bruises. I've tried so hard to throw myself into this, to enjoy myself and be enthusiastic, to love snowboarding as much as everyone else seems to but—

But . . . I just don't. I'm not enjoying myself and I don't love it and I don't know what's wrong with me. A tear escapes and I brush it away quickly before anyone notices. The worst bit is I know I'm lucky. Most girlfriends would chew their right arm off to be taken away on an all-expenses-paid trip to the French Alps for the weekend. It's my fault I'm not enjoying it. It's not anyone else's. And it's certainly not Seb's.

I think about him now at the top of the mountain. He'll be with his friends, having glorious alpine adventures full of sun and scenery, and breaking to enjoy the best bars and restaurants on the upper slopes.

At the very thought I suddenly feel completely alone. More alone than I can ever remember feeling, wearing this silly outfit, miles away from home, with no one to talk to but lots of French-speaking children.

It's all I can do to fight back the tears as I glance back at François. But he's given up on me and is busily flirting with a suntanned blonde in hot pink salopettes. Probably one of the mothers of the cannonballs, I reflect, watching them laughing together. I might as well not be here.

In which case . . .

Throwing my snowboard over my shoulder, I turn and set off slipping and sliding down the slope in the boots that have given me blisters. I'm beginning to think I was right the first time. I'm beginning to think I should never have come.

29

I find an internet café and order myself a hot chocolate. And a slice of that delicious-looking cake. Well, I have been exercising. If you can call falling over 'exercising', I wince, easing my aching body into a chair.

After the freezing cold of the slopes, I've never been more grateful for the cosy warmth of inside and, taking off my sodden gloves, I warm my hands against the cup and take a sip. It's delicious. Sometimes there really is nothing that hits the spot like a mug of thick, creamy hot chocolate.

For the next few minutes I do nothing but sit there in a sort of trance-like daze, eating cake and drinking hot chocolate, feeling myself slowly coming back to life. Gradually thawing out and feeling a bit better, I glance absently at one of the computer terminals. Actually, while I'm here I might as well check my emails, I decide, putting down the cup and reaching for the keyboard.

I'm just logging on when I hear my mobile beep. It's a text from Fergus:

How's your mini-break?

Reading it I feel a beat of pleasure. Getting a text from a friend never fails to cheer me up. I start texting Fergus back but my fingers won't work properly, the result of being previously frozen solid, and it's taking forever with all the fiddly buttons. I give up. I'll just call him instead. Vodafone have sent me a text telling me I've got some new special cheap rate to use my mobile abroad, plus right now I could do with hearing a friendly voice.

I dial his number and he immediately picks up.

'Don't tell me, you're in some swanky hotel in Paris, surrounded by champagne and red roses,' he quips in his Irish accent.

Why does everyone keeping saying that? Fiona said exactly the same thing when I called her while I was on my way to the internet café, to check on Flea, and didn't even try and hide her disappointment when I told her the truth. Her voice dropped about two octaves, from all high and excited to all flat and bored-sounding, and she suddenly said she had to go as there was someone at the door.

'Not exactly,' I say, shifting my damp bottom in my chair. 'You got the country right, but I'm not in Paris. I'm in Chamonix, snowboarding.'

'Crikey.' He sounds impressed. 'I didn't know you snowboarded.'

'I don't, I'm rubbish, it's Seb who's the expert,' I sigh, then realising I sound like I'm complaining, I try to be more positive. 'It's my first time. I'm having lessons; hopefully I'll be a quick learner.'

'Well, good on you,' he says supportively. 'Never fancied it myself. Give me a beach any day . . .'

Not for the first time, I feel myself silently agreeing with Fergus.

'So anyway, come on, forget about me, don't keep me in suspense, how was your audition?' I ask, switching topics.

'It was great craic!' He sounds suddenly galvanised. 'I was in a really good mood as – guess what? – she replied!'

'Who did?' I ask innocently.

'Sara! My Missed Connection!'

For a brief moment I feel a clutch of anxiety, a split second of guilt that zips across my consciousness as I have a sudden recollection of creating that fake email account late last night, pretending to be someone else and writing the email, signing myself as Sara . . .

But then my doubts vanish as I listen to him gabbling excitedly down the phone.

'. . . really gave me that boost I needed for the audition, my nerves completely vanished . . .'

'Brilliant,' I enthuse, feeling a swell of happiness and more than a little relief.

'. . . apparently she noticed me too, but was too shy to say hello . . .'

I've never heard him so happy, sending that email was definitely the right thing to do. I'm so pleased it worked.

'. . . and that she'd love a coffee but she's flying to Thailand next week to go and work in an elephant sanctuary.'

OK, so I admit it's not the best excuse, but it was late and I had to think of a bulletproof reason to let him down gently. It's the best I could come up with under the circumstances.

'Oh well, never mind,' I soothe, 'at least it proves you weren't rejected. And I bet you get the part too.'

'Well, actually there's a rumour they gave it to someone else, I'll find out for sure next week—'

'No way!' I exclaim indignantly. 'But that part was perfect for you!' Now I know how mothers must feel when they think their child is much better than everyone else's.

'It's OK, I'm fine about it—'

'Well I'm not!' I protest hotly. I'm not kidding, I feel like ringing up those stupid casting people myself and asking them what they were thinking! Fergus was *obviously* the best. Of course I'll be polite and everything, I'll just firmly tell them that he's way more talented than everyone else and—

'I think it's fate if I don't get it.'

My imaginary speech in which I'm outraged is brought to an abrupt halt.

'*Fate?*' I echo dubiously. 'What do you mean?'

'I mean maybe I'm not meant to be an actor,' he says blithely. 'I haven't been very successful so far, have I? Maybe I need to do something else, something more fulfilling, something that's really going to make a difference.'

'Like what?' I ask warily. I'm not liking where this conversation is heading; in fact, I'm beginning to feel a bit worried.

'Like going to Thailand to work with elephants.'

Oh god. This cannot be happening.

'Don't you think you might be rushing into things a bit,' I argue hastily. 'OK, so you didn't get this audition, but that's no reason to jack everything in and leave London—'

But he's not listening.

'In fact, I've emailed Sara back.'

Ping.

As I'm on the phone, an email pops into my inbox on the computer screen. With my heart in my mouth, I open it:

> Dear Sara, Wow, what a cool thing to do! I'd love to do something like that. Do they need any more volunteers? Maybe I should come and join you? Fergus x

'I really feel like it's a sign.'

I snap back. '*A sign?*'

Oh god, this is all my fault. It's all because of my email. Instead of making it better, I've made it worse. Much, *much* worse. Fuck. What am I going to do? My mind grapples with a solution. Come on – think, Tess, think. There must be a way to fix this. There must be something you can do.

An idea hits me but I try to bat it away. There must be another option. Another way. But there isn't. There's nothing else I can do.

Making my excuses, I quickly say goodbye then, feeling myself digging a deeper hole, I start typing . . .

I'm going to have to email him back.

I arrive back at the chalet to find Seb, all bright-eyed and buzzing with adrenalin.

'Hey, there you are!' he beams as I walk through the doorway, carrying my snowboard.

And immediately get stuck.

You know that joke with the man with the ladder who turns sideways? Well, that's me.

'Oops, ouch,' I yelp, banging bits of me as I struggle with my snowboard. Some people are born for the slopes – they make it all look so effortless.

I am not one of those people.

'You OK?' he asks, rushing to help me.

'Um . . . yes, fine,' I smile, finally making it through.

'So how was your day?' he asks eagerly.

He's so excited and buoyant, I don't have the heart to tell him it was a disaster, that it was like learning to dance on golf balls and that I hated every cold, soggy, lonely minute of it. Not after all the effort he's made. And not when our relationship depends on it.

Instead, I pin on a bright smile. 'Brilliant,' I nod.

His face lights up. 'I knew you'd love it, I just knew!'

'Yup,' I keep smiling. As if I'm frozen. Which I am, quite frankly, as it took forever to walk back from the internet café with all my blisters. I could feel them popping in my boots like bubble wrap.

'Amazing, isn't it? Like nothing else in the world. That exhilaration, that freedom . . .'

I nod mutely. See, there *must* be something wrong with me. I can't believe we're talking about the same experience.

'And with you doing military fitness, I bet you'll pick it up in no time!'

His eyes are flashing with excitement and he just looks so pleased and happy that all I can do is stand there smiling and nodding, like one of those plastic dogs you see in the back window of cars.

'Well, I should really get out of these clothes,' I say, finding my tongue at last, 'get in the bath, soak these aching muscles.'

'Why don't you jump in the hot tub?' he suggests. 'That's the perfect cure for aching muscles.'

Of course! The hot tub. I'd forgotten all about that. For the first time that day I feel my heart soar.

Except—

'Where are Chris and Anna?'

'Enjoying some après-ski, if I know Chris. They won't be home for hours,' he laughs fondly, then asks, 'Why?'

'Oh, no reason,' I shrug, trying to sound blasé whilst inside I'm doing a Mexican wave.

'Go, jump in,' encourages Seb. 'I'll come join you in a minute.'

'OK,' I smile. Trust me, I don't need any more encouragement, and grabbing my things I head towards the bedroom to get changed.

'Oh, by the way,' Seb calls after me, and I turn.

'I came by the ski school earlier but I couldn't find you. Weren't you on the nursery slopes? The instructor must have got confused as he seemed to think you'd left already.'

Oh fuck. I've been busted. A wave of guilt crashes over me as I realise I must have been tucked up in the café drinking hot chocolate and chatting to Fergus. 'Um . . . yeh,' I nod, 'but they, er, moved me to a different class.'

'Already? Wow.' He smiles proudly. 'See, it won't be long till you'll be able to join me off piste . . .'

'Um yeh, fab,' I smile.

Oh god, I'm a terrible person. Now I feel even worse.

But I'm not going to think about any of that right now, I tell myself firmly. In fact I'm not going to think about anything apart from the lovely bubbling hot tub just waiting for me outside . . .

Almost giddy with anticipation, I peel off my many layers. I didn't bring a bikini as I thought I'd just pick one up at the airport if it turned out to be a spa break, but still, I suppose I can just wear my underwear, I decide, reaching for a towel. Then I pause as a thought strikes. Actually, if it's just me and Seb, I don't need to wear anything at all, do I? And with a naughty giggle I wriggle out of my bra and knickers, and wrap the towel around me.

Outside the temperature has dropped even further. Gosh it's freezing out here, I shiver, glancing over at the hot tub which is lit up on the deck, steam rising invitingly from the gurgling bubbles. I brace myself, then whip off my towel and throw it over a chair. The icy air hits my naked body and I race naked across the snow-covered deck and clamber hastily into the hot tub.

Ahhh, bliss. As soon as the warm bubbles hit me I let out a groan of pleasure. Sinking down into the water, I sit up against one of the jets, relishing the feeling of the water pummelling my aching back. I feel as if I've died and gone to hot-tub heaven. Maybe I was too hasty earlier. Maybe this snowboarding trip isn't so bad. OK, so I'm rubbish at actually snowboarding, and yes it is a bit lonely on your own, but I'm seriously enjoying this part – being out here is just incredible.

Enjoying the experience of it being subzero outside and warm inside, I take in the view. Darkness has descended but I'm surrounded by the snowy mountains, whilst below me the resort is lit up with twinkling lights. I gaze upon it, my breath making small white clouds, then tip my head back. Above me the sky is so dark, so clear, I can see a million stars, twinkling brightly. And, hang on, there's something else . . .

Snowflakes.

As one flutters down and lands on my nose, I'm suddenly reminded of Fergus, and for a moment I'm transported back to his roof terrace. Gosh, was it only last night? It seems like ages ago. So much has happened since then: plane rides, auditions, pretending to be Sara, his Missed Connection . . . Remembering our conversation earlier, my mind flicks back to the internet café and the emails. I wonder if he got my reply?

All at once worry bubbles up inside me, like the bubbles in the hot tub. Maybe I should ask to borrow Seb's iPhone and try to check my emails.

Abruptly I stop myself. What am I doing? I've gone away for the weekend with my boyfriend. I should be thinking about him, not Fergus.

Which reminds me; *where is Seb?*

As if on cue, I hear footsteps. Oh, that will be him now. Good. I need to push all this Missed Connection nonsense with Fergus out of my head. Concentrate on my own relationship, not somebody else's imaginary one.

Brushing my damp hair off my face, I try to rearrange myself a bit. I need to look more like sexy naked girlfriend relaxing casually in the hot tub, rather than knackered achy girlfriend slumped over the jets because every single muscle in her body is killing her.

Stifling a hippo-sized yawn, I recline against the edge and wait expectantly for Seb to appear. His footsteps grow louder, closer. That's funny, but now it almost sounds like two pairs of footsteps . . .

No sooner has the thought struck than I realise with horror that it's not Seb I can hear.

It's Chris and Anna.

'Hey!' yells Chris, spotting me first. 'Look who's here!'

It's like one of those bad dreams where you find yourself naked in a public place. Except this is much, *much* worse. It's not a dream and *I AM NAKED*. Plunging myself as deep into the hot tub as I can go without drowning, I lunge desperately over to one of the jets and pray for bubble coverage.

With the water up to my neck, I poke out a few fingers. 'Hi,' I say weakly, giving a little wave and trying to act, sort of, normal. With any luck they won't notice I don't have any clothes on. They'll just say hi, turn around, and go back to the chalet.

Yeh right. Who am I kidding? Luck officially deserted me on the nursery slopes.

'Oh . . . hi,' says Anna, noticing me with obvious displeasure. She's wearing a bathrobe, which she opens to reveal a white string bikini, a deep suntan and the kind of body that has never seen a Malteser, let alone a whole family-sized bag.

Did I just mention that this is a nightmare? One that I am not waking up from? As they both step into the hot tub – *correction*: Anna steps, Chris strips off to his boxers and sort of dive bombs – my mind scrambles frantically around, looking for an escape route. But there isn't one.

I am trapped. In a hot tub in the Alps. With no clothes on.

And a really bloody bright light shining up my *you know what*, I realise with horror, trying to block it out with my feet.

'So, did you have a nice day?' I enquire politely, as if I'm standing at a drinks party and not squatting in an oversized plastic bathtub with both hands clamped over my breasts.

'Fucking A!' whoops Chris, who's obviously been enjoying a bit too much of the après-ski. 'Totally wiped out on one of the blacks!'

I'm not quite sure what he's saying as he's talking in 'Snowboard', a language which I've discovered is spoken here in Chamonix and which I don't speak, but I'm saved from replying as he turns his attentions to Anna, who's been steadfastly ignoring me. Actually, perhaps *saved* isn't exactly the word I'm looking for, I soon realise, as his attentions are focused mainly on her breasts and they suddenly start . . .

Well, without giving too much detail, I think the phrase they use in America is 'fooling around'.

Personally I have another phrase: it's '*Get Me Out Of Here!!!*'

Cringing with embarrassment, I steadfastly try to ignore them and stare instead at my towel, which is hung over the chair by the door. I'm trying to gauge if I can jump out and grab it before being seen. After all, I can't stay here all night, can I? I can feel myself starting to go wrinkly. Plus, I can hear sucking noises and I have a horrible feeling it's got nothing to do with the hot tub's jets.

Not for the first time do I think about Seb, and not in a good way.

Where the fuck is he? I could kill him.

Mortified, I sit there for a few minutes longer, until I can bear no more and clear my throat loudly. They stop whatever it is they're doing and turn to me.

'Oops, sorry, forgot you were there,' giggles Chris drunkenly.

'Maybe we should go inside, darling,' says Anna with a little tut.

I feel myself go beetroot. How can it be that I'm the one completely starkers, and yet I'm the one made to feel like a prude?

But who cares? They're getting out, I realise, with a rush of relief, as I watch them disentangle themselves and climb out of the hot tub, before disappearing up the path which leads back to the chalet. I wait for a few moments to make sure the coast is clear, then, jumping out, I make a dash for my towel and follow them inside.

I find Seb on the sofa strumming a guitar.

'Hey babe.' As I walk in he looks up, seemingly unaware that anything is wrong. 'How was the hot tub?'

'I thought you were going to join me?' I reply, through clenched teeth.

'Sorry, I got distracted by Chris's twelve-string . . .' He gestures at the guitar as if that perfectly justifies forgetting all about your girlfriend who's outside in the hot tub *naked and waiting for you.*

And don't even get me started on the fact that he should have rescued me from Chris and Anna and their floorshow.

Irritation yaps at my ankles but I try to ignore it. I'm just in a bad mood.

'Let me play you something,' he continues, and without waiting for an answer, he starts playing a series of chords.

Except I can't ignore it. Standing there with an aching body, blistered feet, and water from my hair dripping on the floor and forming a little puddle around me, I realise I've had enough. More than enough. Because it's not all my fault. All day I've tried my hardest to be grateful and enjoy myself, but being dumped on the nursery slopes while he went off to enjoy himself with the others really wasn't much fun. And leaving me waiting in a hot tub for forty-five minutes was even less fun. But expecting me to listen to a bad rendition of 'Wonderwall'?

'Actually I think I'm going to go to bed,' I reply, interrupting his chord progression.

Abruptly he stops playing, and looks up sharply. 'Oh OK,' he nods, with a flash of disappointment, or is it surprise that I'm not going to stay and listen? 'I guess you must be tired, first day snowboarding and all that.'

'I guess so,' I agree. Except it's more than that. It's about how for the first time since we started dating for the second time, I've put me first.

As I walk into the bedroom, he starts up again. I close the door behind me and climb into bed. Except I'm too wound up to fall straight to sleep, so I pick up my Obama book and open it to my page, which is . . .

Page three? *Is that all?*

I try to focus, but I'm distracted by a noise coming from next door. Chris and Anna must be watching a movie. And by the sound of all that screaming, it's a horror film. Honestly, you'd think they'd turn the volume down. They're just so selfish. I try to ignore it, but it's impossible. In fact, it's getting louder and louder and—

Suddenly it dawns on me. *They're not watching a movie.*

Oh, yuk.

Obama makes a loud thud as I chuck the book at the wall in frustration. Not for the first time today does it strike me that my romantic weekend away isn't turning out quite how I expected. And, turning out the light, I put my fingers in my ears and stuff my head under the pillow.

30

Long before the days of Expedia.com I went to a local travel agent's to book a holiday. I was only seventeen and going on a package to Corfu with my friend Suzie, but as we waited our turn, I remember flicking through one of those Winter Sun holiday brochures. The ones with a laughing couple on the front cover, with the toothpaste smiles and colour-coordinated jackets, skiing down a mountain.

For a girl who'd grown up sledging on a plastic bag down the farmer's fields, it all seemed very glamorous. I'll never forget reading about all the fun on the slopes, the benefits of fresh air and exercise, waking up feeling rested and invigorated.

OK, so here I am in Chamonix . . . let's see exactly how much of that brochure was true:

1. Fun on the slopes?

Fall over a lot. Feel like crying. Run away to a coffee shop and eat cake.

2. Benefits of fresh air and exercise?

A bruise that looks like the map of Africa on my left buttock. More blisters on my feet than the last time I walked home from a nightclub in stilettos because I'd missed the last bus. Never again underestimating how much I like sitting on the sofa watching *The X Factor*.

3. Waking up feeling rested and invigorated.

Waking up feeling as if I've been run over by a double-decker bus.

The next morning I can barely move. The word 'sore' doesn't do it justice. It's as if I've aged about a hundred years overnight and it takes forever just to climb out of bed. And to *think* I'm supposed to do it all over again today, I wince, as I shuffle into the shower. At this rate, I'm not going to be able to walk, let alone snowboard.

But after forty-five minutes of standing under steaming-hot jets of water, I've mustered some enthusiasm and am determined to have another go. I can't give up after one day! OK, so yesterday was a bit of a disaster all round, but I'm not going to let it ruin the whole trip. I *can't* let it ruin the whole trip, I remind myself firmly. This is my big chance to prove to Seb that I'm the one for him. I can't blow it now.

Having loosened up enough to be able to put on my socks without shrieking, I make it into the kitchen for breakfast. Only to discover everyone else has finished eating and are pulling on their boots.

'Hey, there you are,' says Seb as I appear. 'We're getting ready to leave.'

'Already?' I check the coffee pot. There's only a dribble left. 'Oh OK, well I'll just have to grab a coffee on the way—'

'No need,' replies Anna sniffily. 'We're going to Les Houches to board the Kandahar.'

'You're doing what?' I ask, ignoring her and turning to Seb for an explanation. Like I said, I don't speak Snowboard.

'Kandahar's the famous World Cup downhill run. We're going to snowboard down it,' he explains.

'Somehow I don't think you'll be able to manage it after just one lesson,' patronises Anna. 'Never mind.'

I've tried my best to like her, I really have, but it's hopeless. She really is a total cow.

'But ride up with us on the cable car,' suggests Seb, who for some reason is completely oblivious to her bitchiness. 'The view is awesome.'

'And you can watch your man fly off the top,' grins Chris, grabbing the last piece of toast before I can reach it and shoving a corner in his mouth.

My stomach protests loudly. Make that coffee *and* toast.

'Then you can ride back down again to the nursery slopes,' finishes Anna pointedly.

I choose to ignore her. 'OK,' I manage limply, 'Well, in that case I'll just go and throw my clothes on and I'll be right with you.'

Despite Anna's comments, I'm really glad I do go, as the view from the cable car more than makes up for having to sit next to her on the ride up there. It's incredible. As is watching Seb launch himself off the top of the mountain. It's a sheer drop, but he casually dives over the edge and disappears with the others, the sounds of their whooping echoing from down below.

If I needed more evidence to prove I'm never going to be a snowboarder, then this is it. It takes me all my courage to even just *look* over the edge.

I take the cable car back down the mountain and grab some breakfast, then make my way to the nursery slopes for my next lesson. Though, to be honest, I'm beginning to have second thoughts. Einstein once said that the definition of insanity is doing the same thing over and over and expecting different results. Which a) perfectly describes my attempts at learning how to snowboard and b) means I must be completely insane.

I'm just struggling to get up from the snow after yet another fall, when I'm vaguely aware of a sort of muffled vibration. Funny, but that almost sounds like my mobile. Hang on, that *is* my mobile, I realise, scrabbling around to find it underneath all my layers. I finally locate it, just before it rings off.

'Hey, I've been trying to get hold of you.'

It's Fergus. It sounds urgent.

'Sorry, I've been on top of a mountain – there probably wasn't any reception.'

'I wanted to talk to you, Tess.'

'You did?' I feel unexpectedly pleased.

'Sara emailed me back.'

Followed by a curious beat of disappointment.

'And I just needed some female advice.'

'Yes, of course,' I reply, quickly gathering myself together.

He clears his throat and starts reading:

'Dear Fergus,

Great to hear you'd be interested in volunteering, but unfortunately the sanctuary is run by Buddhist monks and strictly for practising Buddhists only. Sorry about that. Best, Sara (Karma Dechen Palmo – Radiant Woman of Great Bliss)'

There's a pause, then, 'So, what do you think?' he asks.

I think that coming up with this new excuse wasn't easy and it took *forever* to find that Buddhist name. I was Googling for nearly an hour yesterday in that café!

But of course what I think and say are two different things. I swallow hard. I need to be very careful here. I don't want to make things worse than they already are.

'Well, at least you gave it your best shot,' I say cautiously, accidentally catching the eye of François, my instructor, who throws me a dirty look and motions at my mobile phone. Which is rather cheeky considering his own is permanently glued to his ear. I signal 'won't be a minute' with my gloved hand, and wait for Fergus to answer.

It seems to take forever and then . . .

'Yup, you're right.' Fergus heaves a sigh on the other end of the line.

I've been holding my breath tight inside of me, barely daring to breathe, and now I let it out. Oh thank god. Disaster averted. My whole body sags with relief.

For like a second.

'But then another part of me thinks: you know what, Fergus, if you want something you have to go out there and get it.'

My mouth goes dry. 'You do?' I croak.

'All my life I've been so scared of failure I've never dared go for it. I mean, OK, I tried with my acting, but did I really try? Did I *really* go for it?'

My thoughts are scrambling. 'Um . . . I don't know, did you?' I stammer, but his questions are rhetorical and he's already charged on ahead.

'I don't want to just give up. So I'm going to email her back and tell her I've been doing a lot of thinking—'

'You are?' I interrupt with horror.

'Yes I am,' he says with a determination I've never heard before. 'Ma O'Flanagan won't be happy, or our local Catholic priest, but I've been reading up on it, and you know what? *I think I could become a Buddhist.*'

I open my mouth to say something, I'm not quite sure what, but before I can answer he's gone.

'Fergus? *Fergus?*' I yell down the handset, before I realise we've been cut off. Frantically I try calling him back, which is when I notice the screen on my phone is blank. Oh fuck. The battery is dead!

The rest of my lesson is spent trying and failing to concentrate. I can't stop thinking about my conversation with Fergus, which means I spend even more time on my bum then ever before. I think François is relieved when I tell him today is my last day and I won't be back tomorrow. He says something in French I don't understand, but I don't need any help translating when he throws his arms around me, before waving me off with the biggest smile he's ever given me.

Afterwards I go straight back to the chalet. I want to charge my phone so I can call Fergus back, only after searching through my bag I realise I've forgotten my charger and everyone else has an iPhone.

Something which Anna seems to take great delight in.

'What? You don't have an iPhone?' she sniggers from the sofa where she's draped around Chris, drinking a glass of red wine. 'How vintage.'

'I like my old Nokia,' I say defensively.

'You're going to have to come into the twenty-first century one day,' grins Seb, pulling me towards him for a kiss.

Usually I'd be thrilled by the affection, but now it just irritates me and I pull away.

Seb's grin vanishes and is replaced by a frown. 'What's wrong?'

'Um, nothing's wrong. I'm just tired,' I say hastily, brushing away any doubts. Yes, that's all it is, it's got nothing to do with Seb, I'm just tired and crabby. This weekend has completely exhausted me. 'By the way, shouldn't we start packing?' I remind him.

'I know you don't like to be late, but it's still a bit early for that,' he replies, resuming his smile and reaching for the open bottle of wine. He starts pouring two glasses.

'Why, what time's our flight back to London?' It's probably one of those that don't get into Heathrow until the early hours.

'Oh don't worry, it's not until tomorrow,' he says, passing me a glass of wine.

For a moment I think he's joking. 'Are you serious?'

'Why wouldn't I be?' he replies evenly.

'But tomorrow's Monday.'

'Ten points for a correct answer,' whoops Chris from the sofa, and Anna laughs as if it's the funniest joke she's ever heard.

'And I have to be back at work,' I add for Anna's benefit, whose only job appears to be that of a professional girlfriend.

Scowling at me, she tosses her blonde hair over her shoulder and snuggles up to Chris. I've obviously hit a nerve. To be honest, as much as she's a cow, I actually feel quite sorry for her. I've met girls like Anna before, women who make a career of going out with rich men, but I've noticed a few wrinkles around Anna's eyes and yesterday I caught her looking in the mirror and pulling back her face when she didn't see me watching. I reckon she's a lot older than she lets on.

But what happens when the Botox stops working? When her bottom starts to sag? Chris trades in his girlfriends like his cars and always prefers the newest model. Soon there'll be a different blonde on that sofa, a *younger* blonde. Then what's Anna going to do?

'I'm sure you can square it with your boss,' says Seb casually. 'It's only a day.'

I glance back at him in disbelief. 'I can't just ring up and say I'm not coming in,' I bristle with indignation. '"Sorry Sir Richard, but I'm in Chamonix."'

'Why not?' he shrugs. 'It's not like your job's that important, is it? I don't think you've ever mentioned it, except to tell me you'll be leaving as soon as your boss retires.'

I feel stung. It's true, I hardly ever talk about my job with Seb, but that's because he never seemed that interested in the past.

'But that's not the point,' I argue. 'I might not be the best PA in the world, and it might not be the most important job in the world, but it's important *to me*—'

Until now I've never realised just how seriously I take my job at Blackstock & White. Not because I've got any great career ambitions there. On the contrary, working in an office, *any office*, isn't my dream. And, let's face it, my talents don't lie at the end of a spreadsheet. But I do always try to give something my all, whether I'm good at it or not (snowboarding aside, perhaps . . .). Like it used to say on my school reports,

'Tess might not be the most academic of pupils, but she always tries her best.'

'I can't let Sir Richard down.'

Looks are flying across the chalet at my outburst and Seb takes a sip of wine. 'So what do you want me to do? Change the flights?' He smiles at the very suggestion.

I realise at that moment that the whole truth of why I've never talked about my job to Seb is because he always made it feel so inferior to his mega-successful career.

'Yes . . . I do,' I say quietly but firmly.

For a moment no one speaks, then:

'Oh dude, you're not gonna leave us already,' wails Chris, sticking out his bottom lip like an overgrown schoolchild.

'If Tess needs to get back, Tess needs to get back,' shrugs Seb, but his jaw is set and I can see he's far from happy.

'But can't *you* stay?' suggests Anna, looking directly at Seb. She seems thrilled that I might be leaving.

'Anna's right, I can fly back on my own,' I say evenly, 'it's no problem.' I make an attempt at damage limitation. 'I don't want to spoil your weekend.'

But he's already picked up his phone and begun dialling: 'Hi, is that British Airways Executive Club? I need to change my reservation . . .'

31

As it turns out, all the flights are full and we have to wait until the next morning after all. Which means Seb is happy but I get into the office late and have to work through lunch to try to catch up on all my emails.

Including those from Fergus.

Over the last twenty-four hours he's been as good as his word and hasn't given up. In fact, he and my alter ego Sara have exchanged a dozen emails. I've had to keep checking them at the internet café, the airport, as soon as I got back to the flat, and now at work. It's been quite stressful.

And it's getting to be a real worry. With trepidation, I log in to my fake account and see another one from Fergus waiting for me in my inbox. Anxiety tugs hard. I can't keep emailing him like this. I was trying to save him from feeling rejected; after all, no one knows how that feels more than me, but instead of making things better, I've just made things worse.

I start reading his email, it's the fifth one today: *Dear Sara, it's me again ...*

My stomach knots. I've unwittingly got myself into a cyber-relationship. *With someone who's become a really good friend.* Oh Jesus.

Which is why I'm going to have to kill it once and for all, I decide, as I finish reading the message. Be cruel to be kind and all that. Fergus is going to be hugely disappointed, but ultimately it's for his own good.

With a heavy heart I hit reply and start typing ...

* * *

I've just pressed 'send' when I get a call from Sir Richard wanting to see me. As I hurry over to his office, I find his door ajar and Sir Richard sitting behind his desk, his usual genial mood replaced by a grave expression. Oh fuck. He's angry with me for getting in late today.

'Before you say anything, I can explain,' I blurt. 'My boyfriend took me snowboarding to France as a surprise, only he didn't tell me we were going to fly back today and when I made him try to change the flights they were all busy, so I didn't get in till nearly lunchtime, but I'll stay late tonight and make up for all the time missed . . .'

'Thank you Tess, I'm sure you will,' smiles Sir Richard, 'but that's not the reason I called you in here.'

'It's not?' I look at him in confusion. 'But—'

'Please, close the door and sit down,' he says, gesturing to the chair opposite.

His tone is serious again and, suddenly nervous, I push the door to, then perch myself on the edge of my chair. My mind is racing. Normally in a situation like this I'd be expecting to be told I'm losing my job, only I know that already.

'Can I be assured in the first instance that anything I tell you in this room goes no further?' he asks gravely, pushing his glasses onto the bridge of his nose.

For the first time I notice he's not wearing his old tortoiseshell ones, but a trendy designer pair.

'Um, yes . . . of course,' I nod hastily.

Gosh, I wonder what he's going to tell me? Unexpectedly a thought strikes. Oh no, please don't tell me he's going to confess his online porn addiction! I feel a flurry of panic as he clears his throat and I almost want to squeeze my eyes shut tight.

I swallow hard. Remember, Tess, be calm and mature. *Calm and mature.*

'It's about the company—'

Phew, what a relief!

Sir Richard raises his eyebrows in surprise. 'I'm sorry?'

'Oh, nothing . . . you were saying,' I fluster, realising I'd spoken out loud.

Steepling his fingers, he looks at me solemnly. 'I don't know if you are aware, but my great grandfather, Sir Angus Blackstock, founded Blackstock and White, along with his great friend Ross White, in 1882.'

'Yes, I read that in the company brochure,' I nod diligently.

'Four generations have worked here, each one taking this company from strength to strength, and when I took over from my father and became CEO thirty years ago, it was with the desire to do the same. A desire to pass on a legacy of achievement and expansion. Sadly my son Edmund has never wanted to enter into the family business, choosing instead a different career of sorts . . .'

He doesn't need to finish his sentence. Everyone in the office knows about Edmund, his estranged son, who works in a bar in Ibiza and, according to his Facebook profile, seems to spend his whole time partying and wearing neon vests.

'But regardless, I wanted to leave to my successor, whoever that may be, a legacy of strong growth . . .' He pauses, then lowers his voice. 'However, because of the current economic crisis affecting Europe, nay the world, I am sad to say that that might not be the case.'

He breaks off to clear his throat, then heaves a deep sigh. 'Blackstock and White is in trouble, Tess.'

I jerk my head up.

'Trouble?' I repeat. I might not be the most business-minded of people (I once joined in a conversation with Seb and some of his friends about footsie by merrily regaling how when I'd first met my teenage boyfriend's parents, I'd flirtily rubbed my stockinged foot up against his underneath the dinner table, only to later discover it had been his father's. Which was embarrassing enough, but made more so when I realised they were talking about *the* FTSE.)

However, trouble is trouble, whichever way you spell it.

Sir Richard nods seriously. 'So far I've managed to avoid making any redundancies, but I'm not sure how long this can continue for with the current market trends, which is why my trip to India tomorrow is so crucial. India is one of the largest emerging markets, and in contrast to what's happening in Europe, they've experienced double-digit growth in the alcoholic drinks market over the last two years. If my trip is successful, and we can broker a deal with one of the key players, it could keep Blackstock and White going for another hundred and thirty years.'

He looks at me, his eyes shining, and for a few moments I can tell he's considering the future of the company as a bright one; that he really does believe he can turn the company's fortunes around.

'I probably shouldn't be telling you all this, Tess,' he continues with a smile, 'but as my PA and support this past year, I feel as if we've worked well together as a team. I know all the hard work you've put in to help organise this trip and, before I leave tomorrow, I just wanted to let you know that I really do appreciate it.'

'Why, thank you,' I reply, almost blushing at his compliment.

'No, *thank you*, Tess. This isn't just another business trip, it's much more than that, and I felt it was important for you to know how significant all your efforts have been, and for me to thank you for the part you've played in all this. Especially during what's been quite – how shall I put it? – a *transitional* period in my personal life,' he adds awkwardly.

'Oh, don't mention it, I was only doing my job,' I say breezily, trying not to think about that time I found him on the sofa a couple of weeks back, all crumpled and unshaven. To be honest, that seems so long ago now. Since then he's all smartened up and got his mojo back – it's like he's a changed man.

'I shall miss this company but I shall take solace in the fact that I'm leaving it in the best position it's ever been in.'

'I know you will,' I smile. 'I've got every faith. We all have.'

'Splendid.'

He makes to stand up, which I take as my cue to leave, and I get up out of my chair.

'Oh, and I'd prefer it if we just kept this between ourselves,' he adds. 'I don't want anyone worrying about their job security, especially in this recession. Fingers crossed they won't have to.'

'Of course,' I nod. I think about Kym and her holiday booked to Ibiza next year, the girl in Accounts who's having a baby, John in Marketing who's just got married and is buying a house.

'Oh, and Tess, just one more thing.'

I turn.

'I just had a quick look through all the paperwork for the India trip and it all seems to be in order, except you haven't returned my passport. I know it was sent off to the embassy for the correct visa, so I'm assuming you must still have it.'

'I'll go and fetch it,' I reply confidently. 'I've probably filed it away in a drawer, or in my in-tray.'

'Just as long as it's not been lost in the post,' he chuckles jovially.

'Ha, yes,' I laugh.

Leaving his office, I go back to my desk to get his passport. To be honest, there's been so much going on in the past few weeks that I can't *actually* remember sending it off to the embassy, but I must have, as there are no Post-it notes about it on my computer screen. I only peel them off when whatever it is it's reminding me to do is ticked off my list. Maybe not the most orthodox of organisation systems, but it works perfectly for me.

So if I hadn't sent it off, it'd still be left on there. And it's not, I tell myself firmly, turning my attentions to my in-tray.

I rummage around for a bit, but there's no sign of any passport. How odd. I wonder if the embassy sent it back? Gosh, I do hope so, I muse, feeling a flicker of worry. I quickly dismiss it and start going through the piles of paperwork on my desk instead. I always pay the extra fee to get the visas expedited and couriered back. So it can't have got lost; it must be here somewhere.

Out of the corner of my eye I spot a flash of pink. A scrap of colour almost hidden in the gap between the monitor and the bit where all the cables go. I feel a slight iciness around the bottom of my spine. What's that? I try to reach it with my fingers but it must have fallen down the back and become wedged. Grabbing a ruler, I try to poke it out. The iciness is creeping up my spine but I pay no attention. It's nothing. Probably an old flyer. Or something that's fallen out of a magazine. Nothing important at all.

It's a Post-it note.

All scrunched up and torn where I've stabbed it with the ruler, but most definitely a Post-it note. Realising my mouth's gone dry, I swallow hard, then, with trepidation, smooth it out.

I stare at my scrawled handwriting with disbelief.

VISA

Just one, seemingly innocuous word, but it's enough to send me reeling. Oh no. Please tell me I'm wrong. Please tell me . . . I can't even finish the thought before I'm gripped with panic.

OK, come on, calm down, I instruct myself firmly. Let's not jump to conclusions. So I've found a Post-it. So what? It's a ridiculous bloody system anyway. Sticking Post-it notes as reminders on my computer screen. Honestly! It doesn't *definitely* mean I haven't done it. I've applied for dozens of visas for Sir Richard in the past. Admittedly I always leave it until the last minute to send it to the embassy, but I've never just *forgotten.*

I try to focus, but my mind is spinning. I can't think straight. You're looking for his passport, I remind myself sharply. Yes, of course, I just need to find Sir Richard's passport, check the visa's in there and then I can stop worrying over nothing. It's like when I think I've lost my keys and they're in my bag the whole time, I just can't recollect putting them in there. It will be the same with this Indian visa, I'm sure of it.

I start emptying the contents of my desk drawers, in the middle of which Wendy the Witch strides past and makes some comment about the state of my desk and how 'a tidy desk makes a tidy mind', but I don't answer. I'm too busy frantically rummaging through piles of crap . . . packet of Cup-a-Soup . . . emergency pair of tights . . . mini sewing kit . . . an envelope with some forms inside and – oh my god, here it is! Sir Richard Blackstock's passport!

With a burst of relief I pull it out of the envelope and start flicking through it. It's filled with visas from all his foreign travel. China . . . Hong Kong . . . Australia . . . the rest are blank pages.

No, that can't be right. I went too quickly, I must have missed it. I start again. Slowly this time. Page by page. I reach the end.

No, it can't be.

There's no Indian visa.

I stare at the blank pages in horror. It's not there! The Post-it note must have fallen off my computer screen and I never sent off his passport to the embassy.

And his flight goes first thing tomorrow.

I glance frantically at the clock, but it's already nearly four o'clock. It's too late. By the time I get a taxi to the embassy, it will be closed. Plus, there's no way they'd process it there and then.

Suddenly Sir Richard's voice plays in my head. '*So far I've managed to avoid making any redudancies, but I'm not sure how long this can continue for with the current market trends, which is why my trip to India tomorrow is so crucial . . . This isn't just another business trip, it's much more than that.*' As I start to take in the consequences I feel sick. I've fucked up. I've fucked up big time.

My heart is racing and I feel dizzy.

What the hell am I going to do?

32

'Tess? Are you OK? *Tess?*'

It's like I've dived underwater. Everything has receded and I'm only vaguely aware of muffled noises, but I can't make out what they are. Instead there's a growing sound in my ears as I sink lower and lower into the depths. A whooshing that's getting louder as everything else diminishes. Fades away around the edges. Disappears into the darkness—

'*TESS!*'

I suddenly come up for air to see Fergus peering at me with a worried expression.

'Huh?' I mumble. I feel dizzy. Like I'm going to faint.

'Crikey woman, what's got into you?' he complains.

My mind's like a computer booting up again. Shell-shocked, I stare at him for a few moments. 'I've done something terrible,' I finally manage in a whisper.

'You've done what?' he frowns, leaning closer to hear me.

I swallow hard, trying to slow my racing heart. 'I'm in big trouble,' I say in a low voice.

'Don't tell me, you've been busted for impersonating your voicemail again?' he quips, snapping on a mischievous grin.

'It's really bad,' I'm muttering to myself now as the consequences of my mistake start to run away from me like a line of toppling dominoes.

'What's worse than pretending to be an answering machine?' he laughs.

'Fergus, this isn't funny!' I snap, close to tears. 'This is really serious.'

He looks taken aback by my outburst. 'Sorry, I didn't realise . . .' Coming around the side of my desk, he pulls out my chair. 'Look, sit down, tell me all about it—'

'I don't have time!' I almost shriek.

Kym, who's on her way back from the Ladies, shoots a surprised look across at us.

'What are you two up to?' she asks, raising an eyebrow suspiciously.

God, the last thing I need is Kym finding out what I've done. Or haven't done.

Though she's going to find out soon enough, I realise, a surge of panic rising up again. *Everyone* will find out soon enough.

'Oh, nothing,' I say, forcing my voice to stay level. 'Fergus is just driving me mad as usual.' I give a tight little laugh.

'Ha, ha, yeh, that's right, I'm driving her crazy,' joins in Fergus.

Given he's an actor, that laugh couldn't be more fake. It's like canned laughter, only worse.

'Hmm, right . . .' nods Kym, but she doesn't look convinced. 'Well, don't leave me out if it's some office gossip,' she says, a little sulkily. 'I'm bored rigid.'

'We won't,' I say airily, forcing a wide smile as she continues on to reception.

Fuck. If she wants gossip, how about the company is about to collapse because I've just screwed up the CEO's crucial trip to Delhi, and everyone's going to lose their jobs?

At the thought I go cold and on impulse I grab my coat. Shoving Sir Richard's passport back into the envelope with all the paperwork, I stick it in my pocket.

'Where are you going?' Fergus shoots me a worried expression.

'I don't know . . .' I trail off, shaking my head. 'I just need to get some air. Breathe. *Think.*'

'Wait, I'm coming with you.'

Without hesitation he follows me as I rush outside, past Kym in reception, who looks up from the phone as we hurry past and opens her mouth to say something; but she's too late, I'm already out through the automatic doors with Fergus right behind me.

'What's going on?' he gasps, as the cold air hits us.

I hesitate. There's a part of me that doesn't want to say it out loud. I'm the only person who knows right now, and if I don't acknowledge it I can almost fool myself it's not really happening.

'Tess, tell me!' demands Fergus.

My heart is hammering in my chest. I don't want to tell him, because as soon as I do, it becomes real.

Except, who am I kidding? It's real anyway, whether I tell him or not.

So, taking a deep breath, I blurt it all out: about the passport, the visa, the trip to India, the company hanging in the balance:

'And it's all going to be ruined, because of me, because of my mistake!' I wail.

Fergus's expression is serious. He hasn't spoken the whole time I've been talking; instead he's listened intently, a cleft running down his brow.

'There has to be a way to fix this,' he says finally, shaking his head. 'There has to be.'

'There isn't. The embassy closes at four thirty, and even if we get there, they won't process it in time, it's too late—'

'It's never too late to try to put something right,' replies Fergus, his voice calm and determined. Stooping down, he unchains his bike and turns to me. 'Get on,' he instructs.

I stare at him blankly. 'Excuse me?'

'We're going to the embassy.'

'What? Both of us? But there's only one bicycle.'

'I'm giving you a backie.'

I look at him in alarm. 'Isn't that dangerous?'

'Very,' he nods. Unstrapping his helmet, he passes it to me. 'So put that on.'

I falter. There's no way I want to risk getting on the back of that bike. But I can't do nothing. Even if there's the *tiniest* chance I can put this right, I have to take it. Even if that means getting squashed under a double-decker bus.

'Come on, hurry!'

Strapping on Fergus's helmet, I climb onto the saddle. 'Do you think we'll get there in time?' I gasp, as he jumps onto the pedals.

'I can usually do Victoria in half an hour.' He checks his watch. 'Damn, we've got less than twenty minutes before the embassy closes.'

'Will we make it?'

'Hold on tight, cos we're sure as hell going to find out,' he cries, and with a thrust of the pedals we accelerate off down the side street.

I'm going to die! Seriously, it's going to be *One Day* all over again. Only this time there's going to be two of us. Me and Fergus. Squashed in a mangled wreck underneath a lorry. Or a car that's just pulled out in front of us and we've had to brake sharply and swerve—

Argh!

As I cling on for dear life, my arms wrapped tightly around his waist, Fergus whips the bike safely past the bonnet of the car and shoots down a side street. He's obviously a true professional at this. Not only is he incredibly fit – I swear I have never seen calf muscles like it, they are literally pumping like pistons – but he's also a human GPS. Nipping through alleys, zigzagging down back streets, he whizzes his way across London like a silver bullet, leaving the rest of the grid-locked traffic behind.

Gripping onto him, I watch as the tarmac speeds away beneath us. I'm absolutely terrified. I never take risks. I don't like danger. I'm the one who puts on her seat belt in the back of a black cab. I mean, I know you're *supposed* to, but who does that?

Me. I do.

And yet at the same time, at least the fear is preventing me from thinking about the visa. About what's going to happen if we don't get there in time.

At the very thought I experience another flurry of panic. If I'm going to die, at least I'll escape the fate that's going to be waiting for me back at Blackstock & White, I console myself. I'll never have to face Sir Richard, never have to see everyone's faces when they hear about the inevitable redundancies . . .

No, stop! That's not going to happen, I tell myself firmly. It can't happen! We've got to get there in time!

After crossing Hammersmith Bridge, we race along the Chelsea Embankment, following the Thames as it weaves its path through the city of London. Shafts of sunlight break through the heavy clouds intermittently, like a light display, each winter beam bouncing off the water. We head east, whizzing past the stationary traffic, before cutting up towards Victoria and Buckingham Palace.

There's never a moment's hesitation. This is what Fergus does all day and he knows this city like the back of his hand, taking in beautiful garden squares surrounded by iron railings, white stucco houses, majestic buildings rising up above the city sprawl. Forget any tourist on an open-top double-decker bus: this is how to take in London. Now I understand why he loves cycling so much – it's like the city is a living, breathing thing and you're part of it.

And then, before I know it, we're speeding around a corner and there, just ahead, is the India Visa Application Centre.

'We made it!' gasps Fergus, braking sharply and coming to a halt. He jumps off the pedals. I can't believe his legs don't just crumple beneath him.

'Oh my god, that's incredible . . . we're here already . . .' I stammer in disbelief. Even more incredible is that I'm still in one piece, I think, as he helps me off. My heart is racing and even though I haven't done any pedalling, I'm all wobbly and breathless. Part fear, part anticipation, *part dread.*

We both rush up to the door and I go to push it open, except . . .

'It's locked!' I cry, twirling around to Fergus.

'It can't be! We did that ride in eighteen minutes, I timed it!' he protests, snatching at his watch. 'What time do you make it?'

'Um . . . hang on . . .' I fumble at my wrist. 'Only four twenty-eight!' I cry indignantly. Twirling back around, I hammer on the door.

A security guard appears on the other side of the door. 'We're closed,' he says firmly through the wired glass.

'It's not four thirty yet,' I protest, 'there are two more minutes.'

'Not by my watch,' he says gruffly.

'But I need a visa urgently,' I try to explain, but he's unbudgeable.

''Fraid you'll have to come back tomorrow,' he replies emotionlessly.

'But I can't come back tomorrow!' I wail, my voice getting higher and higher. 'It's for my boss and his flight leaves for India tomorrow morning.'

'Well then he's not going to be on it, is he?' he says with a shrug that shows, quite frankly, he couldn't care less.

I stare at him, feeling both like yelling and bursting into

tears at the same time. 'Please!' I plead desperately. I have no shame. I am willing to start begging.

With a glower he pulls down the blind.

For a moment I stand there, unable to take in what's just happened. And for a moment my hopes remain suspended in the air, like Wile E. Coyote who runs over a cliff and doesn't realise until he looks down.

Then I look down.

And as the reality hits, my hopes go crashing. That's it. It's over. The company will be ruined. People will lose their jobs. *And it's all my fault.*

I turn away from the door, my body sagging in defeat. 'It's too late,' I say quietly to Fergus, who's been waiting anxiously. 'I've ruined everything.'

'Hey, stop beating yourself up,' he says immediately, putting his hand on my shoulder. 'You tried to put it right. Anyone can make a mistake.'

'But not this huge,' I choke, feeling the tears rising up in my throat, 'and not like this. This isn't about me, I don't care about me, it's about everyone else . . .' My eyes are filling up and I have to blink them away. 'People have kids, they've got mortgages . . .'

'Hey . . . hey,' he says, putting his arm around me as I start crying and bury my face in his chest. 'Now come on, they'll understand, they're your friends, they'll know you didn't do this on purpose . . .'

But I don't hear the rest of his sentence because I'm sobbing my eyes out. Big fat meaty tears that stream down my cheeks as if they're never going to stop. I've made mistakes in the past, but not of these epic proportions. How could I have been such an idiot? How? *How?*

I'm not sure how long we stand there, two people in the middle of the pavement, on a cold, grey January day, with the traffic and the world whirling around them. With my eyes squeezed tightly shut I want to block everything out, I don't want to think about anything. Until I become vaguely aware of the sound of a door opening, muffled voices, then the security guard instructing loudly, 'Can you move away from the door so the staff can exit?'

'C'mon Tess, no point standing here.'

I hear Fergus's soft Irish accent in my ear and look up, blearily, to see a few people leaving the building, and the security guard glaring in my direction. He's right, it's pointless. It's over.

Roughly wiping my face with my sleeve, I step backwards. I catch some of the staff looking over, brief curious glances as they wonder fleetingly what the story is behind the girl with the puffy face who's obviously been crying, and the dark-haired bicycle courier trying to comfort her. Before, just as fleetingly, I'm forgotten and supplanted by more important thoughts of meeting friends at the pub, the tube ride home, the children's tea.

But I remain here. Thinking of the fate that awaits me back in the office. About confessing what's happened to Sir Richard. My heart sinks at the thought. The worst thing is he won't be angry, he's too kind a person, he'll just be sad and disappointed, which is much, *much* worse. I'd rather he shouted at me. I deserve it. I let him down. I let everyone down.

'Tess?'

A voice breaks into my thoughts. For a moment I vaguely assume it's Fergus, but then I hear it again, louder this time.

'Tess!'

Realising it's not him, I turn around. Someone is staring at me from a few feet away. A man wearing a fur-trimmed parka and one of those hats with the flaps that cover your ears. I stare at him for a few moments, then suddenly it registers.

'Ali!' I cry, recognising him. Of course, it's Ali from the computer store. I haven't seen him since I picked up my laptop and we poured our hearts out to each other. He walks towards me and I give him a big hug. 'What are you doing here?'

'I came to meet my sister after work; we're going for a bite to eat. To meet my parents,' he adds, looking nervous.

'That's great Ali,' I smile encouragingly. I know how important this is to him. 'I'm sure it'll go really well.'

'Well, that's why I'm taking my sister along as a human shield,' he allows himself a small smile. 'Hey, Rupinda,' he calls over to a girl in a red duffel coat who's being let out of the office by the security guard. 'Come and meet my friend Tess and' – he gestures towards Fergus, and lowers his voice – 'Is this *him*?'

'Oh no,' I say quickly, realising the inference. 'Fergus is just a friend.'

'Hi,' smiles a pretty Indian girl, hurriedly pulling on her gloves as she comes to join us. 'Pleased to meet you.' Politely she extends a mittened hand.

'You too,' I reply, noting the family resemblance between Ali and Rupinda. 'And this is—' I'm about to say Fergus, but Rupinda suddenly gives a loud shriek and, withdrawing her hand, clamps it over her mouth.

'Rupes? What's wrong?' Ali's face is suffused with concern. 'What's happened?'

But she's rendered speechless. Her dark eyes flashing brightly, she shakes her head back and forth as if she can't believe her eyes.

'Rupes!' he demands, and then slips into a torrent of Punjabi.

'Is she OK?' asks Fergus, shooting me a worried look.

'I don't know.' I shake my head and look back at Rupinda, who's just standing on the pavement, frozen like a statue. At the sound of Fergus's voice, she takes a gloved hand away from her mouth and opening her mouth, finally stutters, 'It's him!'

'Who?' I ask, puzzled.

Raising her hand, she stares directly at Fergus and points a finger. She looks as if she's seen a ghost. 'The man from the advert.'

'Advert?' repeats Ali in confusion.

Rupinda's eyes have now gone glassy and it dawns on me that it's not horror she's experiencing, but excitement. '"*We get to the bottom of those bits that need pampering . . .*"' she gushes, repeating the line from the ad with a look of wondrous awe, '"*gentle yet strong, we go on and on and on . . .*"'

I look at Fergus with amusement. He's gone bright red.

'You were in a commercial?' says Ali, slowly registering.

'For bog roll,' Fergus nods, looking shamefaced.

'He's an actor,' I say loyally.

'Oh my goodness me, I love you!' Rupinda exclaims suddenly, coming back to life. 'I've watched that advert a million times! The bit with you and the kitten, it's so cute . . .' She trails off dreamily.

'I think you've got a fan,' I whisper, my mouth twitching in amusement.

'Thanks, I'm glad you liked it,' says Fergus self-consciously.

'I just can't believe I've met you,' she continues. Letting out a deep sigh she gazes at him lovingly.

'Your *biggest* fan,' I hiss, correcting myself.

Fergus is looking so embarrassed, shifting around from foot to foot and blushing to the roots of his hair, until all at once something comes over him. Throwing back his shoulders, he pushes back his hair off his temples and flashes her the smile he uses for all the girls in the office. I call it his 'leading man' smile.

'So do you work here?' he asks, in a voice that's suddenly dropped about three octaves.

I look at him in surprise. What's going on?

'Um . . . yes,' nods Rupinda, who's visibly trembling, and it's nothing to do with the icy temperatures.

'Is that so?' Fergus raises an eyebrow, Sean Connery-style. 'And would you have anything to do with the visas?'

Oh, so *now* I see where he's going.

'Yes, absolutely!' she nods fervently. 'I process them.'

'Well in that case,' he flashes her another leading man smile, 'I wonder if you could do me a favour . . .'

33

'You're a miracle-worker!'

'Oh, I don't know about that,' grins Fergus modestly.

'Trading your autograph for a business visa?' I exclaim. 'It was brilliant!'

'Well I'm just glad she's happy and you're happy.'

'Happy?' I grin. 'I'm ecstatic!'

A couple of hours later we're in a pub, celebrating. Rupinda was more than happy to do us a favour in exchange for Fergus's autograph, and after less than twenty minutes she reappeared with Sir Richard's passport, including his brand-new business visa, valid for travel tomorrow. After saying a huge thank you, I rushed back to work (in a cab this time), just before the office closed, and gave it to Sir Richard.

'Sorry about that, it was in my drawer,' I said with as much nonchalance as I could muster. 'I must have overlooked it.'

'Not a problem,' he replied cheerfully, flicking through to check his visa. 'I knew everything would be in order.'

I had a flashback to the frantic last couple of hours which had seen me desperately racing across London on the back of a bicycle, pleading tearfully with security guards and group-hugging Fergus, Ali and Rupinda with heady relief as we exchanged an autograph, a visa and our goodbyes.

'Yes, all perfectly in order,' I smiled brightly, before wishing him a safe trip and heading gratefully to the local pub.

Where I'd arranged to meet Fergus who, for the first time since I'd met him, had left his bike at home and caught the bus.

'Well, cycling while under the influence is never a good idea,' he laughed, getting in the first round.

'Here's to India!' he's saying now, raising his pint glass.

'And still being alive after that bike ride!' I grin, chinking my glass against his.

'Hey, you were fine, I was the one without a helmet,' he protests, taking a swig of his Guinness. 'I risked my life for you!'

I realise he's joking around, but as his words register, I also realise that that was exactly what he did and it's no joke. 'I know,' I say gratefully, falling serious for a moment. 'I don't know how to thank you.'

'Don't worry, another pint should do it,' he quips, and proceeds to drain the rest of the current one in one go.

'It's a deal,' I laugh as he waggles his empty glass. I'm buzzing with happiness, not to mention with wine. I've only had one glass but it's already gone to my head and I feel a bit tipsy. And I intend to get even tipsier, I decide, turning towards the bar before letting out a groan.

'Oh no, look how busy it's got,' I tut, suddenly noticing how the pub has filled up with the after-work crowd. The whole place is heaving and there's a crowd of people queuing at the bar waving tenners. 'I'll never get served.'

'Don't worry, I know the barmaid,' smiles Fergus. 'I'll get them.'

'What? In exchange for an autograph?' I tease, and he laughs.

'I can't help it if I've got fans,' he protests mockingly. 'Now what are you drinking? Same again?'

'No, let me get this round,' I protest. 'I can't have you doing everything.'

'Well if you insist, but I'll come with you, help you carry them.'

'I can manage, I've got two hands.'

'What if I want a bag of salted peanuts as well?'

I start laughing. 'OK, I give in,' I acquiesce, and together we start excusing our way through the crowd towards the bar. Gosh the place is packed.

'By the way, it's all over with Sara . . .'

'Who?' Spotting a space by the bar, I quickly squeeze in. 'Oh, your Missed Connection, of course.' With the visa crisis I'd totally forgotten about all that, but now I snap back.

'She said her plans had changed at the last minute and she was leaving for Thailand immediately.' Squeezing in next to me, Fergus turns to face me. 'And she said she wouldn't be able to send any more emails as there's no internet at the elephant sanctuary, or phones, or even regular mail. She's totally uncontactable.'

That was my last email and, as much as I'd worried about it hurting Fergus, I'd had to write that. I had no choice.

'That's a bummer,' I console, 'but don't take it personally. It's not you, it's just bad timing.'

He nods, his expression thoughtful. 'I guess you're right,' he agrees quietly.

'Didn't you know? Women are always right,' I quip, trying to lighten his mood.

It works. His expression breaks and he lets out a throaty laugh. Hearing it I feel a sense of huge relief. Despite all my fears, everything has worked out great in the end. Sir Richard gets to go to India and save the company and I got to save Fergus from a broken heart. All's well that ends well.

'To tell the truth I owe her a big favour,' he confesses.

'A favour?' I repeat, taken aback. 'Why?'

He chews his lip thoughtfully. 'Don't get me wrong, I was made up when Sara first emailed me. I couldn't believe my luck that she'd replied to my ad, I thought it was fate, and then when she said she was going to Thailand – well, I admit I got a bit carried away . . .' He breaks off sheepishly and heaves a sigh. 'But so much has happened since I posted that Missed Connection ad, and in a way it's thanks to her that I've realised I wasn't being honest with her, or myself.'

Hang on a minute. I stare at him feeling wrong-footed. I thought I knew what Fergus was thinking all along, but now, sitting here, it dawns on me I might have been mistaken.

'You weren't?' I say uncertainly.

'No,' he admits with a shake of his head, 'and she doesn't deserve that. Sara was always honest with me and I wanted to be truthful to her, to explain. Which is why I wrote back.'

I stiffen. *He wrote back?*

'When?' I try to ask casually, but my mind is scrambling. I never received another email. When did he send it? *What did it say?*

He shrugs. 'Oh, it was just before I saw you in the office . . .'

So that's why I didn't get it. I was too busy having a nervous breakdown about Sir Richard's visa. It must be still in my inbox. *Unread.* For a split second I wish I'd listened to Seb all those times he told me to get an iPhone. Now I could rush into the loos and read my emails, instead of standing here wondering what on earth he needed to thank me for and explain.

'But anyway, it's over, I'm never going to see her again,' he says, batting it away with his hand. 'So, come on, what's it to be? More wine?'

'Um . . . yes, please . . .' I smile, brushing the vague doubts inside of me under some cerebral carpet. He's right, it's over. What's there to worry about?

'Coming right up,' he smiles cheerfully, turning towards the barmaid, before letting out a cry. 'I can't believe it!'

I glance at Fergus, whose smile has frozen, and follow his eyes.

And it's as if someone has just dropped a heavy weight on my chest.

Oh my god, it just can't be . . .

But it is.

Standing across from us at the bar, it's her.

The girl from the café.

For a moment everything stops. As if I've just pressed pause on the DVD recorder of life and everything freeze-frames. Time stands still and I have this weird sensation of being removed from the situation, of looking down from above, and seeing the inevitable sequence of events that are about to happen whilst being powerless to prevent them. Of holding my breath deep inside of me. Of being suspended in that split second that divides life into before and after.

Then all at once someone presses play again.

And, like a car crash, it happens.

'Sara!'

'Fergus, wait . . .' But before I can stop him he's already made his way across to her. I rush after him.

'I thought I'd missed you. I thought you'd left already!'

Fergus is jabbering away in joyous disbelief while the girl is staring at him in bewilderment.

'Excuse me, do I know you?' She glances unsurely at her friend, who looks back blankly.

'It's me, Fergus,' he blushes beetroot. 'Sorry, I got a bit carried away, I should've introduced myself properly.'

She's looking at him uncertainly, as if trying to place him, while at the same time coming to the conclusion that there's no way she'd forget an attractive Irishman and he must be either drunk or trying out some crazy chat-up line, neither of which is appealing.

But Fergus is too busy grinning from ear to ear to notice. He looks so happy to see her. So excited. My heart plummets into the depth of my boots. Oh god, what I have done? *What have I done?*

'I'm sorry, but I really don't know you . . . Fergus,' she's saying now.

'The guy from the café . . . Missed Connections . . .' he adds, lowering his voice with embarrassment.

'Sorry, but I don't know anything about any Missed Connection,' she replies, firmer this time. 'And my name isn't Sara.'

Doubt flickers, like the flame of a candle. 'But the emails . . .' he begins.

I can't bear it any longer. I've been standing here for the last minute, not saying anything, not doing anything, but now I've got no choice. I was the one that got him into this mess, I have to get him out.

'It was me,' I blurt.

Three little words, but their significance is huge.

For the first time he seems to notice I'm standing behind him and, turning away from the girl, he looks at me in confusion. 'Tess, what are you talking about?'

I swallow hard, my heart hammering in my chest. 'I wrote the emails,' I say, hardly bearing to meet his eyes.

He stares at me in bewilderment. '*You're Sara?*'

I nod wordlessly.

For a moment neither of us speaks and I watch the flurry of emotions scudding across his face as he struggles to absorb what I'm saying, what this means. I wait for the impact of my words to hit. It seems like an eternity—

'Oh, I get it.' His voice is unrecognisable. Hard and steely; it makes me flinch. 'So this was all some kind of joke at my expense, was it? Thought you'd have a good laugh with everyone in the office—'

'*What?* No!' I cry with horror. Oh god, this isn't what was supposed to happen at all, how could he even think that? But even as I'm asking myself these questions, I'm suddenly seeing how this could be viewed from another perspective and it's making me go cold. 'You've got it all wrong.'

Our voices are raised and everyone in the bar is turning around to see what the commotion is.

'You've got a nerve,' he fires back. '*I* got it wrong?'

I feel frantic. Instead of explaining, I'm just making it worse. 'Please, Fergus, it wasn't like that . . .' I try again, but he shoots me a look that stings.

'Oh really? What was it like?'

'I was trying to stop you getting hurt, to save you from being rejected . . .'

The moment the words come out of my mouth, I hear how they sound and know immediately I should never have said them. But it's too late.

He recoils like a boxer who's been struck, then recovering he looks at me, his jaw set hard. 'Fuck you Tess, I don't need your pity.'

And turning away he pushes blindly through the crowds of people who have stopped to listen, and storms out of the pub.

34

For a moment I'm frozen, too shocked to move. I can't believe what's happened. It's all gone so wrong, so horribly *horribly* wrong. I cast a wild look around me; everyone is staring, but I don't care, I don't care about anyone but Fergus.

'Are you OK?'

I hear a voice and notice the girl he thought was Sara, her face creased with concern. 'Um no . . . I'm . . . I'm so sorry, I didn't mean to drag you into this,' and stammering my apologies I rush after Fergus.

Outside it's started to rain and I can see his figure up ahead, across the street.

'Fergus, wait!' Running down the steps I race across the road, dodging traffic. A car horn honks loudly, its driver yelling obscenities at me, but I barely notice. 'Please, wait, I know you're angry but let me explain!'

He doesn't turn around. He keeps striding up the street, determined to ignore me. I try to catch him up but the rain's coming down heavier and the pavement's slippery. 'It was never out of pity, you've got to believe me,' I'm shouting at his retreating figure, desperately trying to make myself heard above the traffic. 'I would never do that, you're my friend—'

Abruptly he stops dead and twirls around. 'Friend?' he cries scornfully. 'You call yourself a friend? What kind of friend does that?' His chest heaving, he breaks off and glares at me through the sheet of rain.

I've never seen him look at me that way before and I can feel my eyes smarting with tears, but I can't let them fall. I have to explain, to make him see.

'A friend who didn't want you to get hurt,' I reply, swallowing hard and trying to calm the storm of emotions that is threatening to overwhelm me. 'When you posted the Missed Connection ad and didn't get a reply, I couldn't bear seeing you so down about it. And then you had your audition, and you were so good, and you kept talking about getting rejected . . .' My voice wavers but I force myself to steady it and carry on: '. . . and I wanted to give you some confidence, I wanted to give you a boost, to make you realise what a great guy you are.'

I raise my eyes to Fergus's but he's not looking at me, he's staring down at the pavement, his jaw set hard. 'So I thought I'd write back and pretend to be her . . .' I trail off. At the time it had seemed like such a good idea, but saying it out loud now, it seems like such a stupid, thoughtless one. 'I thought it would give you a boost, make you feel good about yourself.'

'Don't patronise me.' He looks up at me, hurt pride flashing across his face.

'I'm not,' I protest. 'You're getting all this out of perspective, you're overreacting.'

'*I'm overreacting?*' He spits the words back at me and I flinch.

'Fergus, I didn't mean . . .'

Oh god, what's the point? I throw my hands up to my face, pressing my forehead against my palms. Instead of making things better, I'm just making them worse. It's like a car careering out of control and I don't know how to stop it.

But I have to try.

'I didn't want you to get hurt,' I say again quietly, taking my hands away and daring to meet his gaze. 'I know what it's like to feel rejected.'

'Yeh right,' he snaps. 'How would you know how it feels to be rejected?'

I pause. I can't tell him. I can't tell him about Seb, he'd never believe me.

'I . . . I can't explain . . .'

'Funny that . . .'

'But it's true, I do, you have to believe me,' I plead, fighting back tears.

'Believe you?' he cries scornfully. 'Why should I believe you? You don't even believe in yourself.'

His accusation catches me by surprise.

'You work some office job you're no good at because you don't have the guts to believe you're talented, to follow your dream, to even try what you *are* good at . . .'

I stare at him speechlessly.

'I saw that bag at your granddad's. It was amazing, you've got real talent, but you're just wasting it, throwing it away because you don't have the balls to believe in yourself, because you think you're not good enough—'

'*Says you!*' I retort with a snap of impatience, suddenly finding my voice. 'You didn't have any confidence before that audition, *you* didn't think *you* were good enough.'

'But I still went, didn't I?' he argues. 'I still tried.'

'Because I sent you that email,' I fire back.

'Oh please, don't flatter yourself Tess,' he replies, his voice hard. 'I would have gone anyway. You think I'm not used to rejection? I would have put myself out there, I would have tried, because if you don't try, you've failed anyway.' He pauses to sweep a hand through his hair, which is sticking to his face with the rain, then peers at me intently. 'What are you so scared of, Tess? Why are you so scared of being you?'

'I'm not scared of anything,' I say hotly.

'Is that why you spend the whole time pretending to be someone you're not?' He looks at me across the darkened street, his eyebrows raised pointedly. 'I thought I was supposed to be the actor.'

Somehow, somewhere, this conversation has turned around and now the focus is on me and I don't like it.

'I don't know what you're talking about.'

'The movie? The concert?' he challenges. '*Snowboarding?*'

I'm suddenly reminded of our conversations: talking about the *Star Wars* DVD he helped me find and me admitting I didn't like sci-fi; the time I confessed to wearing earplugs to listen to Seb's indie band, liking naff music instead, and him making me laugh about the Nolans; how happy I was to get his text when I was sitting alone in that café in Chamonix, calling him up to hear a friendly voice, confiding how I really felt.

'And there was I thinking Sara was the fake,' he says with a hollow laugh.

'I'm not a fake!' I cry defensively, snapping back. 'You don't know what you're talking about.' But even as I'm denying it, I know he's said something out loud that I don't want to hear, voiced some of the doubts that have been growing inside that I don't want to face up to.

Then, for a moment, neither of us speaks and we just stand there under the streetlamps, our ribcages rising and falling, the rain soaking through our clothes. Hurt and anger hanging in the air, thick like exhaust fumes, forming an impenetrable wall between us. Once so close, now so far apart.

'You sure about that, Tess?' he says finally, after a long pause. 'Because I'm not so sure. I thought I knew the real you, the person underneath it all, but now I don't know. I don't know what's real and isn't real.' He flicks his eyes up to meet mine. 'Do you even *know yourself* any more, Tess?'

As our eyes meet, I see something that makes my heart constrict. Disappointment. Then he turns and walks away. Only this time I don't call him back. It's too late. Standing motionless in the rain, I watch his figure gradually getting smaller and smaller, blurring into car lights, as he disappears out of view, out of my life. Gone.

When I finally arrive home, the flat's cold and empty. Fiona's left a note saying she's out with Tallulah at obedience classes and, tired and wet, I run a bath, then curl up on my bed with Flea and my laptop.

That's when I find the email.

With everything that's happened, I'd forgotten all about it, but now with a heavy heart I open it:

Dear Sara,

Thank you for being so honest with me, and now I want to be completely honest with you. When I first saw you in the café I thought you looked adorable, and I couldn't stop thinking about you. In fact I was probably a bit obsessive. Not in a scary-stalker way, but in a that's-all-I-can-think-about way.

But now I've realised it was to stop me from thinking about someone else. To try to stop myself from falling in love with them. I didn't do it deliberately, if that's what you're thinking – at the time I wasn't aware of what I was doing. But it didn't work anyway. To tell the truth it did the opposite.

You see, in a funny kind of way it took a 'missed' connection to make me see a deep connection I already have, to finally face up to the fact I'm in love with someone. And that someone is my friend, Tess. Only the thing is she's in love with someone else.

Anyway, this is probably too much information so I'll stop. I hope you don't think I've led you on, or messed you around, and I'd like to think we can part friends, even though we never met. It was never my intention to deceive anyone; as it turns out, the only person I was deceiving was myself.

I wish you all the best with your life in Thailand, and the elephants (btw I know you made that bit up about the Buddhist monks – I admit you had me going at first, but thanks anyway for trying to let me down lightly). Oh, and one last thing, a piece of safety advice: how do you stop a charging elephant?

Take away its credit card.

(The bad jokes are always the best.)

Fergus

I smile as I finish reading the email, but tears are blurring my vision. I didn't think I could feel any worse than I did. But I was wrong. Like I've been wrong about so many things, I realise, a sob rising in my throat.

I stare at Fergus's words on the screen, watching them blur and smudge like a watercolour left out in the rain. I feel dazed, like it's almost too much to take in. I had no idea he felt this way about me, was in love with me – *WAS*, I remind myself sharply. The past tense. Because whatever feelings he had for me are gone. I saw to that. My mind throws up an image of us in the street, the way he looked at me, and my heart aches. He's been so honest, and I've been so *dis*honest. How can he ever forgive me?

How can I ever forgive myself?

A single tear breaks free and spills down my cheek. Followed by another, and another. I don't try and stop them. I couldn't even if I wanted to.

35

A plane flies overhead, streaking a trail of white across the unbroken stretch of clear blue sky. I watch it for a moment, squinting in the sunshine, then open my compact to check my make-up. Oh dear. Despite the lashings of mascara and concealer, my eyes still look puffy and bloodshot. I add a bit more red lipstick, then dig out my sunglasses from my bag and stick them on. There's nothing else for it, I'll just have to hide them.

It's lunchtime the next day and I'm sitting on a bench outside St Mary's Church. It's surprisingly mild, as if winter suddenly got mixed up with spring overnight, and a few confused crocuses have poked their heads above ground, lulled into a false sense of security that the last of the frost is gone. Snapping my compact shut, I return it to my backpack and pull out a carrier bag. Inside is a pair of black satin stilettos I found in a charity shop. They were still in the box but had these ugly buckles on the front, so I replaced them with a pair of gorgeous art-deco butterfly brooches that I found in a junk shop instead. I tug off the boots I wore to the office, and slip them on. They go perfectly with the dress I'm wearing.

All done, I check my watch. I'm early for once. But then I made a special effort, after all.

There's the sound of crunching gravel and I look up to see a car approaching down the driveway. A silver mini, an old-style one, is rattling towards me, the suspension bouncing up and down as if its two passengers are on a trampoline. It comes to a halt with a rather worrying grinding of brakes, and the door is flung open.

'Well, here we are,' comes a cheery voice, and a head of brightly coloured dreadlocks emerge. 'Made it finally!'

It's Mel, from Hemmingway House, all smiles and dangly earrings.

'Sorry we're a bit late, completely my fault.'

'No it's fine,' I smile, jumping up from the bench and giving her a hug.

'Oooh, fab shoes,' she gushes, looking down at my feet. 'Very snazzy.'

'If you'd paid as much attention to my directions, we would never have got lost,' grumbles a voice from inside the car.

'Hi Gramps,' I smile, popping my head inside and leaning over to give him a kiss. 'Hang on, let me come round and help you out.'

'Nonsense, I can get out myself,' he protests, swinging open the door. Over the roof of the mini I see his walking stick waving around in the air. 'What do you think I am, an old man?'

Mel and I exchange grins, before rushing to his aid. Despite a lot of insisting that he's fine and can manage himself, he finally allows us to help hoist him out.

'See, nothing to it,' he announces, eventually standing upright. He glances at his reflection in the windscreen and begins adjusting his trilby.

'Well, I'll leave you two to it,' says Mel, lowering her voice and turning to me. 'I'll just wait in the car.'

'Are you sure you don't mind?'

'For Sidney? Of course not,' she grins. 'Take as long as you want.'

I give her a grateful hug, then turn back to Gramps. 'Ready?'

'Yes, I think that's everything.' Satisfied with the angle of his hat he smiles, then suddenly looks stricken. 'I forgot to buy flowers.'

'No, you didn't,' says Mel, pulling a bunch of bright yellow chrysanthemums out of the car. 'We bought them on the way, remember?'

'We did?' he says doubtfully, scrunching up his forehead. 'I don't remember.'

'They're beautiful,' I say swiftly, before he can get upset at his failing memory. Linking my arm through his, I give him an encouraging smile. 'Come on, let's go.' I wave to Mel. 'See you in a little while.'

Waving back, she climbs back into her car and I hear the soft sound of the radio playing as we set off walking arm in arm, Gramps with his cane, me in my stilettos, along the small path that leads behind the church to the cemetery.

'You look wonderful darling,' he says, as soon as we're by ourselves.

'So do you,' I smile, returning the compliment.

Gramps has never looked more dapper. Underneath his single-breasted overcoat, he's wearing his best charcoal grey pinstriped suit, 'made from the finest Italian cashmere, I'll have you know', with a purple silk lining and a matching cravat, perfectly pinned over a crisp white shirt.

'Who starched those collars?' I ask, both impressed and a little worried. Last time Gramps did his collars, he left the iron on and nearly burned down Hemmingway House.

'Miss Temple kindly offered,' he says casually.

'*Miss Temple starched your collars?*' I echo in disbelief. 'Are you sure it wasn't Mel?'

'No, it was Miss Temple,' he insists. 'She's been very helpful of late – practically a changed woman.'

I feel a beat of concern. There's no way Miss Temple would do anything as kind as starch his collars. He's obviously confused. 'Are you feeling OK today, Gramps?'

'Don't fuss dear, I'm fine,' he reassures, patting my hand. 'Oh, I nearly forgot, she wanted me to pass on a message. Now, what was it . . . ?' He taps his head with his forefinger. 'Ah yes, she says the next time you visit, you must join her in the staff room for a sherry; something about forming closer bonds with friends and family.'

'That's a message for me?' I'm astonished. Miss Temple has never shown any enthusiasm for forming a bond with me on any previous visits. On the contrary, she can't seem to wait to get rid of me.

'Yes, for you and that nice chap you brought with you the other evening.'

So *that's* what all this is about. I feel both relieved and sad at the same time.

'You mean Fergus,' I say, feeling a pang at the mention of his name. I haven't heard from him since our row last night, and I don't expect to.

'I mean your new boyfriend,' he replies with a raised-eyebrow look.

Oh, god. I'd forgotten about that.

'Ah yes, there's something I need to tell you,' I confess.

'Now now, I'm only pulling your leg,' he winks, before turning back to focus on the winding path. 'You don't have to explain anything, I'm just happy you've found someone.'

'Well that's the thing,' I try again, 'you see, there's been a bit of a misunderstanding because of Phyllis . . .'

'Has she been interfering again?' he frowns.

'Oh, don't be a meanie, Phyllis is such a sweet old lady,' I chastise. 'And she likes you,' I add, nudging him teasingly.

'She likes everyone,' he dismisses with a tut. 'She got caught in Billy Rothman's room at the weekend.'

'So?' I challenge.

'Well, they weren't playing Scrabble,' he says, glancing sideways at me over the tops of his glasses.

'No!' I gasp. To think I was taken in by her shortbread fingers, I realise, feeling shocked. And, I have to admit, secretly rather impressed. She must be eighty if she's a day. Talk about Girl Power.

We keep walking, the sound of our footsteps crunching on the gravelled path as we enter through the iron gates into the small graveyard. It's nice here. Too often cemeteries are depressing and gloomy, all marble mausoleums and plastic flowers, but this one is surrounded by trees and close by the river.

'So come along, tell me, what has Phyllis been up to this time?' he says after a pause. 'I hope she didn't cause any trouble between you and your new fellow.'

'No . . . no, not at all,' I shake my head, figuring how to explain about me and Fergus.

There's no easy way, I'm just going to have to come straight out with it.

'Because I haven't seen you look that happy in ages my dear,' he continues, before I have a chance to say anything, 'and anyone in that room could see how he felt about you.'

My chest tightens. 'They could?'

'And how you felt the same way.'

What?

'I know you thought you could hide it from me,' he chuckles, misreading my astonished silence for admission, 'but you can't hide feelings like that. And I should know, that's how I felt about your nan.'

'I know, but . . .' Flustered, I open my mouth to deny it, to tell him he's been silly, that he's got it all wrong, but I don't want to hurt his feelings or disappoint him, not today of all days . . . Except, that's not all. There's something else stopping me. I falter, trying to make sense of my conflicting emotions as a flicker of doubt illuminates something buried deep down inside of me that I didn't know was there until just now; that I hadn't *admitted* was there. A feeling that maybe he hasn't got it wrong, *I have.*

'Well, here we are.'

I focus back to see we've stopped walking and are standing in front of a small, simple headstone:

ENID CONNELLY
1930 – 2007
BELOVED WIFE, MOTHER AND GRANDMOTHER
OUR BODIES MAY NOT BE ETERNAL
BUT THANKFULLY OUR LOVE IS

I've read those words so many times but they still bring a lump to my throat.

'I do miss her,' he says quietly.

'I know you do,' I say, reaching for his hand and squeezing it tightly.

I help him place the flowers on her grave, the bright yellow blooms standing up proudly in a vase, just as Nan liked them, and then for a few moments we just stand there, arm in arm, lost in our own private thoughts and memories. So often in life we have to find the right words, say the right thing, but there are some times when words aren't necessary. You don't need to say anything. You just need to feel it.

After a little while he pulls out his silk handkerchief and dabs his eyes. 'Right, enough of this sad stuff,' he says, pinning on a smile, 'we're here to celebrate.'

'Absolutely,' I nod firmly, swallowing the lump in my throat. 'Why do you think I wore these stilettos? So I can kick up my heels . . .'

He laughs gratefully at my bad joke and I smile supportively.

'And that's not all . . .' Unlooping my rucksack from over my shoulder, I rummage inside, then pull out a half bottle and two plastic tumblers.

'What's that?' he asks.

'Champagne, of course. What else do you drink on your wedding anniversary?'

His face lights up with astonishment and delight. 'What would I do without you, eh?' he chuckles.

'Well that's the thing,' I reply, unwrapping the foil and grabbing hold of the cork, 'I'm afraid you're never going to find out as you're not getting rid of me yet.'

The cork makes a loud pop and fires across the cemetery.

'Flaming Nora, you'll be having us arrested,' he jumps.

I laugh, quickly grabbing a glass as the frothing liquid spills out of the bottle.

'Your nan loved a bit of fizz.'

'Well here's to Nan. To both of you,' I say, pouring out two large glasses and passing him one. 'Happy anniversary.'

We chink our plastic tumblers and then for a moment we're silent as we both drink the champagne, savouring the cold bubbles as they explode on the tongue.

'We would have been married fifty-seven years,' he says, after a pause. 'I know my memory isn't what it used to be, but that's a date I don't forget.'

'Wow, fifty-seven years, that's incredible.'

'Not really,' he smiles. 'Being married to your nan was easy . . . though we didn't always see eye to eye.' He laughs and shakes his head. 'She could be a bloody feisty woman, that's for sure, but that's what made Enid Enid, and I loved her, warts and all. I wouldn't have changed a single thing about her.'

As he talks about her, his face becomes animated and I can see the love shining in his eyes.

'If I had my time again, I wouldn't change a single thing about the fifty-seven years we had together. Not a single thing. Not even the arguments, and we had some right humdingers, I tell you.' He chuckles at the memory. 'We even had a barney the first time we met.'

I glance at him with a surprised smile. 'You never told me that before.'

'It was at the pictures. I'd gone with my friends Bobby Wincup and Fred Lester. I can't remember what we saw now, but that's probably because I was too busy staring at your nan. I saw her as soon as we walked in. Afterwards I plucked up the courage to ask if I could walk her home and tried to steal a kiss—'

'Gramps!' I gasp, with mock indignation.

'I was a bit of a bugger in those days,' he confesses, 'but my word did she put me in my place. I was terrified.'

'Why, what did she say?'

'I can't remember now,' he says, furrowing his brow, 'but I do remember how she smelled. She wore lily of the valley in those days and I remember thinking she smelled like a summer's day . . .'

He trails off, smiling fondly to himself, and I can see he's back there now, back to that moment in time when he was a cocky young man in his twenties, flirting with the pretty young girl who was to become his wife.

'From then on I could never imagine life without Enid. We never spent a night apart once we were married, even the kids were born at home . . .' He pauses, and I watch as his smile falls away. 'Not until she went into hospital . . .' Swallowing hard, he stares into the middle distance, his voice barely a whisper. 'I'll never forget walking into that ward and seeing her there . . . I was so scared and she was so brave . . . losing her was the worst day of my life.' He turns to me, his eyes red and glistening with tears. 'I thought I'd die of a broken heart, you know.'

My chest tightens: seeing him so upset breaks my own heart. 'Don't you ever wish you could make that bit go away?' I say, feeling angry at the past. 'That you could erase those painful memories, forget they ever happened, just remember the happy times you had together?'

'You must never say that,' he reprimands sternly.

'But why not?' I look at him in surprise.

'Because it's the bad memories that makes you appreciate the good ones. Don't ever wish them away. It's like your nan always used to say, "You need both the sun and the rain to make a rainbow".'

He looks at me, his face determined. 'I don't want to forget *anything*. All I've got left of your nan are memories. Good or bad, I don't want anything to take those away.

'And nothing will,' I say quickly. 'We'll never forget Nan, none of us will.'

'But that's just it . . .' His eyes meet mine. 'I know what everyone's saying.'

'What?' I frown.

'About me going doolally . . . what do they call it these days? Alzheimer's.'

'No, we don't think that at all,' I protest, but inside guilt kicks in, as I think about the meeting that's taken place between my parents and the nurses, the talk about him seeing a doctor, my own recent admission to Fergus. I don't ever want to lie to Gramps, but how can I tell him? How can I tell him the truth?

'I've seen the leaflets, I know Cyril down the hall has it, he can't remember where he is any more . . .' He shakes his head in dismay. 'And it does scare me, Tess – it terrifies the life out of me.'

For the first time in my life I see the fear in Gramps's face, see how distressed he is, and I desperately want to comfort him.

'You'll be fine, Gramps,' I try to reassure him.

'Will I?' he asks. 'Every day I remember less and less. My memories are being stolen from me and I'm trying bloody hard to hang on to them' – he clenches his bony fist as if they're in the palm of his hand – 'but they're slipping away and I can't do a damn thing about it. I forget names, times, places . . .' He sighs with exasperation. 'We're the sum total of our memories, Tess. Memories are the most precious things we have. Good or bad. That's what make us who we are. What would we be like without them?'

He looks at me, and I can see the anger and frustration in his eyes. And the panic. 'I worry that I'm going to forget her. I'm not going to remember what she looks like, her voice, the moments we shared—' His voice trembles and he breaks off.

I put my arm around his shoulders and draw him close. I can almost feel his fear and I rail against it. Gramps has looked after me since I was a little girl: comforted me, reassured me, made everything safe. Now it's my turn.

'You'll never forget her,' I say resolutely. 'Never in a million years. If you love someone your heart will always remember them. Even if the mind doesn't, the heart never forgets.'

I can almost feel him draw strength from my words. 'Never in a million years,' he repeats quietly, determinedly.

The sun dips behind a tree and, as we fall into shadow, I feel the temperature drop. I notice our glasses are empty.

'It's getting cold, let's go back,' I say.

'Yes, let's,' he nods.

And, clearing everything into my rucksack, we link arms and walk slowly back to the car.

36

Arriving back at the flat I fumble for my door key. Fiona's home, I can hear her inside talking to someone, she must have company . . . I dig around in my bag. Hang on a minute, was that a moan I just heard? I pause to listen. And is that . . . *heavy breathing*? Finding my key, I put it in the lock with trepidation. Well, it wouldn't be the first time I've walked in on something I shouldn't.

Closing the door loudly behind me, I walk into the kitchen to find Fiona sitting at the table. As usual she's hidden, apart from the top of her head, behind the screen of her laptop. I feel a stab of relief.

Unlike Fiona.

On looking up and seeing me she lets out a shriek. 'Oh my god, you gave me the fright of my life!' She lunges frantically for her mouse and there's lots of hasty clicking.

'Sorry,' I apologise quickly, 'I didn't mean to scare you.' I've taken off my sunglasses and, despite lashings of concealer, my eyes are still puffy with dark circles from crying last night. Gramps was just being kind when he said I looked nice. I look a complete fright.

'No, it's not that, I just wasn't expecting you back so early . . .' She breaks off as if she's said too much.

'Is someone here? I thought I heard you talking to someone.'

'Really?' She fidgets uncomfortably. 'No, there's no one here, I was just Skyping with my editor about my column.'

'But isn't your editor a woman? I'm sure I could hear a man's voice—'

The shrill ring of her BlackBerry interrupts me and she snatches it up. 'We got cut off, I'll call you straight back,' she hisses into the mouthpiece. 'Anyway, I was just going out,' she says in a loud voice, turning back to me.

I peer at her dubiously. 'Where are you going?' .

'Oh, I'm just going to take Tallulah for her usual evening trot around the block,' she replies, avoiding my gaze and closing the lid of her laptop.

'In your underwear?' I gape as her body is revealed. Minus its clothes.

Two spots of colour appear high on her cheeks. 'Ah yes, of course, silly me, I forgot . . . um . . . it was so hot in here I had to take my clothes off!' she exclaims, and starts fanning herself.

'Whilst talking to your editor?' I raise my eyebrows.

'Well . . . um it's all very liberal at *Saturday Speaks* . . .' She gives a tinkly little laugh as she grabs her discarded clothes, lying in a pile on the floor next to her chair, and starts hastily pulling on her woolly tights and sweater dress. 'Well, see you later.' Hurrying past me into the hallway, she grabs her coat from the rack.

'Aren't you forgetting something else?'

With her hand already on the latch, she turns.

'Tallulah?' I prompt.

'Oh, yes, of course, silly me,' she gabbles, rushing back into the kitchen and returning with Tallulah scooped up in her arms. 'Bye,' she cries. Then she's gone, the door slamming behind her.

I stare at it for a moment, my mind ticking over. Skyping with her editor? Feeling so hot she took her clothes off? Having to take Tallulah for a walk? Yeh, right. What does she take me for? She was obviously Skyping with a man and it was all getting a bit hot and heavy. Why else would she be sitting there in her bra and knickers? And now she's rushing off to call him back. I wonder who it is? And why is she being so secretive?

Maybe she's seeing Henry VIII again and she doesn't want me to know. Or perhaps she's changed her mind about Quasimodo and it's the bell-ringer from Sassy Soul Mates.

Mulling it over, I go into the kitchen and have just flicked on the kettle when I hear a knock on the door. That'll be Fiona. No doubt she's forgotten something else, including her keys, I muse, padding back into the hallway.

'So come on, what's the big secret?' I demand teasingly, pulling open the door.

Only it's not Fiona, it's Seb.

'I haven't got any secrets,' he replies, looking confused.

'Oh god, sorry . . . I thought you were my flatmate Fiona,' I start hastily trying to explain. 'She just left.'

'I know, we met outside,' he smiles, relaxing. 'She let me in.'

'Right, yes, of course . . .' I nod, feeling flustered. Seb's visit is totally unexpected. We haven't seen each other since we got back from our mini-break, and him just turning up like this has thrown me.

'So are you going to invite me in?' he prompts.

I realise he's still standing there in the doorway. 'Er yes, of course . . . come in. I'm just making a cup of tea . . .' Hurriedly I step back so he can enter.

'I've been trying to call you all day but your phone was turned off,' he says, closing the door behind him and following me into the kitchen.

'I was with my granddad, we went to visit Nan's grave.'

'Oh, I'm sorry,' he says, throwing me a look of sympathy.

'Don't be.' I find myself smiling as my mind flicks back. It was a happy afternoon, not a sad one. 'We went there to celebrate.'

'Celebrate?' Seb looks confused.

'Today was their wedding anniversary,' I explain. 'They would have been married for fifty-seven years.'

'Wow, that's longer than most life sentences, hey?' he quips, expecting me to laugh at his joke about marriage.

But whereas before I would have joined in his laughter, this time I ignore him and instead turn my attentions to the kettle.

'Do you want tea or coffee?' I ask, changing the subject.

'How about a lychee martini instead?'

Unhooking two cups off the mug tree, I look at him blankly.

'Come on, let's go for dinner at Mala.' Taking the cups from me, he puts them back on the mug tree. 'I could kill their spicy Szechuan noodles, couldn't you?'

Oh, god, no. Those noodles will kill me, not the other way around.

'Actually I'm not hungry, I already ate with Granddad.' I go to grab the mugs again.

'Oh OK.' He looks slightly surprised by my lack of enthusiasm. 'What about a movie instead? There's that new 3-D sci-fi film with Will Smith . . .'

'Um, no thanks,' I shake my head, 'I don't really feel like going out.'

'Well, in that case why don't we stay in . . . ?' Moving closer, he slips his hand around my waist and starts nuzzling his face into my neck. 'I actually bought you a little gift . . .' He pulls a small pink-and-black Agent Provocateur bag from his pocket and waggles it at me. 'Seeing as we've got the place to ourselves, maybe you could put this on . . .' he whispers flirtily into my ear.

'Um, you know, I'm not really in the mood,' I hear myself saying.

'C'mon, it'll be fun . . .'

'I'm actually a bit tired . . .'

'You could do that amazing thing with your tongue . . .'

'Seb, stop it! I don't want to!' I burst out. All at once something snaps inside me and I pull sharply away, pent-up emotion exploding out of me like the cork out of a bottle. 'I don't want to do any of those things.'

Shock flashes across his face. 'Why? What's wrong?'

Stunned by own outburst, I take a moment to recover. Me and my big mouth. Why did I blurt it out like that? I look at Seb and feel a sudden anguish. He looks so bewildered. 'I'm sorry . . . I didn't mean to snap . . .' Wracked with guilt, I try explaining. 'You see it's just—'

'Is this about the snowboarding weekend?' he interrupts.

'What? *No!*' I exclaim.

'Because you don't have to worry about cutting short our trip. I got us both season passes!'

Oh god. I stare at him, frozen with horror. I don't know what to say. But at the same time I know I have to say something. And not just about the snowboarding, but about everything, I suddenly realise. Gathering up my courage, I try to think of a way to tell him, to try to explain. He looks so pleased with himself that there's no easy way to say this.

So I just come out with it.

'Seb, I hate snowboarding.'

'What?' He furrows his brow, as if he's misheard.

'And spicy food. I can't eat it. In fact, I think I'm allergic to chillies.'

'But I don't understand. You said you loved it – you told me you loved both those things.' Seb is shaking his head as if he's got water in his ears.

'And I don't like science-fiction films either.'

'*You don't?*'

I shake my head. 'No, to tell the truth I find them a bit boring. No, that's not even the truth; the truth is I find them really, *really* boring. All those silly costumes and spaceships that look like something you've made from a Fairy Liquid bottle on *Blue Peter* . . .'

Now I've started I can't stop. It's as if there's a tiny, cramped room inside of me where I've been hiding the real me, where for the last few weeks I've been stuffing my true feelings in an attempt to make them disappear. Piling my opinions and thoughts so high until there's no more space left. And now someone's unlocked the door and they're all coming tumbling out in a torrent.

'And as for all that sexy lingerie,' I roll my eyes, 'I don't really wear underwear like that the whole time, it's too uncomfortable.'

'Uncomfortable?' He looks perplexed, as if he'd never considered such a thing.

I nod. 'G-strings cut right up my *you-know-what* and I only wore that nipple-less bra once and talk about chafing . . .'

'But I thought you enjoyed wearing it,' he says, glancing in confusion at the Agent Provocateur bag sitting redundantly on the kitchen counter.

'Because that's what I wanted you to believe,' I confess. 'I mean, would you enjoy wearing bum floss?'

If I'm hoping to lighten the atmosphere by making a joke, I'm unsuccessful. Raking his fingers through his hair, Seb looks at me wildly. 'This isn't making any sense – *you're* not making any sense.' He turns away from me and sits down on the sofa, looking dazed.

'Look, I'm sorry, it's all my fault, everything's my fault . . .' I break off and stare hard at the kitchen lino. I feel awful, but at the same time I also know this is the first sense I've spoken for a long time. Swallowing hard I look up at him. 'I think we should break up.'

'Break up?' cries Seb, aghast, swivelling his gaze across me like a strobe light. 'But why? We get along so well, we like all the same things—'

'No, don't you see? That's what I'm trying to explain. We don't like the same things, Seb. I just pretended to like them so you'd like me.'

He stares at me in confusion, not computing what's going on. How can he? How can he begin to understand we dated once before and he broke up with me and I've been dating him all over again, doing things differently, hoping that this time he'd fall in love with me.

'But this is crazy! I'm in love with you!'

His words ring out loud and I freeze. He's never said that before, and for a moment my heart skips a beat. It's what I've always wanted him to say. What I've waited so long to hear. Last time when we dated he'd tell me I was beautiful, or he thought I was adorable, or that he loved being with me. But he never told me he loved me. He never said those three little words.

And now he has.

Now I've got what I always dreamed of.

But at what price?

I take a breath, holding that moment where his words hang suspended in the air, enjoying that moment I've waited so long for, breathing them in, seeing what it feels like, trying them on for size.

Before I brush them away.

'You're not in love with me,' I say quietly, shaking my head.

'Yes I am!' he protests indignantly.

I glance over at him sitting on the sofa, just as I once sat on his. Only now the roles are reversed. Yet if ever there was a moment I thought I might find some pleasure in the way the situation has turned around, I couldn't have been more wrong. Dating Seb again was never about trying to get some warped kind of revenge. I was just following my heart; it was impossible not to. But although Seb might have broken it when he finished with me, there would be no satisfaction in breaking his.

'No, you're not,' I say firmly. 'You're not in love with the *real* me, you're in love with the person I became, the person I changed into, the person I tried to be. Trust me, I'm not the girl you fell in love with. That's not really who I am.' A sob rises in my throat – saying the words out loud is making me face up to what I've become and the reality is hard to face. 'You're in love with a fake. *I'm a fake.*'

As I spit out the words, I think about Fergus. He was right all along and yet I refused to believe him.

'I thought I wasn't good enough. That there was something wrong with me. That I needed to change for you to love me, to be different, *to be more . . .*'

I can feel my eyes welling up as I remember those emotions. When we broke up the first time I blamed myself. It was all my fault. If only I'd tried harder, done things differently, been funnier, sexier, cleverer, more enthusiastic, sporty, successful . . . *more everything*, then Seb would have fallen in love with me.

Because somewhere, somehow, something got buried deep down inside of me, an insecurity, anxiety, self-doubt – call it what you want – that made me feel I didn't deserve to be loved, that plain little old me could never be a success, that somehow I wasn't worthy. And for all these years I've been carrying that feeling with me.

'Only now I've finally realised I *am* good enough,' I say determinedly and, hearing myself say it out loud for the first time in my life, I suddenly know it to be true. 'I'm *more* than good enough, and I don't need to change. I just need to accept and love myself for who I really am. Because how can I expect someone to love me if I don't love myself? For someone to think I'm good enough if I don't think I'm good enough?'

But Seb's not listening. He doesn't want to. 'Is there someone else? Is this what it's all about?'

It's like biting down on tinfoil: every cell in my body jumps. 'No, of course not,' I protest quickly, but my mind betrays me by throwing up an image of Fergus.

I still haven't heard from him. He was so angry and upset I don't think he'll ever forgive me, especially now he knows I'll have read that email he sent to 'Sara'. My chest tightens. I still can't believe he felt that way. I had no idea.

Except . . .

My mind flashes back to us both on the terrace, snowflakes whirling around our heads, my breath held tight inside of me. A feeling of magic, anticipation and something else . . . only I can't put my finger on it. Not that it matters. Whatever it was has gone now. I made sure of that.

'No, no there's no one else,' I say quietly.

Then for a few moments neither of us moves or speaks and there's an awkward silence. I become aware of the loud humming of the fridge, the slow drip of the tap, the muffled drone of an overhead plane.

'Are you *sure* it's not about the snowboarding weekend,' he says after a pause, 'because Chris did mention something about the hot tub—'

'Please, Seb,' I gasp and he falls silent again. 'Trust me, this isn't about the weekend, or the hot tub, or you . . . it was *never* about you, it's about me.' My voice softening, I walk over and sit next to him on the sofa. 'You're a great guy, but I'm not the girl for you.'

'You don't mean that, you're just saying it,' he says huffily, his earlier hurt being replaced by indignation. Folding his arms, he angles his body away from me. 'That's what everyone says when they break up with someone.'

He has a point. If I remember rightly he said a similar thing to me.

'No, Seb, you're not listening, I really *do* mean it,' I say firmly. 'You like exercising and keeping fit, and I like slobbing on the sofa watching *The X Factor*.'

'What about military fitness?' he demands, as if he's caught me out.

'I went once and pulled my hamstring.'

'But you go running.'

'No, *you* go running, I just pretended to go. The only thing I've ever run for is the bus.' I pause as I catch his expression; I'm finally admitting who I am – to both of us.

'I'm a girl whose favourite food is boring old beans on toast, and when I'm not setting about three alarm clocks and wearing two watches, I'm always late—'

He tries to protest, but I won't let him. 'No, really I am . . . and I love listening to Abba, not indie bands that all sound the same, and wearing my ratty old T-shirt bras and big comfy support knickers.'

He blanches.

'I'm a girl who only got to page three of that Obama book you gave me before I realised it's never going to change my life and I'd rather read *OK!* and look at celebrity cellulite in bikinis.'

'Celebrity *what*?'

'And my favourite film isn't *Star Wars*, it's *Dirty Dancing*. Or anything with Johnny Depp in it.'

Seb stares at me aghast. I might just as well have said I'm an alien from outer space.

'But plenty of couples have different interests,' he says, finally finding his voice. 'Opposites attract, remember?'

I smile. 'I know they do, and I've thought the same thing, but it's more than that, Seb. We're not just opposite, we're totally different, we believe in different things . . .' My mind flashes back to Gramps, standing with him this afternoon in the graveyard.

'Like I do believe in marriage. I believe in falling in love with someone who makes you feel like the luckiest person alive, in making a commitment to that person in front of the whole world, and going on this mad, crazy journey called life together . . .' I pause as I remember the look in Gramps's eyes when he talked about Nan. 'And I can't think of anything I want more than to be married to someone for fifty years who loves me for who I am, warts and all, and for me to feel exactly the same about them.'

I break off, my heart thudding. I feel almost breathless. But I feel something else. Liberated, exposed, *lighter*. As if the pressure of trying to be someone else has been lifted from my shoulders, like a heavy overcoat that's been weighing me down, stifling who I really am.

And then for a moment there's silence. We both sit side by side, neither of us saying anything, both studying our feet. I realise I'm still holding the two mugs.

'So you didn't really like all those things,' he says after a long pause. 'You were just pretending?'

Finally he gets it.

'I'm sorry,' I nod.

'Well, I guess I should go . . .' He gets up from the sofa and I follow him down into the hallway. 'Bye Tess.'

'Bye Seb.'

We kiss each other awkwardly on the cheek but he's only halfway out of the door when he pauses and clears his throat.

'What about that night you had five orgasms? Was that fake too?'

His handsome face is suffused with uncertainty, and crossing my fingers behind my back I shake my head. 'No, that was for real.'

His features relax. 'I knew you couldn't fake that,' he says with a little nod of satisfaction and, turning, he walks out of the flat and closes the door behind him.

Dear Diary,

Seb and I broke up.

Well, that's not strictly true. He broke up with me. He said he loved me but wasn't in love with me, that it would probably be better if we break up, how he hopes we'll always remain friends . . .

But you know the worst thing of all? When he told me he couldn't see a future with me. That pretty much broke my heart.

I'm not sure what to write now. Shall I write that I still feel numb? That it's only been a few hours and I still can't believe it's over? That I know that soon the shock is going to wear off, like an anaesthetic at the dentist, and I'm terrified of the pain?

Or shall I write that I know it's all my fault. That there are so many things I wish I'd done differently. So many regrets. So many 'what ifs'. But now it's too late. I've never loved anyone like I love Seb, and now I've lost him.

I miss him already.

37

If someone had told me, when Seb was breaking up with me, that a few months later I'd be breaking up with him, I would never have believed them. I would have said it was impossible, inconceivable, ridiculous. I would have accused them of being crazy.

I would have—

Well, you get the picture.

After Seb leaves I make myself a cup of tea with two sugars. Actually, make that three. Well that's what you're supposed to do when you've had a bit of a shock, isn't it? Except, in this case, I've shocked myself. I had no idea I was going to break up with Seb. When I woke up this morning I had no intention of ending our relationship. I didn't scribble a reminder on a Post-it note and stick it to my computer (though after yesterday I'm going to *totally* rethink that method).

In fact, if breaking up with someone was a crime, I'd plead 'not guilty, your honour', as it wasn't premeditated. It's just the moment I stopped focusing on Seb and what he wanted, and focused on myself and what I wanted, I realised it wasn't Seb. I want someone who loves me for who I really am – and he doesn't.

And in that moment, everything changed. Like pulling a thread, our whole relationship began to unravel, like the stitching on a hem, and fell apart.

Then suddenly there we were, breaking up. *Again.*

Only this time it's different. I'm different. Sitting on the sofa, nursing my cup of tea, I re-read my diary, only it's almost as if it's been written by somebody else. I'm not that heartbroken girl who blamed herself for everything any more.

'*He told me he couldn't see a future with me.*'

I read the words again and this time I can't miss the irony. By some weird, inexplicable twist of fate I might have erased our past, but Seb was the one who couldn't see our future.

And now, this time, for the first time, neither can I.

After the major upheavals of the past couple of days, the rest of the week passes in relative calm. Which is not a bad thing. To be honest, I don't think I could take any more shocks to the system. I feel like when I was six years old and used to play that game where they blindfold you and spin you around, then whip off the blindfold and you stagger about, trying not to fall over.

But it's fine, I just need to get my bearings again, I tell myself firmly. I just need to sit still and regain my balance; in fact what I need is a bit of boringness.

To tell the truth, I think boring is very underrated. Sometimes in life you need a bit of boring, a bit of trundling along without anything jumping out and blindsiding you and turning your world upside down. Everyone tells you change is good, but right now I could do with a little bit of dull, thanks very much.

So, keeping with the theme of dull and boring, I decide to spend the weekend tidying up my room and having a total clear-out. Since New Year's Eve I've let things slide: there's tons of washing that needs doing, a pile of ironing; my wardrobe is bulging with clothes that I don't even wear . . .

I open the door and glance in it with dismay. Is it just me, or does no one wear at least seventy-five per cent of their clothes?

It's 8 a.m. on Saturday morning and I'm already up, caffeinated, and rifling through the hangers, spying things I haven't worn for ages, if ever. That's it, I'm never going to buy anything ever again, I tell myself sternly, grabbing handfuls of clothes and shoving them in a bag for the charity shop. Look! There's still something that has its price tag on! Wincing, I avert my eyes quickly. OK, so what else needs to go? I cast my eye around the room and it falls on the Obama book sitting on my bedside cabinet, still unread. Correction: *never to be read.*

Well, maybe it can change someone else's life, I decide, adding it to the pile of clothes with a sense of relief and satisfaction. Oh look, and there's the lingerie Seb just bought me. I look inside the bag and unwrap the tissue paper – it's a diamanté G-string. I hold it between thumb and forefinger, like a catapult. It almost makes my eyes water imagining where the diamanté bit goes – thank god I'm never going to have to wear it.

The bag is full now so, grabbing an old cardboard box, I drop it inside, along with the Obama book which is threatening to break the already stretched-to-bursting bin liner, and I start looking around for more things to give away. Like, for example, here's that piece of driftwood I got from when we went to the beach; maybe someone would like that. I stick it in the box, then suddenly pause . . .

Hang on a minute . . .

Still holding the box, I rummage around the room for a few moments, collecting different bits and pieces. On my dressing table I spot the cork from the bottle of red wine lying next to the plastic wristband from the concert; next to the fire is the box of matches from Mala; one of Seb's plectrums has found its way into my holdall, along with the stub for my snowboarding lessons . . . and what's this in my jeans pocket?

I pull out the ticket stubs from when we went to see *Star Wars*, and chuck them in the box. What else is missing? Oh right, yes, the photo from the wedding. Going to the wardrobe I feel inside my jacket and pull out some old confetti, and with it a Polaroid of Seb and me. I drop it in the box. That's it. That's everything.

I stare at the contents. How funny. It's just like before. Like the first time we dated. Except it's not – because this time when I look through all the mementos, I don't feel sad, or regretful, or sentimental. Instead I just remember how bored I was watching *Star Wars*, not to mention that entire boxed set afterwards; having to stuff my earplugs in so hard at that concert that they were still jammed in on the way home and not having a clue what Seb was going on about; the Polaroid from the wedding where we look so damn miserable is because we *were* so damn miserable.

I have a flashback to throwing back the bouquet and the look on the bride's face . . .

And suddenly, out of nowhere, a giggle escapes, then another, and another, until tears of laughter are streaming down my face as my mind flicks through all the different memories attached to each item.

You had to be there. And I was. *Twice.*

Only when I've finally dried my eyes do I rescue the book and the G-string. Those can go to charity. And the rest? I unceremoniously throw the whole box in the bin. Like I said, it's just junk after all.

Three large bin bags, two cardboard boxes and several hours later, I'm finally done and I drag it all to the charity shop. I do it in a sort of relay system until, by the time I've dropped off the final bag, I'm exhausted.

On the other hand, the woman who manages the shop is elated.

'Thank you *sooo* much, this is all *sooo* wonderful,' she coos, swooping down upon my piles of clothes and immediately starting to sort them into colours. 'Ooh, and I love this cardigan.'

I glance across to see her holding up a lovely little mohair three-quarter-sleeve number with pearl buttons and feel a pang of regret. I always do that when I give things away. As soon as an item of clothing is in the charity bag, something weird happens. I suddenly love it again and can't live without it.

It's a shame there isn't the equivalent of a charity bag for people. It would save so many relationships that are in trouble: just pop your partner in a charity bag and, hey presto, you've fallen in love with them all over again.

'Um, can you wait till I'm gone . . . before you go through it all,' I plead, somewhat awkwardly.

She stops holding up the cardigan and clutches it to her chest. 'Of course, I *totally* understand,' she confides, then lowering her voice says solemnly, 'One can get *very* attached, can't one?'

'Yes, one can,' I nod, trying not to smile.

The doorbell goes, interrupting us, and a petite, grey-haired woman enters. She can't be more than five feet tall but she's pulling a shopping trolley almost as big as herself. 'Oh, please, let me,' cries the manager, dashing over and holding the door for her. 'I'll take that . . .'

'*Non, non*,' replies the woman in a strong French accent, 'I am perfectly fine.' She looks across at me and winks. 'Very old, but perfectly fine. Like a vintage claret.'

She lets out a little peal of laughter, showing off two rows of tiny, perfectly straight teeth which I notice are all her own. For someone her age that's pretty amazing, but then she's not your typical old lady. Dressed all in black, with lashings of red lipstick and her hair swept elegantly into a chignon, she's the epitome of chic.

'I've brought some things.' She opens her shopping trolley. Unlike me she has no second thoughts, and starts piling everything onto the counter. Which is when I spot a flour sack.

'They're yours!' So this is the mystery French lady I've heard all about.

'*Oui*,' she nods, 'and I have many more.' She digs in her shopping trolley and brings out a whole stack of them.

'Wow!' I gasp with delight. 'Where did these all come from?'

'From when I was a little girl, we lived on a farm . . .' She trails off, smiling at the memory. 'I keep too many things, but now I'm moving out of my house as it got too big, my children grew up and left, my husband died . . .'

'Oh, I'm so sorry.'

'*Non*,' she shakes her head. 'He was not well; it's better this way. It's like a dance, life. Such fun, but sometimes you get tired and forget the steps . . .' She trails off again with a shrug. 'Then it's time to take a rest.'

As she talks about dancing I remember the red dress and glance across to see it hanging on the rack. She follows my eyes.

'You should try it,' she nods.

'Oh, I'm way too big for it,' I protest.

'Nonsense.' She shakes her tiny, birdlike head, and with surprising agility crosses the shop floor and unhooks it from its hanger. 'Take off your coat.'

I'm not used to having strange little old French ladies boss me around, but wordlessly I do as she says.

'The fabric is silk; it stretches, like this, you see?' Looping it over each of my arms she starts wrapping the swathes of fabric around me with the skill of a seamstress. 'On me it was much longer, that was the fashion in the fifties . . . but on you – *parfait*!'

She steps back with a flourish of satisfaction, and we both look at my reflection in the mirror propped opposite. The dress is on top of my jeans and T-shirt, and I'm wearing my scruffy old trainers, my hair tied up in a ponytail, but such is its magic, everything else seems to fade into the background.

Everything disappears, and all I can see are the folds of luscious scarlet fabric that hug and cling, smell its scent of perfume and days gone by, and for a brief, glorious moment I'm transported back to Paris in the fifties, a dance floor, a band playing . . .

'All you need now is someone to dance with,' nods the shop manager approvingly.

I snap back to see I'm in Oxfam in Hammersmith with Rihanna playing on the radio.

'Um, yes . . .' I nod, feel slightly embarrassed.

'I'm sure she has lots of men to dance with,' laughs the old French lady gaily, looking across at the manageress. 'Remember when we were young? There were so many men, *n'est-ce pas*?'

Having no doubt spent her youth organising church jumble sales, the manageress colours at the mere suggestion. Not to mention that even though there's probably twenty years between them, it's pretty evident she didn't enjoy the same popularity with the opposite sex as the French lady with her red lipstick and silk dress.

'Well, I don't know about that . . .' she laughs awkwardly and, avoiding the old lady's gaze, chooses to look at me instead. 'So, tell me – how would you like to pay for that?'

38

After buying the red dress and the rest of the cotton sacks, I leave the shop and make my way home. On the way I make a bit of a detour. Well, actually it's less of a detour and more of a completely-the-wrong-direction. But there's nothing else for it, I've tried everything else. Turning down a street in Shepherd's Bush, I walk along the pavement, counting the number of the houses, until finally I reach the one I'm looking for.

Number seventy-four.

Fergus's address.

With my heart hammering in my chest, I stop outside the redbrick building. The last few days I've done nothing but think about Fergus and what happened. I still feel terrible for hurting him, and I don't blame him for being angry, but I've finally stopped beating myself up about it. What I did might have been stupid, but it was stupid for all the right reasons, and although I don't expect him to forgive me, I just want him to know that. I *need* him to know that.

My eyes sweep upwards to the top flat where he lives. I'd hoped I could explain when he came into the office this week, except a different courier came instead, and when I asked where Fergus was, he said he was new and had no idea; he'd just been assigned our deliveries and pick-ups. So I sent him an email and waited for him to reply. But he didn't. So I sent him another one. Nothing. He didn't reply to my texts either. Or pick up when I called.

Which is why I'm now here, standing outside his flat, trying to pluck up the courage to go and ring the doorbell. Well, that was the plan. Only now I'm here, I feel a lot more nervous than I thought I would. I mean, he obviously doesn't want to see me or speak to me, does he? He's avoiding *and* ignoring me. Which begs the question, what the hell am I doing here? He'll probably just tell me to go to hell.

I feel my courage slipping away. This was a stupid idea. Yet another one, I think, kicking myself. I seem to be getting pretty good at them, don't I? Turning around, I start walking away, but I've only taken a few footsteps when I hear Fergus's voice in my head: *It's never too late to try to put something right.*

I hesitate. What have I got to lose? Turning back around I stride up to the front door and ring the doorbell. I brace myself. I'm just going to come out with it. Even if he slams the door in my face. I'm going to give it my best shot.

Only there's no answer. I wait for a few moments, then scribble a note asking him to call me. I slip it through the letter-box. Let's hope he was right about it never being too late.

By the time Monday morning rolls around I've sorted a lot out, emotionally and practically. My head is clearer, my room is *certainly* a lot clearer and I'm feeling a lot more positive. Which is good as I need to get into the party spirit.

With Sir Richard still away in India and his retirement party looming, I spend the rest of the week busy making sure the final arrangements are all in order. After what happened with his visa, I've changed my Post-it note way of doing things, and now have a list on which I'm ticking things off. Balloons? *Tick.* 'Happy Retirement Sir Richard!' banner? *Tick.* Caterers serving organic, sustainably farmed food? *Tick.* Alcohol? Well, that bit's easy. *Tick.*

All the staff are excited. Despite the sadness at losing a

much-loved boss and still not knowing who's going to replace him, it's an opportunity for the girls to wear their new spangly dresses, the boys to try to impress with their dance moves, and for everyone to get drunk at the expense of the company. Me? I just want everything to go smoothly.

By the time I turn off my computer on Friday evening, everything on my list has been ticked off, not just once, but twice. I'm not taking any risks this time. Sir Richard is due to arrive back this evening – he changed his flight so he could have a few extra meetings in Delhi – and a car is picking him up from Heathrow and bringing him straight to the party. So there's no room for mistakes; everything has to be perfect.

And it will be, I reassure myself, flicking on the radio to help calm my nerves and get me in the mood. I'm in my bedroom, getting ready for the party. I invited Fiona as she always loves a party and I'd rather not go alone. Well, actually I didn't have to ask, she volunteered, as she said she needed to talk to me about something 'and it would be a good opportunity'.

A flashback to a few days ago and her mentioning it to me as I left for work, all shifty body language and avoiding my eyes, triggers a feeling of doom. I suppose I should have asked her outright what it was, there and then, but to be honest, I didn't want to know. God, I hope it's not that she's selling the flat or something, and wants me to move out. The timing would be terrible as I'm out of a job in less than two weeks. But then, aren't things supposed to always come in threes? No boyfriend, no job, and now no home?

Not that they're *all* bad, of course. Breaking up with Seb was definitely the right thing to do, and it's not as though I was ever going to make a career out of being a PA, but even so it would be a bit of a triple whammy. Plus, more importantly, despite the overflowing ashtrays, bizarre foodstuffs left in pans and the fact that Fiona still hasn't got round to putting a lock on the bathroom door, I've grown rather fond of the place.

Finishing applying my mascara, I stand back to check my reflection. I'm wearing the red silk dress from the charity shop and now it's not on top of my jeans, I can see the old French lady was right, it does fit perfectly. Humming along to the radio, I do a little twirl, watching how the folds of silk whirl out like a parasol. Then pause as the fabric falls against my legs – hang on, what's this song I'm humming?

Is that . . . ?

The Nolans, 'I'm in the Mood for Dancing'.

I'm suddenly reminded of Fergus. I've been so busy with organising the party it's helped keep me distracted, but now there's nothing to prevent me from thinking about him and he comes crashing into my mind. He never replied to my note. Part of me didn't expect him to; it was a long shot anyway. Still, I wonder if he's going to be there tonight? He was sent an invitation along with all the other regular couriers Sir Richard employs. Deep down inside, I allow myself to feel a morsel of hope. Maybe, just maybe . . .

Gosh, is it that time already? Noticing my alarm clock, I pull myself together. Quickly grabbing my coat I reach for a gold clutch. Then change my mind. It's far too small, I'll never get everything in that. I know, I'll take my bag!

My bag.

I feel a flash of unbridled pride. Finally, after weeks of hard work, I put the finishing touches to it last week and, though I say so myself, it looks great. The leather handles that I made from the braces of the dungarees give it this great vintage quality, and then you've got the silk ribbons, and embroidery and the mother-of-pearl buttons and . . . well, quite frankly I could go on forever gushing about it. More importantly, where is it?

I rummage around my bedroom looking. Shit, at this rate, if I can't find it we're going to be late! Now I'm longer dating Seb, I've abandoned the two watches and it's all fallen apart again quite quickly and I've gone back to my default setting of always running ten minutes behind. 'Hey Fiona,' I call out, 'have you seen my bag?'

'What?' She pops her head out of her bedroom. She's wearing a tight black cocktail dress and a pair of killer heels.

'Wow, you look fantastic!' Not that Fiona doesn't normally look good when she goes out, but tonight there's a sort of shiny glow about her that I've never seen before.

'Thanks,' she giggles happily. 'So do you.'

I smile gratefully. She's been very supportive over my break-up with Seb. She didn't judge, or try to pump me for details, she just gave me a reassuring hug and told me he wasn't that good-looking anyway and she was sure his teeth were veneers. She also very sweetly left me a copy of a magazine with an article on celebrity cellulite on my pillow, 'as it's something no girl should miss out on and will make you feel heaps better'.

'So, you ready to go?' she asks.

'Nearly, but I can't find my bag. Have you seen it?'

'What does it look like?'

'You know, the one I made with the leather straps and silk lining.'

Immediately her happy shiny face is replaced by one of guilt.

'Oh, *that* bag . . .'

I feel a tug of anxiety. 'What do you mean, *that* bag?'

'I think I might have borrowed it.'

'*Think?*' I fix her with a look.

'Sorry.' She throws me an apologetic smile.

I roll my eyes; it's one thing her borrowing my stuff, but she never puts it back.

'Well where is it?' I say.

'Well that's the thing . . .' she says slowly. 'I borrowed it last week when I went to a shoot and the stylist saw it and wanted to use it in the photographs with the model . . .' Her voice has speeded up and she's now falling over herself trying to explain. 'I'll get it back, promise,' she finishes.

'*Fiona!*'

We're interrupted by the beep of a text message popping up on my phone. I snatch it up and glance at the screen. 'It's from the minicab service telling us the taxi's here,' I say, reading it. 'Come on, let's go.'

'Wait, I need to get Tallulah.'

'You can't bring her,' I exclaim.

She stiffens and juts out her chin. 'Wherever I go, Tallulah goes,' she says firmly.

Tallulah, it seems, has become a permanent fixture in the flat. We've had her for a month now and there's been no word from Pippa about coming back to collect her. However, whenever I tried to bring up the subject with Fiona, she refused to talk about it in front of Tallulah. 'How would you like to be abandoned?' she hisses, covering Tallulah's ears.

'Oh, all right,' I sigh, giving in and grabbing my clutch bag. I stuff as much in as I can, then shove the rest in my pockets and hurry downstairs. Fiona follows me, her stiletto heels clacking away on the steps like a pair of castanets, hugging Tallulah to her chest. Until finally we're outside and climbing into the stuffy warmth of the minicab.

'Don't worry, I'll get the bag back, I promise,' she says, looking across at me.

'You'd better,' I threaten, then soften into a smile. 'I can't believe you didn't tell me!'

'Well actually, that's not all . . .'

I look at her, uncomprehending.

'There's something else I've been meaning to tell you.'

My stomach drops. I knew it. 'You want me to move out, don't you.'

She frowns in confusion. 'Move out? Why would you think that?'

'Well you looked so uncomfortable when you said you had something you needed to talk to me about . . . I just put two and two together and—'

'Got about seven hundred and fifty,' tuts Fiona. 'No, of course I don't want you to move out, I love having you as a flatmate. Even if you did use my Diptyque candle,' she adds with a raised-eyebrow look.

I feel myself colour. 'Ah, yes, I've been meaning to tell you about that . . .'

'Another time,' she shushes me and I smile gratefully.

'So what is it you want to tell me?'

'I've met someone,' she admits rather nervously.

'Oh, well I *knew* that already,' I reply, feeling both relieved and a little smug. 'Doggy classes indeed,' I tut, shooting Tallulah a look. Perched upright on Fiona's knee, she stares jauntily back. We've never quite seen eye to eye.

'Well, actually it's a bit more than that.' Anxiously vacuuming her throat, Fiona stops stroking Tallulah to hold up her hand. She waggles her fingers.

Correction: *finger*.

In the dimness of the minicab, I see a flash of something.

Wait a minute. I peer closer. *Is that . . . ?*

And at the exact same moment as I spot a large, sparkly diamond sitting on her finger, I hear her cry,

'I'm engaged!'

39

If I had a mute button I'd press it now, because for the next few minutes all I can hear are the sounds of me and Fiona doing lots of excited shrieking and screaming and 'Oh my god I can't believe it!' on a continuous ear-splitting loop, joined on backing vocals by Tallulah's high-pitched yapping.

Pity the poor cab driver. I'm surprised he's got any eardrums left.

Finally, with our throats sore and exhausted from shrieking, we both wind down like clockwork toys and flop back against the back seat of the cab.

'Oh my god, I can't believe it,' I say for the millionth time, staring at her in stunned amazement.

'I'm still pinching myself,' she grins madly, clutching her ring. 'Isn't it beautiful?'

I can't answer. I've got a million questions whizzing around in my head: *Who? How? When? Where?* I don't have a clue where to start.

So I take a deep breath. 'OK, so first we need to rewind,' I say firmly.

Well, someone's got to be sensible here, otherwise we're going to spend the entire cab ride oohing and ahhing over the rock on her finger and I'll still be none the wiser by the time we arrive at the party.

'It's all been a bit of a whirlwind, I met him online on Sassy Soul Mates a couple of weeks ago and we just clicked.'

'So come on, tell me about him, who is he?'

She needs no encouragement. 'His name's Ricky and he's not my usual type at all,' she begins excitedly, 'but there was something about him, something about the way he made me feel. He's really romantic and old-fashioned and he made me feel special, he made me feel attractive' – as it all comes pouring out, she smiles, almost embarrassed to be admitting it – 'and not attractive if I was skinnier, or if I lost those ten pounds, or I could fit into my "thin" jeans, but attractive just the way I am.'

'But why the big secret?'

'I didn't want to jinx it,' she confesses. 'I've had so many false starts in the love department, I didn't want to say anything until it was official . . . plus you were so caught up with Seb we've hardly seen each other . . .' She breaks off. 'Sorry. I shouldn't have mentioned him.'

'It's OK, I'm not upset about us breaking up,' I smile reassuringly. 'It's different this time.'

'*This time?*' She frowns.

'Er . . . I mean, generally speaking.' Realising what I've said, I correct myself hastily.

'It's different this time for me too,' she nods earnestly, and I feel a beat of relief that she's loved-up and relating everything back to herself. 'Before I was always attracted to the handsome players, I thought they were exciting and sexy and a challenge. Now I realise they were just a waste of time.' She looks down at her hands and touches her ring.

'Ricky's so different to all those other guys I've dated. I thought he wasn't my type, but it turned out that actually he *was* my type, it's all the others that weren't. I finally found what I was looking for, and I've realised I was looking in all the wrong places. Including the Quality Street tin,' she adds sheepishly, shooting me a rueful smile.

'Well, I had my suspicions,' I grin, and she blushes guiltily.

'I'm sorry I tried to blame Flea.'

'Don't worry, he's not the type to bear a grudge,' I reply, and she laughs.

'Oh Tess, I'm just so happy!' she beams, her face breaking into her default grin. 'Me! Getting married! I still can't believe it . . . and you'll be my maid of honour, won't you?' She looks at me, her eyes shining excitedly.

'Wow, yes, of course, that's great, but . . .' I pause. I have to tread softly here. Fiona can get very defensive when it comes to her love life. I still remember the time she had a crush on Gary Bishop in year six and bit my head off when I pointed out he was playing kiss chase with Lorna McClellan. Plus, I don't want to put a dampener on things. It's just . . . oh sod it, I can't sit here and not mention what I'm thinking.

'Isn't it a bit, *well*, soon?' I venture.

'You can't put a timescale on love,' she replies sagely, suddenly falling serious. 'When you know, you just know.'

I can see her mind's made up, and to be honest, maybe she's right. If the last few weeks have taught me anything, it's that the things I thought I knew, I didn't really know at all.

'Well you have to wait a little bit,' I protest, smiling. 'I haven't even met him yet!'

'Well that's the thing . . .' She pauses, as if searching for the right words. 'You have.'

'*I have?*' I look at her, taken aback. I thought we'd got over the surprises.

'Sorry to interrupt, love.' The cabbie's voice comes over the speaker. 'But we're here.'

We've been so engrossed in our conversation, neither of us has realised we've pulled up outside the party venue, a private members' club in Mayfair.

'Oh, right, thanks,' I say hurriedly and, signing the chit for the fare, I push open the door and step outside into the cold night air. My mind is racing, trying to think where I could have met Fiona's fiancé. 'Are you sure?' I ask, as she joins me on the pavement.

'Well yes,' she says, seeming uncharacteristically nervous. 'I didn't realise at first, but it turns out you know him and I've been wondering how to tell you . . . I didn't want it to be awkward—'

'But I don't know anyone called Ricky . . .'

I don't finish as the large black door of the club swings open and we're greeted by Sir Richard. His face lights up when he sees it's me. 'Darling, I've missed you!' he cries, throwing open his arms.

I do a double take. *What the hell?* I know we have a good working relationship, but still . . .

'You too!' exclaims Fiona.

Only he's not smiling at me, he's beaming at my best friend, and as he gathers her up I can only stand on the doorstep, my mouth hanging open in astonished disbelief.

Then, abruptly, it registers.

Ricky is Sir Richard?

After I've got over the initial shock of discovering my boss is engaged to my best friend, Fiona and Richard (I can drop the 'Sir' but I'm sorry, I draw the line at calling him Ricky) are keen to share their story, and it all comes out about their dates, and how they met.

'So it wasn't internet porn at all! He was online dating!' laughs Fiona, as we walk together through the lobby. Fiona and Sir Richard with their arms entwined. Me trotting alongside, like a bewildered Labrador.

I go bright red. Now it's all slotting into place, the webcam, the subscription email . . .

Sir Richard bursts out laughing. 'Ha, yes, Fiona told me you thought I had an addiction!'

Oh my god, this is *sooo* embarrassing. Plus, if I remember

rightly, it was Fiona who was convinced he had a porn addiction. I shoot Fiona an I'm-going-to-kill-you look but she just collapses into giggles.

'So you haven't been going to dog obedience classes?' I say quickly, trying to steer the conversation away from my boss and online porn. Never a good combination, trust me.

'Sorry, that was a bit of a fib,' she blushes, 'though we have talked about it. Ricky's got a red setter called Monty, you know.'

'Yes I do,' I nod. 'He cocked his leg up on my Swiss cheese plant when he came into the office last week.' Despite tons of Baby Bio, it's still not recovered.

'Oh I don't think he'll dare misbehave around you darling,' he laughs, giving Fiona a squeeze around the waist.

'Are you saying I'm bossy?'

'Forceful,' he corrects.

'Well, someone had to get rid of that suit,' she grins.

'It was bespoke—'

'It was horrible!'

I watch them both laughing and chatting away, tripping over each other to finish the other one's sentences. Sir Richard is almost unrecognisable from the man he was a few months ago. Gone is his wispy comb-over. Instead there's a short, fashionable haircut with, dare I say it, a little product in the front? Not only that but he's flashing a pearly white smile that could only be the product of some expensive bleaching at a Delhi dentist. Together with his trendy designer glasses and expensively cut suit, the metamorphosis I've been noticing over the last few weeks is complete.

'I've given him a makeover,' says Fiona proudly, catching my amazed expression as I take him in.

It's incredible. He looks like a completely different person to the Sir Richard I used to know. Probably because he is a completely different person, I realise. Whereas before he always had a faintly musty air about him, like something that's been left sitting on the shelf for too long and has been forgotten about. Fiona has come along, dusted him down and breathed fresh life into him, and now he's happy and in love.

'Well you both look amazing, congratulations, I'm really happy for you,' I smile. 'But I have one question: How did you propose if you were in India?'

'Skype!' grins Fiona.

Ah yes, Skype, I'd forgotten all about that, I think, getting a flashback to Fiona in her underwear at the kitchen table.

'I had the ring couriered to your flat and had Fiona open it on camera,' he says proudly.

'Then he popped the question!'

'And she said yes.'

They both smile happily, and I get another flash of his pearly whites. Now he looks, dare I say it, attractive. Not that I fancy Sir Richard, I think, hurriedly scratching that thought as we walk into the party together.

Grey's is a prestigious gentlemen's club, but with Sir Richard's family being members for three generations, they were more than happy to host his retirement party in one of their private rooms. It's all very grand: huge crystal chandeliers hang from the moulded ceiling; eighteenth-century oil paintings fill the walls, and at one end there's a large marble fireplace, whilst at the other French windows lead onto a private terrace.

Across which is strung a large glittery banner that reads, 'Happy Retirement Sir Richard!'

Well it can't be too grand, can it? *It's a party!*

I glance across the room, taking in the dozens of helium balloons shaped like giant tequila, rum and whisky bottles that I found on some random website in the States and had shipped over, the DJ I hired who's set up in the corner (complete with glitter ball and flashing lights) and the waiting staff who are flitting around serving up the delicious 'Sir Richard' cocktail that I had concocted especially.

And which everyone seems to be enjoying, I note, watching Kym finishing one off while simultaneously reaching for another, a few girls from Marketing who already look as if they've had more than a couple and are jigging around on the edge of the dance floor, even though the DJ hasn't started yet, and some serious flirting which seems to be going on between one of our account directors and his PA.

'Tess, I have to say a big thank you,' says Sir Richard, as Fiona disappears to powder her nose. 'You've done a wonderful job tonight.'

'Oh, don't mention it,' I smile. 'It's my pleasure.'

'I also wanted to thank you for giving us your blessing,' he continues, before lowering his voice. 'And to reassure you about any concerns. I realise this might appear to have been quite a recent development . . .' he clears his throat awkwardly and I know we're both remembering him on the sofa in his office, 'but in fact divorce proceedings from Lady Blackstock were started some time ago and, although I'm not quite yet a free man, my intentions towards Fiona are completely honourable—'

'Oh, yes, I'm sure,' I interrupt him quickly, before he confides in me any further. He's been a brilliant boss, and I'm sure he'll be a great husband, but I'd rather not hear any more about his intentions, honourable or otherwise, towards Fiona. 'Absolutely. I don't doubt it.'

'Marvellous.' He looks as relieved as I am not to have to talk about it any more. 'Well then, let's enjoy the party shall we?'

Grabbing a drink, I start chatting to people. Everyone seems to be having a good time. Except of course for Wendy the Witch who, unlike everyone else, has forgone the party dress and is wearing her usual head-to-toe black and is standing in the corner, glowering at everyone. She's still smarting from the fact she hasn't been called to a second interview for Sir

Richard's job. 'As if I should have to do an interview in the first place! I'm the obvious successor,' she complained loudly afterwards, to anyone and everyone who would listen.

She catches my eye but I pretend not to see her and spend the next half an hour avoiding her and mingling, before it's time for Sir Richard's speech.

'Ahem . . . ladies and gentlemen . . .' Clearing his throat, he takes to the little makeshift stage with all the theatrics of a seasoned performer at the Old Vic, and starts bowing and waving to the crowd, who immediately burst into a big round of applause.

'First of all, I'd like to thank everyone for coming to my little retirement shindig,' he begins when they've finally stopped clapping. 'I'm not going to bore you with a long speech as I think you've had quite enough of me these past thirty years . . .' Cue lots of whooping and cheering. 'But I want to make two announcements.'

Immediately people quieten down. Despite the party atmosphere, everyone loves Sir Richard and his retirement has caused more than a few concerns amongst the staff. For months now, everyone has been wondering who will replace him as CEO and how it will affect the company, and more importantly their jobs.

'Now, do you want the good news, or the good news?'

It's a terrible joke, but everyone laughs.

'The first is that my recent trip to India went better than I dared hope and was extremely fruitful. As you know, I have always had a global vision for this company, a desire to see it grow even stronger and further improve as the market leader. Because of this, I believe it's extremely important to expand into the developing markets, and therefore I am thrilled to announce that Blackstock and White has secured ongoing relations with Patak Patel Ltd, one of the key players in the drinks market in India. It has also been decided, reflecting this exciting new development, that my successor will be Mr Sanjeev Patel, a remarkable man who I'm sure you will all love, and who I'm sure will take the company to a whole new level . . .'

There's a huge round of applause and a lot of chattering breaks out as people take in the news. There are a few surprised looks and some raised eyebrows, but mostly there's a mixture of relief, excitement, and a lot of huge grins from the Accounts department. The only person who doesn't look pleased is Wendy, whose jaw sets hard as she claps with teeth clenched.

'And now for the second piece of good news,' continues Sir Richard, after the buzz from his first announcement has died down slightly. For a moment he looks nervous as he glances across at Fiona and holds out his hand, but she rewards him with a delighted smile. 'I'd like to take this opportunity to introduce my wonderful fiancée—'

As Fiona joins him on stage, the whole place erupts. For a moment I think the carefully moulded ceiling might actually blow off, as people whoop with astonished delight and congratulations. Most people have heard rumours of his divorce, and assumed Fiona was his new girlfriend, *but a new fiancée*? And one who's half his age? The men look on in disbelief at the hot young blonde with her arm around their boss, whilst the women who've already been commenting on his makeover at work over the past few weeks suddenly look at Sir Richard in a whole new light.

'So that's why he wasn't interested in going on a cruise like my nan and granddad!' Kym looks across at me indignantly. 'I can't believe you didn't tell me he was going out with your flatmate! C'mon, spill all the gossip!'

'Well that's the thing, I didn't know—' I begin to try and explain, but I'm interrupted by Wendy who appears by my elbow.

'Your friend marrying the boss won't make any difference, you know,' she scowls. 'He's still leaving next week.'

'I don't know what you're talking about,' I reply, trying to ignore her, but knowing it's impossible.

'Your job. Don't think you'll be getting any special favours, if that's what you're after.'

'I'm not thinking that,' I reply stonily. 'And anyway, I've already got some freelance work lined up.'

'Well I hope they're not our competitors – there could be a clash of interests. You could get in serious trouble if it's discovered you're passing on trade secrets,' she threatens.

Somehow I don't think babysitting for the neighbour's eighteen-month-old is going to clash.

'So *who are* you freelancing for?' she asks, narrowing her eyes.

Oh god, this is all I need. For over a year I've had to put up with Wendy's nasty jibes and constant criticism, but I draw the line at interrogation.

'Actually, if you'll just excuse me, I need the loo.' And before she can start shining a light in my face and pulling out my fingernails, I make a break for it.

40

Dashing to the safety of the Ladies, I find a long queue. And Fiona.

'What are you doing here?' I smile, relieved to see her.

'I just needed to escape for a few minutes; it got a bit overwhelming being the centre of attention,' she grins. 'And I've drunk so many of those cocktails I'm dying for a pee.' She crosses her legs. 'Gosh, I wish they'd hurry up.'

I glance at the two cubicles. On one is a sign that says 'Out of Order', and behind the other I can hear several girls talking.

'Bali was totally fabulous . . . I'm going to get Daddy to buy a villa out there, I want to show my jewellery . . .'

Fiona crinkles her brow. 'Hang on, isn't that . . . ?' Abruptly the door is flung open, and a gaggle of blondes spill out of the cubicle, sniffing conspicuously and wiping their nostrils.

'Pippa!' she gasps in astonishment.

A tanned blonde, dressed in the kind of designer ethnic chic that costs an absolute fortune, twirls around, and there's a split-second pause, almost as if she's trying to place her, then she breaks into a smile. 'Fifi, darling!' She makes a big show of planting two loud mwoah-mwoah kisses on each of her cheeks.

'What are you doing here?' asks Fiona, looking puzzled.

Clutching at the strings of love beads around her neck, Pippa flashes her a fake smile. 'I'm here with some friends and Daddy, having dinner. He's a member,' she adds pointedly, and I catch her looking me up and down and wondering how on earth I got in.

'I thought you were in Bali,' says Fiona, still uncomprehending.

'I just got back, I was going to call you first thing.' She suddenly spots Tallulah, who's tucked inside Fiona's bag. 'My baby!' she whoops. 'Mummy's missed you! Poor darling, have you been missing Mummy too?'

I see Fiona stiffen and hug her closer. 'She's been fine,' she says tightly.

'Wait a moment, where's her Swarovski crystal collar?' demands Pippa.

'It was too tight, it was damaging her trachea. Puppies need a thinner, nylon collar, which will allow enough space so you can fit two fingers underneath . . .'

As Fiona is speaking, Pippa is looking at her with astonishment, not because she knows so much about dogs, but because she's daring to answer back.

'Says who?' she snorts.

'Well, I've been doing a lot of research on the internet . . .' Aware of Pippa's obvious displeasure, Fiona's confidence is fast disappearing and she starts looking all nervous and stammering, '. . . and I bought this book—'

'Well you won't be needing any of that,' says Pippa sharply, and Fiona jumps. 'I'm afraid you've wasted your time and money as I'll be taking Tallulah back home with me now.' Turning back to her blonde friends, she rolls her eyes and says under her breath, 'Honestly, you leave your pets with some people and they just can't be trusted.'

But it's said loud enough for me to hear and I feel my hackles rise. Nobody could have looked after Tallulah better than Fiona. I admit, at first I was worried, especially after Gerbilgate, but she adores Talullah and Tallulah adores her.

I see panic flash across Fiona's face. 'But you can't,' she cries.

Pippa rounds on her. 'What? Are you telling me I can't take my own dog home?'

Fiona looks shocked by her own outburst. 'No, it's not, it's just . . . well . . . all her toys and things are at my flat . . .'

But Pippa is ignoring her. 'Lickle baby-waby missed her mummy didn't she . . . ? ' she coos, puckering up and bending down to kiss Tallulah, '. . . she doesn't need that nasty-wasty nylon collar, does she . . . ?'

Tallulah, however, who all this time has been sitting quietly and well-behaved in Fiona's handbag, has other ideas. Seeing Pippa's lip-glossed pout, she suddenly bares her teeth and tries to bite her.

At which point, all hell breaks loose.

'Argggghhh!' Pippa jumps back, shrieking. 'She bit me! That fucking dog bit me!' She clutches at her face. 'I'm bleeding, I know it, I'm bleeding. Oh my god I'm going to be scarred for life! I'm never going to be able to go to another party again!' Shaking and wailing, she dashes to the mirror while her friends rush to comfort her, worried looks flying between them.

Though I'm sure they're more worried about the threat of no parties than their friend's potential disfigurement. Having seen them in action at our flat, something tells me they're only in it for the invites and freebies.

'Call an ambulance! I need a doctor! Get Daddy, he'll call Mummy's plastic surgeon!'

'Here, let me look,' I say, trying to calm her down. 'I've done some first aid.'

But she's hysterical, and for a moment I think she's going to ignore me and carry on shrieking, until dutifully she takes her hand from her face.

There's nothing. Not even a mark.

'It must have just been a little nip,' I say matter-of-factly.

Blotchy from crying, she looks at me wildly. 'What? There's no blood?'

'Nope, no blood.' I shake my head. 'It didn't even break the skin.'

There's a moment of relief, and then:

'That dog's a vicious animal! It needs to be put down!'

Fiona blanches and covers Tallulah's ears with her hands. At which point, Pippa's Botoxed forehead puckers slightly. 'What's that?' she demands, peering at her fingers.

Suddenly I realise; she's spotted *The Ring*.

'Oh yes,' says Fiona, blushing, 'it's my engagement ring.'

For a brief second Pippa is rendered speechless, before quickly snapping back. 'Let me look at that,' she snorts, snatching up Fiona's finger. 'It can't be real.' With her free hand she starts scrabbling around in her bag and pulls out her little magnifying glass, used for looking at gemstones. Like a sort of posh, blonde Sherlock Holmes, she peers at the ring. Her face turns puce. 'But that can't be . . . it's real,' she gasps incredulously.

'Five carats, antique, *worth a fortune*,' I stage-whisper to her.

I exchange looks with Fiona, who blushes.

Releasing Fiona's finger, Pippa draws herself upright. 'Congratulations,' she says stiffly. 'And who's the lucky guy?'

'You haven't met him,' says Fiona, her face lighting up at the mere mention of him.

'His name's Sir Richard,' I butt in.

'Well, I call him Ricky,' corrects Fiona, blushing some more.

But I can already tell what Pippa is thinking, and it isn't about whether his name is Richard or Ricky. Underneath that expensive Bali tan she's gone as white as a ghost. Because that's something I've found out about the high-and-mighty Pippa. She might be a serious heiress, but I looked her dad up online and it appears he made his fortune from bingo halls – not quite the pedigree she'd like everyone to believe.

'Which means Fiona's going to be a lady,' I say, trying not to gloat. Pippa's money might be able to buy a lot of Fendi handbags, and a lot of friends, but the one thing it can never buy is the one thing Fiona will, quite inadvertently, have: a title.

Pippa looks as though she's about to collapse and has to

steady herself against the side of the washbasin. One of the blondes rushes to her aid. 'Pips sweetie, are you OK?'

'I don't feel well. I think I need a tetanus,' she blusters.

She's so ridiculous, I actually feel pity for her. Especially with friends like those, I note, watching how they're now all fawning over her.

'Probably best to be on the safe side,' I nod.

She glowers and I smile sweetly.

'And if it's all right with you, I'm going to keep Tallulah,' says Fiona, suddenly emboldened.

I glance at her proudly. Finally it's happened. She's sticking up for herself, and I can see in her expression, it's because something's changed. She doesn't want to be one of them any more, she's happy being herself

'Whatever. Do what you like with the stupid mutt,' Pippa scowls, 'just as long as you keep her away from me.' And, supported by the blondes, she's swept out of the toilets.

Leaving Fiona and me by ourselves. For a moment neither of us speaks. Both slightly stunned and still absorbing what just happened, we just look at each other. Fiona cracks first. Her lips start twitching. After that it's hopeless. Exploding into loud guffaws, we double up laughing, clinging onto the hand-dryers, our faces streaming with tears. Somehow, I think that's the last we'll be hearing of Pippa.

Afterwards, we go back outside to rejoin the party and Fiona goes off to find Sir Richard, linking her arm through his with the ease of someone who's been doing it for years. Observing them from across the room, I look at them together, and now my initial shock has abated, I have to say they actually make a good couple. Sir Richard is obviously besotted by her, he keeps getting her nibbles and gazing at her adoringly, whereas Fiona is picking invisible threads off his jacket, subtly motioning to him when he has crumbs on his chin.

I feel a glow of pleasure. My best friend's in love, Sir Richard got his deal, the party is a huge success . . . the DJ has started up, and I watch everyone busting out their moves on the dance floor. Everything has worked out brilliantly, except – I let my eyes wander around the room, hoping they'll fall upon a tall, six-foot-something figure, with broad shoulders and a shock of messy black hair.

Where are you Fergus? As I ask myself the silent question, I'm well aware I don't know the answer. I've been trying not to think about him all night, but with each passing hour I've found myself glancing at the doorway, hoping he might turn up at the last minute. But no. He hasn't come.

'Thought I'd come and say hello.' I turn to see Fiona at my side. 'I've sent Ricky off in search of more of those delicious spring rolls.' She flashes a smile, then frowns. 'Hey, are you OK?'

'Just a bit tired,' I fib. 'I think I'm going to go . . .'

'Already?' Her face flashes with disappointment.

'I don't want to turn into a pumpkin.' I try to crack a joke, but there's no fooling Fiona.

'Do you want me to come back with you?' she asks, concerned.

'No, of course not!' I protest quickly. 'You stay, it's your night.' I smile encouragingly. 'By the way, do the spring rolls mean no more rainbow food?'

She laughs. 'No more, I promise. No more stupid fad diets, no more secret eating, no more trying to find blue food.' She shakes her head in disbelief.

'Congratulations, best friend,' I say quietly, and this time I'm not just talking about the engagement, but about the battle she's been waging with food ever since I've known her, and which, finally, she might have started winning.

'You'll be next,' she says firmly.

'Oh, I don't think so,' I smile ruefully.

'Trust me, there're plenty of fish in the sea. Look at me and Ricky,' she encourages. Now Fiona is in love, she's evidently determined that everyone should share her good fortune. 'When you least expect it, you'll find someone.'

'But that's the thing, Fi, I already did.'

She's had a few too many cocktails, and she squints tipsily at me. 'Huh?'

'Oh, it's a long story . . .' I quickly dismiss it. 'I'll tell you some other time. Now you go and have fun.' Pinning on a smile, I give her a hug, before waving goodbye and weaving my way through the rest of the partygoers towards the large mahogany double doors.

I push them open. On the other side, the lobby is quiet and empty, and as I walk to the cloakroom I catch sight of myself in the red dress in a large, gilt-edged mirror. Sadness kicks in. I might have the dress, but it's like the charity shop manager said: '*All you need now is someone to dance with.*' And if life is like a dance, then there's only one person I want to dance with.

Fergus.

And finally it hits me. I can't deny it any longer. I love Fergus. I love every single thing about him. I love the way he made beans on toast taste like the most delicious meal in the world; the way he hates New Year's Eve and transforms other people's junk into something wonderful; the way he risked his life racing across London on a bicycle to help a friend. And the way he loved me for who I truly am. I never had to try with him, I could always be myself.

But now it's too late.

I've found myself, but I've lost Fergus.

Collecting my coat I pause, listening to the sounds of music and laughter floating out into the lobby, before pulling up my collar. I step outside into the cold night. And taking a deep lungful of frozen air, I set off walking and leave the party behind.

41

And so life goes on.

Because that's the thing about it: life won't let you lie in bed feeling sorry for yourself. Life's a bit like my mum when I was a teenager and she used to vacuum outside my bedroom door at the weekend to make me get up. All bossy and pushy, life won't take no for an answer.

Oh no, *siree*.

Life doesn't give two hoots if you're feeling depressed or unhappy, heartbroken or upset, or just generally like things haven't turned out the way you wanted them to. It's not going to stop the world turning so you can get off until you feel better. On the contrary, life rolls up its sleeves and demands you carry on and get on with it.

And so that's exactly what I do. What's happened has happened. Now I have to try and put everything behind me and get on with it.

Because that's all you can do, isn't it?

It's been a week since the party. Sir Richard has officially left and so it's all change. On Monday we were all summoned into the conference room to meet Mr Patel, our new CEO. He seems like a really nice guy and afterwards he made a special effort to talk to me and encourage me to reapply for my job as PA. Which was really kind of him, but I've decided not to and am working out the rest of my notice until the new PA starts. If finding myself proved to me one thing, it's that I have to be true to myself – and that means not being a PA any more.

Plus, quite frankly, Mr Patel had a lucky escape, I muse, glancing at my inbox, which is overflowing with unanswered emails. Including one from Fiona that's just popped in entitled 'Sassy Soul Mates.' I can't resist opening it. Since she met Sir Richard she's been evangelical about online dating and has been trying to get me to join, but I'm steadfastly ignoring her.

> Hi Tess, look what I've found! I thought I recognised her at the party, but couldn't place her, then I remembered where I'd seen her. It was when I was checking out the competition on Sassy Soul Mates. I've attached the photo and profile. Don't you know her???

Curious, I start scrolling down. Calling herself, 'Pussinboots' and listing her 'likes' as 'domination, whipped cream and prickly objects', it's a photo of a woman wearing thigh-high PVC boots, a frilly blouse unlaced to her navel, and a studded dog collar. Carrying a whip, she's suggestively holding a very phallic-shaped cactus . . .

I get the fright of my life. Oh my god. For a few, stunned, horrified seconds I just stare in disbelief.

And not just because of the phallus-shaped cactus.

As I look at her pouting into the camera, my stomach lurches in recognition.

It's Wendy!

For a moment I'm frozen, then I clap my hand to my mouth to stifle a giggle. Well, I'm sorry, but it's just too funny. It's Wendy the Witch as you've never seen her before.

> Oh my gosh, imagine if anyone ever saw this? It's one of our managing directors!

I type hurriedly in response to Fiona and hit reply.

Trying to brush the image from my mind, I turn back to the rest of my emails. Bloody hell, I've got so many, they're like magic porridge. No sooner have you deleted one then another one appears—

My train of thought is suddenly interrupted by a loud snort of laughter. I glance up from my computer to see Kym, her hand over her face, which is creased up with laughter. Hmm, I wonder what's so funny? I turn back to my emails and am just clicking on one headed Marketing Strategy; detailed notes, when I hear a shriek from one of the girls in the Marketing department, followed by more guffaws of laughter.

What *is* going on?

Then all at once there's this big commotion and everyone starts snorting with laughter and shrieking, 'Oh my god, have you seen it?' 'I can't believe it' 'Bloody hell!' 'Does she know?' 'Has Wendy seen it?'

Oh. God.

Suddenly I realise what all the uproar is about. The photograph. I've sent everyone Wendy's photograph by mistake! I feel hot and cold all over. I don't know how I did it but in my haste, instead of hitting reply, I must have hit forward and somehow it's gone to my entire address book. Which means it's gone to everyone in the company.

Thank god I've resigned already.

By the time I leave the office that evening the commotion has only just died down. Wendy is understandably both furious and hugely embarrassed. I own up straight away, and after shouting abuse at me she finally calms down when Kym offers to make her a cup of tea, which she accepts with a grateful smile. To be honest, it's the first real smile I've ever seen from Wendy. Maybe now this will make her a bit nicer to everyone. Well, if she wants the jokes about little pricks to stop, anyway.

After work I catch the bus to Hemmingway House to visit Gramps. I find him in the common room playing Scrabble with Errol and Pearl, a West Indian couple in their eighties, both of whom have snow-white hair and the loudest laughter you've ever heard.

'Ah, just in time to help me with a seven-letter word,' calls out Gramps, as he sees me walk in.

'Where's Phyllis?' I ask, giving him a kiss on his whiskery cheek and pulling up a chair beside him. 'I thought she was the expert.'

'Haven't you heard? She's got herself a lover,' replies Errol, erupting into deep, velvety laughter.

'Wash your mouth out with soap,' cusses Pearl, slapping him on the arm. 'Not in front of the young girl.'

'It's OK, I heard,' I smile, colouring slightly. 'And I'm not that young.'

'You're a baby,' dismisses Pearl, fixing me with her megawatt smile. 'Now, when you get to be old coots like we are . . .'

And then she's off. Shoulders heaving, head thrown back, her loud, raucous laughter starts ricocheting around the common room. And who knows how long for, if she hadn't been interrupted by the arrival of Melanie who appears at the doorway.

'Hi everyone. I'm just showing around a new member of Hemmingway House who I'd like to introduce . . .'

We all stop what we're doing and look up.

'Sidney, Tess, Errol and Pearl, I'd like you to meet Cécilie.'

There's a murmur of cheery hellos as a small lady with grey hair scraped into a chignon, and pillar-box red lipstick, appears next to her.

I recognise her immediately.

'You're the French lady from the shop,' I exclaim delightedly, hurriedly jumping up to welcome her.

'Ah yes, you're the girl who bought my dress,' she smiles in recognition. '*Quelle belle surprise!*'

We hug as if we're old friends, bonded over a shared love of a red silk dress.

'Gramps, this is the lady I was telling you about,' I say excitedly, turning to him, 'the one who has all the vintage flour sacks that I made my bag from . . .'

Easing himself up from his chair, he walks over to join us.

'*Enchanté*,' he smiles, kissing her hand.

She blushes. '*Le plaisir est pour moi*.'

'You speak French?' I stare at him in astonishment.

'I used to have quite a few customers from Paris when I worked in Savile Row,' he reveals. 'Though I'm afraid I'm a little bit rusty.'

'Not at all,' protests Cécilie, and I see Gramps's chest swell.

Watching them both, I feel a strange sort of tingle . . . Hang on a minute, is something happening here? Standing in the middle of them both, I suddenly feel rather green and hairy, like a gooseberry.

'Ah, you're playing Scrabble,' she says, noticing the abandoned board.

'Why, do you play?'

'A little, but being French I'm not so good with the words,' she smiles apologetically and shrugs her shoulders. Then, leaning closer she whispers, 'I'm much better at cards.'

Gramps jumps back, his face lit up with delight. 'Well, now you mention it I've got a deck right here. What about a game of Whist?' He turns around to look at the others.

'As long as you let us win for once,' laughs Errol, and Pearl joins in.

'What fun,' smiles Cécilie, clapping her hands delightedly.

'Well, that's decided then,' announces Gramps, looking pleased, before his gaze falls upon me. 'Oh, but there's Tess' – he looks at me as if suddenly remembering I'm here – 'and it's only for four players.'

Only this is one time I don't mind him being forgetful. I'm

more than happy to be forgotten. 'Don't worry about me, I'll leave you to it, have fun,' I smile, giving him a kiss and waving goodbye. 'Bye.'

But Gramps is already bent close, dealing out cards with Cécilie, both of them chuckling and smiling. I haven't seen that spark in him since Nan died. Smiling to myself, I walk away. This is the first time I'm not a bit sad to be leaving him. It's a good feeling.

It's getting late by the time I get back to the flat. As usual there's barely anything in the fridge, apart from a packet of half-stale pitta, so I toast some in the vain hope it will make it more edible, then pad into my bedroom and flop on my bed. I dislodge Flea who's curled up on my pillow, and he gives a little squeak.

'Sorry buddy,' I whisper, tickling his ear and showering him with pitta crumbs. He gives another little grumble, then curls up again, tucking his tail neatly underneath him so he resembles a big, hairy orange croissant.

Picking up the remote, I turn on my little portable TV and start flicking absently through the channels, while munching on half-stale, half-toasted pitta. There's nothing on, just a bunch of soaps and bad reality shows and I'm just ruminating over the important topic of where would I be without pitta bread and Flea, which are the two main staples of life – well, apart from Gramps *of course*, when I see it.

It's some entertainment show and they're doing a news bulletin about some actor who's got a part in a new hospital drama:

'*From bog roll to dream role . . .*'

I stare rigidly at the TV as the presenter begins his introduction.

'*. . . an actor whose previous claim to fame was a certain commercial is set to become a new hearthrob as Dr Lawrence in* Accident and Emergency, *a new prime-time series . . .*'

A photograph flashes up on the screen.

Oh my god. *It's Fergus*. He got the part after all! No wonder he hasn't been into the office lately, he must have left the courier company when he got the role.

'Tess?'

Vaguely I hear the door slam and Fiona's voice call out, but I can't answer. I'm staring at the screen, transfixed.

'Tess, are you home?' She appears at my bedroom door, all breathless and flushed.

'There you are!' she exclaims.

I'm still glued to the TV and she glances at the screen.

'That him, isn't it?' she says after a pause. I told her all about the long story that was Fergus this past week.

I nod wordlessly.

'I take it you haven't heard from him, then?' She raises a hopeful eyebrow.

I shake my head. 'And I'm not going to,' I say resignedly.

She plonks herself down on the bed, and gives my arm a comforting squeeze.

'Well, it's lucky I'm here, because I've got something that will cheer you up,' she says, encouragingly, flashing me a smile.

'It's going to take more than a bag of Maltesers this time,' I smile ruefully, knowing her tried-and-tested cure-all.

'No, it's a lot better than that.' She starts rummaging around her bag, which is gigantic and filled to the brim with who knows what, until finally she pulls out a magazine. '*Ta daaah!*'

I look at it blankly. 'A magazine?'

'Not just any magazine, it's my magazine! It's not on sale till tomorrow but I got an early copy and look, it's my article,' she says, quickly flicking to the page and spreading it out in front of me.

'Oh that's great Fiona, well done,' I nod, my eyes glancing over the photographs of models posing with different beauty products. And it is great – though to be honest, Fiona has done hundreds of shoots, I don't know why she's so excited about this one.

'No, I'm not talking about *my* stuff,' she exclaims, as if it's perfectly obvious what she's going on about it. She flicks over a page. 'I'm talking about your bag! Look!' she demands, jabbing it with her finger.

I look at where she's pointing, and there, sure enough, taking up the whole page, is a glossy photograph of a model with my bag slung over her shoulder.

'Wow, yes,' I say, feeling a surprised rush of pleasure. Fiona gave me back the bag a few days ago, but it's strange to see it in a photograph in a magazine. 'It looks good, doesn't it?'

'Good? It looks bloody fantastic!' tuts Fiona, flicking over onto the next page. 'And look, the stylist loved it so much, she used it here as well.'

Gosh. So she did. Somewhat stunned, I stare at all the different colour photographs: there's one where my bag is filled with beauty products; another where they're spilling over the sides and you can see the lining; another close-up where you can see the tiny sequins; one with the model and the leather handles against her bare skin . . . I feel myself swell up with pride. I knew I'd done a good job, but even so, it looks so much better than I ever dared dream.

'And that's not all,' announces Fiona. Turning over the pages to the end of the shoot, she points out the credits. *Photographer: Jean-Claude. Model: Amy@ TrueInc. Stylist: Amy Woods. Beauty Writer: Fiona Mannering. Bag by Tess Connelly.*

'Oh my god!' I gasp. I stare at it in amazement. I got my name in a magazine, and not for me, but for my bag, for something I made.

'Isn't that great?' enthuses Fiona.

'Wait till I tell Gramps, he won't believe it,' I say excitedly. But knowing Gramps, he will. He always said I had a gift; he always believed I could do it. Just like Fergus. As he flicks back into my mind, I feel a prick of sadness. I can't tell him. I can't share this with him.

I glance once more at the TV, then turn it off. 'You know, I think I'll get an early night,' I say, closing the magazine.

'Too much excitement, hey?' grins Fiona.

'Yeh, something like that,' I smile back. And it's true, it is exciting. My bag in *Saturday Speaks* magazine. Not bad for a first effort. You never know, this might be a first step towards my dream of actually selling one. Hope flickers like a flame. I've been thinking about work and I'm not sure what I'm going to do, apart from sign on with some temp agencies, do some dog walking, a bit of babysitting. But maybe now if I work on my bags in my spare time . . . maybe this is a start . . . maybe one day I'll get a whole photoshoot with my bags.

Well, a girl can dream, can't she?

Leaving Fiona, I go into the bathroom to wash and get ready for bed. I'm in the middle of cleaning my teeth when I hear Fiona's phone ringing. It's probably Richard; they're never off the phone from each other, when they're not spending all their time together. I'm getting used to it. Though I've made Fiona promise she'll put a lock on the bathroom door before he stays over. After what happened last time . . . Fair enough, he might not be my boss any more, but bumping into Sir Richard on the loo . . .

I shudder.

'Sorry, it's who? Oh . . . yes . . . no . . . don't worry, it's fine to ring so late . . .'

Hmm, wonder who she's talking to? Not Richard, there would have been about five 'darlings' by now. Plus, she's suddenly put on her posh voice.

'If you'd care to hold the line one moment.'

She appears at the bathroom door, her hand clamped over her BlackBerry.

'It's for you.' Her face has gone a funny pink colour.

I pause, mid-brushing. 'Who is it?' I ask, through a mouthful of spearmint froth.

'Super Chic.'

'Who's Super Chic?'

Fiona looks at me in shocked disbelief. 'You've never heard of Super Chic?' she exclaims.

Something tells me I should have. 'Um . . . no,' I shake my head.

'It's only the hottest, most talked-about fashion website! It has its own online store – everybody uses it . . .' She breaks off and looks at me, obviously remembering I'm a charity shop junkie.

'Oh I see . . .' I nod, then frown in confusion. 'But why do Super Chic want to speak to me?'

She's going a really funny pink colour now, *and is she trembling*?

'It's the head buyer,' she gasps. 'She saw your bag and she's sorry to call so late but she's too excited to wait until tomorrow morning and . . .' She breaks off, almost breathless, before the rest of her words come tumbling out. 'You're not going to believe this, *but they want to place an order*!'

What?

Stunned, I stare at Fiona. For a moment I can't take her words in; it's as if they remain floating above me in giant bubbles. I can't believe what she's just said, what this means, how a dream can just come true in the blink of an eye.

And now she's holding out the phone to me, and with nerves, excitement, joy and disbelief fluttering in my stomach, I take it from her.

'Hello, Tess Connelly speaking.'

They always say you've got to start somewhere. When they interview famous businesswomen, successful entrepreneurs, or even novelists, they always talk about how they started out in their garage, or set up their business in a spare bedroom, or did their writing in a café to keep themselves warm. For me, it was in our bathroom that didn't have a lock.

Because there, standing on our shaggy bathmat, in my Snoopy pyjamas with a mouth full of toothpaste, I take my very first order of what is to become Bags by Tess Connelly Designs.

And that's only the beginning.

42

New Year's Eve

Outside the temperature is minus god-knows-what and sleeting. I swear, sleet has to be the worst kind of weather known to man. Rain isn't too bad, so long as you've got an umbrella, and snow can be lovely when it's all fresh and white and powdery. But the combination of the two is freezing, slushy ice pellets that soak you to the skin, ruin your shoes, and make every single cab in London disappear into thin air.

I'm not kidding, I can't see one single yellow light. But I can see tons of girls in party dresses and fake tan. Shivering and trying to shelter, they're searching vainly for a cab to take them to their parties before a) it hits midnight or b) they freeze to death or c) both. Seriously, it's hell out there.

Which is why I'm so happy to be inside, all snug as a bug in a rug, I smile to myself, drawing my face away from the window and the scene below on the street.

It's New Year's Eve and I'm in my flat with the central heating full on so it's like the Bahamas. After going home to spend Christmas at Mum and Dad's, which meant listening to my little brother, who's back from his gap year, say every five minutes, 'Would you believe it, but this time last year we were sitting on Bondi Beach', I finally decided to come out and admit I didn't like New Year's Eve.

Mum was a bit upset. She couldn't understand why her daughter wanted to go back to London to stay in on her own, when she could be joining them at the local village hall, 'as they're having a disco and everything'. But after last year, I decided that this year I was going to finally be true to myself, and that meant no more crappy parties, no more fighting traffic and no more trying to look as though I'm having the most fun ever whilst wishing I was at home in my pyjamas.

Which is why I turned down all the party invitations and will be spending the evening at home with Flea, drinking a bottle of Cava, eating takeaway pizza and watching the new Johnny Depp movie on DVD. *Whilst already wearing my pyjamas.* I can't wait.

Plus, it gives me a chance to reflect on the past year – and believe me when I say it, it's been quite some year.

So much has happened since Fiona got that phone call from Super Chic all those months ago. I've gone from making one bag with Gramps on his old sewing machine, to owning my own business and employing a small team of people (including Gramps, whose new title is Creative Consultant) and producing hundreds. I've even got my own logo and a website that Ali set up for me, and orders are flooding in. We can hardly keep up. Plus we've got all these new designs and fabrics, and I've got so many different ideas . . .

I have to stop myself before I get carried away. I get like that. Sometimes I almost have to pinch myself just thinking about it. It really is a dream come true.

And that's not all that's changed. I glance at a photograph above the fireplace. It's a picture of Fiona and Sir Richard on their wedding day, together with Tallulah and Monty with flowers in their collars. They got married this summer on his family's estate in Scotland, and he's wearing a kilt, whereas Fiona fulfilled her bridal fantasy of wearing her grandmother's dress. Apparently she'd never been able to fit into it before, but since meeting Sir Richard, she's dropped a couple of dress sizes. Not that he cares about her weight, but that's probably why. It's as if, as soon as it ceased to matter, the pounds just melted away.

Well, until recently, but now she's started putting them back on. Only this time she's got a good excuse: Fiona's four months pregnant. Sorry, I mean Lady Blackstock. God, I still can't believe it. Fiona is now a lady! Not only that but she's swapped her stilettos for a pair of Hunter wellies and is now living in the country. I'm now renting the whole flat from her – well, there didn't seem much point in moving out. Flea likes it here, plus I've turned Fiona's bedroom into my design studio.

But Fiona isn't the only one who got lucky in love. Gramps and Cécilie are never apart, although their love is of a different kind. His heart still belongs to Nan, as it always will, but in Cécilie he's found someone to share his love of poker; and in Gramps she's found someone to dance with again. On weekends they have tea dances at Hemmingway House, and they're always the first to take to the floor, waltzing around the common room in their finest suits and dresses.

As for his health, with Cécilie's help we finally got him to see a doctor, and as we feared, he's in the early stages of Alzheimer's. The good news – if there is any good news with this disease – is that no one knows how quickly or slowly it will progress. So far he's doing well; he's got Cécilie to jog his memory and, like she always says in that wonderful French accent of hers, 'We are all making new memories every day.'

I'm distracted by 'Auld Lang Syne' playing on the radio. To this day, I've never understood what that song means, the words don't really make sense, but I think it's about remembering old friends. And old boyfriends, I reflect, listening to the song and thinking about the round-robin email I received from Seb, wishing me Happy Holidays. Just like last year. Except this year I didn't get upset, I just smiled and emailed back, 'You too'.

Then again so many things feel different to last year, at least from what I can remember. I can't be sure as I lost my old diary a while ago. I don't have a clue where it went, and my memory's dreadful, but it disappeared around the time Fiona moved out, along with the disk. Maybe it got thrown away, who knows?

There's lots of things I don't know. Like, did it really happen? Did wishing I'd never met my boyfriend really erase our relationship? And did I really date him all over again, only differently this time? It sounds crazy. It *was* crazy. Looking back now, I almost can't believe it happened, and sometimes, just before I fall asleep at night, I think maybe it didn't happen – maybe I dreamt it all, maybe I blurred the lines between my imagination and reality.

Except, I know that can't be true. I don't need a diary to prove to me that something happened to me; somehow I magically got a second chance at love, but the twist was, it was myself I learned to love. It's just a crying shame I learned it too late to be with Fergus.

The doorbell goes and I snap back. Ah, that will be the Cheese Feast and garlic bread I ordered. Hurray for Mario's pizza delivery!

'Coming . . .' I yell, dislodging Flea, who gives a disgruntled meow. I hurry into the hallway. 'Hang on, I just need to find my wallet . . .' Grabbing my bag, I start digging around with one hand, while I grip the door with the other.

I pull it open, my head still in my bag. I must do a lighter silk lining next time; this navy blue paisley is too dark.

'Aha, here it is!' I look up, waggling my wallet triumphantly.

A tall figure is standing in my doorway. I notice the scuffed boots first, followed by the long limbs, then the dark suede coat. My chest tightens. Somewhere inside me a pulse starts beating urgently as my eyes peel upwards. Unruly black hair is flopping over his face, almost hiding his eyes. It's got much longer than I remember it.

'Fergus,' I manage after a pause. 'What are you doing here?'

I suddenly feel absurdly nervous. And stupid. *For god's sake, whose stupid idea was it to wear pyjamas?*

'Oh I dunno,' he shrugs, trying to sound nonchalant, 'I just happened to be passing.'

My mind is racing. I can't believe he's here. Standing in front of me. After all this time. There's so many things I want to say.

'How did you know where I live?' But all I can do is ask stupid questions.

'I was a courier, I used to find addresses for a living—' he begins, then breaks off. 'OK, I confess, I used my charms on the dragon at Hemmingway House.'

'You mean Catherine?' I can't help the beginnings of a smile. 'As in our future Queen Catherine?'

'Aye, that's right,' he smiles sheepishly, and for a moment we both fall silent, our minds flicking backwards.

'But it's New Year's Eve. Don't you have a party to go to?'

'That's why I'm here. Who else do I know who hates New Year's Eve as much as I do? I thought maybe I could *not* celebrate with you?'

I find myself smiling. 'I'm afraid I'm just staying in.'

'Grand,' he grins. 'Don't we have a date? "Next New Year's Eve, my sofa or yours",' he reminds me, raising an eyebrow. 'Only I don't have a sofa.'

'What happened to your chaise longue?'

'It's in storage. I moved out of the studio as I've been filming in Manchester mostly. I'll have it back soon though – I'm buying a house. Nothing fancy but I think you'd like it—' He breaks off awkwardly.

'Wow,' I say, pinning on a bright smile, 'the acting must be going really well.'

'Yeh, I suppose so,' he shrugs modestly. 'And I heard about

your bags – well, I saw one, a girl was carrying one and I rushed over. I think she thought I was trying to snatch it.'

I laugh. 'We both got our dreams, didn't we?' I say, after a pause.

'Yeh,' he nods. 'Sort of.' He pauses, stuffing his hands awkwardly in his pockets before clearing his throat. 'Look, I wanted to say I'm sorry.'

'No, *I'm* sorry, I was an idiot to send those emails,' I blurt, before he can stop me. 'It was stupid of me, I didn't think.'

'No, I was an idiot not to see the reason why you did.'

Now the small talk is over, the dam is broken and our feelings are pouring out.

'I was the one who didn't think,' he finishes, shaking his head.

And then there's a pause, as if we've run out of words. After what feels like forever, Fergus finally speaks.

'Can we pretend like it never happened? Start over?'

As his eyes search out mine, I feel a tug deep inside, but I know for certain I can't.

'No,' I shake my head firmly.

'No?' He looks crushed.

My chest tightens as I think about everything we've gone through together, about all the good things and the bad things, and it's like Gramps says: never wish any part of it away. However painful, our memories and the times we spent together have made us *us*, and I don't want to erase a single thing.

'Let's just carry on where we left off,' I say quietly.

For a moment his brow furrows, as if he's trying to figure out what's going on, then his face softens in understanding. 'And where would that be?'

'Hmm, well, let's see . . .' I pretend to think. 'Well we've met, got to know each other, and then we had the big row . . . so . . . what comes after the big row?'

His mouth twitches and he raises an eyebrow. 'The making up?'

Our eyes meet, and we both break into giddy, nervous smiles. As finally, after all this time, after everything that's happened, he reaches out and wrapping his arms around me, pulls me towards him.

Desire, that's what I felt on his roof terrace, I suddenly realise, feeling him next to me. That sensation I couldn't put my finger on. It was desire.

'There's just one more thing,' I say, and he pauses. 'From now on we have to be totally honest with each other.'

'OK, well in that case I have something you should know,' he says, suddenly serious.

'You do?' I feel a prickle of panic.

'I'm in love with you, Tess Connelly.'

I feel a rush of happiness. 'Well, it's funny you should say that. I'm in love with you too.'

Then, with him holding me tightly, we fall back against the door. And as it closes behind us he bends down and, with his warm mouth on mine, kisses me like I'm his leading lady.

Believe me, this is something I'm *never* going to want to forget.

ALEXANDRA POTTER

Me and Mr Darcy

He's every woman's fantasy . . .

After a string of nightmare relationships, Emily Albright has decided she's had it with modern-day men. She'd rather pour herself a glass of wine, curl up with *Pride and Prejudice* and step into a time where men were dashing, devoted and honourable, strode across fields in breeches, their damp shirts clinging to their chests, and *weren't* into internet porn.

So when her best friend invites her to Mexico for a week of margaritas and men, Emily decides to book a guided tour of Jane Austen country instead.

She quickly realises she won't find her dream man here. The coach tour is full of pensioners, apart from one Mr Spike Hargreaves, a foul-tempered journalist sent to write a piece on why Mr Darcy's been voted the man most women would love to date.

Until she walks into a room and finds herself face-to-face with Darcy himself. And every woman's fantasy suddenly becomes one woman's reality.

HODDER

ALEXANDRA POTTER

You're the One That I Don't Want

How do you know he's The One?
Are you getting butterflies just thinking about him?
Have you dreamt of marrying him?
Do you just *know*?

When Lucy meets Nate in Venice, aged 18, she knows instantly he's The One. And, caught up in the whirlwind of first love, they kiss under the Bridge of Sighs at sunset. Which – according to legend – will tie them together forever.

But ten years later, they've completely lost contact. That is, until Lucy moves to New York and the legend brings them back together. Again. And again. And again.

But what if Nate isn't The One? How is she going to get rid of him? Because forever could be a very long time . . .

A funny, magical romantic comedy about how finding The One doesn't always have to mean happily ever after.

HODDER

ALEXANDRA POTTER

Who's That Girl?

If only you knew then what you know now . . .

Imagine you could go back ten years and meet your younger self – would you recognise her? And what advice would you give?

- Wear sunscreen
- Back away from those PVC trousers
- DON'T give that idiot your phone number
- Lemon juice won't bleach your hair – it just attracts wasps
- He's The One – don't let him get away

For Charlotte Merryweather, there's no need to imagine. She's about to find out for real. With some surprising consequences . . .

Alexandra Potter's deliciously funny and enchanting romantic comedy looks at life, love and what might happen if you could turn back time . . .

HODDER

ALEXANDRA POTTER

Be Careful What You Wish For

'I wish I could get a seat on the tube . . . I hadn't eaten that entire bag of Maltesers . . . I could meet a man whose hobbies include washing up and monogamy . . .'

Heather Hamilton is always wishing for things. Not just big stuff – like world peace or for a date with Brad Pitt – but little, everyday wishes, made without thinking. With her luck, she knows they'll never come true . . .

Until one day she buys some lucky heather from a gypsy. Suddenly the bad hair days stop; a handsome American answers her ad for a housemate; and she starts seeing James – The Perfect Man who sends her flowers, excels in the bedroom, and isn't afraid to say 'I love you' . . .

But are these wishes-come-true a blessing or a curse? And is there such a thing as *too much* foreplay?

HODDER

ALEXANDRA POTTER

What's New, Pussycat?

What would you do if your boyfriend proposed?

– Say yes and throw your arms around him
– Text everyone with your good news
– Take out a subscription to Brides magazine

Delilah does none of the above. Instead she packs her bags and heads to London in search of a new life, and a new man. Only she meets two. Charlie, the sexy media mogul and Sam, best friend and confidante.

Everything seems perfect. Thrown into a whirlwind of glamorous parties, five-star restaurants and designer penthouses, Delilah couldn't be happier. After all, it's a million miles away from her old life. And her old self. Which is exactly what she wanted.

Isn't it?

Do you wish this wasn't the end?

Join us at www.hodder.co.uk, or follow us on Twitter @hodderbooks to be a part of our community of people who love the very best in books and reading.

Whether you want to discover more about a book or an author, watch trailers and interviews, have the chance to win early limited editions, or simply browse our expert readers' selection of the very best books, we think you'll find what you're looking for.

And if you don't, that's the place to tell us what's missing.

We love what we do, and we'd love you to be part of it.

www.hodder.co.uk

@hodderbooks

HodderBooks

HodderBooks